FIREHAMMER

Ric Hunter
Colonel USAF (Ret)
Fighter Pilot

BASED ON A TRUE STORY

RIC HUNTER

"It was that quality that led me into aviation in the first place —
it was a love of the air and sky and flying, the lure of adventure,
the appreciation of beauty. It lay beyond the descriptive words
of man — where immortality is touched through danger, where
life meets death on an equal plane, where man is more than
man, and existence both supreme and valueless at the same
instant."

~ *Charles A. Lindbergh*

i

ISBN 978-1-937958-45-9 Trade Paperback

ISBN 978-1-937958-46-6 ebook

ISBN 978-1-937958-47-3 iBook

LCCN: 2013940165

Red Engine Press (www.redenginepress.com)

Bridgeville, PA

Edited by Joyce Gilmour

Layout by Joyce Faulkner

Printed in the United States

CHINA

Red River

Caobang

Dongkhe

Dien Bien Phu

Langson

Hanoi

LAOS

NORTH VIETNAM

Gulf of Tonkin

Vientiane

DMZ

Hue

THAILAND

Da Nang

Mekong River

Korat RTAFB

SOUTH
VIETNAM

Bangkok

CAMBODIA

U-Tapao
Air Base

Tonle Sap

Phnom Penh

Tay Ninh

Koh Tang

Saigon

Bien Hoa

Gulf of Thailand

South China Sea

Southeast Asia 1975

Major Battles

LCPL - E3 - Marine Corps - Regular

Length of service 2 years

Casualty was on Jul 20, 1966

In QUANG TRI, SOUTH VIETNAM

HOSTILE, GROUND CASUALTY

GUN, SMALL ARMS FIRE

Body was recovered

Panel 09E - Line 45

This book is dedicated to Lance Corporal Timothy S. Davies, USMC, who gave his life for his country and his fellow Marines. He was the inspiration for this book and my next door neighbor growing up. He was my high school best friend, and we also dated best friends. We were young then and mischievous, but not bad. The day I learned of Tim's death was a low point. I have visited his grave site in Mobile, Alabama, and his name on the Vietnam Veteran's Memorial several times. He was a strong, good-looking young American who volunteered for the most dangerous job in the squad as radioman. He is forever one of my heroes. Semper Fidelis.

Chapter 1

JULY 20, 1966

"Here dead lie we because we did not choose
To live and shame the land from which we sprung
Life, to be sure, is nothing much to lose,
But young men think it is, and we were young."

—*A.E. Housman*

The sniper left the lush jungle undergrowth behind and started climbing the highest tree in Quang Tri Province. He chose it for its height and its thick cladding of large, heart-shaped leaves that would provide a chance for escape. As he made his way up from limb to limb, he pinched leaves and shoved them into the webbing of his helmet. His Asian pale skin was now black with streaks of grease. A drab-green headband kept sweat out of his eyes. Always with three points of contact with the tree, he moved like a cat stalking its prey, slow and deliberate, till he found a broad limb to stand on and hooked one elbow over another limb to lock himself to the tree. He wrestled the Soviet-built Dragunov 7.62X54 rifle from his back with his free hand and laid it across a cradle formed by overlapping branches. Secure on his perch, he took the lens covers off the PSO-1 optical sight. Like putting on an old glove, he slipped his right thumb through the hole in the stock and brought the rifle to his shoulder to check its condition and his own balance after the long, tough climb. As his cheek settled on the smooth, oiled stock he peered through the crystal clear, four-power scope to study the illuminated rangefinder that gave him capability to 1300 meters. It looked fine. Chevrons in the middle of the scope for bullet drop compensation and windage marks to the left and right of the center reticle all were in good shape. The sniper was methodical and took minutes panning the distance for high-value targets, looking for officers, tank commanders, senior NCOs — or radio operators. Every movement was purposeful and slow so as not to catch the eye of a counter-sniper. Seeing no targets, he unwound his left arm from the webbed nylon sling and placed the Dragunov back down like putting a sleeping baby in a cradle. *The Americans keep coming,* he thought, taking a long pull from his canteen. *One more kill will make 30. Maybe then I can visit my wife...*

＊

For the first time, Lance Corporal Tim Scott carried his unit's PRC-25 radio, nicknamed a "prick." Knowing the life expectancy of Marine radiomen in a firefight to be about 15 seconds — that antenna wagging in the breeze was like saying, "Here I am, shoot me!" Tim, 19 years old, bulletproof, and invisible volunteered anyway.

Sweat soaked Tim's utilities, beaded down his arms to his fingers and dripped on the M-14 rifle clutched between his knees. On this air assault, his squad was part of India Company, 3rd Battalion, 4th Marines. Like other members of his squad, he was sitting on his helmet to protect his ass from groundfire that might penetrate their UH-34 Seahorse helicopter. The *thwack-thwack-thwack* of the helo's rotors beat a hypnotic rhythm in the thick tropical air as it shuttled them to a hot landing zone, or LZ, three miles south of the demilitarized zone separating North and South Vietnam.

Tim grinned. The *thwack-thwack* sound triggered memories of the tire tread separating and smacking against the wheel well of his folks' car the night after he and Randy drag raced a friend's Supersport. His dad figured it was a faulty tire and took it in for replacement. Tim's grin faded. He'd tell his dad the truth about that tire sometime when he got back to the world.

The Marines started a final check of their equipment. Lance Corporal Steve Matthews, sitting next to Tim, was his buddy and had a rare sense of humor that kicked in when tensions were high. Holding a make-believe microphone to his lips, he leaned over to Tim's ear and shouted above the engine noise and whirling rotors.

"Ladies and gentlemen, it's 0700 at the DMZ airport. It's 110 degrees with a humidity of 87 percent. As you can guess, LZ Crow, for this here Operation Hastings, is hotter than a two-peckered goat. Just right for us gyrenes."

Tim nodded and gave a thumbs-up as Steve continued. "Control tower's reporting light to moderate groundfire in all quadrants. Please remain seated until I turn off the seat-belt sign. Enjoy your stay, and we appreciate the chance to serve you on Phouc Yu Airways!"

Tim forced a smile and nodded. As a standing joke in the squad, he shouted, "Why are you here, Marine?"

"Just doing my duty, SIR!" Steve shouted back.

Tim had made LZs against Viet Cong, but never against NVA, and never one this hot. Staff Sergeant Williams, platoon leader, told them that as part of Task Force Delta they'd be facing NVA, North Vietnamese Army regulars. After decades of fighting the French, they were lethal and skilled at jungle warfare. Always an elusive enemy, when the regulars could be located the U.S. forces engaged them with all they could bring to bear. Dressed in their pith helmets and green uniforms, the NVA moved like shadows through heavy foliage. Hard to see, harder to kill.

What the sergeant knew but didn't tell them was that they were headed to "Helicopter Valley." The third platoon of India Company had just nicknamed it the day before when a twin-rotored CH-46 Sea Knight was hit by 12.7mm machine-gun fire and collided with another CH-46. A third helo maneuvered to avoid the pair and slammed into a tree. Later that day enemy fire struck another CH-46. Belching flame and smoke, it hit the ground. India Company's position was under pressure from three sides, leaving one way in and out to the south. They had suffered 100 casualties, 18 dead and 82 wounded. Tim's squad was fresh reinforcement for the beleaguered company.

In-country for almost six months, Tim killed before but was growing numb. The addictive adrenalin rush of those first few kills had faded... as had the guilt. Now he needed more danger to fuel that addiction. Only to his God did he admit he was scared shitless carrying the prick.

The door gunner glanced at them over his shoulder and shouted, "Too much incoming, we won't touch down. You'll have to jump." He raked the lush tropical rainforest with a deafening burst from his M-60, scattering empty shell casings on the helo's floor. "All right! Get ready to un-ass this bird!"

"Lock and load!" At the squad leader's bellow, a flurry of nervous hands slapped ammo clips into M-14s and cycled bolts, the metallic sounds carrying to every ear, even above the din of the chopper. Nobody made eye contact, game faces — nobody smiled.

Tim pulled the operating rod on his M-14, chambered a round, then tightened the straps on the prick. As he started to put on his helmet, he held it in both hands gazing behind its webbed lining to stare at his favorite photo of Dory, the first and only girlfriend he'd ever had. She was thunder, he lightning. They fit together like two spoons. Her blonde hair in pigtails, she sported a boy-melting smile as she stood waist deep in the surf at Dauphin Island just south of Mobile. He smiled, remembering the love they'd made in the middle of the day, on a beach towel between sand dunes covered with sea oats.

PFC "French" Thibodeaux sat on Tim's left and crammed a third piece of chewing gum in his mouth. "Helps my noives," he shouted in his New Orleans Cajun accent. Steve Matthews sat to his right checking pins in the grenades on his flak jacket. Restless, Steve wiped sweat from his forehead then unsnapped a canteen and took a long slug. The helo's engine strained; the heavy staccato beat of the rotors added to the noise level as it slowed and tilted.

The door gunner shouted a stream of profanity and unleashed another burst. An enemy round grazed the shoulder of his flak jacket and splattered into the ceiling above Steve's head. The blow spun the door gunner sideways against the cockpit bulkhead. "Goddam fuckin' gooks!" he shouted as he lunged back to his machine gun swinging on its pedestal in the doorway.

Tim's reflexes made him duck from the ricochet. He rolled his helmet on and cinched the chin strap. Out the gunner's door he saw tall elephant grass thrashing in the rotor wash.

The pilot came in low and slow, the door side tilted down for the Marines. "Go! Go! Go!" the gunner screamed between bursts, ripping fire at a tree line 200 meters away.

The nine Marines bailed out. Tim landed, staggering to keep his balance. Steve tumbled, rolled, and crouched to his feet. Adrenaline mainlining their veins, they scrambled for a shallow creek bed 50 meters away. Their only place to hide, it seemed like 50 miles away as they faced a wall of hot lead.

The pilot increased RPM as the helo's rotors clawed for air. The door gunner's M-60 dueled with a torrent of enemy automatic weapons, their chatter a toxic exchange, a devilish crescendo. Tracers flew green and red-hot back and forth across the LZ.

Packs, loaded with fifty pounds of gear, pulled at the Marines' shoulders and slowed them. Tim ran in a half-crouch, his PRC-25's antenna a bullet magnet. Shots snapped in his ears as others plowed the earth at his feet. He felt the shock wave and heard the crack of a round as it just missed his throat. Hearing a sickening *thud* behind him, Tim hesitated and watched in horror as French tumbled forward catching a round in the chest from an AK-47.

With the ditch just meters away, everything rolled in waves of slow motion. *Armageddon*, Tim thought as he dove into the ditch and rolled. A withering hail of automatic weapon fire cut a tree in half on the bank above him.

The belly-high ditch served as a trough for monsoon rains. Now it held only a trickle of water mixed with the fetid smell of human waste from a nearby village. The banks weren't much, but right now they offered a world of protection. Of the nine Marines aboard the helicopter, six made it to the ditch. They faced the North Vietnamese Army in a godforsaken hellhole 12,000 miles from home.

"Where's French?" Steve shouted above the din.

A heavy barrage of mortar rounds exploded where a minute before the helo dropped the squad. Rocket propelled grenades, RPGs, exploded just meters away. Ears rang and heads ached.

"He's hit!" Tim screamed.

"If that was Armageddon, this is the gate to Hell," Tim whispered to himself, as he peered over the top of the ditch.

Staff Sergeant Williams stumbled over the edge and rolled against the bank. He shouted, "Scott, get the prick working! We need air support — YESTERDAY!"

"French went down about thirty meters back, Sergeant. He's hit bad. I don't think he's gonna make it," Tim replied, extending the prick's antenna.

"Yeah, I know. Get us some air." The veins in William's neck bulged from exertion. His eyes riveted on Tim's radio just before he held his M-14 over his head and fired for effect over the embankment.

Tim worked the frequency for help while his mind went into basic training at Parris Island automatic mode. "Jolly Roger, Jolly Roger, this is Spade One-One, over." Zipping and popping rounds cracked overhead and chewed up the bank as the NVA zeroed their position. The world was coming unglued and his left hand trembled holding the mike. He knew the one tether to outside help was his radio.

"The gook bastards got our location now," Steve shouted. "Where the hell's the rest of the company?" One knee braced against the embankment, he slammed the M-14 into his right shoulder and emptied the magazine.

"Jolly Roger, Jolly Roger, this is Spade One-One. Come in," Tim shouted, sticking his finger into his right ear to muffle the noise. "Request immediate air support, NOW!"

Tim looked at Steve. "I can't reach them from down here. Gotta get this antenna up where it can do some good." The sound of incoming fire changed to a deeper tone and dirt flew from machine-gun rounds that peppered the crest above their heads.

"That's .51 caliber. Bad shit," Steve said.

"Oh, God," French screamed from the elephant grass.

"Gotta get the antenna higher!" Tim yelled to Sergeant Williams, then scrambled halfway up the embankment. He hesitated near the top, then twisted around to look back across the ditch searching for French.

"Stay down, Marine!" Williams screamed.

Tim ducked from reflex as rounds whizzed overhead.

The others, seeing Tim's movement, began crawling to the top of the ditch. Lance Corporal Rodriguez shed his pack, then crawled out of the ditch and into the elephant grass toward French.

"Shit!" Williams shouted. "Lay down cover fire!"

Tim looked above him to see the antenna rising just inches above the crest. He cradled his M-14 across one knee, covered one ear and shouted into the mike, "Jolly Roger, Jolly Roger, this is Spade One-One. Come in."

Sergeant Williams joined the rest on the bank as they unleashed lead at the enemy. He glanced back to see that Rodriguez had reached French. Rodriguez gave them a thumbs-down. French was lost.

Seeing Rodriguez's sign, Tim boiled with anger and emptied his magazine at muzzle flashes in the tree line. He crouched below the crest, ejected the magazine, and slapped in another and chambered a fresh round. "Not fuckin' French," he muttered, then tried the prick again.

*

The sniper was well hidden high atop a leafy tree behind the NVA position. He scanned the edge of the ditch through the Dragunov's scope searching for a Marine with a radio. When the swinging antenna blade caught his attention, he marked its location a meter left of a pale red rock. Satisfied, the sniper raised his eye from the scope, looking for a rest to steady the rifle in that position. A slight movement downwards brought it into a Y-shaped cradle formed by a branch. The sniper hunched down, peered through the scope, found the rock, the antenna, the helmet. He tightened like there was an egg between his finger and the hair trigger. He wanted the report to surprise; that would be a good shot. He exhaled half his breath and held it. The reticles were rock steady and almost covered the helmet at 400 meters.

The first round tore through the target's esophagus. His body lurched to a standing position, then his knees buckled as he crumpled and sat on the bank. In profound shock, little by little the target turned his head and stared downward into the ditch.

The sniper never removed his eye from the scope. As his semi-automatic rifle recoiled it ejected the spent round and chambered another. The empty brass tumbled off one branch to another below him. He settled the scope back on the target, eager to get off a second insurance round.

*

As if frightened, Tim's eyes opened wide, then rolled back. His jaw dropped. The second round hit above his right eye and spun him sideways. He lay face up, stretched across the bank, the PRC 25 still on his back.

7

"Spade One-One, Spade One-One, this is Jolly Roger. I read you now. Come in." The microphone swung back and forth below the edge crest of the ditch, its umbilical still connected to the radio underneath Tim. The relentless fire never skipped a beat for the dead nineteen-year-old.

In the movies, the hero crumples to the ground in slow-motion, in silence. On this day in a real war, the crackling of bullets punctuated every poisonous moment with the sound of a hundred Fourths of July. The hot Southeast Asia air hung heavy with the acrid smell of cordite from spent ammunition, the stench of seared flesh torn by high explosive incendiary, and the foul breath of human waste wafting from the ditch bottom.

*

Eleven time zones away, Randy Houston buffed Blue Coral on his black Buick Special convertible. Fraternity party that night. Hot date. With the Buick's top down, Randy hummed as the radio blasted "The Sounds of Silence" by Simon and Garfunkel. He sat, legs folded, rubbing the waxy haze to reveal the gleaming, jet-black finish of the driver's side door. His mind wandered as he saw his own face in the reflection.

He helped Tim polish his folks' new Plymouth Savoy to high-gloss the Saturday before they sneaked it away to the drags on the unopened interstate. Randy grinned; he recalled how Tim's dad exchanged one of the tires the next day, thinking it was bad.

"We peeled too much rubber, bud," Randy mumbled, glancing at his watch. Ten after three. Plenty of time to finish the job and get cleaned up. The little date window showed 20. Despite the July heat, a chill climbed his sweaty bare back from the base of his spine to the nape of his neck. It startled him and made him tremble a bit, though he didn't know why. He thought of Tim, who was somewhere in Vietnam, killing commies.

***

"Sometimes it's good to have a crazy friend like you, Jan," Dory said, wiping off her eyeliner. "I feel sort of awful. I miss Tim so much."

"Write him," Jan suggested.

"I do, every day. I can't stop thinking about him. I'd give up air to kiss him just once, to talk to him, to hold him in the backseat of the car," she sighed. "Today's worse than usual for some reason." She pulled a box of flowery note cards from under her pillow and started a letter to Tim in her loopy feminine script. She began as always: "My Dearest Tim, I love you so much. Come home to me as soon as you can…"

"No! Stay down!" Steve half-shouted, half-cried as he strained to reach Tim's blood-covered shoulder on the rim of the bank. Another sniper round slammed into Steve's helmet, ripping it from his head. Dazed, Steve watched as it flew across the ditch, landed upside down, and rocked back and forth. He rolled onto his back and slipped down the embankment. A hoarse "Goddamnit!" was all he could utter, as the butt of his M-14 slid into the rancid sludge in the bottom of the ditch.

Randy merged the Buick into traffic on Government Street and headed toward town. Top down on a balmy summer evening, feeling good, he hummed along with the radio. The mysterious chill behind him, he was eager to pick up his date. Tonight it was boilermakers at the frat house.

*

The Dragunov's flash suppressor was good, but there was a faint sparkle when seen from head on. The sniper knew he had been there too long and the Americans would soon zero his location. He used his free arm to position the gun's sling across his chest, but the Dragunov's magazine dug into his back. He reached down and with his hand grasping its butt, rotated the rifle sideways to lay against his back. Like a big green cat, he started down. With purpose he placed each boot on the next limb. *One confirmed kill, one probable*, he thought. *Maybe I can go home…*

*

Dory put on fresh "Love That Red" lipstick and kissed the bottom of the perfumed letter to Tim just below the inscribed "S.W.A.K." She wanted him above all else and the gnawing ache wouldn't go away — ever. He'd been in Vietnam six months. A lifetime.

*

On July 20, 1966, in a firefight near the demilitarized zone, time stopped for Tim Scott. In Alabama it would be days before they knew.

*

Navy A-4 Skyhawks and Air Force F-4 Phantoms pounded and napalmed the NVA position until they disengaged from the Marines. LZ Crow was now cold. Steve helped muscle Tim's poncho-covered body onto the floor of a medevac chopper while rotor wash beat the air into a dusty red storm. The wounded sat or lay atop the dead.

A small scrap of something blew from Tim's helmet and fluttered across the LZ. Steve ran after it, then fell on his knees to trap it against the ground. He held onto it with both hands. Through dust-burned eyes he saw it was a photo of Dory standing in the surf; a drop of Tim's blood colored the lower right corner. On the back he read Tim's schoolboy scrawl:

"And I heard the voice of the Lord, saying: Whom shall I send? and who shall go for us? And I said, Lo, here am I; send me." Isaiah 6:8

Steve kept Dory's photo inside the webbing of his helmet until he rotated home three months later.

*

That night Tim's mother bolted upright from restless sleep. Even with her heart pounding and her breathing shallow and ragged, she'd heard her beloved Tim call his familiar middle-of-the-night words, "Mom, I'm home."

***

Chapter 2

HE CALLED IT HIS

FIREHAMMER...

"To be a good soldier a man must have discipline, self-respect, pride in his unit and in his country, a high sense of duty and obligation to his comrades and to his superiors, and self-confidence born of demonstrated ability."

—George S. Patton, Jr.
General, U.S. Army

I signed and dated the retirement request for my best technical sergeant. "Damn, I hate to lose a good man," I muttered, setting the pen down on the ancient oak executive desk as I looked out of the huge window at the end of the room. Old Glory stood straight out from the pole like a sheet on a clothesline. *Another windy day at Kansas University,* I thought.

"Colonel Houston?" Joyce, my secretary, peered through the doorway, her glasses perched at the end of her nose as usual.

"You have a phone call from a Mr. Steve Matthews. Wouldn't say what he wanted."

I thanked Joyce, gave her the papers I just signed, reached for the phone and hit the speaker button. "This is Colonel Randy Houston."

"Hello, Colonel, this is former Lance Corporal Steve Matthews, United States Marine Corps. Did you fill out an 'In Touch' request a couple of years ago to get information on Tim Scott?"

I could feel my heart rate pick up and an instantaneous rock formed in my stomach. "Ah... yes..." I felt a mixture of curiosity, flush, and dread all in the same instant. *Am I finally going to know what happened?*

"I put Tim on the evacuation chopper when he was killed in Vietnam."

It was involuntary, my eyes swelled, my mouth went dry and a lump as big as a golf ball stuck in my throat. I reached for the mute button. *After thirty years, I may learn what really happened to my best high-school friend.* "Joyce, please shut my door!" I said trying not to let my voice crack. I hit the mute button again to turn on the speaker.

"Sir, are you still there?" Steve asked.

"Yes, please go ahead. When was that, Steve?" I asked, my voice breaking. I needed to verify the person on the other end of the phone was talking about my Tim Scott since it was not an uncommon name.

"July twentieth, nineteen sixty-six, in the DMZ. He was my best friend."

"He was mine too, Steve, many years ago. I don't want to be a prick... just need to know for sure you're real. This is too important. Can you tell me something about Tim that a best friend would know?"

"Ah, let me think..."

"I know it's been almost thirty years, just something that you and I might know about him," I coaxed.

"He had a Zippo lighter he called, 'Firehammer.'"

My eyes shot to a Zippo on my desk. The answer hit me like a ton of bricks. At once I knew this was real. A touch of the rage I felt when I learned of his death flared in my gut. I swallowed hard and tried to compose myself. "I have mine sitting on my desk. Had it engraved, 'July 20, 1966.' Tim's girl, Dory, named his Firehammer because he would often flip it open and shut and it sounded like a metal hammer to her." I took my glasses off and wiped my eyes. I needed the silence Steve provided just then. "Steve, I want to hear everything you can tell me. I need a little time to gather this in. I really appreciate you taking the effort to call. Can I call you back in a bit?"

"Yes, Sir, I'll give your secretary my phone number. I have the battle report I can send you."

"Good — ask Joyce for the address...and Steve, thank you very much for calling. I'll call you soon."

I hung up the phone and stared at the Zippo. I picked it up, cocked it, and then banged it shut: its characteristic metal on metal sound. Firehammer. In one short phone call all my priorities changed. Depressing paperwork and an important seminar faded toward the horizon as I remembered the night I learned of his death.

It was 7:30 and I had parked the Buick. While I was grabbing a case of Bud out of the trunk, Jimmie had his arms around our dates escorting them to the front door of our apartment. That's when Terry tapped me on the shoulder.

"We need to talk, Randy."

"Okay, Terry, but first grab the other case of beer, will you?"

"It's important, Randy."

"Let's get this beer in the fridge first, Terry."

He followed me through the front door and down the hall to the crowded kitchen. After putting one case in the refrigerator, I broke open the other and offered a beer to Terry. Out of character, he declined.

"Are you sick, or something?" I had never known Terry to turn down a free beer. After popping a can for myself, I turned to Terry. "So, what's so important?"

He just looked at me and said, "Let's go in the bedroom."

"Don't flatter yourself, Randy."

We sat on my bed. I took a long swallow of my beer. I can still remember, the only sound then was the window air conditioner fighting the hot July, lower-Alabama heat. "Okay, Terry, let me in on the big secret."

He looked up. "It's not good, Randy."

"What's not good, Terry? For God's sake, spit it out!" My mind jumped to my parents and younger brother in Bangkok, only a few hundred miles from the war zone in Vietnam.

"It's about Tim. He's...dead."

"Don't fuck with me, Terry. This is not funny." He was always the practical joker and liked to amuse himself at other's expense. He wasn't above this kind of shit.

"It's no joke, Randy, honest."

I looked into Terry's eyes. They confirmed that he wasn't joking.

"Tim's mom called while you and Jimmie were picking up the beer." Terry drew in his breath. "She was crying and could hardly talk. She said all they knew was that Tim was on patrol somewhere near the DMZ and was shot by a sniper. It happened a couple days ago, but the Marine Corps just notified her last night. They couldn't tell her anything else. I think you should phone her, Randy. She's really messed up."

Disbelief turned to shock, then to rage. I punched a nearby lamp. It flew across the room and shattered against the wall. I bent over and picked up a coffee table and slammed it against the same wall. "Motherfucking gook bastards!" I screamed as my fist went through the sheetrock near a doorway. Terry wrapped his arms around me from behind. "Stop it, you're gonna hurt yourself and you've already gone through our damage deposit!"

Then as now, my whole life pivoted on its axis. Steve's saying he put Tim on the chopper brought back the sound of the Huey's rotors in Southeast Asia. They're distinctive: you never forget it — the *wop-wop-wop* sound is burned into your brain. It was what Steve must have heard as he put Tim on board and heard the medevac lift off.

***

Chapter 3

REAL MEN EAT

FLOWERS

"How Air Force pilots regard Navy carrier pilots: Next time a war is decided by how well you land on an aircraft carrier, I'm sure our Navy will clean up. Until then, I'll worry about who spends their time flying and fighting."

—*Dave English, cliché, Slipping the Surly Bonds*

Morale was so low it could have fallen off a dime. It was attitude. It's what's left when you cut away the bullshit. After ten years of fighting a war that nobody understood and few wanted to fight, it was a puzzle as to why they were there. They had all lost friends, sons, fathers, or daughters to the Vietnam "conflict"; now they had lost the ground those people had died for. What the hell were they were supposed to do? Just sit next-door in Thailand and watch it happen?

May, 1975. The North Vietnamese had swept through South Vietnam, steamrolling everything in their path. In Phnom Penh, Cambodia, and next-door Saigon, South Vietnam, Americans had been evacuated and the country left to the communists. The 34th Tactical Fighter Squadron, flying F-4D Phantoms from Korat, Thailand, did everything asked of them. It didn't matter. The South still fell. It cost America her youngest and finest, more than 58,000 killed in action, over 2000 unaccounted-for POW/MIAs.

*

Thailand, January 3, three months before Saigon fell, Captain Randy Houston stepped off a huge, T-tailed C-141 onto the steaming tarmac of a flight line crowded with F-4D, F-111A, and A-7D aircraft.

These are war birds, built for killing. Do I have what it takes? During the steamy fifty-yard walk to base operations, his 1505 khaki uniform shirt darkened with perspiration.

At just under six feet, he still had the imposing frame and athletic build of the linebacker he'd been in high school and college. His air and the slightest swagger came from Top Gun in F-4 training. His outward self-assuredness camouflaged the building anxiety he felt the closer he got to the war zone.

The wet heat of the tarmac was suffocating. During jungle survival training in the Philippines, instructors told them about the monsoon in Southeast Asia. It rained every afternoon and the sun boiled the moisture into a Turkish bath. A bead of sweat meandered down Randy's neck. This was the monsoon. What the instructors hadn't mentioned was the smell — the ripe stench of human dung used as fertilizer floating on the weak Asian breeze.

Randy stopped and turned toward the runway as two F-4s thundered by, afterburners shaking the ground under his feet. *The sweet sound of freedom. Good to hear it.* He was in-country as a brand new F-4 pilot fresh from training at Homestead Air Force Base, Florida. By the time customs inspectors finished pawing through his footlocker and B-4 bag, he knew he was in a whole different world. Razor wire ringed the operations compound. Drug dogs sniffed and slobbered through his underwear. Even the conversation was different.

"What's happenin' back in the world, Captain?" a stubby first lieutenant greeted him, offering a casual salute that sort of fluttered away from his right eyebrow.

"Same old shit," Randy said, returning a hurried salute between shoving handfuls of underwear back into his footlocker. "Who are you?"

"I'm John Flasch, your sponsor, call sign Jumpin' Jack. What's yours?"

"I don't have one yet. My instructor told me not to screw up in training. Said I wouldn't like the call sign it'd earn me."

"Ha!" The lieutenant nodded approval. "Your instructor was dead right. And let me give you a word of advice, don't try to dub yourself with one. It just has to materialize over time. We had a backseater show up last month and introduce himself to the ops officer as Mad Dog." The lieutenant was grinning widely now as he handed Randy a roll of socks that had fallen on the concrete floor.

Randy started to thank him but the lieutenant was working up to the punch line.

"So, the ops-o just looked at him and said, 'We got a Mad Dog, you're Blow Dog!' Guess what he's stuck with for life? Anyway, I'll help you get around the first few days, and if you're lucky, I'll be your backseater when you start flying day after tomorrow."

"Monday? Great! Pretty quick, isn't it?" Randy liked the cockiness of this backseater. *No milquetoast here*, he thought.

"You'll get used to it. Things happen fast in a one-year tour," the lieutenant said, helping Randy gather his stuff. "By the time you get combat ready and checked out as a flight lead, you only have a few months 'til you're outta here and back to the world."

"What's it like flying these D model F-4s?" Randy asked, dragging his heavy footlocker to a faded blue Air Force jeep. "In training we flew Es with slats and the 5-5-6 switchology mod." The flying lingo helped him forget how tired he was from the flight.

"By the way, you can call me Jumpin' or Jack, if you like. Yeah, I hear those new Es are nice. These are dumb Ds. They came from Ubon. Been in Southeast Asia for most of the war. Some of 'em have been shot up pretty bad, and they do some squirrelly shit. Every now and then a fuel tank blows itself off the wing or a motor falls in the engine bay. Other than that, they fly fine." He grinned, begging for a reaction from the new guy.

"About the worst thing I saw in training was when my leader's F-4 pitched down, then up and out of close formation when we were night flying," Randy said, as he and Jack heaved the footlocker into the back of the jeep. "All we saw were position lights on his aircraft streaking up and down, then poof, he was gone above us. We found out later the autopilot went batshit in pitch control. If it had gotten sick in roll and pitch at the same time, we'd've been dead meat. Anyway, where we headed?"

"We're gonna drop your stuff off at the hooch and get to the O'Club before the kitchen closes. There's only two places to eat: the club or the Thai restaurant on the other side of the base. The Rams have a table in the club dining room, so you might meet some of the guys. Plus, it's sorta like American food." Jack started the jeep and pulled away from base operations. "We don't want to break you in too fast! I've never gotten used to the reconstituted milk or Thai lettuce. We call it *klong grass.* Chews like rubber."

"What's a klong?"

"They're canals you'll see running everywhere. The locals dump everything in 'em, and I mean everything."

"Is that what I smelled on the ramp?"

"Partially. They also use their sewage to fertilize crops. They grow a lot of rice and tapioca around here. The smell's called *honey bucket* because of the wooden buckets they use to carry the crap to their fields. Pretty soon you won't even notice the smell." Jack stopped the jeep on the side of the road next to a group of one-story wooden buildings, uniform in shape, with metal roofs. "You'll notice there aren't many parking places. Part of the adjustment is that nobody here has cars; therefore, you don't need parking places. Us commoners walk or ride bikes; a few of the brass have these blue-steely staff jeeps." Jack grinned and pointed. "This one's Raptor's, he's the squadron commander."

"Raptor?"

"Oh, yeah. Prince of a guy. You'll enjoy him." Jack pointed to some low buildings. "These are our hooches. Home sweet home."

Randy noticed bare aluminum roofs and weathered wood siding in need of paint. Each building sat on short concrete block pillars. In the center, each hooch had a screened breezeway and communal latrine. Standing alone in the middle of the four hooch buildings was a smaller one with lawn chairs scattered about its door. A few yards away was what looked to Randy like a ping-pong table, but only about two feet high with a dugout pit of muddy water off one end.

"Well, you're here. That's your hooch over there by the tennis court. I'll help you lug this stuff to your room."

"What's that smaller building with the beads hanging in the door and the red lights inside?"

"That's the party hooch. It has a bar and a Thai guy that mixes drinks and keeps it clean. Like my great-great-grandpappy, William Tecumseh Sherman said: 'War is hell.'"

"What's that thing that looks like a ping-pong table?" Randy asked, pointing.

"That's the *deck* we use for carrier landings. It gets greased up with Mazola Oil, then you take a run and land on your belly." Jack pointed at a coiled pile of webbed hose on the ground near the deck. "The *barrier crew* uses that old piece of fire hose to catch your legs. That's if they like you — AND you've already been in the mud at least once. When you miss the *trap*, you end up in the mudhole. That's also where we pour the leftover beer, so it smells real weird. That's about all there's to do around here on Sunday afternoons. The Thai maids think we're *clayzy Amelicans* because we parade around in our uniforms and shiny jungle boots six days a week, then we're drunk and covered with mud on Sundays. Ain't it hell?"

"Sounds like fun." They each gripped a handle at the end of the footlocker and headed toward the nearest hooch. "Speaking of war, what's the chance of seeing some action?"

"Well, that Vietnamization thing in the South didn't work. We gave the South Vietnamese airplanes and tons of equipment, then pulled out." The two set the footlocker on the ground outside the door of the end room. "They did okay for a little while, but are getting their butts kicked now. I think the North Vietnamese are just waiting for the right time to take over the country. When that happens, we might see some action."

"I hope so. I don't want to spend a year over here killing monkeys on the bombing range."

Jack knocked and a tall, bespectacled, and balding man came to the door. "'Lo Jack, who's this?"

"Randy Houston, your new roommate. Just in from the world and he got to celebrate Christmas at home!" Turning to Randy, he said, "This is Eldon Lufkin."

"Christmas at home, huh? Must be nice. No white Christmas here, just a whiskey front that blew through with Santa Claus. Let me help you with your stuff, Randy. Your bed's by the door here. Mine's over there by the air conditioner. Squatter's rights."

Randy glanced at the air conditioner. "Glad to see that machine. Must be tough to sleep in this heat without it."

"Yep," Eldon said.

The dark room had only one window at the end by the door. They each had a dresser and a desk that bore the abuse of new guys moving in and out every few months. Randy's had chipped veneer, an assortment of cigarette burns, and drink stains. The hooches were built to last five years because the planners thought the war would be over by then. Ten years later the hooches were still standing, adorned with resident gecko lizards crawling on the walls.

The trunk was stowed at the foot of Randy's bed, and then the trio walked a block to the O'Club. In the dining room they made their way to an extended table along the right wall. A big squadron patch was painted on the wall behind the table. Randy noticed the large white ram on a black background in the middle of the patch. It blew smoke from its flared nostrils. The "34th Tactical Fighter Squadron" inscription on the bottom.

"'The Rams,' huh, Jack?"

"Yeah, or, like the other squadrons call us, 'The snot-blowing goats.'"

"Not many people here tonight," Eldon said. "Everybody kind of does their own thing on Saturdays. If you're not flying, you're off on Saturday afternoons. A lotta guys go downtown or to Bangkok." Eldon pulled a chair out to sit across from a bulky man at the squadron table. "This is *Animal* Thompson. Animal, meet Randy Houston, fresh meat from the States."

"Hi." Randy reached across the table to shake hands.

Animal's rough hand felt like a country ham. Randy's fingers stung from the big man's grip. Animal had competed for the U.S. Olympic weightlifting team in college. Years later he still rippled with muscles and his short-cropped, black crew-cut block of a head merged with his shoulders on a neck like an oak stump. His pockmarked face looked like someone had put out a fire with an ice pick. His t-shirt had a phantom with a cape, flipping a bird, and underneath it read, "Eat shit and die."

Randy sat across the table from Animal, his view obscured by a vase filled with red and white flowers. Animal shoved it aside, as if he were clearing the area for battle.

Animal eyeballed Randy, sizing him up and emitting a guttural belch. "What's your call sign?"

"He doesn't have one yet," Jack said. "He's just out of training at Homestead."

"Well, we'll have to do something about that," Animal said.

Randy looked at Animal. "How did you get yours?"

"Uh, oh," Jack muttered.

Animal cracked a smile. He reached for the vase, slowly wrapped his hand around some of the flowers, and jerked out a handful. Eyes fixed on Randy, he crammed carnations and roses into his mouth and began to chew. Pieces of flowers fell to the table and a white petal stuck to the corner of his mouth. He rolled his eyes, swallowed most of the bouquet, then wiped his mouth with the back of his hand. "Questions?" he mumbled.

"Pass the pepper, will you?" Randy said, pointing to the shaker at Animal's elbow. Randy jerked the remaining flowers from the vase, unscrewed the lid on the pepper shaker and dumped its contents on the flowers. Shoving them in his mouth, he winked at Animal. "I like lots of it on my salad." Randy grinned as tears started running down his cheeks.

"Shit-hot!" Animal bellowed, then waved to the bar waitress across the dining room. "Li-Li, bring my friend here a drink and make it a double scotch-nam." Turning to the others at the table he yelled, "Serve swill to the rest of these buggers!"

"What the hell's a scotch-nam?" Randy asked, choking down the last bud.

"Scotch and water," Animal said. "'Nam' means water." He stared at Randy and broke into a smile. "Know what, Randy? You just picked up a call sign. I'm gonna nominate you to the ops-o as 'Pepper' Houston!"

✳✳✳

Rain pounded on the aluminum hooch roof like a kettledrum roll. Randy groaned and tried to shake off the jetlag and the scotch from the night before. He rolled onto his back wondering where he was and looked at the alarm clock: 1100. He'd been in a dead man's sleep for 12 hours. He had never heard rain so relentless. It was dark with the shades pulled, but squinting, he could see that the bed at the end of the room was empty. Then he remembered. *Oh yeah, Eldon, he's gone. At least I know where I am.* He pulled the covers over his head and sank back to sleep.

A couple of hours later the door to the hooch flew open and smacked the wall. It sounded like a thirty-aught-six gunshot.

"Get your lazy ass up, Pepper!" Animal shouted. He jerked the covers off and vise-gripped Randy's right ankle.

"Who the hell are you? One of those prison *goons*?" Randy asked, his voice raspy from hours of snoring.

"That's right, and I'm about to expose you to the Vietnamese mud-pit torture trick. Put your pink ass in some shorts and join the squadron formation behind your hooch, or you'll have all the flight commanders in here dragging you to the pit by your hair. I only saved your butt because you like pepper on your flowers."

"Maybe that's why my tongue tastes like a doormat in a shit storm." Randy kicked his leg loose from Animal's grip. Rolling out of his bed, he planted both feet on the floor as he sat for a moment trying to stay vertical. "What's the mud-pit torture?"

"That's when you make your first carrier landing. Of course, you don't get trapped and you end up in the mud pit. Since it's your first, you have to sit in the pit while the next ten guys hit the mud."

Head throbbing, Randy made a face. "Wow, sounds like a helluva lot of fun."

"Piece of advice. Just roll with it, call 'Bingo fuel' every now and then so somebody brings you a beer. No whining. When your ten is up, pick up a couple of handfuls of mud from the bottom of the pit and throw it at anyone who's around. Try to hit the squadron commander, Raptor. The one with 'Zacary' disease. His head rook zacary rike his ass — it's shaved smoother than a baby's butt. He's one micro-managing, anything-you-can-do-I-can-do-better — ASSHOLE."

"Okay, thanks for the intel. I'll be out there in a minute."

Animal shut the door. Randy flipped the light on and found the watch he'd bought in the Philippines after attending jungle survival school. He chuckled to himself remembering his F-4 instructor's words: "That's how they can tell you're a fighter pilot, Houston — big watch and little pecker." Randy fastened the Seiko's heavy gold band on his left wrist, then pulled on a pair of cut-off jeans and headed out the door.

There was a loud splash. Catcalls and laughter ricocheted off the hooch next-door as he rounded the corner to the carrier landing pit. The first guy to see him was Jumpin' Jack.

"Hey, new guy!" Jack shouted.

"Let's all say hello to the new guy!" Animal chimed in, and things momentarily grew quiet.

With twenty pairs of eyes on him, Randy raised his hands in mock surrender. A rousing, "HELLO, ASSHOLE!" the traditional welcome to new guys, echoed off the four hooches forming the open quadrangle. Realizing he was officially "one of the guys," Randy joined their laughter. He instantly felt like he was back in his crazy college fraternity days surrounded by characters, booze, and foolish antics.

Someone screamed, "New meat." Another said, "Ready the deck with some fresh hydraulic fluid!"

"Local Thai beer. It has formaldehyde in it to kill the bugs," Animal said, shoving a cold can of Seng Ha into Randy's hand. "Now, I want you to meet somebody."

He gestured to a Neanderthal-type with matted hair, standing in front of Randy, dripping dirty water and wearing a dingy brown jock strap.

"This is Maggot. He's a backseater, a weapons system operator, or Woooozo. And a helluva one at that."

"Hi. Billy Grubb. I'll be your instructor for your first carrier landing." Maggot extended his filthy right hand. His left held a naked rubber chicken hanging by its long neck.

Randy wondered what he had gotten into. He shook Maggot's hand and said, "What the hell is that thing?"

"Oh, just in case you're thinking about passing on the carrier landings, you get to wear this around your neck until you ship outta here," Maggot said, just crawling out of the mud, white teeth framed by his chocolate-milk-colored, muddy face.

"No way am I wearing that thing for a year!"

"Good, and let me explain something else. We can tell you're a new guy by those nice cutoffs that still have some color to them. The longer you're here, the longer the maids have to beat on your clothes and the more respect you get. You can tell the old heads by how faded their clothes look. That's why I wear this jock strap; nobody can tell I've only been here a month."

Randy's gaze drifted down to Maggot's crotch. "What if women see you in that thing?"

"Don't worry, there's not many around. There's only three round-eye American chicks on the base. They're nurses, so they've seen it all anyway. Come on, chug that beer and I'll start your checkout on becoming a certified, Yew-nited States Navy carrier pilot."

Randy watched as man after man ran a half-circle, as if flying a landing pattern, and then slid down the gray carrier deck on their stomachs. Sometimes they would catch the old fire hose barrier with their calves bent at right angles to their legs like an upside-down or inverted tailhook. At other times the barrier crew would sling the hose out of reach so the would-be carrier pilots had no choice but to slide off the deck into the water-filled mud pit.

Randy looked toward the party hooch and saw Jack talking to an older man who had just stepped out the door. Jack pointed in Randy's direction, still talking. Randy figured the stocky, once muscular and now slightly overweight man who ambled toward him was squadron brass. As he drew closer, Randy could read the inscription on the man's t-shirt. Guns blazing, an F-4 rode his barrel chest. Printed below was, "If you don't fly Phantoms, you ain't shit. Richtofen."

"You must be the new frontseater fresh from the world. I'm Lieutenant Colonel 'Stump' Collins, ops officer of the Rams. Welcome aboard."

"Thank you, Sir. Glad to be here. I've waited a long time to be in a fighter squadron and I'm anxious to get in the air."

"Well, first things first. You need a call sign." Turning to the group, he shouted, "Hey you snot-blowing goats! Listen up! I'm told Captain Houston here likes to eat flowers and he likes a lot of pepper on 'em. He's been nominated by Animal for a call sign of Pepper. I approve that. From now on he's called Pepper unless he does something stupid. Let's say hello to Pepper."

"Hello, Asshole!" again echoed off the hooch walls, followed by, "in the pool!" And, "Nice cutoffs!" from two guys wallowing in the mud pit.

"Ready for your first carrier landing?" Maggot asked, grinning.

"Yep," Pepper said, setting his empty beer bottle down on a weathered cable spool that served as a table.

"Remember your radio calls; call base with a gear check, and be sure you get clearance to land, or they'll wave you off." Pointing toward the deck, Maggot continued, "As you approach, get in a kind of half-crouch so you can hit the deck at a grazing angle instead of belly-flopping and maybe breaking some ribs. You could break some ribs. It's slippery, but hard." Maggot pointed at the approach end to the deck. "Oh yeah, careful with that area as you approach: it gets wet and turns to mud. Pig Farmer got grounded last week after he slipped and crashed into the front of the deck. Dislocated his shoulder. We had to lay him on the deck and I.V. Mekong whiskey to kill the pain."

"Be a helluva note, wouldn't it?" Pepper said. "Get grounded in Southeast Asia before I ever get airborne."

"Just be careful and watch how I do it," Maggot said, tossing the rubber chicken on the spool table. "I'll be a good instructor and demo the pattern and landing for you — once."

As he began to jog the semi-circular pattern, Maggot's muscular, naked, mud-covered butt reminded Pepper once again he was a long way from the world.

"Maggot's base with gear, full stop," he said, as if talking to a control tower. Looking over his left shoulder as he jogged the semicircle, his eyes locked on the approach end of the deck. He began a half-crouch as he lined up on final.

"Cleared to land!" shouted one of the barrier crew holding the fire hose.

Maggot slid on the slippery, painted plywood deck with practiced ease; his arms extended in a diving position, his hands turned up to shield his face from the hose. His legs caught the cable. He stopped just short of sliding off into the mudhole at the end. Two guys sitting in the watery pit threw brown, grit-filled water in his face anyway and shouted, "Waves over the bow!"

Pepper peeled off his t-shirt revealing bulging pecs and a pale, hairy chest.

"Man, cover your eyes," Animal hollered, putting his hands over his eyes. "Your whiteness is blinding."

"New meat…new meat…new meat," the crowd began to chant.

Looking like a tarbaby and wiping muddy water from his eyes, Maggot walked up. "Any questions?"

"Yeah, just one. What's the chance of that barrier crew catching me on the first run?"

"About the same chance you have of getting laid tonight by a round-eye. Slim and none. Just watch this end of the deck and don't run into it."

"Off we go into the wild, blue yonder…" Pepper sang as he started his run. His pulse quickened. He didn't want to screw up with everyone watching. "Pepper's base with gear, full stop," he shouted with undeserved confidence.

As he lined up on final in a half-crouch, one of the barrier crew dropped the hose. Skipping sideways and waving his arms over his head, he shouted, "Wave off, wave off, no clearance to land. Cable is down, cable is down!"

Pepper did the natural thing as if he were in an F-4, and just ran on by the deck. He started another circular pattern to try again and made the gear check call approaching base. This time he heard, "Pepper's cleared to land" on final.

Bent over at the waist and trotting, Pepper lunged. His right foot slipped in the mud and he hit the deck harder than he intended. The oil sped him along as he slid with palms turned up and head turned to the side to avoid catching the barrier with his face. He felt the hose touch his bent calves and for an instant thought it might stop him from plunging head first into the mud pit.

Suddenly, the hose went slack and he heard a chorus of laughter. Disappearing beneath the foul surface he tasted rancid, week-old Seng Ha mixed with mud and water. The earthy smell was like the puddles he'd played in as a child.

Pepper retched, but tried to laugh. Duly baptized, he had just become part of the torn and cratered Southeast Asia landscape of the Vietnam War. It would forever be a part of him...

Chapter 4

FIRST FLIGHT

"When once you have tasted flight, you will always walk the earth with your eyes turned skyward; for there you have been, and there you will always be..."

—Leonardo da Vinci 1452-1519

W hen a new fighter pilot arrives in a war zone things happen fast. A normal three-year tour is crammed into one year and the squadron gets him in the air as soon as possible. Moving household goods into storage, then traveling halfway around the world and stopping for pipeline training like jungle survival school, it was usually a month or better since they last flew. The jet was similar, but everything else was different. The flying procedures changed, the runway was different, the terrain and weather as well. A new pilot was task-saturated easily, and flew with a seasoned instructor pilot on his first hop. An unconscious desire always rode along. *I've got my hands full just flying this jet, I hope nothing catastrophic happens...*

*

"Ram One-One, this is Korat Tower, wind one-eight-zero at eight knots, cleared for take-off runway one-three."

Pressing the microphone button on the right throttle, Pepper answered, "Ram One-One, roger," and nudged both throttles forward. The Phantom's engines instantly responded with their characteristic scream as mountains of air were sucked through the intakes. The control stick was located between his legs, and holding the nose gear steering button on it he guided the jet onto the active runway to line up on centerline.

"Remember, these D models are faster than the Es you came out of," Pepper's instructor pilot, Captain 'Jasper' Emmons spoke through the intercom system from the backseat. "Be ready to pick up the landing gear sooner on take-off so we don't over-speed their limits."

"Roger that," Pepper said, pumping the top of the rudder pedals to hold the brakes as he eased each throttle forward one at a time to 100 percent, military power. Engine thrust with both throttles to 100 percent, or mil, would cause the tires to turn on the wheel rims, so he set both throttles at 80 percent and quickly scanned the twin banks of engine instruments. *RPM, exhaust temp, oil, hydraulics, and nozzles look good. Green for take-off.* "I'm ready," Pepper said, leaning forward to punch the button on the clock to start the elapsed timer.

"Let's roll," Jasper snapped. "We're taking too long on the runway."

I'm sluggish, behind the jet. Haven't flown in over a month. Gotta speed up. He pulled his feet off the top of the rudder pedals releasing the brakes, then shoved the throttles outboard to the left side and forward into afterburner. An invisible hand shoved him back into his seat as the Phantom hurtled down the runway, thousands of horses surging toward take-off speed. Centerline dashes merged into a solid line as the airspeed indicator passed a hundred knots in only seconds. The rudder was effective now, and Pepper steered the aircraft back to centerline with the pedals, At 120 knots he pulled the jet's control stick all the way back to the stop. The Phantom's nose began to rise, and he eased the stick forward to hold the nose at take-off pitch. At 160 knots he felt marshmallow cushiness and knew he was no longer tied to the ground. Brain cobwebs cleared a little as his mind caught up to the speed of the thundering jet.

Pepper reached forward to raise the landing gear with his left hand. He liked the F-4 gear handle. It was big, and not easily missed in the rush to accelerate to climb speed of 350 knots. He rotated it up to retract the gear. As he fumbled and searched for the flap switch, three green lights in a triangle on the instrument panel extinguished, telling him the gear had unlocked, then the red light in the gear handle went out indicating the gear doors were up and locked.

"Gear up, flaps up, pressure's good, through three-hundred, going to three-fifty," Pepper said. "Sorry, Jasper, I talk to myself when I'm behind the jet."

"No sweat, I do the same thing. It lets the wizzo know what I'm looking at."

Pepper pressed the microphone button. "Korat Departure Control, Ram One-One's airborne, climbing to three-thousand, runway heading."

"Ram One-One, departure. Radar contact. Turn right to zero-three-zero, climb and maintain one-five-thousand."

"Zero-three-zero, one-five-thousand, Ram One-One," Pepper said, easing the phantom into a thirty-degree banked right climbing turn. *Damn, I'm rusty. Chasing that airspeed all over the place. Gotta get it back down to three-fifty. Everything else looks okay.*

"Better watch that airspeed," Jasper said on the intercom.

"Yeah, I'm working on it. My mind's still back on the runway." *Instructors! Why do they always tell you what's wrong two seconds after you've started to correct it? Man, those clouds are beautiful. Air under my ass feels good.*

"Ram One-One, departure. Cleared into the working area. Squawk One-Two-Zero-Zero, monitor this frequency for advisories."

"Ram One-One, roger."

"Squawk set," Jasper volunteered from the backseat. "Take a look at that road down there to our left. If you work along it between those two villages, we'll stay in the working area."

"Got it." *This jungle all looks the same. If it wasn't for the rice paddies and an occasional road, I'd be lost. No big cities or large features like in the States. Just flat and green.*

"Okay, Pepper, let's start with some maneuvers so you can get your hands back and see how this D-model is different. Why don't we start out with a rig, stab-aug check and then maybe do a barrel roll?"

"Sounds good, rig, stab-aug check complete. Yaw Aug is off. Fuel and oxygen is good." *Feels good to be making these radio calls. Talking pilot shit again.* "I'm going to roll around that cloud at eleven o'clock. It's a 400-knot entry, right?"

"Roger. Use whatever power you want."

Pepper dropped the nose of the Phantom and pushed the throttles to mil. Four-hundred knots came quickly. He began a rolling pull, keeping the puffy cumulus at the same location on the canopy. It was a basic maneuver he'd taught many times to students in pilot training.

"Okay, good job, Pepper. Now let's do some turns and jog your memory on how the hard wing of the D talks to you differently than the slat wing E. Like we said in the briefing, where the turn rate was greater in the slat, you'll find the D starts to buffet more, and at a higher airspeed. That's the primary handling difference."

Pepper completed his left turn to stay in the training area, then rolled wings level. Setting the power at 85 percent on each engine, he nudged the control stick to the left to set the bank angle at 60 degrees. "I'm just going to hold this bank and let the airspeed decay. Sound okay?"

"Yeah, that's fine. At about 200 knots you'll start to feel some buffet. Just try to hold level flight into the heavy buffet to get a feel for it."

The Phantom still carried nearly a full load of fuel, a condition that would cause it to slow down faster in turns. As the airflow left the wing from decreasing airspeed, he knew he could expect a shudder or buffet of the jet to tell him a stall was imminent. With airspeed decreasing below two-hundred knots, Pepper felt the jet start to buffet.

"Okay, there's the tickle," Pepper said. "I'm going to ease the stick all the way back into my lap in this turn."

"Once you get there with the stick, you can only turn with the rudder," Jasper said, his voice shaking slightly from the jet's tremor. "If you try using the stick instead of the rudder you'll depart dear old controlled flight."

"Okay, there's the heavy buffet," Pepper said as the instrument panel in front began to shake. "The E-model was smooth compared to this."

"Now turn back the other direction while you stay in the buffet."

Never having flown the hard-wing D model, Pepper instinctively leaned the stick to the right to counteract the left turn, but he didn't use enough rudder. Instead of turning right as commanded, the Phantom snapped farther left and rolled on its back with the nose dropping toward the ground. The sky was no longer visible. Only dark green jungle filled his windscreen.

"Okay, no sweat, just ease off the back pressure and try rolling upright with rudder," Jasper said.

Instincts again told Pepper to pull the nose up to level flight, not let off while it pointed at the ground. *Damn, she's shaking hard. What's the altitude? Fifteen-thousand. Good. Okay, sweetheart. Here we go, fly right for Pepper. Off the back pressure and here's the right rudder. I'll be damned, she turns good that way!*

"That's it. Let the airspeed build before you start pulling the nose to the horizon."

Shit, you'd think I've never stalled an airplane before! "Okay, I'm pulling right at the edge of the tickle," Pepper responded, easing the nose of the Phantom up to level flight. "That was fun, let's do some more!"

"Come right to stay in the area and let's set up for a pitchback and sliceback. Get four-twenty-five on the knots and start whenever you're ready."

Pepper lowered the nose of the Phantom and pushed the throttles to mil. The airspeed shot through 380. Approaching 425 knots, he practiced making the usual radio call, "Ram One-One's got a blue bandit, right five o'clock, low. Ram's in a right slice, engaged." He slammed the throttles outboard, then to afterburner. Simultaneously he snapped the Phantom into a steep diving right-hand turn with the aircraft nearly on its back. He felt the thump of the 30,000 pounds of afterburner thrust. A quick look at the airspeed indicator told him he was maintaining the 425 knots needed to give him the optimum turn radius. Five Gs came fast. He overshot to six. The oxygen mask sagged on his face, sweat rolled down his forehead, the anti-G suit around his legs inflated with air and squeezed to hold blood in his upper body. He grunted to fight tunnel vision as blood reacted to gravity and flowed from his eyes. "Damn, this hurts so good!" he shouted, then pulled the F-4 up to level flight and checked airspeed — still 425.

"Okay, let's set up for a pitchback. If you line up on that dirt road down there, we can see how close to 180 degrees you can get on this one," Jasper said, just as the MASTER CAUTION light came on and the emergency telelights on the instrument panel lit up like a Christmas tree...

***

Chapter 5

ERRANT PHANTOM

"To put your life in danger from time to time…breeds a saneness
in dealing with day-to-day trivialities."

—Nevil Shute, Slide Rule

A fighter pilot knows that when things start to go wrong with his
jet, they often continue, even snowball. The loss of one important
system affects others until the aircraft is a flying derelict looking
for concrete before it falls from the sky. No matter how long a pilot flies,
the initials IFE (In-Flight Emergency) never lose their gut-wrenching
force. When a car acts up, the driver can just pull over, lift the hood, and
investigate. As a shark must swim incessantly to live, an aircraft has to
be moving forward to remain airborne. For a Phantom, that's about 300
MPH to be safe. During an IFE the pilot has to rely on warning lights
on the emergency telelight panel to get a sense of what's failing. He then
has to trust his airmanship and knowledge of aircraft systems to get the
bird home. The initial adrenaline shot is similar to that of combat. His
first thought: *Is this the one that's gonna get me?*

*

"Damn. What's that left engine doing?" Jasper snapped over the intercom
from the backseat.

Pepper's eyes shot to the double bank of engine instruments. "There's a
MASTER CAUTION…left generator and utility hydraulic light. And…

RPM and exhaust temp on the left engine are winding down. We got a flame-out."

"Shit, we didn't do anything wrong, the good old General Electric J-79 just quit," Jasper mumbled. "Point our nose toward the base — now. We've got problems, Pepper. You fly it from up there and I'll do the talking. Listen up when I do."

"Roger, I've got the aircraft, Korat's on the nose." Pepper leaned forward and punched the left engine ignition button attempting a restart before it went to zero RPM. "We shouldn't have utility hydraulic failure just because the left engine quit."

"I know, we'll sort that out in a minute. How's the right one look?"

"Good. The left RPM is near zero. Left throttle is idle." Pepper ran his left hand around the cockpit checking switches, flying the Phantom with his right hand on the control stick. "Forty-eight miles to Korat, restart on the left is a no-go, it's tits-up, throttle's coming off."

"Start dumping fuel — now," Jasper said as he switched frequencies and keyed the mike.

"Korat Tower, this is Ram One-One with an in-flight emergency. We're presently 45 miles northwest descending out of one-five-thousand. Our left engine is flamed out and will not restart. We also have utility hydraulic failure. We'll be engaging the approach-end cable on landing. Better roll the fire trucks."

"Korat Tower, roger. Understand you're going to take the cable and will be closing the runway in about five minutes."

"That's affirmative, Tower."

Jasper returned his attention to Pepper. "Okay, hit the emergency checklist. We'll need to put the arresting hook down and take the approach-end cable. You ever want to land on a carrier?"

"Sure, piece of cake. Carrier pilots are way overrated."

"Well, it ain't no piece of cake. Let's get busy up there, new guy. You've gotta make this landing. I can't see the friggin' cable from back here. We've got about three minutes to get our shit together. Keep dumping fuel until I tell you to cut it off. We've got to get our weight down or we'll tear the cable loose when we hit it."

Pepper had the checklist strapped to his left thigh and open to emergency procedures. "Okay, I ran the checklist. Do your descent check and stow loose items in the back. My shoulder harnesses are locked. Check yours." Pepper hesitated, his mouth getting dry. "The only other thing is to put the command selector valve in AFT INITIATE so you can eject us both if this gets worse."

Ordinarily, the Phantom needs utility hydraulic pressure to lower the landing gear and power the wheel brakes. Without it, the pilot must lower the gear by emergency air bottles and hope they would free-fall into place and lock down. But once lowered, the landing gear can't be picked up again. It takes skill to fly on one engine with the landing gear stuck down. It was like a car hitting on half its cylinders, pulling a heavy load up a mountain.

"Checklist says problems recovering an F-4 with a combination single engine and utility failure are severe," Pepper noted. "No shit."

"Yeah. True. Flight controls are half-ass workin', including the rudder. We really need rudder on one engine, too. Make all your turns away from the dead engine to keep from rolling or yawing out of control. That means only right turns up there, nose gunner."

"Roger that."

With no braking system, Pepper would lower the tailhook from the front cockpit and plan a touchdown in front of the steel cable stretched across the runway. He was rusty; he hadn't landed an airplane in over a month, and had never put a Phantom in the cable. Doubts swept him, then disappeared in the flurry of flying the jet and searching in the monsoon haze for the runway. He had a sick bird and one chance to make the nest.

"Helluva first flight, huh?" Jasper chided. "Leave the flaps up and plan a straight-in approach."

"Okay, will do." *Right engine, keep turning.* Pepper inched the right throttle forward to maintain 250 knots. "I'm glad I left a coat hanger in my locker so Jack can use it to rake my wallet out of our burning rubbish."

"Nah, this is gonna be a piece of cake," Jasper said. "Let's stay on this glide path all the way to touchdown so we don't have to use much power on the right engine. Get the gear down and the hook, we're about six miles out. Stop dumping now."

Pepper moved the hex-head dump switch to normal which stopped the venting of fuel. He reached to the left chest pocket of his flight suit and felt the outline of Tim's lighter. *Do some magic...* "Okay, emergency gear handle is out. Gear coming down — I hope. The nose and left main are down. Damn, no green light on the right gear. I'm holding 170 knots."

"This is gonna get real ugly if we catch a cable with one main gear unlocked," Jasper said. "Okay, keep your airspeed steady, and slowly feed in right rudder to yaw the aircraft to the right. Maybe we can get that 170-knot air to catch the gear door and pull it down. Be careful, yaw can get away from you flying on one engine."

"Here goes the rudder, there won't be much more available anyway. I already had some in from carrying power on that right engine."

"Got the hook down?"

"Not yet." Pepper's feet were on both rudder pedals. He held the right pedal in until his leg began trembling. The control stick occupied his right hand and the remaining good throttle his left. He moved his left hand to flip the tailhook switch on the instrument panel. He quickly put his hand back on the throttle to add power as the tailhook came down in the slipstream and added drag. "There it goes. Tailhook's down. No green light in the right gear yet...come on, baby."

"One mile to touchdown. Keep'er comin'," Jasper advised, then pressed the radio button.

"Tower, Ram One-One. Can you put your glasses on us and see if the right main looks down and locked? We're indicating it's unsafe."

"Ram, it looks like you have three down and a hook."

"Pepper, test that light bulb and see if it's good."

"Bulb's good, but still shows the gear's unsafe."

"Okay, we're gonna take our chances. The right engine could decide to quit. Put her down just in front of the cable. If we miss it, we'll try to catch the one at the far end of the runway. If we miss that one, we're ejecting. Got it?"

Pepper swallowed hard, a bead of sweat trickled down his forehead and onto his oxygen mask. "Roger that."

Pepper aimed the F-4 to a touchdown point half a football field before the cable. He'd seen carrier landings in the movies and imagined an eyeball-popping experience when the cable caught the jet. Locked shoulder harnesses would hold his body back, but his head and eyeballs would drop forward in the instantaneous stop. If the right gear wasn't locked and folded on touchdown, they would miss the cable and go careening off the side of the runway in a cloud of dust, smoke, and fire. They would be riding a 150-knot, 37,000-pound sled slowed only by scraping along the ground, hitting obstacles, or worse yet, tumbling.

Pepper used the button on top of the control stick and trimmed the Phantom so it would virtually fly itself to the runway. They were on short final now, only a few hundred yards from touchdown, airspeed set.

"Once we touch down, keep the right wing up as long as you can," Jasper encouraged. "It'll ease the pressure on that unsafe gear."

"Copy." Pepper's gaze shifted constantly between the AIRSPEED INDICATOR and the runway. He added a little power to hold the decreasing airspeed at 168. A fire truck was in position near the approach end. He could see others speeding to their locations farther down. *Hope we don't need 'em...*

"Ram One-One, Korat Tower, cleared to land, cleared cable engagement... good luck."

"Ram, roger," Jasper answered the radio in practiced instructor pilot calmness.

Mouth dry as sand, pulse racing toward 180, concentrating on nothing else, Pepper touched the Phantom down 200 feet in front of the cable. *Come on, baby, hold.* He held left pressure on the control stick to reduce the weight on the right main gear. Just before passing the cable the nose gear came down and touched the runway. *Shit hot! It's holding!* They both felt the right main holding its weight. Then there was a falling lurch to the right. Because of the jet's leaning angle, the tailhook skipped over the 2"-thick cable crossing the runway.

The right wing continued to fall as its landing gear retracted. The Phantom yawed right from the friction of the wing scraping the concrete surface of the runway.

"Oh, shit," Jasper uttered.

Pepper fought panic as adrenaline coursed his veins. He jabbed full left rudder and struggled with both hands on the control stick to hold full left in a feeble attempt to combat the Phantom's impending slide off the right side of the runway. Instantly the right gear door ripped from its hinges as wing panels tore away from the underside. Jasper snapped his head to the right and saw fire billowing from the wing's fuel tank.

Firefighters stood by on the taxiway and began to respond. With a monstrous scraping, tearing sound, the Phantom smashed through runway lights and hit a distance-remaining marker with a big number six on it. As the Phantom plowed through grass, air scoops underneath sucked dirt and pumped it through the ventilation system. Dust filled the cockpits. Pepper and Jasper began to choke, they no longer could see where the errant Phantom was headed. Acrid smells of burning rubber, plastics, fuel, and insulation filtered through their oxygen masks. They banged forward and to the left side of their cockpits when the right wing struck the runway. As the jet skidded off the runway, the left main gear plowed a furrow in the earth, savagely reversing their rotation. Both pilots were brutally thrown around their cockpits like marbles in a can. A sick, sinking feeling hit Pepper's stomach.

The landing gear wrenched from the wing and the tire unceremoniously bounced through the infield grass on a lonely, hundred-knot mission to nowhere.

Pepper clutched the control stick with all his strength, dampening the impact of his shoulders on the unforgiving steel canopy rails. In the backseat, Jasper had nothing to hold onto. His helmet struck the left side of the heavy Plexiglas canopy, shattering its plastic viser and knocking him unconscious. As the Phantom spun in the opposite direction, his head whipsawed and struck the right side of the canopy.

"Let's get the hell out of here," Pepper shouted as the severely damaged aircraft came to rest in a billowing cloud of dust and smoke. For a moment their luck held, the dirt extinguished most of the fire under the right wing. But as they came to a stop, a hot titanium wing panel re-ignited leaking JP-4 jet fuel.

Pepper reacted from drilled procedures: pulled the right throttle up and over the shutoff detent and switched the battery off. Reaching between his legs with his right hand he rotated the ejection seat safety lever up. At the same time, he used his left hand to free himself from the burning Phantom. A fiery fuse licked at the three tons of jet fuel still aboard the disintegrating aircraft. *Gotta get outta this thing!* He jerked open the canopy handle. In a panic to escape, he pushed on the glass to speed its slow yawning.

Pepper scrambled from the cockpit and saw that the rear canopy was still down. "What the hell? He's not moving." Pepper stepped onto the engine air intake and pounded on the canopy. Pain shot through his hand as it bounced off. "Jasper, get outta there! The fuckin' thing's burning!" *Think! Pull the canopy jettison handle and blow it.* Pepper opened the small door labeled "Danger." He stepped back on the spine of the fuselage and buried his face in his arm. He jerked the lanyard and flinched as 1200 pounds of compressed air exploded, propelling Jasper's canopy skyward.

Flames spread over the right wing and 2000-degree heat boiled like a blast furnace as Pepper shielded his eyes with his arm and inched forward to unstrap Jasper from his ejection seat.

The concussion from the blown canopy shook Jasper from unconsciousness. Through blurred vision he saw flames leap up from the right wing toward his cockpit. Instinctively he felt for the ejection handle between his legs and pulled. Dazed from the crash, he was still slumped right, out of proper position as the powerful Martin-Baker seat blasted up its rails.

The blast knocked Pepper off the engine air intake to the ground eight feet below. Pain jolted through his left shoulder. Stunned and in shock, he crawled his way from the building inferno, dragging his left arm.

Pepper felt someone grab his collar and looked up to see a hulk of a man in a shiny foil fire suit dragging him along the ground. Behind them, Pepper's front ejection seat succumbed to ravaging heat and blasted up the rails. Almost in concert, a fuel tank in the right wing exploded, shocking the ground, and rocketing a chunk of wing panel hundreds of feet into the air. Pepper cringed and glanced at the panel to see only the "US" part of USAF still left on it.

The firefighter let go of Pepper who rolled to his side, looking up for Jasper. The seat performed its automatic sequence and separated from him 100 feet in the air. The parachute snapped full of air as he descended. His arms hung limp like a rag doll, his head rolled listlessly as he got half a swing in the chute before hitting the ground in a heap only yards away from Pepper.

"No!" Pepper screamed. He disconnected his oxygen mask and hurled it away. His smoke-smudged face was streaked with sweat as he stumbled to get to his feet. He steadied enough to watch a silver-clad firefighter run to capture Jasper's billowing parachute as fire wind drug Jasper's body across the ground. Another firefighter grabbed Jasper's parachute risors and worked feverishly to release him from the harness. With Jasper finally free, the fireman threw Jasper's limp form over his shoulders and carried him away from the exploding cauldron behind them.

Martin-Baker seat can break your back...he was in a bad position. Dammit, Jasper...

Chapter 6

DISTANT EYES

"What freedom lies in flying, what Godlike powers it gives to men...I lose all consciousness in this strong unmortal space crowded with beauty, pierced with danger."

—Charles A. Lindbergh

Pepper moaned as the firefighter rolled him onto a stretcher. Pain raced to replace shock. A coal-black medic in a starched white uniform with three stripes of an airman first class took over and shoved Pepper's folding stretcher in the back of the ambulance. The medic clambered in, reaching for the stethoscope around his neck.

"How's Jasper...where is he?" Pepper asked.

"The flight surgeon's lookin' at him, Sir. He'll be here in a minute. Where are you injured?"

"Not sure," Pepper said, rubbing his left arm. "My shoulder and arm hurt like hell."

"Okay, you ain't gonna die from that. I'm goin' to take off your helmet, see if your head's on straight. Let me know if anything else hurts, okay?" The medic unsnapped Pepper's chin strap, then rotated the helmet forward and off. "Anything hurt when I did that?"

"No."

"Good. If head and heart are workin', you're all right. I'm gonna take your blood pressure, Sir."

"What's your name, airman?"

"I'm Airman First Jedediah Monroe, Sir," he said, wrapping the cuff around Pepper's right arm. The airman flinched as another jarring explosion from the Phantom racked the ambulance. Monroe's "damn!" was drowned out and Pepper jerked as a heavy piece of the jet slammed onto the ambulance roof.

A second stretcher bumped the back of the ambulance and started to fold. "Out of the way! Coming in!" a flight surgeon shouted. He held a clear plastic oxygen mask over Jasper's mouth with one hand, and tried to lift the stretcher with the other. A medic rounded the corner of the ambulance and helped as they rolled Jasper in next to Pepper.

The flight surgeon, now inside and still holding Jasper's oxygen mask, twisted around and shouted at the driver, "Get on the horn to the ER. Tell 'em we've got two injured pilots: one has severe head and spinal, the other has shoulder trauma. We need radiology standing by and someone working on a medevac flight for the major. Let's go, driver!"

Pepper turned his head toward the other stretcher. "Jasper, *Jasper!*"

"He's out. He can't hear you." The flight surgeon grabbed for the stretcher's handle as the ambulance surged forward and the siren spun to a wail.

"Is he gonna live, Doc?" Pepper asked.

The surgeon shrugged. "Yeah, he'll live. Can't tell about his injuries, though. No way of knowing until we get some x-rays and run some tests."

"Did the ejection seat get his back?"

"May have. He came around a minute ago and couldn't feel his legs. But that could be a lot of things. That damn Martin-Baker is good for trashing lower thoracic and lumbar vertebrae."

"Will he fly again?"

"Time will tell, time will tell. Anything is possible, from paralysis to complete recovery."

"Will I fly again?"

"You're lucky. Arms and shoulders can be fixed. If that's all, you'll be fine."

"I hope he'll fly, Doc. I hope he'll fly…"

*

That night Pepper lay on cool white sheets in a hospital room. Besides the bed there was only a gray metal desk chair and a small bedside stand with a dim lamp. They were keeping him overnight for observation. A stranger to hospitals and being sedated, he occasionally awoke to unfamiliar disinfected smells. Whenever he saw a nurse or medic he asked about Jasper. The answer was always the same: "The doctor will see you in the morning and explain everything."

It was bright the next morning when Pepper awoke to someone taking his pulse. "Hi, Captain Houston. I'm Doctor Lilly, a flight surgeon. Good news. You got a pulse." The doctor put Pepper's hand down on the bed. "We rode together in the ambulance yesterday. I understand you have some questions about your friend Jasper."

"Yeah. I remember now. I go by Pepper. You?"

"Boots. Ask me no questions about it, I'll tell you no lies. You seem to be doing better this morning. How's the shoulder? Getting used to the sling?"

"How's Jasper?"

"I'll tell you about him in a minute. Got any pain?"

"Not bad," he said, leaning on his good elbow to prop himself up. "I forget about it, then move and zing-o. I get a pretty good jab in my upper arm."

"You've got some pretty bad bruising where you landed, and maybe a slight fracture of your arm. You're in pretty good shape. That's what probably kept you from getting hurt worse. Did you play ball in college?"

"Yeah, a couple of years as linebacker."

"Did you play at the Air Force Academy? I remember a Houston there a few years back."

"No, for the Tide at 'Bama. I never got out of second string though. The scholarship ran out and no way I was headed to the NFL."

"Well, toughened up playing ball did you a favor," he said, studying the chart on the clipboard as he sat in a desk chair. "That's probably what kept you from getting a serious injury when you piled up that F-4."

"That's good to know. Is Jasper gonna make it?"

"He's hurt pretty bad, but he's stable. He's in and out of consciousness."

"The last thing I can remember from yesterday was you saying something about his back. Is it going to be all right? Will he fly again?"

"X-rays showed two thoracic vertebrae compressed and two lumbar fractured," Dr. Lilly said, continuing to study Pepper's chart. "He's been through a lot. He may have trouble walking again. It really depends on the individual at this point."

"Damn. I should've held the right wing up longer to keep the weight off the gear, or not landed so soon. Maybe I shouldn't have blown his canopy and just waited for the firefighters."

"You did everything you could." Dr. Lilly laid the chart in his lap and looked at Pepper. "Once a Phantom touches the ground, there's no flying it. From what I heard about your engine and utility problems, the jet needed to be down pronto before something else quit. Just as we pulled up you were popping the canopy. The fire was spreading fast, and the jet could have blown any second. Pulling the canopy jettison lanyard was the right thing. A firefighter would have done it 15 seconds later anyway, but then it would've been too late."

Pepper lay on his back and stared at the ceiling. "But when I blew the canopy that made him pull the ejection handle."

"Egress training teaches us that, remember?" Dr. Lilly stood and hung the chart on a hook at the end of the bed and turned to face Pepper. "If you're surrounded by fire, the best reaction may be up and outta there. Jasper just resorted to his training instincts. He was disoriented and barely conscious when he pulled the handle."

"When can I see him?"

"There's a medevac C-9 in this afternoon to fly him to Clark Air Base in the Philippines. Maybe you could visit him for a few minutes before it takes off."

*

The C-9 Nightingale is the military version of the Douglas DC-9 and was equipped to transport severely sick and injured personnel to medical treatment centers. Pepper had seen the gray and white medevac many times before on its routine stops. The red cross on its vertical tail always gave him a warm feeling. He'd never really thought about why; now he understood. It was comforting to know medical help in the form of a fast jet and trained staff could whisk an F-4 driver away if wounded or injured.

One of the C-9's engines was running as Pepper walked up the stairway to find Jasper. He carried a small book tucked in the sling. A blast of cool air and a flight nurse with shoulder-length red hair and babydoll-blue eyes met him as he stepped through the doorway.

"Your medical records, Captain?" she said, scanning down a roster on a clipboard she held. "According to the manifest everyone is already aboard."

She's drop-dead gorgeous. Pepper stood mesmerized… "Oh, I guess this sling threw you off. I'm here to see Major Emmons before you take off." *It's been a while since I've seen a round-eyed American woman…wonder if I could get on the manifest?*

The nurse looked up with a slight smile. "You'll have to hurry; we're taking off in about five minutes, just as soon as the pilots finish their preflight." She pointed to her left down the aircraft. "The major's down the aisle. Follow me and I'll take you to see him. Remember, no more than five minutes, okay?"

"Roger that."

As she turned to lead him toward the rear of the aircraft, Pepper's eyes feasted on the beauty in front of him. Light from the doorway bounced off a highly polished medical storage cabinet and made her auburn hair shine. His gaze moved down her back following her tailored and well-fitted green fatigues to where they gathered around a narrow waist. There was a delicious flare around her curved hips.

"Okay," Pepper said, turning sideways in the aisle to let an attendant with an I.V. bottle rush by. *Damn, what a knockout!*

"My name's Randy Houston; they call me Pepper."

"Nice to meet you," she said, smiling, turning her head to the side.

"I guess your name's classified information?"

"Yep. 'Secret, no-foreign dissemination,' and you're still foreign." She turned and pointed to a lower bunk. "Here's Major Emmons. You don't have long." As she brushed by him toward the front of the C-9, she whispered, "My name's Robyn…" Her last name was drowned out by the roar of two Phantoms on take-off in full afterburners.

The space was tight inside the C-9. It looked to Pepper like a medical submarine with hospital beds stacked up like bunks on both sides of a narrow aisle. Jasper was on a bunk with special apparatus for back injuries holding his head rigid. At the foot of his bed, Doctor Lilly was making final adjustments on traction to keep pressure off his spine. Jasper's head was shrouded by a heavy white gauze bandage down to his eyebrows. A sheet and an olive-green blanket with U.S. printed on it covered the rest of him.

Pepper stopped short of the bed and stared. Flirting with Robyn evaporated as the scene came back to him of the exploding Phantom and that one wing segment spinning through the air. It had U.S. on it too. His dad always said that meant "us." Now it was "us" on a medevac, with Jasper clinging to a thread of life, possibly never to walk again. Pepper took a deep breath to counteract the sinking feeling in his stomach. He glanced at Dr. Lilly, then at Jasper.

"Hi, Jasper."

"You'll have to lean over so he can see you, Captain," Dr. Lilly said. "He can't move his head."

Pepper leaned over and looked into dull eyes that moved little and seemed focused miles away. "You're going back to the world, Jasper, but they're gonna take a good look at you in the Philippines first."

Distant eyes, bloodshot with pain, moved slowly to meet Pepper's. There was no expression, pupils were narrow.

"As soon as I know where to write, I'll send you a letter, let you know what the squadron is doing. That way you'll be up to speed when you get back." Pepper struggled to keep his voice from cracking. *Damn. He's really hurtin'…and I caused it.*

Jasper tried to speak, but the whisper was lost in the noise on board. Pepper leaned closer, "Say again, Jasper."

Jasper's voice was barely audible. "We didn't do anything wrong."

Pepper nodded, fighting back tears. "I know. I've thought about it a million times." *We could've flown longer, the result would've been the same. That gear wasn't gonna lock down. Maybe we'd have been better off to just punch out together. You wouldn't be here now and the jet would've made a smokin' hole in the jungle instead of trashing the runway.*

Jasper stared at the ceiling of the C-9. His lips tried to move again. Pepper flushed with emotion, his eyes misted as he leaned down to listen with his good hand on his knee. "We didn't do anything wrong…write my wife…tell her what happened…I'm okay…love her."

Pepper took Jasper's limp right hand in his as if shaking hands and squeezed. There was no response. "I will. You're in good hands — the best there is. If the nurses look as good as the one I just met, you're gonna have plenty of nice scenery. Hang tough, buddy. I'll get to Clark to see you soon." Pepper squatted down to speak directly into Jasper's ear. "I'm leaving a copy of *Jonathan Livingston Seagull* on the bed here for you. You'll fly like him one of these days."

Robyn touched Pepper on the shoulder. "Captain, we're ready for take-off. You'll have to deplane now."

"Okay," Pepper said as he stood upright in the aisle, never taking his eyes off Jasper.

"Keep your mach up, partner. I want to fly with you again."

Jasper's eyelids closed as he drifted away under the sedative Dr. Lilly injected into the I.V.

Maybe I should tell him about the North Vietnamese starting an all-out push toward Saigon…he wouldn't hear me now anyway. Pepper felt empty as he followed Robyn toward the C-9's door.

She turned to let him by. "Don't worry, we'll take good care of him." She patted his good shoulder.

"Thanks. We need him back. He's a good fighter pilot," Pepper said, noticing "GREER" for the first time on the uniform nametag above her breast. "My mother's maiden name was Greer. Any chance we're related?"

"Maybe. I was born in West Virginia."

Pepper turned to face her in the doorway. He tried not to get lost in the stunning blue eyes that seemed to look into his soul. "I was born in a little town in western North Carolina called Boone. What's the chance we're *kissin'* cousins?"

"Slim to none," she said with a wry smile.

Pepper grinned. "Well, fly safe and maybe I'll see you on the next trip. He turned to grab the handrail of the stairs, hesitated, then looked back. "Can I call you if I get to Clark?"

"Suit yourself, but I'm not there much. We gotta go. You be safe, too."

"Bye. I'd appreciate you taking extra care of Jasper. We crashed an F-4 a couple of days ago. I walked away, he didn't."

Robyn smiled. "I'll consider it my privilege."

He turned and made his way down the stairs as Robyn stood lost for a moment. Her hands dropped to her sides, she stared at his back as he descended. She turned and reached for the locking handle of the C-9's door. She muttered to herself, "He looks nice in that flight suit. Wonder if our paths will ever cross. I hope it's not in a hospital."

Reaching the tarmac, Pepper turned and gave her a short flyboy salute. Robyn smiled, then slowly locked the door in place.

Chapter 7

TARGETS AND

FIGHTERS

"Up there the world is divided into bastards and suckers. Make your choice."

—*Derek Robinson, Piece of Cake*

The 34th Tactical Fighter Squadron commander's office, a murky boar's nest tucked away at the end of the hall, was not visitor friendly. Squadron pilots wanted no part of the commander's office. They dubbed it the "turning room" because of the military facing movements demanded of them when reporting to the commander and again when leaving — assuming they were still in the Air Force.

By virtue of "G-series" orders from the president, the commander was judge, jury, and executioner. He could demote, confine, even sentence a subordinate to hard labor. Worse than that, he could rip a pilot from the cockpit and ground him.

"Who's next?" Lieutenant Colonel William R. Offal bellowed to his administrative sergeant sitting out at his desk.

"Sir, the colonel is ready for you now," the sergeant said, then added quietly, "Don't forget to report in a military manner."

Pepper straightened up from the stained, bile-colored Naugahyde easy chair that was one of the first supply items to arrive when the war spun up ten years ago. Perspiration broke out as he strode briskly into the CO's office. The colonel's "I love me" plaques and pictures randomly hung across the pale-green walls. Pepper spotted a painting of a peregrine falcon, talons extended, diving on unseen prey. Scale models of an F-4 Phantom and an F-105 Thunderchief perched on the commander's desk, their noses pointing at Pepper's groin. *I'm standing in their line of fire.*

Pepper clicked the heels of his flight boots together and snapped a salute with his good arm, fingertips touching his right eyebrow, quivering ever so slightly. "Captain Houston reporting as ordered, Sir."

Ignoring Pepper, Lieutenant Colonel Offal stood behind his desk, hands on hips, intent on gazing out a large picture window at the flight line. He was built like a huge fireplug: a tough-looking package, bulletproof and Teflon-coated. His slick-shaven head reflected the fluorescent lights, and his pointed, drooping eagle's beak of a nose was mirrored in the glass.

The colonel's eyes were padlocked on two of the squadron's Phantoms taking off in bobbing, sloppy formation. "Weak dick — shit!" he mumbled. "A baboon could take off cleaner than that. Who the hell's number two?" He jerked a copy of the flying schedule from the leg pocket of his flight suit and scanned it hungrily. "Hmm, Duster Flight, Lieutenant Johnson again as number two." He pivoted to his desk, leaned over and pressed the intercom button for the operations officer, his second in command. "Stump, listen up."

"Yes, Sir," a reedy voice piped, partially drowned out by the background noise of the launching Phantoms.

"Stump, I just watched the most deplorable take-off in fighter aviation history. Same way, same day ain't good enough in this squadron. My schedule says that was Duster Two on the wing, Johnson with Animal leading. Is that right?"

"That's affirmative, Sir."

"Well, you tell Animal I'm going to send him and that sorry wingman of his to the Wet Nurse School for the Blind if I see another take-off as weak as that one. How the hell are they supposed to fly combat if they can't even make a decent take-off?"

"Okay, I'll talk to them when they get in. Maybe they need a little basic formation flying before they can drop bombs like real men."

"Goddam right! No call sign for Johnson until he shows up for work as a fighter pilot one of these days. Clear?"

"Yes, Sir."

Colonel Offal released the button and glared at Pepper who was standing at rigid attention, still saluting. "Who the fuck are you?"

"Sir, Captain Houston reporting as ordered."

"Houston, huh? I got a blowjob there once. Worst I ever had. The bitch sank her teeth like a damn vampire. Haven't trusted a hooker since. Don't plan to, either. Are you from Houston, *Houston?*"

"No, Sir. From Mobile, Alabama, Sir."

"That's too damn close to Houston for me."

Offal rounded the corner of his desk and his steel gray eyes closed in on Pepper. Eyes like an acetylene-cutting torch boring through tempered steel. Pepper stood saluting, braced at attention, working to hold his hand steady. Offal got in his face, exhaling breath that stank like day-old gin from a dirty glass.

"Houston, what's your call sign?"

"Pepper, Sir."

"What's mine?"

"I'm not sure, Sir."

"That's mistake number three for you," he said, moving closer. "Do you know what happens with three strikes, *Pepper?*" Droplets of spittle landed on Pepper's right cheek.

"No, Sir."

"You're out, Captain." His face flushed red. Beads of sweat glistened on his forehead. "Your first fuck-up was trash-canning one of my jets, the second was wiping out one of my best instructors, the third is you're too stupid to learn my call sign before marching your shiny pink ass in here. It's Raptor. Do you know what a raptor is, Houston?"

"Some kind of bird, Sir."

"Put your arm down," he ordered. "I'll return your salute when you're worth a shit." The colonel took a step back and put his hands on his hips, his eyes never leaving Pepper's.

Pepper dropped his arm to his side.

"A raptor is a bird of prey; they snatch other critters for food, right out of the air." His fist flashed in Pepper's face. "That's what I do, Houston. Somebody screws up, I have 'em for lunch."

He's eatin' me...

"You fucked up. You crashed one of my jets. Now, instead of going to war with 18 Phantoms, I go with 17. That ain't enough. Hell, we haven't even engaged the enemy and thanks to you we're minus a jet." He paced to the side and threw his arms in the air. Suddenly he lunged back in Pepper's face, their noses only inches apart. Raptor's pupils were as big as dimes; that close his breath was even fouler. "Goddam. At this rate all the gooks have to do is sit there and watch us kill ourselves."

Pepper swallowed hard. *He's getting off on this...*"Sir, we — I didn't do anything wrong. I had to get the jet on the ground. That gear would never have locked down. We tried everything."

"How many hours do you have in the F-4, Houston?"

"I have about 60 hours, Sir."

"Sixty? How do you fuckin' know you tried everything with only 60 hours in the jet? You think you know it all, Houston? Hell, I've got two thousand, and I learn something every time I strap on a helmet."

"No, Sir, I don't know it all, but I was the outstanding graduate in F-4 training, Sir."

Raptor's face broke into a smirk. "Well, I'll tell you what, Houston. That and a quarter might just buy you a cup of coffee at the O'Club. Stand at ease, and listen." Raptor backed away and stomped around his desk, stopped on the other side and turned to face Pepper. "The next time you have a serious in-flight emergency, get on the radio and talk to the squadron supervisor of flying. Make damn sure you've tried *everything* before you put a Phantom in the cable. Understand? Son, if you ain't gonna do this right, you ain't gonna fly with the Rams." Raptor leaned forward, fists planted on his desk. "You could have put some Gs on that jet and maybe got the gear down, or at least had another Phantom driver come up close to see if it was locked. So, you *didn't* try everything. Did you?"

"No, Sir."

"Take this to the bank, *outstanding graduate.* I need every one of my Phantoms. You put a scratch on one of 'em again and I'll personally cut your balls off. Got it?"

"Yes, Sir."

"I need every pilot I've got, too. You cost me Jasper. Now you're gonna do the work of two. The North Vietnamese are making an all-out push to capture Saigon. It's just a matter of days until the little bastards are knocking on the ambassador's door. Get yourself ready for war, to kick some gook ass. And remember one fuckin' thing, if you can, *outstanding graduate.* This ain't no training school. Up there are only targets and fighters. Targets bore holes in the sky and get their shit blown away. Fighters have to think. Which are you, Houston?"

"Fighter, Sir."

"Good. Maybe you are trainable. One more tip since I'm being so nice, Captain. There'll be an accident board convened to investigate your crash. Tell them the truth, but don't volunteer a damn thing. Dismissed."

"Thank you, Sir." Pepper snapped and held a salute.

Raptor stared across the desk. "What? I'll give you a salute when I see a fighter pilot. Not until then. Get the fuck out of here," he said, reaching for a sheath of papers.

Pepper dropped his salute. Hot fury boiled up, flushed his face as he took a step back, turned on his right heel and marched out of the room.

Raptor. Good call sign for him, the sonofabitch. By God, I'm still flyin'. Fighters and targets? I ain't no target. Maybe he's trainable too. "Stand by for a fighter pilot — asshole!" He planted his flight cap on his head and stepped out of the squadron's front door and into a sticky, sultry Southeast Asian afternoon.

Chapter 8

WHITE COUNT

"Will Rogers never met a fighter pilot."

Aviation cliché

The bar at the Officers' Club was crammed with green flight suits. A thick layer of cigarette smoke hung under the dim ceiling lights. A lone Thai girl, wearing only a G-string and pasties, danced on the stage in the corner. The juke box blasted Jerry Lee Lewis screaming, "Great Balls of Fire," as the girl gyrated for a lone, forlorn second lieutenant wearing fatigues sitting at a small round table. No one else seemed to notice. Pilots and wizzos huddled in small groups at the longest bar in Southeast Asia. Most talked of the North Vietnamese Army's push south toward Saigon from the former American air base at Da Nang.

Pepper didn't know many faces yet, but recognized Animal standing at the corner of the bar with two other captains.

Animal's hands were imaginary airplanes as he described an aerial attack and demonstrated his famous out-of-control guns defense maneuver.

"When the guy's got me in his pipper about ready to put the trigger down, the stick's already in my lap from a hard turn, and I instantly push it forward at about one negative G and slap rudder opposite to the direction I was just turning. It kinda turns the jet inside-out, and there's no way he's gonna track me with his guns. Of course, tryin' to recover the plane from out of control can be a real pisser."

Animal looked up and saw Pepper approaching. "Hey, Pepper. Good to see ya out and about, bud. That last landing of yours was a real beaut. Didn't quite walk away, did ya?"

"Thanks, Animal." Pepper offered a short, flyboy salute. "I appreciate your support. I make one landing in a month and trash a Phantom. Can't afford to waste time making a reputation. It's a short tour here, you know."

Animal laughed and slapped the bar. "Pepper, I want you to meet a couple of your squadron mates. They've been at Clark doing the flight simulator thing. This is Paco Gibson and Judge Bean. Paco's a weapons school grad, Judge is his backseater. Judge is an electronic warfare officer, the dreaded E-WO."

"Sounds like you had a wild ride the other day," Paco said, shaking Pepper's hand.

"Yeah, wildest I've been on."

"How's Jasper doing?" Paco said, putting his beer down on the bar. "Heard anything?"

Pepper's eyes averted. He looked down and leaned forward on the bar with one elbow, then stirred remains in the bottom of an ashtray with his index finger. "Doc Lilly said they won't have to rebuild his skull. The concussion was pretty bad, but he'll heal in time. They won't know about his back for a while. They've got him in traction, waiting for the swelling to go down. That could take some time."

"Wanna drink?" Animal asked.

"Yeah, thanks," Pepper said. "They're flying his wife to Clark to be with him until he's good enough to go back to the States."

"Will he fly again?" Judge asked.

"Doc says it depends on his back. I'm keeping my fingers crossed."

"We may need him," Judge said. "The gooks are rolling down Highway One toward Saigon like they were on a Sunday afternoon drive. The South's pretty much given up. We'll get action soon."

Animal handed Pepper a double scotch-nam on the rocks. "This is getting entirely too serious, man," he said. "I say we have some whiskey. Then I'm going to introduce you to Southeast Asia's greatest fringe benefit. The fighter pilot cure for a bum arm is a Thai rub 'n scrub by a couple of lovely young hard bodies."

*

The Osaka Inn was the only Americanized building on the street. It nestled between junky Thai nightclubs with red lights and beads dangling in their doorways. Rickshaw drivers lined both sides of the busy street as the grubby yellow Datsun taxicab carrying the four aviators stopped in front.

"We call this place *Osaka-to-me*, the finest rub 'n scrub north of Bangkok," Animal said. He grinned, then gulped a double slug from a pint of Mekong whiskey and passed it around one last time. "Argh, that's good stuff, smells like turpentine, tastes like JP-4. Let's go get your white count down, Pepper."

"White count?"

"Yeah, after what you've been through, your white count is way too high. One of these Thai honeys is just what Doctor Animal ordered."

The wobbly airmen swaggered through big double doors held open by two raven-haired, dark-eyed Thai women in mini-skirts and halter tops.

Pepper's eyes scanned the bar. It didn't look too threatening. Besides, Animal was twice as big as anyone there. The periphery was dark with small round tables and a half-dozen men sitting at them drinking and smoking. They were facing a long glass wall. Behind the well-lighted glass storefront panels, young women were in various stages of undress. They were talking and mixing as if at a slumber party. Each had a number hanging from a small chain around her neck. The four took a table in the front and ordered drinks. Pepper couldn't take his eyes off the scene behind the glass.

"Man, I've never seen anything like this," he said, wide-eyed, disbelieving. "This is one helluva fishbowl."

"Yeah, war *is* hell, ain't it?" Judge said. "For a hundred baht, or what we call a red note, five bucks American, they'll give you a bath, a massage, and take your *white count* to zero. That's two-days' wages for most Thais.

Good deal for them; really good deal for you." He pointed to the left of the fishbowl to a Thai man standing in the shadows. "Just tell that guy, the *tour guide* standing over there, which one you want."

Pepper leaned forward to see. "Shit, man, really?" he said.

"If you ain't with the one you love, you gotta love the one you're with," Animal retorted, then drained the bottle of Mekong. He took out a red note, licked it, plastered it to his forehead, then walked to the glass and put his hands on his hips. He stared at number six, a petite girl, probably in her late teens, clad only in black panties. She moved slowly to the glass. She delicately fondled both snow-white breasts, then squeezed the dark brown nipples with her fingers. Her ebony eyes locked on Animal's. Her tongue slowly edged its way around full red lips.

"Whoa, this one's okay," Animal said to the glass wall, then turned his head toward the tour guide. "Six is my lucky number, always has been. So is seven and eleven. I want all three. Here's my red notes," he said, peeling one off his head and pulling two more out of his pocket.

At six feet and 220 pounds, Animal dwarfed the three oriental women. They stopped briefly to speak to the tour guide, then walked arm-in-arm down the dimly lit hallway. "Yee haw!" Animal shouted. "I'll see you guys in about an hour. Come to Papa, ladies. Thunder Lizard is my name. Pleasure's my game."

Pepper ordered a double Johnny Walker and water and wondered if he'd ever see Animal again. *I've never done this. One more drink and I'm liable to do anything, it's been a long time...*

The tour guide intercepted the waitress bringing drinks and carried the tray to the table himself. "Gentlemen, Mr. Thunder Rizard wanted you to guess his rucky number for surprise. He said first one to get it wins, and to start with you." He was pointing at Pepper.

"Uh...nine," Pepper said.

"Ahhh, numbah one G.I. You win!" he said and held up nine fingers to the girls behind the glass. A comely, bronzed, ponytailed charmer in a babydoll-white negligee walked around the glass wall and handed her number to the tour guide. She looked at Pepper, smiled, took his hand, and led him down the hall.

Man, she smells good...soft hands...

Pepper downed his drink for courage before entering the room. There was a large bathtub on the left and what looked like a padded massage table in the middle of the room. A small statue of Buddha sat on a corner ledge about head high.

"My name Dawn. What you?" the seductive brunette purred, leaning at the waist, hips swaying as she turned on steaming hot water at the tub.

"Ah...Pepper."

"That funny name. What you real name?" she said as she started unbuttoning his shirt. "What you want me to do?"

Pepper groped for words.

"What wrong with arm?" She helped him out of the sling"I fell off an F-4 and landed on it. It's pretty sore, but I'm not feeling much right now."

"I be careful. You want bath? Dawn make you feel number one, G.I." She unbuckled his pants and let them drop to the floor.

"Okay, I guess a bath would be all right. Besides, warm water and rubbing that shoulder might do it some good.""You get in tub now. What you want Dawn do? You want make ruv? You want hand-job? You want fuckee? You want lound-the-world?" *Holy shit, Batman. I'm getting dizzy.* She eased the negligee off her shoulders and let it slip to the floor, standing in front of him with only thin white satin panties draping her tiny hips. Pepper stared at beautiful, rounded breasts and dark, full nipples as she took his hands and placed them on her breasts. "What you want, G.I., huh?" she cooed, doleful ebony eyes probing his.

"I want a hot bath and a massage, Dawn. That's all."

"You sure, G.I.? I make you feel good all over. Get white count down? It okay."

Whoa, I better steady myself against this tub a minute. Don't let her know, you can get rolled in here. "You do blowjob?"

Dawn's answer was matter-of-fact, almost automatic. She pointed to the small brass, pot-bellied Buddha in the corner. "Buddha not rike brojob."

Pepper rested his bad arm around Dawn's shoulders to steady himself and led her to the statue. He reached with his right hand and turned the Buddha around facing the corner. "Buddha not see," he assured.

She turned to press her tight, lithesome body against his, on tiptoes she raised both arms around his neck. Her lips met his and her tongue quickly explored inside. He caught the faintest hint of cheap perfume. This time it smelled good. Pepper's lips flared warm and his right hand touched the silky skin at the small of her back. His fingers instinctively slid under her panties and felt the curve of firm, rounded hips.

Dawn eased from the embrace to pull his shorts down and then quickly kissed him again.

He swayed, senses reeling.

"You get in tub now, G.I." She smiled, gently stroking his erection.

Damn. That feels really good…been a long time…hope I don't pass out.

Pepper eased into the steaming tub as Dawn began to wash his back with a soapy natural sponge. It smelled of lilacs, fresh and clean. She pushed him gently back against the tub and washed his injured left shoulder.

"This okay? Not hurt?" she asked, then moved to his chest. "You have nice muscles, G.I."

Pepper laid his head back on the tub and closed his eyes. "Played… linebacker at 'Bama…thanks…"

She slid the bar of soap slowly down his firm, rippled abdomen to between his legs.

"You hard as lock, G.I."

Pepper drifted, then was gone. Johnny Walker had spirited him away…

Chapter 9

KILL ME IF YOU CAN

"A fighter pilot's breakfast is two aspirin, a Mars Bar, and a puke. Let's fly air combat."

Animal

Pepper rubbed his sore shoulder and the pain reminded him of the conversation with Raptor when they had passed in the hallway: "You're lucky, Houston, I'm going to need every available pilot for combat operations and evacuating Saigon. I'm going to approve you to fly training missions pending results of the accident board investigation. Get your ass in gear and get qualified ASAP."

North Vietnamese steamrolled toward Saigon. According to intelligence reports, some forces in the South resisted, but many just threw down their weapons and faded into the rice paddies and jungles. At Da Nang, only 300 miles north of Saigon, squadrons of highly capable American-supplied F-5 fighters were left intact and fully armed for combat. North Vietnamese pilots had only to climb in, take off, and engage U.S. forces with them. Ironically, American-built jets were considered the primary air-to-air threat to U.S. forces. To prepare for possible engagements with the North Vietnamese, squadron pilots began mock-fighting each other in air-combat training.

Dr. Lilly checked the injury and range of motion of Pepper's shoulder then cleared him to fly. By early April, his scores on the bombing range had improved to qualification status. But his last phase of training would be even more demanding, requiring aerial refueling with a KC-135 tanker aircraft, and air combat on the same mission. Pepper would be one-on-one against another Phantom flown by a highly experienced instructor pilot. The last air combat mission would be a checkride flown against Raptor. If he passed, Pepper would be a fully combat qualified F-4 driver.

They briefed for an hour in small rooms that secluded flight members from the bustle of squadron operations. It was sacred — a time for flight leads to cover in detail the mission objectives for all members. Flying time cost about $10,000 per hour for a two-ship of Phantoms. Every air minute was precious, and maximum training was wrung from every one of them. Pilots and backseaters were wrung out too. The taxpayers nearly always got their money's worth.

Backseaters are weapons system officers, or wizzos. They're navigators, not pilots, and run the aircraft radar and navigation systems. They're also an extra set of eyeballs, important in finding an enemy that is often only a speck against the sky.

Animal was the air-combat instructor for the Rams. Pepper had a final mission to fly with him before going head-to-head with Raptor. Pepper was paired with Jumpin' Jack Flasch as his wizzo; Animal was paired with Maggot.

Animal hulked over a tabletop briefing podium, brow furrowed with concentration. Behind him was a chalkboard covered with blue and red circles depicting aerial engagements that were planned for the mission. Three other flight members sat around the rectangular briefing table taking notes on times and radio frequencies for the demanding air refueling and air-combat mission. Animal flew as hard as he played. In the air he was all business.

Animal began his wrap-up: "Okay, let's review high points before we step to the jets. Let's do a formation take-off and make it look good so Raptor doesn't jump our asses again. Our tanker will be in orbit on Chestnut Track just west of the Mekong River. There are fighters ahead and behind us. Let's be on time." Animal's eyes shot daggers across the table. "Maggot, you may be the best air-combat wizzo in this squadron, but fuckin'-A, *on time* means just that. You were thirty seconds late for this briefing. Don't pull that crap in the jet."

Maggot flushed and nodded sheepishly.

Animal turned to the blackboard behind him and pointed to a hand-written list of events they would accomplish. "From the tanker we go to the training area for three engagements. Pepper, your first will be an offensive attack on me. I want you six- to nine-thousand feet behind and thirty degrees off my tail. You'll achieve radar missile and heat missile parameters, followed by a gun attack solution and a separation from the fight. I'll be defending against you, no-holds-barred. So don't get too close."

To emphasize his point, Animal picked up two pointing sticks with miniature models glued on the ends, one an F-4, the other a MiG-21 Fishbed. He held the Phantom in front and the MiG behind as if it were attacking. "The second engagement will be with you out front, defensive to start. Remember, I never think of myself as *defensive*, even out front. I'm going to kill the son-of-a-bitch behind me, it's just going to take a little longer. You are full-up defense — kill me if you can."

Animal laid the models on the briefing table. "The last set-up will be neutral to begin with. We'll turn away for some separation, then turn toward each other to meet head on. May the best man win." He looked squarely at Pepper. "When you fight Raptor on your next hop, remember, this is his favorite attack. He'll do the unexpected, trip you up, then bust you on the ride. That proves Chrome Dome's still got balls at his advanced age. Let's go around the table. Questions?"

Pepper was the only one to speak. "When I'm on the defensive engagement, I understand that I have to kill you. I won't pass by just defending against the missile and separating from the fight?"

"Affirmative. If you start off defensive and can just get away, it normal-ly means you've won. Today you have to kill me. If Raptor can't kill you in the neutral engagement, sometimes he'll put you in the tougher position — defensive. He likes to watch his prey squirm. He's sure to get a shot — and maybe a kill that way. Once again, if he makes kill parameters, you bust the mission. If you go from defense to offense and shoot him, you may not have a career left. It's a pressure-cooker ride. If he gets one missile shot on you — you live. Two, you're a dead man. He took two Sidewinders, or what we call *heaters* on Rocky Stone last month that sent the boy back to basic fighter maneuvers. Damn humiliating. Rocky's got five-hundred hours in the F-4 and Raptor broke him down like a twelve gauge. Rocky gave up in the end."

Animal turned to the board and started to erase it. "In this business you gotta have a fighting spirit. Even if you lack other things, you can make up for it with fighting spirit. That's why you're probably better off to go offensive and get the kill on Raptor. Just don't hammer him too hard if you get the opportunity." He turned back toward the group. "More questions?" Animal smirked at the silence around the table. "Let's go kick ass."

*

They stopped by the operations desk for aircraft tail numbers and then signed out for the mission. On the way to life support to don flight gear, Jumpin' Jack caught up to Pepper.

"On that defensive engagement, I'll be twisted around looking back, watching Animal when he calls 'fight's on.' Be in full afterburner on the throttles, and bend the jet around hard when I call for a break turn — we'll put it in his face. We want to force him to overshoot below and behind us."

"Yeah, got it."

"When I tell you, do a nose-high reversal back into him. Have your switches already set for guns. Guaranteed you're in a knife fight then. The rest is up to you. Do some of that pilot shit up there; fight him with your rudder pedals when it gets slow. Gun his fuckin' brains out. Pretend he's Raptor."

Pepper grinned and nodded. "I can do that. The bald-headed asshole really pissed me off the other day in his office. He did the same thing to me on the ground that he did to Rocky in the air, with one major difference: I don't give up." Pepper pushed open the door to life support and walked in. "Raptor can eat shit and die. Animal won't be expecting it; you give me the right call on the reversal, and I'll get us in a knife fight."

"Missiles are for queers," Jack quipped. "Going for guns gets you up close and personal. Remember, I can't see what's happening once you have him out front and things happen fast. Watch out for target fixation and pressing in too close. If you get inside the five-hundred foot minimum range on Animal, you might bust the ride, and that shit's dangerous."

"Okay, at that point my fangs'll be out...I'll watch it."

*

Pilots stored their flight gear in the life support section of the squadron. Anti-G suits, parachute harnesses, and helmets hung in their lockers. Donning the G-suit was like a cowboy putting on a pair of leg chaps before climbing onto the saddle. Where chaps protected the cowboy against brush and limbs, the G-suit protected the pilot internally. Air bladders in the suit automatically inflated and squeezed the pilot's waist and legs, restricting blood flow.

During hard turns in the Phantom, the body succumbed to centrifugal forces and blood was forced into the legs from the head and upper body. To fight blacking out, the G-suit combined with the pilot's grunting and strenuous isometric flexing of stomach and leg muscles kept blood flowing to the head. The G-suit was worn skintight and had an umbilical hose that attached to the aircraft's pneumatic air system once the pilot got into the ejection seat. Leg bladders would then inflate automatically and pockets in the calves held checklists, gloves, or maps. Without chaps a cowboy's legs might be cut and bleeding by the end of the day. Without a properly functioning G-suit, a pilot might experience blackouts or even unconsciousness — sometimes within a few seconds. Such were the rigors in the F-4 air-combat game.

Pepper latched and zipped a 10-inch-wide waistband of the G-suit in front and spun it around so the heavy-duty waist zipper ran down his left hip. He leaned down to zip each leg on the inside from his thigh to his ankles. Then he went to the outside zippers on each thigh that tightened the bladder snugly against each leg.

Pepper pulled on his helmet and walked to the test station used to check oxygen masks under pressure and earphone and microphone functions. Helmets were covered with camouflaged tape. A double visor housing in front of the helmet enabled the pilot to roll down a dark lens for day or a clear lens for night. Pepper clicked the bayonet connections of the oxygen mask with its built-in microphone into both sides of his helmet. *This thing's gotta fit good. Sweat and Gs will pull it down...won't be able to talk.*

The mike in the mask allowed the pilot to communicate with his wizzo through the intercom system, and to the outside world through the jet's radios. Pepper plugged the mike, oxygen mask, and G-suit umbilicals into the tester. He jerked connections loose to make sure they'd break apart if needed during ejection.

Pepper donned the last pieces of flight equipment, the survival vest, and the parachute harness. The harness, constructed of strong nylon webbing, fit each arm like a jacket, then latched at the chest and strapped across each thigh. *Gotta cinch these straps tight, might get thrown around the cockpit defending against Animal's guns...*

Once in the Phantom, the pilot and wizzo attached their two shoulder fittings to the parachute system that was integral to the ejection seat. Fittings were double-checked by the flight member and triple-checked by the crew chief. The fittings served as the only connections to the life-saving parachute and survival gear contained in the seat pack.

The last attachments to the ejection system were the cords secured to each calf. On ejection, the cords would savagely jerk the pilot's legs from the rudder pedals into the seat so they wouldn't be severed by hitting the instrument panel as the seat's ballistic charge launched it up the rails.

*

The formation of two Phantoms used a call sign of "Hammer." They completed preflight checks and took to a sky of cotton-like cumulus clouds, or cu, that rapidly built thousands of feet above them. During the steaming monsoon season, cu seemed to start forming earlier each day. By take-off that afternoon, towering clouds were roving thunderstorm bullies that pounded anything in their path.

Animal and Maggot flew the lead Phantom, Hammer One, while Pepper and Jumpin' Jack were the wingman as Hammer Two. Air refueling was scheduled for Pepper's practice, as it had been over a month since he did it in training. He was erratic at first and grew impatient trying to hold precise position close beneath the big tanker. As his touch on the controls softened, the Phantom settled down and the boomer plugged in. Each fighter took on 5000 pounds of fuel before Animal eased the formation away from the lumbering KC-135 Stratotanker and headed for the center of the air-combat working area 60 miles to the west.

"Hammer Flight, ops check, fence check, go tactical," Animal called over the UHF radio.

As wingman, Pepper acknowledged with the customary "Two," and rolled his Phantom to the right — away from Animal. Their flight paths diverged until Pepper reached the "tactical" formation position of 6000 feet. It allowed good lookout visibility in all quadrants. Now four sets of eyeballs could scan the sky for threat aircraft which could attack from any direction.

Jack began checks, talking to Pepper over the intercom. "Okay, Pepper, check fuel and oxygen. Green up armament switches. We'll be real close on these set-ups — maybe inside a mile and a half. We should forget radar missiles and set up for heaters and guns. MASTER ARM on?"

"Roger that. It's on." Feeling good after a successful air-refueling hookup, Pepper launched into a monologue: "Ladies and gentlemen, this is your captain speaking —"

"Oh, not that airline shit again," Jack said.

"I need to inform you that our AIM-9 heat-seeking Sidewinder missile, commonly called a heater, is selected with a low growl, and our MASTER ARM is on. Your armament panel is in the green. Please remain seated and locate your barf bags. We'll be spilling coffee in your laps and generally tossing you about as we maneuver to engage Animal and Maggot, turning them to toast!"

"Never saw a fighter pilot who lacked confidence," Jack retorted. "I guess you're no exception."

"Sometimes it's hard to be humble. But like Raptor said, up here are only fighters and targets. We ain't targets. Let's kick some ass."

A super-cell cu towered near the center of the area like a giant lighthouse and helped the crews stay oriented. With the two Phantoms traveling at 500 knots, Animal maneuvered the formation to miss the buildup, and aligned the Phantoms for their first engagement. Pepper flew about a mile and a half behind and slightly off to one side.

Animal called, "Okay, Hammer Two, you are offensive on us for the first engagement. We'll be out in front of you. Right-hand turn. Hammer One's ready."

"Hammer Two's ready," Pepper challenged.

"Hammer, fight's on."

Pepper was pumped. "Okay, Jack, fuckin'-A, let's go to war."

"Kill us a MiG. We're locked on. Radar ranging is good, you're at eight-thousand feet and closing at two-hundred knots in the turn. Missile selected?"

"Heater, Jack. There's the high growl. It's got Animal's exhaust, she's going to fly."

Pepper called the practice missile shot, "Fox-Two," then spoke to Jack. "Animal's turning hard, Jack. I don't think we're going to get the second heater for a kill. I'm going to lag back, stay behind and try to get another shot. Gun's selected."

Jack answered, "Okay, range is 32-hundred feet, still closing at two-hundred knots. I can't see him from back here. Under the nose?"

"Yeah, I've got him. Animal's good. He's keeping his smash up and giving me too many angles for the shot. I can't get another heater for the kill…maybe a snapshot with the gun. Then let's leave. I'm coming down hard to the right and into him." With the quick descending turn, Pepper's G-suit started to inflate. Reflexively, Pepper tightened his leg and stomach muscles, grunting, trying to keep blood flowing to his eyes.

Pepper aligned his Phantom directly behind Animal's, raking his gunsight through for a practice snapshot with the Phantom's 20-millimeter, six-barrel Vulcan cannon. Just as Pepper squeezed the trigger, the picture flip-flopped. Instantly, he went from looking at the top of Animal's Phantom to eyeballing its twisting belly. *Shit! What happened?* Animal had shoved his control stick forward and thrust his left leg to the stop for full left rudder. He appeared to stop in midair. Pepper's closure doubled to 400 knots and Animal's jet filled Pepper's windscreen.

"Holy shit!" Pepper yelled as he rolled and pulled away, trying to avoid Animal's out-of-control Phantom.

"I hate it when you pilots say *holy shit*," Jack groaned.

"Animal really put it in my face, the prick."

"Yeah, that's his patented gun defense — a last-ditch maneuver. We better get the hell outta here or he'll be gunning us. I've seen this flick before."

"Okay. Time to be stinking cowards." Pepper slapped the Phantom into a hard-left turn. He shoved the throttles outboard, then forward to the wall for full afterburners. Pepper and Jack were pressed back into their ejection seats as the jet responded. The distance between the two Phantoms opened quickly.

Animal called, "Good separation. You're out of range. Let's knock it off."

"Hammer Two, knock it off," Pepper parroted the required response.

"Did you get a gunshot, Hammer Two?"

"Negative. You surprised me. I done good to avoid a midair."

"Okay, remember your objective. You need to achieve a kill on me. You didn't do it. If you'd repositioned instead of going for guns and been a little more patient behind me, you could've gotten the second heater shot. Poof. I'd've been a dead man."

"Copy." *Patience, hell! I want to kill you...*

"Okay, Hammer Two, let's set up for your defensive engagement. Stay where you are and check your rearview."

Pepper twisted in his seat and spotted Animal a mile and a half behind his right shoulder. "Damn, Jack, he's getting in the saddle on me for this engagement. He's going to be hard to shake from that position. He wants *me* to achieve a kill?"

"No sweat. Remember what I said. Put it in his face to start, then listen for my reversal call. Be ready for guns."

Pepper switched to guns on the armament panel. "Time for a knife fight," he said. *This is what I've been waiting for. Slap the jet around, go for the throat, get up close and personal. Canopy to canopy.*

"Set smash at 450. Hammer One, ready," Animal advised.

"Hammer Two, ready," Pepper said, slamming the throttles into full afterburner.

"Fight's on," Animal called.

"What's *smash*, Jack?" Pepper asked.

"Another name for speed. Remember, speed is life to a fighter pilot."

"Knife's in my teeth," Pepper muttered. *This time I'm gonna be in his face.* Pepper jabbed the wings right, then pulled the stick hard back in his lap. The sharply turning Phantom pressed him into his seat. His neck muscles burned from the strain of looking over his shoulder. *Stay ahead of the Gs, grunt, harder, GRUNT! Tunnel vision...come on G-suit!*

Airspeed's bleeding, 280. Blacking out, GRUNT! Ease off a little. Now I can see. "Where's Animal?"

"He's deep behind us." Jack coached, "It's time for a nose-high reversal left, go!"

Pepper kept the control stick centered near his crotch, while his leg extended for full left rudder. His midair pirouette cost him 100 knots, but it surprised Animal and put them canopy to canopy only 800 feet apart. In two moves, a hard break turn and a reversal, Pepper had gone from a solid defensive posture and neutralized Animal's advantage.

"Animal says he's offensive even when he's on defense. We are too," Pepper grunted. "Time to die, you simulated Raptor sonofabitch."

Jack grunted and coached, "Check minimum range. Five-hundred feet. Don't bust it. Watch your fangs."

Okay, Pepper, hold the stick centered. We're slow. Knife fight time. Use rudder. We're in a scissors, back and forth. He's sliding out front a little. Gunsight's ready. He's too slow for his infamous last-ditch maneuver. Be patient. Roll back with left rudder. Aligned with him. Ride him like a red-headed stepchild. Sight's on...time to die! He's getting big — fast. I see both helmets, Korat's JJ on the tail. "Hammer Two, guns, guns, guns — kill." *Too close, roll or we'll hit...*

Animal returned the call, "Hammer Two, knock it off. You're inside five-hundred feet. Way inside. Pepper, don't do that again. Going from defensive to a gun kill was a good move, but busting that five-hundred feet can get us killed for real."

"Copy," Pepper replied. *Way too close. Target fixation. His jet was as big as a barn when I turned on the gun. If it'd been a MiG, I'd've flown through the debris and trashed my own jet. Control the fangs.*

"Hammer, let's set up for the neutral engagement. Raptor's favorite," Animal called. "We'll turn into each other and meet head on, I'll go slightly high at the pass. Okay, turn in. Fight's on."

"Copy. Fight's on," Pepper acknowledged. "Jack, let's kill us a Raptor. Hang onto your ass and tits. Time to rock 'n roll."

"Animal likes the high road at the pass so he can keep his energy up when he turns on you," Jack coached. "Going downhill first keeps his smash so he can use it later. He'll use it. You think you have him, then he cashes in speed for turning capability to get the kill. Just because you meet at the pass with fifteen-hundred knots closure doesn't mean you'll keep it very long. Fight your best fight."

"Thanks for the info."

Three miles apart when the two Phantoms turned to meet head on, Pepper could see Animal's smoke trail disappear as they pointed at each other. He locked into afterburner early, going for maximum smash at the pass.

"Hell, he's already in burner," Pepper said.

"Betcha he enters this fight fast and leaves faster," Jack said.

Pepper slammed the throttles into afterburner. "We're late on the burners." He was a precious 150 knots slower than Animal at the pass and below him. *Climbing. Turn into Animal. Gain smash? At the same time?* With only a hundred hours in the Phantom, Pepper knew he was outmatched. Animal had over a thousand hours. Raptor, two thousand. Pepper knew they were about to be had. *If this were combat, we would die.*

"Damn, Jack. We're trapped. Animal'll come out of this engagement blowing our shit away," Pepper said, looking up and to his right as Animal rolled and started diving to engage. "We're slower. He's higher. Not good." Instinct told Pepper to turn toward Animal's jet and start a circling fight, to keep him from achieving missile parameters.

"Go straight. Get as much speed as you can. Come back at him for another head-on. You need to be higher than him next time."

"That takes balls. If we don't get out of range by the time he gets his nose on us and fires, we're dead."

"Nobody said this would be easy. Turn into him now, we're dead meat. Guaranteed."

"Okay, let's go for it. We're blasting through this fight. We'll come back with the high ground. Keep him in sight back there. Smash is six-hundred now."

"I can't see him anymore," Jack said.

"Give me bore sight radar up-front and I'll get a quick lock-on when we're pointed at him again. Maybe we can surprise him with a radar missile in the lips before we get to the pass."

"You got it. Bore sight radar's up front. He's hard to see, probably about four miles at six o'clock. Animal's getting his nose on us now."

Pepper glanced at the airspeed. "Okay, we're at 700 now. I'm coming back into him and climbing. We'll lose some speed, but that's okay, we got a ton of it. Jack, stay ahead of the Gs, we're gonna be there a while."

Pepper rolled the Phantom to the right and started its nose up in a pitch-back maneuver. At their high speed, the Phantom could turn hard for a long time, but it was the humans on board who limited turning capability. Pepper's G-suit surged with air, squeezing his midsection and legs as he pumped his feet hard against the rudder pedals, grunting to force draining blood back into his eyes. At full mental and physical exertion, adrenaline coursing through his veins, and the fear of dying at the end of Animal's missiles pumped Pepper to a razor's edge. Every sinew in his body strained; every neuron in his brain fired. Screaming, he stopped the draining blood from his eyes at tunnel vision.

While he twisted and looked over his right shoulder to keep sight of Animal, Jack's G-suit umbilical unplugged, its air bladders emptied. With the high speeds, the G-force onset was rapid. Sustaining 7 Gs in the turn, they felt the equivalent of more than three high-performance carnival rides at once. Jack's body, at seven times its normal weight, drained blood from his head, to blackout, then to unconsciousness.

Coming out of the pitch back and with tunnel vision, Pepper lost sight of the other Phantom. "Where's Animal? Jack, you got him? I've lost him. Jack!"

The intercom was silent. Using the canopy bow mirrors, Pepper looked into the back cockpit. He could see only the top of Jack's helmet. He was slumped forward, hanging in his shoulder harnesses. "Jack! Wake the hell up! Animal's two miles on the nose." *Shit! He looks like Jasper did.* "I'm locked on. Radar missile shot. "Hammer Two, Fox One," Pepper called over the UHF while pressing the trigger to simulate release of an AIM-7 radar-guided Sparrow missile.

Once Pepper released Gs coming out of the hard turn, Jack quickly regained consciousness. By the time Pepper called the shot, Jack's legs and arms were shaking uncontrollably, a sign that part of the brain was starting to get blood. "What the hell?…How many Gs did we pull?" Jack asked.

"We were at seven for a while. You all right? Animal's under my nose now. Do you want me to stop the fight?"

"Shit, I should be able to handle seven. I'm only twenty-six. Am I getting old? Damn! G-suit's unplugged. Cord's in my lap. I'm okay. Just a headache. Keep fighting. Kick his ass. I'm plugged."

"That's what I call a fighter-wizzo, Jack. This is war! I'm engaging Animal down and to the right. One more missile and he's a dead man. No more 'this is your captain bullshit.'"

This time Pepper flew to where he wanted to be at the pass, higher than Animal, and his airspeed 525 knots. Animal reacted turning toward Pepper to take away his advantage. Pepper countered by rolling, setting the Phantom's wings to turn hard. Like two boxers, the pilots used their Phantoms to jab and circle, trying to land punches to vital areas. Stamina and attitude would win the fight. Missiles and bullets were the pilot's jabs; stamina was airspeed. Animal's attitude was cold and calculating, based on experience. Pepper's was based on the will to win.

"Okay, Jack, we've got some advantage at the pass. That's muy grande. Your G-suit working?"

"Affirmative. Press the attack," he said between loud grunts to fight blackout.

Pepper, not quite ready to go for the kill, kept 400 knots in full afterburner and continued the descending right turn. Twisting in the seat and grunting, he could see Animal over his right shoulder across the circle. Sweat poured down his forehead and dripped off his oxygen mask. His leather gloves were soaked. It was grueling work, but Pepper was gaining some critical angles for a heater shot.

Animal turned hard to try to hold Pepper off. That cost airspeed. Starting lower than Pepper, Animal's Phantom was now below 250 knots.

"Okay, Jack, time to cash in some smash and get our nose on 'em. I'm gonna tighten the turn and take a heater shot."

"You're at five Gs now. I'm okay. Go for it!"

Pepper pulled even harder on the control stick and the Phantom responded like a thoroughbred, tightening its turn. Airspeed bled to 300 knots, still enough to do the job. The Sidewinder's infrared sensor began a high growl as it detected heat from Animal's jet. Pepper quickly checked the range at 6000 feet. "We've got the range; we're in the heart of the envelope, the missile likes what it sees. Fox Two, kill for Hammer Two."

Animal called back over the UHF, "Hammer, good kill. You took your time, got the advantage and flew your jet. Do that with Raptor tomorrow."

"Rogahh! Copy!" Pepper was pumped; it was hard to quell the excitement in his voice on the UHF. He slapped the Phantom into a quick victory roll. "Jack, we're ready to kick Raptor's ass!"

"Think so? He's got tricks nobody's ever seen. He never does the same thing twice."

Undaunted, Pepper replied, "I guess we'll see what the Raptor bird can do…"

Chapter 10

OIL AND WATER

DON'T MIX

"The duty of a fighter pilot is to patrol his area of the sky, and shoot down any enemy fighters in that area. Anything else is rubbish."

—Baron Manfred Rittmeister von Richtofen
"The Red Baron," 1917

Most fighter pilots train their whole flying careers, never to duel in true air combat. If they go to war and engage an enemy aircraft, it's icing on the cake. Practice duels in air combat are relentless and real, death or not, as real to the pilots as breathing. Blood is not spilled perhaps, but it might as well be. If they perceive they have met death in the air, they bleed spiritually. It is genuine. They are driven to be the best, and defeat in the air is crushing. Fighter pilots don't give a damn for those not sharing their passion. They embrace it in themselves and respect it in their adversaries.

Raptor's and Pepper's personalities repelled like oil and water, but they both understood the need to be aggressive. To them, training and reality were the same. One-on-one air combat, a deadly ballet of climbs and dives, whirling circles, pirouettes, and sprints across clouds is a lethal duel...to the finish.

*

There was a private squadron briefing room available, but the uninterrupted sanctity of the mission briefing room, of course, didn't apply to Raptor. He preferred to hold briefings in his office with flight members gathered around his desk as in a staff meeting. He demanded that his flight leaders and instructor pilots be thorough and professional in their briefings, but his personal rules were different.

A routine briefing took a minimum of 50 minutes, with every detail of the mission covered. Raptor expected his backseater to brief the essential numbers for timing, frequencies — everything. His wizzo for the mission was Major "Tiny" McLain, at six-feet-three, 240 pounds, he struck an imposing figure. Raptor's portion of the briefing lasted about 10 minutes, most of which was given with his back to the flight members as he watched the activities on the flight line from his picture window. He was often interrupted by phone calls from higher-ups in the chain of command, and from subordinates accustomed to his vexing micromanagement of their activities.

Tiny covered the mandatory items for the mission: "Take-off time is 1210 hours. Our slot in Korat Operating Area One begins at 1230 and goes to 1315, with altitudes of eight to twenty-five thousand feet."

Raptor sat in an executive chair behind his desk, peering through his window to the world of flight line operations. Those in the briefing could see only the top of his glossy head above the chair. He swiveled slightly and barked over his right shoulder, "Okay, Tiny, that's enough on the numbers. I expect everybody in here can write them down off the ops board without being too confused.

"Pepper, by the time you fly with me you're supposed to know how, or my instructors aren't doing their job. We'll use standard procedures to and from the training area where I will summarily kick your ass in three neutral engagements. If you happen to get lucky and achieve a valid, gun-camera-documented kill shot, then you *may* pass the ride. Otherwise it's back to kindercare for you. Questions?"

Pepper's face flushed, jaw muscles twitched. *You flaming asshole! You may summarily kick your own ass, but you ain't kickin' mine. Kindercare? He better fly as good as he talks.* "Just one, Sir. That valid *kill* I plan to get is either two missiles in the heart of the envelope or a gun-tracking shot, correct?"

"Right. And, per my squadron standards, which you're supposed to know, those missiles have to be more than five seconds apart. Watch the closure and the 500-foot minimum. We start engines in twenty minutes. That's all."

Raptor's back received no salutes.

*

Pepper, Jumpin' Jack, and Tiny sat on benches in the crew van, a bread box on wheels. The Thai driver picked his way through a maze of fuel trucks and aircraft maintenance activity on the flight line to deposit the three in front of their Phantoms. Fashionably late as usual, Raptor had an NCO drive him to his Phantom in the commander's jeep, his own personal limousine service.

Small talk tailed off as the driver approached the green and brown camouflaged war birds. Fading words were drowned by the deafening scream of jet engines louder than the pit area at the Indy 500. Hot JP-4 exhaust reeked of kerosene and saturated the air. The fliers began thinking ahead as they glimpsed their jets in sheltered revetments across the flight line. Routinely traveling at mach 1 speeds demanded that mental processes stay ahead of events. They scanned their Phantoms at a distance for proper configuration, looked to see if starting units were hooked up and ready to go.

A black flag flying from one of the aircraft revetments indicated the heat index had passed 100 degrees. Sweat soaked them. Pepper wiped a bead of sweat running into one eye. "Damn, it's hot out here."

"Wait 'til summer," Jack said.

With no air conditioning in the van, the long-sleeved, fireproof flight suits, G-suits, and harnesses stifled air circulation.

Jumpin' Jack opened a barrel-shaped cooler and grabbed three frozen rolled-up hand towels. He tossed one to Pepper and one to Tiny. "Pry it open and wrap it around your neck," he said to Pepper. "It's poor man's air conditioning. Just before take-off use it to wipe your forehead so the sweat doesn't roll into your eyes, and take a good slug from your frozen water bottle. When we're doing 160 knots on the runway, I like my pilots to see."

"See ya in my gunsight, Tiny," Pepper hollered over his shoulder as he hopped from the crew van and walked toward the jet. The fully loaded Phantom lived up to its nickname, "Rhino," 38,000 pounds of rippled muscle, ready to charge. The centerline fuel tank hanging from its belly always looked like a huge bomb.

"Jack, those heat-seeking missiles are fuckin' lethal darts. I love this double-ugly thing."

The crew chief stood by the cockpit ladder with the aircraft forms binder in his left hand. He snapped a salute with his right. Both officers returned the salute. Pepper asked him how the jet had been flying.

"Great, Sir. Radar's been a little quirky, but I think we got it fixed."

Jack took the forms and handed Pepper another frozen towel. "Looked like you heated up in there with Raptor. Here's an extra one. You may need it between fights. That's part of his psych game. He likes to put pressure on, kinda like combat. See if you can handle it and still get the job done. Just hang onto your fangs and fight 'em smart like you did Animal. Do that and we'll get the kill."

*

Pepper did his best to be the perfect wingman en route to the air-combat training area, vowing to prove his squadron commander's first impressions wrong. Their call sign today was "Ram One Flight," used only by Raptor. Pepper's radio check-ins were crisp and sounded good as "Ram Two"; he labored to keep his Phantom in perfect fingertip formation position. Usually, Pepper could trim his jet with nose-down pressure, and use wing trim into his leader to make for a heavier-feeling stick. Now he seemed to be all over the place. He had difficulty holding the Phantom solidly in position. He kept his head frozen looking left to fly close formation on Raptor as they sliced through the air at a ground speed of 500 knots, wingtips only three feet apart. It took razor-sharp focus and concentration, like a horse with blinders. Raptor could have called for spread formation to ease the workload on his wingman, but stubbornly flew his jet as if Pepper's Phantom weren't there.

"Jack, is it me, or is he rough as a cob?" Pepper asked. Before Jack could reply, Raptor jerked his wings into a sharp right turn. Surprised, Pepper's jet rode high on Raptor and now angled into him.

"Shit!" Pepper said, quickly pushing down and rolling right to avoid collision. The negative Gs caused sediment and dust in the cockpit to float in the air.

"It's him. The bastard could care less about his wingmen. He'll leave them jammed in close forever. I hear he tried out for the Thunderbirds once and they made him fly close formation for an hour. He didn't make the team, so he gets back at the T-birds by beasting his wingmen. It's part of wringing you out before we get to the area. More of his damn psych game."

"Okay, I'll just weld us to his wing like we're one Phantom. You keep an eye on the instruments and I'll stay visually locked."

"I'm watching them, we're all right. Stay on him like stink on shit."

As they entered the air-combat area at 20,000 feet, their formation flew in and out of fog-like cirrus clouds. At times, Pepper lost sight of Raptor's Phantom only feet away, especially when a white shroud of moisture momentarily blocked out all but a wingtip light on his aircraft. In clouds, a good leader will look at his wingman to see how thick they are and not roll his jet until they clear.

"Raptor wants his wingman tight no matter what," Jack said. "He's the leader...and leaders do no wrong."

Clouds darkened as Raptor once again rolled into Pepper. "Shit, Jack. I've lost him. Nothing but white there. Gonna hit. I'm outta here." Pepper twisted his head from looking at Raptor to his instrument panel loaded with gyro-stabilized attitude, heading indicators, and rows of gauges. In an instant he analyzed their altitude, attitude, airspeed, and direction, and rolled just enough to prevent a collision while trying to avoid vertigo. On the edge of task overload, he pressed the microphone button on the right throttle and made the required call, "Ram Two is lost wingman. Turning right to heading 165, leveling at nineteen thousand."

Raptor flared with impatience. "Ram Two, go to squadron common frequency. ASAP!"

"Two," Pepper acknowledged.

Jack quickly dialed in the channel. "Here we are, *lost wingman,* still in the clouds, trying to find which way is up and Raptor gives us a channel change. What an asshole. Maybe he'd like it better if we just clobber him."

"Trust me, this is better. He told me if I ever scratch another Phantom I'm toast. Bumping him now would shit-can *two* more jets."

"Ram check," Raptor barked.

"Two."

"Ram Two, is my lead not *smooth* enough for you?"

"No, Sir. I mean, yes, Sir. I just lost sight in the clouds."

"Well, Ram Two, you are the first pilot in this squadron to ever go 'lost wingman' with me leading. Since you were an outstanding graduate, it must be my fault, correct?"

"No, Sir. Permission to come aboard your right wing? I have you in sight."

"Cleared to join, if you think you can stay around, Ram Two."

Jack chuckled, "More of the psych bullshit. He's really on his game today."

"Screw him to the wall. 'Fighters and targets,' is what he told me in his office. Well, this jet is my desk and this sky is my office. He can bug me on the small stuff, but we ain't a target. He's going to be one pretty soon. I'm gonna kick his ass."

After making Pepper fly close formation the rest of the way to the air-combat area, Raptor finally called for spread. Cloud banks billowed everywhere, but as the Phantoms swept through the area, Raptor found a five-mile clear space. "Okay, Ram, we'll work here. Remember the rules of engagement. Stay clear of clouds in the fight. Ram Two, turn away now for separation."

Pepper slapped the wings into a right turn to acknowledge. "Jack, let's make sure we're greened up. Betcha Raptor didn't call for the checks so we'd forget and blow the first engagement." Pepper leaned forward to the instrument panel. "MASTER ARM is coming on, radar missile selected and tuned. I'm ready up front."

"I'm ready here too. Radar is up front to you, you're bore sight, get us a visual lock-on. Looks like we've got about three miles separation. We'll be turning in soon."

Raptor called, "Ram Two, with weather moving in, we'll have to return to base with more fuel onboard in case we have to divert to Udorn Air Base. Bingo fuel is now 4500 pounds. We'll only have time for two engagements. Make 'em count."

Raptor was off Pepper's left shoulder now, a dark speck against white cumulus clouds as the distance between them grew to five miles. They were surrounded by bulbous mounds of clouds and thunderstorms with the occasional cloud-to-cloud rapier of lightning. It was a fishbowl of clear air, but between them was a singular vertical column of billowing cottony cumulus much like the center pole in a tent. Pepper discounted it from being much of a factor, but thought it might be close to where the Phantoms would pass in the first engagement.

"Ram, fight's on," Raptor called in a sullen monotone.

"Fight's on."

"Okay, Jack," Pepper said, "it's time to turn big parts into little parts with this simulated MiG. Comin' hard left. Let's try to get two Sparrows on 'em before the pass. I want a couple of white fence posts stuck in Raptor's beak before he ever gets to the fight." Pepper jammed throttles into afterburner and rolled out, pointing his Phantom at the speck that was Raptor climbing through the horizon. A glance at the instrument panel told him their speed was 525 knots and that the radar had found its target. *We're locked. Missile's ready. Let 'er rip.* He squeezed the trigger on the stick and pressed the mike button on the right throttle. "Ram Two, Fox One." The gun camera automatically started to run.

"I can't see him anymore," Jack said from the backseat.

"Got him. Right one o'clock."

Jack went into air-combat data transfer. "We're still at 525, five seconds to the second missile. Closure is twelve-hundred knots, we'll be close to minimum range. Two...one...Fire!"

Pepper pulled the trigger in RADAR mode. In combat, another Sparrow would have launched. "Took the shot, but I'm not calling it. Too close to minimum range. I can't afford to call a bogus kill on Raptor."

While Pepper was preoccupied with achieving Sparrow parameters, he didn't notice Raptor's subtle climb during his turn. Pepper had an optimum look-up Sparrow shot, away from ground interference, but Raptor had the advantage at the pass. He was about to use it.

"That column of clouds is now on our left...Raptor high right one o'clock, one mile. This ain't good," Jack mumbled.

Raptor rolled his Phantom very early, way before he passed. Narrow trails of moisture peeled off his wingtips as the Gs increased in his hard turn down and into them.

"We can't turn left with the clouds," Jack said. "Raptor's taken away the right turn option. We're sandwiched. The sonofabitch trapped us with the rules."

Yep, we should be diving into that cloud right now to get away. "He's lead-turning the shit out of us," Pepper said, and hesitated an eternal two seconds. "I've never seen anybody turn that soon. I've got to come up and into him. We can't separate, he's got too much turn out of the way." He slapped the wings right and pulled the stick toward his lap. Moisture in the air close to the cumulus turned Pepper's Phantom into a ball of fog as he laid on Gs, telegraphing his hard turn. "I'm trying to steal some of Raptor's advantage. Jack, watch him behind us. We're losing knots fast."

"Okay, he's at our deep six o'clock low now. I've lost sight in the turn. Last I saw, he was headed toward that cloud."

"I'm bending it around." *That's the last place we saw him — I'm going to point right at that cloud. Still in AB, going downhill. Come on, build knots faster, Rhino, goddamit!* "Try to get a visual on him ASAP. If we lose sight much longer, we're dead meat."

Jack scanned the sky on either side and above as far as he could see. "Where'd he go? The sucker pulled the disappear switch." They were screaming down straight at the building cumulus. Airspeed was back to 525.

Pepper fought panic and searched the quadrants in front for any sign of movement. They were getting close to the cumulus. Suddenly Pepper caught sight of Raptor's Phantom. "Oh, shit. I'm visual at three o'clock. Raptor must have come out of the cloud. He's got us." *I can't go right, the damn cloud is there. He's got us for sure if I go left. Gotta go up...and pray for a miracle.* "Climb, baby. Like a homesick angel. Climb. Get me outta this mess."

"Pepper, you better do some of that pilot shit up there. He's gonna gun us in a second."

"I can't see him back there anymore. Let me know when, and I'll try Animal's last-ditch gun defense."

"Oh, shit. We'll be out of control then. If you're going to do it...better do it now. We're about to get our brains gunned out."

Their Phantom was pointed 60-degrees nose high, and airspeed bled rapidly. Pepper shoved the stick forward. Just as he fed full left rudder they heard Raptor on the UHF, "Guns, guns, guns, and more guns — kill!"

Pepper's jet flopped nose down and yawed sickeningly to the left. They were a falling leaf, first tumbling tail over nose, then yawing and rolling in circles.

"Oh, shit," Jack muttered.

"I don't know what that first flop was, but this looks like a flat spin, Jack," Pepper said.

Maps flew around the cockpit, dirt and debris suspended in midair. The horizon was alternately spinning and then bucking up and down. More spinning, more bucking up and down. The cockpit filled with the smell of exhaust fumes from the engines still in afterburner. MASTER CAUTION, generator, and oil pressure lights flared on the emergency telelight panel. *This is what Animal meant about 'out of control.'*

"How much altitude do we have?"

"We're at fifteen thousand. We'll have to eject at ten. Shit, Pepper, recover the damn thing!" Jack hollered.

"Stick forward, aileron, and rudder neutral, *hold the goddam stick centered!*" Pepper yelled.

"Ram, knock it off," Raptor called. "This fight's over. Recover your jet."

"Recover my jet? What the hell do you think I'm trying to do? Enjoy the fuckin' ride?" Pepper said, without hitting the mike button. The Phantom continued plunging, rolling, and pitching like a shot-gunned duck. The two men bounced about their cockpits like pinballs. "Throttles are in idle. Keep the motors runnin'. Any ideas, Jack?"

"Deploy the drag chute…maybe it'll drop our nose…we can fly out. If not, we'll be stepping over the side."

"Ram Two, you're passing twelve thousand. Recover your jet! Stick forward, ailerons, and rudder neutral."

Shut the fuck up; already done it. Pepper groped for the drag chute handle with his left hand. *Where's the damn thing! Never had to find it thrashing around like this.* Finally he felt it, grabbed hold, and yanked.

A small door in the jet's tail popped open, and the drag chute fell from its compartment. It snapped open for an instant before ripping away by hurricane-force wind. It provided just enough resistance to pitch the Phantom's nose down. Once pointed at the ground, wind again flowed over the wings, and knots quickly increased through 160.

Pepper took a deep breath. "We're flyin'!" He pulled the Phantom's nose up to the horizon.

"Ram Two, I'm behind you off your right wing," Raptor called. "That was a great airshow, but we're not here for aerobatics; we're here for air combat. Now that you've learned how to fly straight and level, how does your jet look?"

"We nearly planted this jet in a rice paddy," Jack mumbled. "That sonofabitch would choke his grandma."

"Sir, the jet's okay," Pepper called. "Generator and oil pressure lights are out, and the engines look good. We're probably minus our drag chute."

"Okay, Ram Two, you lost me in the clouds, then went out of control with that weird gun defense maneuver, so it's *kindercare* for you. We're heading back to base. Affirmative on the chute. Door's gone too."

"Goddamit! I ain't goin' to no stinkin' *kindercare,* you asshole!" Pepper blurted over the intercom.

"Stay cool, Pepper," Jack advised. "Press that mike button now, your career *and* your flyin' are over. You should take that other frozen towel and use it to cool down. How about I fly the jet a minute?"

"Okay, you got it." Pepper shook the stick to confirm, then rolled his helmet forward and off. His hair dripped with perspiration. The frozen towel felt good; its icy shock taking his mind away for a moment. He reached for his good-luck piece, Tim's Zippo, in the chest pocket of his flight suit. He could feel its familiar rectangular shape. *Listen, weak dick. If Tim could slug it out knee-deep in rice paddies — and get blown away, there's gotta be one more fight left in you.*

He fished the still cool water bottle from the left leg pocket of his G-suit and took a long slug. Rolling his helmet back on, he queried, "Jack, you got another fight left in you?"

"Shit, man. Mama said I was born fightin'."

"All right. It's time to shake 'n bake." Pepper snapped his chin strap and cinched the oxygen mask to his face. He shook the stick to take control, then called Raptor. "Ram One, we're not bingo fuel yet. We've got enough for one engagement. Sir, request we give the taxpayers their money's worth and use the gas we have left for training."

Raptor paused. He maneuvered the flight around some clouds and was ready to depart for home base. "Ram Two, what's the checklist say for a popped drag chute in flight?"

"Sir, it says to return and land as soon as possible. But, I always thought that was because the door would still be open in flight. You eyeballed it gone. If this were the real thing, Sir, I couldn't go home and land. I'd keep fightin'."

"Remember what I told you? You just trashed one more of my jets."

Keep your mouth shut for once. Stay right here on his wingtip. You've asked, that's all you can do. Damn, I wish he'd say something.

"I'll tell you what, Ram Two, if you think you can handle it, we'll do another engagement. Who knows? You might get lucky. Turn away for separation."

Pepper jammed the stick and slapped the Phantom in a hard right turn to acknowledge. "Shit-hot, Jack. We ain't done yet!"

"Let's go for it. Forget the radar missiles in the lips. Keep it simple. Heaters and guns."

"We're armed in the green, good growl on the heater." Pepper yanked his lap-belt strap to cinch down tighter.

"He's getting hard to see. We must be about five miles now."

"Ram, turn in, fight's on," Raptor called.

"Fight's on."

"Okay, Jack. Comin' hard left. Goin' for the high entry at the pass this time, see what happens. We gotta do something different. Looks like he's going to pass off our left side."

The two pilots pointed their steeds toward each other, knights on muscled thoroughbreds. They slammed throttles into afterburner, spurring them to charge. Each looked for chinks in the other's armor. Neither found an advantage. Instead of toppling each other with lances, it was now a knife fight. Raptor was low just before the pass. Pepper set his wings in a hard slicing left turn down into him. At the same time and just as aggressively, Raptor jammed his Phantom up and into Ram Two. The closure was fast — a blink at a mile's separation — they had passed.

Pepper's mind raced. It was all on the line. "Jack, they're in a climb, turning left behind us. Now I can't see them anymore." *We're not supposed to do this, might give him the advantage...* "I'm reversing turn back to the right. I'm betting the old buzzard can't see us right now either. Maybe he'll lose sight of us down low. If not, he'll have angles on us, and eat us for lunch. Here goes."

Gs were relentless as they entered a hard left turn, then reversed quickly back to the right. Normally the G-forces diminish as hard turns bleed airspeed, but going downhill kept their energy high and the G's constant. Both fliers grunted, screamed, and flexed to keep blood in their heads. Pepper twisted, straining his neck under to see over his right shoulder. He jammed his helmet between the canopy and ejection seat headrest to cut its weight. He couldn't move his head, but he could roll his eyes farther up to find Raptor. Pepper was at his physical limit. Through graying vision, he searched to find his foe high to his right. *It's do or die time, Pepper. Screw it up, you're toast. Dammit, where is he?* He scanned frantically for telltale signs of the opposing Phantom. Eyes straining, he sought the dark, camouflaged profile. Nothing. The sky was empty.

Pepper pointed a gloved finger to the edge of the curved canopy, high to his right. "Jack, I've lost a visual on Raptor. He should be right about there, but he's not!"

"I've got him!" Jack yelled. "He's farther back. Hot damn, Pepper. It worked! He's still turning, belly up. He doesn't see us. Keep climbing to the right and I'll point you straight at him...Okay, there. On your nose, high. Still turning away."

"I'm visual. He's not. Let's slam this heater right up his ass."

The AIM-9 Sidewinder heat-seeking missile hissed, then emitted a thunderous growl as Pepper, dead at Raptor's six o'clock, captured the Phantom in his sight, square in the heart of the missile's envelope. He held the sight steady and squeezed the trigger to simulate firing the missile, then pressed the mike button on the throttle. "Ram Two, Fox Two."

Pepper knew Raptor now had their position. He watched as Raptor rolled his jet on its back, pointing at the ground in a missile defense break turn. Raptor would lose precious airspeed turning so hard, but he had to defeat the incoming missile and prevent Pepper's second shot for the kill.

On the offensive now, Pepper knew he hadn't won yet. He'd never seen a Phantom roll that fast. "...three...two...one...there's the second missile on 'em right at the edge of the envelope. I'm not calling it, but there it is. He should be a dead man flyin'. I'm gonna lag behind him, then close for guns. I want Raptor to know I'm staying behind him."

"Watch min-range, five-hundred feet," Jack warned. "That'll bust us for sure."

"Rajahh. Ladies and gentlemen, the Vulcan Gatling gun is selected and armed. You'll hear the sound of ripping canvas as we send six-thousand rounds per minute of twenty millimeter into the MiG, now on the run, a mere eight-hundred feet at our twelve o'clock. Relax and enjoy the kill."

Eat shit and die, Raptor — payback's a bitch...

Pepper and Raptor were now two fencers feinting and whirling in counterpoint. No more talk or radio chatter. Wizzos knew that living and dying at this point in combat was entirely in their pilots' hands. Nothing they could say or do would help. Fencing was now a back-alley knife fight — whirling circles and total concentration for the two pilots dueling on high.

Pepper rotated his wrist around the stick's pistol grip so that only his fingertips controlled the 18-ton jet. The stick was an eggshell he dared not break. Such high speeds and aggressive maneuvers required paper-thin precision. He wanted the gunsight and camera focused precisely on Raptor's cockpit. Slowly, he walked it down from the nose of Raptor's jet, then across the radome to the windscreen. With the sight fixed on Raptor's helmet, he squeezed the trigger. In combat, at least 200 rounds of high-explosive incendiary would eviscerate Raptor before his jet exploded — teeth, hair, eyeballs, and black vapor would be hanging in midair. Gasping for air under the Gs, Pepper wheezed, "Guns tracking, tracking, tracking — Kill!"

There was a tense hesitation before Raptor replied, "Ram, knock it off. We're goin' home."

*

Returning to base, the Phantoms rejoined and picked their way through the weather. Pepper was pumped from winning, but still wondered if his flying career might be over. He'd hammered Raptor with the most difficult of all attacks: a gun-tracking shot. They had been "up close and personal." There was no doubt Pepper had achieved parameters in the swirling, diving, rolling, high-G contest. Now it was a matter of how Raptor would handle his toasting. Animal was right, this *had been* a pressure-cooker ride.

Pepper and Jack hung up their flight gear in life support and walked across the compound to squadron operations. There was no sign of Raptor; after parking his Phantom, he'd been chauffeured directly to his office. Pepper knew he'd be waiting, blood in his eyes.

They walked in the broiling Asian sun on a pebbled sidewalk bordered with white painted rocks. "Jack, I appreciate the job you did today — the way you pulled me out of a rough spot with that towel. Thanks."

Jack shrugged. "No sweat. Pun intended. Hey, it was a tough hop. We walked away from it, didn't we? Besides, we whupped his ass," he chuckled. "Felt damn good. Don't brag, though. The old man gets real touchy when he's hammered. Watch it."

On the sidewalk to the squadron they met a lieutenant. On the end of the lieutenant's shiny leather leash stood Roscoe, the base mascot.

Pepper had heard about the pup and dropped to one knee as Roscoe sauntered up, wagging his tail, his stiff, aging hips swaying back and forth. He licked Pepper's hands affectionately while Pepper rubbed the retriever's furry ears. "How you doin', buddy?"

Pepper glanced up at the lieutenant. "You must be the latest Roscoe Control Officer."

"Yes, Sir. Second Lieutenant Penix, the RCO."

"What do people call you, Penix?"

The young officer reddened. "My friends call me PeeWee, Sir." Squatting next to the dog, he continued, "Roscoe got his rabies shot this morning. I just gave him a weekly bath."

Pepper looked into the mascot's eyes and stroked his head. "PeeWee's taking real good care of you, Roscoe. You smell good. Is it true, PeeWee, that Roscoe came here in a fighter pilot's lap? A single-seat F-105?"

"Yes, Sir," PeeWee said, stroking Roscoe's furry back. "It was about ten years ago. Roscoe was just a puppy. The pilot picked up the jet from overhaul in Taiwan and flew him to Korat. Some people say he flew with him in his lap the whole way. After that Roscoe would go to the runway in the commander's jeep and watch all the jets launch for the Rolling Thunder Operation. One day his master didn't come home. That's when they made the junior lieutenant on base the RCO."

"I hadn't heard the whole story. Thanks."

Pepper held Roscoe's ears in both hands and looked close into his brown, all-knowing eyes. "Can you bring me some good luck, huh? I need it. See you in the dining room tonight? Come by the Ram table and I'll buy you a steak."

"Sir, the new club officer from the *world* put up a sign on the dining room door at lunch today." He panned his hand in front of him like reading a marquee. It says, 'Roscoe not allowed in the dining room,' signed '*The* Manager.'"

Pepper jerked and looked at PeeWee. "You're kidding! Well, screw him. We'll put up our own sign." Pepper panned his arm. "I'll say, 'Manager not allowed in dining room,' signed, 'Roscoe.'" *What the hell, my flying's over anyway.*

"Great idea, Sir. With your permission, I'll go ahead and post that sign. Anybody asks, I'll say some captain in a flight suit told me to do it. They all look alike to me."

"Roger that, PeeWee."

"See ya, Roscoe." *Time for Raptor...*

∗

Pepper and Jack stood with their backs to the wall outside the commander's office. The door was open. They could hear him inside bellowing on the phone.

"Yes, Sir, I know that's another one out of commission. We'll have to cannibalize a drag chute door off one of the jets in maintenance. We'll order one top priority from the States and should have it before Saigon falls. If not, we'll keep cannibalizing until it comes in. Yes, Sir, I know it's the second jet he's trashed. It won't happen again."

Raptor slammed the phone down and bellowed, "Ram Two, you better damn well be out there. Get your asses in here!"

As they entered, Tiny slumped in a chair beside Raptor's desk, staring at the floor. Raptor wasn't looking out the window this time. Glowering, he was on his feet, leaning forward with clenched fists planted on the desktop, arms ramrod straight.

His shiny head flushed red, Raptor ignored their salute and snapped, "Sit down! First you weak dicks fall off my wing in a little weather. That's the first time any pilot did that to me in my two-thousand hours flying the Phantom. Next, you let me blow your shit away with the gun. Finally, you morons put on the damnedest airshow I've ever seen. You cost us a door and a drag chute, and you just got my ass chewed by the Wing King. Helluva ride, boys!"

Pepper's jaw tightened. He fought the urge to reply. *Also saved your goddam jet, and I learned something, you sonofabitch. If I'd defended a second sooner, you wouldn't have gun-tracked me. I saw Animal do that, and there's no way you could've stayed back there in the saddle.*

Raptor plodded around to the front of his desk, folded his arms across his chest, leaned back and half-sat against the desk. "Pepper, you're a flyin' accident waiting to happen. Hellfire! I guess it's already happened. You piled up one of my Phantoms, remember?" He never blinked, never took his eyes from Pepper's. "I have one question: How did I lose sight of you in that last engagement? On top of everything else, did you violate the rules of engagement and jump in a cloud?"

"No, Sir."

"Well, speak up. What *did* you do?"

Be careful, stupid. Make or break time. "Sir, when we passed each other I was high, then dove low behind you in my hard left turn. I was betting you couldn't see me for a second, and that you'd look for me to come out of the turn the same way I went in. So, I reversed my turn and came back right instead of left. Jack picked you up visually, belly up to us, and I entered deep at your six o'clock for the heater, followed by the gun."

"Was that a good gunshot?"

Here it comes. Tell him you muffed it and you may fly again. Tell him it was good and it's all over. Done. Finis. You're outta here.

"Sir, there was no cloud to jump into like the *previous* engagement. It was hard to follow you, but guns were good. Min-range was seven-hundred feet."

Raptor locked his steel-blue eyes on Pepper's. There was a long, painful silence. Screaming jet engines on the flight line began fading as if ending a concert. Slowly, Raptor's facial muscles relaxed, his jaw muscles no longer flexed. Arms still folded, he turned his back and walked to the picture window behind his desk. "You showed me a little something, Houston. You got hammered in the first engagement. You came back. You got the gunshot. Everything else is rubbish."

Raptor wadded up his mission data card and threw it across the room into a trash can ten feet away. "Two points." His voice rose. "Now, get the hell out of here, and get yourself ready for Saigon. Remember one thing: don't ding any more of my jets, understand?"

"Yessir!" Pepper and Jack rose to salute. They held them...waiting. For a long moment, Raptor stared at their reflections in the window, then snapped a return, his back still to them.

Thank you, Roscoe...

Chapter 11

YELLOW STAR

"Nothing makes a man more aware of his capabilities and of his limitations than those moments when he must push aside all the familiar defenses of ego and vanity, and accept reality by staring, with the fear that is normal to a man in combat, into the face of Death."

—Major Robert S. Johnson, USAAF

I n preparation for the evacuation order, the crews had been arising at midnight and briefing missions until dawn. Each time all week, they stood down from launch posture and tried to rest during the day amongst the clatter of an active air base. Sleep was scarce; tensions rose. With every intelligence briefing, they watched the situation in South Vietnam worsen. *The Stars and Stripes* was filled with details of a giant American C-5 aircraft loaded with Vietnamese children. No one knew whether "Baby Lift" had been shot down, or had crashed outside of Saigon, killing all on board. Rumors were rampant about the North Vietnamese steamrolling through the South from Da Nang, the former American air base. They were now nearing the capital of Saigon. The war was lost. It was only a matter of time before the NVA would surround the South's capital and begin the expected annihilation.

On the double-teak doors to the Officers' Club dining room hung a poster that said: "MANAGER NOT ALLOWED IN DINING ROOM—ROSCOE." The yellow Lab was sprawled under the Rams' table, gnawing contentedly on a T-bone from Pepper. The room was abuzz with at least a hundred people, all talking at once. It was Friday night, time for managers of destruction to blow off steam.

The highest ranking officer in the room was a chubby major from the supply squadron. The rest were aviators and aircraft maintainers wearing captains' or lieutenants' bars. The rowdy pilots at the two fighter squadron tables and the AC-130 Spectre Gunship table lobbed wine-soaked dinner rolls at each other, as frazzled waitresses ducked and dodged to deliver their meals. A petite Thai barmaid carried a tray of drinks between the Spectre and Ram tables.

Animal was describing to Pepper how to prevent the aircraft from going out-of-control during guns defense maneuvers in the Phantom. "It's okay to push the stick forward and use full rudder, but don't hold the rudder too long." Animal's hands were dogfighting, his right hand blazing away at his left. "Just get it rolling in negative-G and take the rudder right out again."

Pepper leaned toward Animal. "I think I get it. The only way is to try it until it works. You really watered my eyes when you put it in my face."

A flight-suited choir of Spectres sang, "Yippee-yi-yay, yippee-yi-yo... Ghost riders in the sky..." as they launched a fusillade of Ripple-soaked rolls at the Rams' table. The barmaid carrying a tray of drinks was caught in the middle. Backpedaling to avoid the incoming rounds, she slipped and went airborne. Seeing the tray of high-octane cocktails fly from her hands, Maggot shot from his chair to catch a glass in each hand. He landed astride the waitress, whose dress and apron flipped up to her face.

A soggy roll fast-balled through the space formerly occupied by Maggot, ricocheting off Animal's rising hand, spattering his nose. Things grew quiet. Maggot grinned, still atop the wide-eyed waitress on the floor. When the silence hit him, he sat one drink on the floor, lightly covered her mouth with a hand, smiled, and whispered, "Shhh."

Animal wiped his face with a napkin, then grabbed an orange from the fruit bowl in front of him. Unfolding slowly to his six-feet two-inches, he was a grizzly on its hind legs. He tossed the orange from hand to hand, scanning the room for the culprit. As he hulked there in the silence, no one dared launch another soggy missile.

Pepper eased his chair back, ready to dive under the table if needed. Only the distant rattling of dishes behind the swinging kitchen doors disturbed the silence.

Having failed to spot the enemy, Animal scowled and sucked in a deep breath. "DEAD BUG!" he roared. Metal chairs clattered as dozens of airmen hit the floor. On the way down, Animal grabbed Pepper's collar, yanking him from his chair. Dozens of laughing men and women in flight suits and camouflaged fatigues lay on their backs and thrashed their arms and legs in the air like dying insects. By tradition, the last person on the floor had to buy drinks for everyone else and a hundred of them wouldn't be cheap. This time the action was so frenzied a loser could not be declared. A Thai waitress came unglued, dropped her tray, and ran screaming into the kitchen. Roscoe chewed his bone oblivious to the bedlam. He belched contentedly, lifted a leg, stretched his neck, and licked his freckled balls.

Maggot still enjoyed his position atop the waitress. A dead-bugging Spectre pilot stopped thrashing next to him and bellowed, "Look, Maggot's *not* queer anymore! He likes girls now." Laughter rang out. The room was a slippery mess, but tension was now on vacation.

Suddenly the wing commander, a full-bird colonel and highest ranking officer on base, burst through the dining room doors talking to someone over his hand-held radio. "ROOM, TIN HUT!" the supply squadron major shouted. Everyone snapped to attention. The room grew quiet again as the colonel finished his call, "Korat One, copy. Oh-one-hundred hours." Hands on hips, he eyed the carnage. Officers at rigid attention faced in all directions, many holding chairs they'd just retrieved from the wet, food-strewn floor. Then, with eagles glistening from his collar, his expression glaring and stone-cold, he finally spoke. "Clean up this mess and get some rest. I want you ready for a mass briefing at 0100 hours." He glanced at his watch and added, "That's in five short hours, ladies and gentlemen."

The colonel turned to leave, then suddenly halted. He spied Roscoe under the Rams' table, crunching Pepper's T-bone. A tall man, he stepped to the table and squatted to the old dog's level. Roscoe stopped gnawing as the two made eye contact. The colonel spoke loud enough for all to hear, "Roscoe, you *and* the club manager are allowed in here."

He stood and looked across the rabble. "Carry on. I want you and your people ready."

The only facility large enough to hold all flying personnel and aircraft maintenance supervisors was the base theater. Five minutes before the intelligence briefing, the room was chatter-filled, everyone eager to get the latest on what was happening in Vietnam.

As usual, the rumor mill cranked overtime. Excitement and anticipation filled the room. The lights were full bright; on stage a large American flag scrolled down in front of the movie screen. Talk fell to a murmur. Then a voice boomed from the back of the room: "Ladies and gentlemen, the wing commander!" The clatter of spring-loaded seats and 600 boots hitting the floor rocked the room as men and women snapped to attention.

Wearing a green flight suit with camouflaged patches and black eagle insignia, the colonel walked briskly down the center aisle. Taking the steps to the stage two at a time, he turned to face his command. "Take your seats," he ordered.

The colonel scanned the room for a few seconds, hands on his hips. He turned and strolled toward the left side of the stage, eyes on the wooden floor as if seeking precise words. The only sound was the whisper of air conditioning. He reached stage left and turned to face the flag.

"Ladies and gentlemen," he began, eyes still on the flag, "to me the red stripes on Old Glory mean bloodstained snow at Valley Forge where a young American patriot lay clad only in rags, a single musket ball left in his pouch. The last word from his throat was 'freedom.' Those stripes are for a private from the Army of Northern Virginia sprawled across a boulder at Little Round Top near Gettysburg, his lifeblood seeping into holy soil, blending with that of thirty-thousand other Americans."

The colonel turned, walked slowly to the center of the stage and faced his audience before continuing: "Those bars are for the infantry lieutenant washed ashore by bloody surf at Omaha Beach. They're for the F-86 pilot whose Super Sabre was blown from under him near the Yalu River in North Korea. They're for the F-105 Thud driver who lay starving on the floor of a rancid cell in the Hanoi Hilton. What do they all have in common? They gave their best.

"Some of you have fought here before. Others, it's your first time. What I'm asking all of you to do when we launch for MiG Sweep and then eventually evacuate Saigon…is give your best. We've all been touched by this damn war. Many of us know fathers, sons, daughters, and friends who have served. Some have been wounded, some have died here. They all did their duty. Now it's time for us to do *our* duty and finish this war."

With his hands still on his hips, the colonel turned sideways and sauntered across the stage as he continued, "I want you maintainers to give our aircrews the best jets you can. We don't fly trash. If they're not safe, leave 'em on the ground. Load them with ass-kicking ordnance and triple check the weapons systems. Aircrews, make sure you have what you need. Ensure aircraft systems are working properly. Have your weapons armed and ready. When you satisfy the rules of engagement and it's time to meet the enemy…don't hesitate. Bring your full might and fury down on them. Make them wish they had never heard of the United States Air Force. But do it smart. I want all of you back here when this is over."

He turned to face the audience once again. "I'm returning to the command center. I've asked Captain Dana Bonham to give you the intelligence briefing that she gave to the battle staff earlier. A lot has happened, and she'll tell you what you need to know. Carry on."

The colonel made his way down the steps, then stopped and leaned down to speak to Raptor who sat on the aisle seat of the front row. His shiny head nodded affirmative. The colonel then strode briskly to the back of the theater where a sergeant held the door open for him.

As the lights dimmed and the flag retracted, Captain Dana Bonham stepped from behind the curtain to the podium on the far left side of the stage. She was illuminated by a single spotlight. Known for swimming endless laps for exercise, "C-tone" delighted in driving her perpetual poolside audience wild by rubbing Coppertone tanning lotion on her long, toned legs. Her honey-blonde, shoulder-length hair was accented by a deep tan, her uniform was starched and pressed. C-tone had recently been awarded "Best Intel Officer in Pacific Air Forces." She was a complete package and knew her stuff; the most important was enemy capabilities.

She began, "Over the last two weeks I have briefed you on the North Vietnamese Army's relentless progress toward Saigon." A large map of Vietnam flashed on the screen. "Presently, Saigon is surrounded by two armored divisions and one infantry division, with a second marshaling northwest of the city. We suspect their objective will be to roll down Highway 1, seize the capital and the American Embassy. You have been briefed on the surface-to-air missile and anti-aircraft artillery overlapping Saigon. An additional SAM-2 site is now operational at Tay Ninh northwest of the city. Headquarters Air Force Intelligence at the Pentagon tells us that Saigon is now the most heavily defended real estate in the world."

When C-tone pressed the remote control in her hand, a 15-foot-tall bust of an iron-faced, North Vietnamese colonel filled the screen. He wore a powder blue flight suit. "Gentlemen, this is what you *haven't* been briefed on. This hard-core killer is Ho Van Chieu, call sign Yellow

Star." She stepped from behind the podium and stood beside the photo to underscore her words. "He's deadly enough to sport North Vietnam's national symbol as a call sign. Chieu is a MiG-21 driver with nine confirmed American kills, mostly Phantoms. He would like to finish this war with 'You Yankee Air Pirates' as a double-digit ace or better. He disappeared from PhucYen Air Base outside Hanoi over two weeks ago. Yesterday our sources placed him in Da Nang, the former American and South Vietnamese Air Force base. As you know that's only a half-hour north of Saigon for Yellow Star."

Barely visible at the edge of the shadows on stage, C-tone turned facing the audience. "You may remember from a previous briefing, the VNAF left a squadron of American front-line F-5 Freedom Fighter aircraft intact and fully armed at Da Nang. These jets are armed with our Sidewinder missiles and 20mm cannon and now they are a threat to you. Even worse, friendly VNAF pilots farther south are pigeon-holing their families into the single-seat cockpits to flee toward Thailand. So, before you fire, rules of engagement today require a visual identification. By the time you can ID it as an F-5, and know that it's not one of the friendlies escaping the country, you'll be forced into a close-in knife fight."

C-tone turned from the screen and walked slowly toward the podium. She stopped under a ceiling floodlight and faced them, her blonde hair glistening. "Gentlemen, let me remind you, the F-5's turn rate is five degrees per second faster than the Phantom's. Its maneuverability is superior. Your Phantoms have long-range radar missiles. The F-5 doesn't, but they're useless in a visual ID situation. Your best advantage is speed. Those who have fought Yellow Star and lived, say he attacks with surprise from out of the sun or from far below. You're forced to turn to defend, which costs you speed. Fly proper tactical spread formation so that you can see the enemy attacking your wingman before it's too late. Fly as fast as you can until engaged. *Keep your smash up.* If an F-5 is moving sideways on your canopy or windscreen, that means he'll pass you. If it's stationary, his nose is on you...attacking.

"Yellow Star's personal MiG-21 is polished silver. It has a bright red vertical tail with a yellow star on it. Once in the fight, he wants to be noticed. In Russian media he's been quoted bragging, 'When my enemy knows who he is engaged with, it's too late.' It's a psych ploy. The Da Nang F-5s are silver like the MiGs, and hard to see against clouds or the sky. A recent RF-4 reconnaissance photo confirmed that one of them now has a red vertical tail.

"During Operation Linebacker II, the Triple Nickel Squadron had two F-4s engaged by Yellow Star. His trademark was a barrel-roll maneuver to achieve firing position behind them. That F-4 wingman was his eighth kill. As you know, it takes finesse to do it right, and most pilots won't try." C-tone flashed a smile to ease the tension and continued, "He's made an art form out of it, kinda like Animal's last-ditch guns move."

Everyone looked to Animal sitting in the third row. He sported a rare blush and slumped down in his theater seat. He said loud enough for the back row to hear: "A bottle of Jack Black for anyone who cooks him before I do!"

When the catcalls died down, C-tone continued, "If Yellow Star is in the saddle from that barrel roll, your best hope is that your wingman can fire before the bad guy launches a heater." She walked over and set the remote control on the podium and faced them once again. "Gentlemen, I wish you good luck and Godspeed today. Be careful out there. That concludes my briefing…"

Her last words trailed off to Pepper's thoughts…Yellow Star looked proud, certain, secure. He slid into Yellow Star's eyes like sliding into a craggy, dark cave. Tense, he realized his fingers were squeezing the armrests. He had read all the Top Secret "Red Baron" combat engagement reports in the intelligence vault. The number of North Vietnamese aces had stuck with Pepper. Thirteen. He remembered that Yellow Star attacked at very high speeds, and would turn to maneuver for the kill when other MiG drivers wouldn't stick around. Reports said he was unshakable. His "ice-cold aggressiveness" was what made him the North's leading Phantom killer. Pepper understood every word C-tone said, but he had never fought another aircraft except the Phantom.

A wave of self-doubt washed over Pepper like a premonition of danger. It's been play fighting up to this point. *Now…you fuck up, you die.* One thought consumed him: *this guy looks like the face of death…*

Chapter 12

ROSCOE GETS HIS RIDE

"The smallest amount of vanity is fatal in aeroplane fighting.
Self-distrust rather is the quality to which many a pilot owes his
protracted existence."

—Captain Eddie Rickenbacker

Before major air operations such as the evacuation of Saigon, it was
U.S. doctrine to first fly offensive counter-air missions to take out
as many of the enemy's airfields and aircraft and basically cripple
their air arm so that other U.S. aircraft had a better chance of succeeding
in their missions. Those "other" missions might be bombing enemy troop
concentrations, attacking lines of communication and in Saigon's case,
effecting an evacuation of U.S. and Vietnamese personnel. One of the
offensive counter-air, or OCA missions, was MiG Combat Air Patrol,
MiGCAP, also known as MiG Sweep. F-4s were to take off from bases
in Thailand, cross "The Fence," the Mekong River, and patrol for enemy
aircraft such as MiGs, or in this case also American F-5 fighters that the
North Vietnamese captured. Once the fighters engaged the enemy, it was
like an old western duel to the death. The two principals, the flight leaders
on both sides, would be assisted by their seconds, or "wingmen." If this
duel didn't happen exactly this way — it could have. The fighter crews at
Korat had been reporting to duty around midnight for the last couple of
weeks to start mission prep, get intel briefings on the North Vietnamese
Army's thrust into the South and brief their individual missions. Since
there had been no decision to evacuate up to this point, military leaders
planned for a worst case scenario of a very early morning launch to
maximize daylight for the evacuation attempt. Good military leaders

try to let their men and women get as much rest as possible before big missions. These missions often started with a telephone recall to report for duty.

Where's the damn phone? Pepper tripped over his jungle boots as he fumbled around the darkened room. The fog from only two hours sleep still thick in his head, he finally located the phone next to the lighted clock which read 0900.

"Hello."

"Captain Houston, this is the operations center. We are under a recall. Draw your weapon at the armory and report to the squadron immediately, Sir."

"Okay." Pepper stared at the receiver and tried to get his bearings. *Damn, I'm tired. This must be the real thing. I hope so — no more games.* He went through the automatic, hurried motions of zipping his flight suit and tying his boot laces. His mind was working to process the change in plans. *I wish my head would clear! Think! Do you have everything? You may not be back in this hooch for a while. Hell, you may never be back.* From sheer habit he planted a flight cap on his head, the characteristic fighter pilot ducktail crease in back. Checking his watch, it read 9:18, on the twenty-ninth. *April 29. Might see combat today. Been briefing a bombing strike mission every day this week. Get pumped…I'm ready.* He fumbled for the worn Zippo in his left chest pocket. *Got your Firehammer, Tim. Nine years. Like you Marines say, 'payback's a motherfucker.' Gonna deliver 500-pounders to the NVA today.*

Pepper stepped through the doorway of the fighter squadron operations room and into pandemonium. The large counter was surrounded by pilots and navigators copying down changes in missions. Briefing rooms were strewn with maps, checklists, and flying gear. Shouts echoed down the halls: "Let's step, we're late."

"Get your shit together. Push it up!"

Pepper turned and bumped into his wizzo racing out the door with another pilot. "Jack, where the hell are you going?"

"The whole thing's changed, man. They paired me with Paco a few minutes ago and told us to step to the jets. Check with the duty officer at the desk to see what's shakin'. We gotta go."

"Pepper, glad you're here!" said Lieutenant Colonel Brad "Mad Dog" Smith, the operations officer on duty.

"Sir, isn't it rare to have this much brass behind the operations counter?"

"This is the real deal."

Adding to the chaos, a brand new backseater, who was also an electronic warfare officer, EWO, burst through the door. Captain George "Queer-Tron" Speckling tripped, dumping his ditty bag of flying gear on the floor and blurted, "Who's filing the flight plan to Saigon?"

Mad Dog rose from behind the counter and stared at the mess on the floor. "Tron, are you wacko? You don't file flight plans when you go to war!" Then he looked at Pepper and grinned. "You're in trouble, Tron's your new backseater, and you're no longer flying strike. You're flying MiGCAP on Raptor's wing."

"MiGCAP?" Pepper croaked, "I've been briefing strike for a week, and now I'm flying combat air patrol against MiGs? With Raptor, ah, Colonel Offal?"

"Here he comes," Colonel Smith said, busily shuffling papers. You may get your chance to fly that strike mission later, we need to clear the area of MiGs first."

Pepper's pulse went into afterburner. So did self-doubt. *To live, a MiGCAP pair has to work as a team. Raptor and me? With a green wizzo? Shit! And Raptor's already suited up.*

Raptor stopped at the counter to jot down tail numbers on his line-up card. Without looking up he said, "Let's go, Houston, we gotta step to our jets. I'll brief you en route to Saigon. I want a good wingman. All I want to hear from you is: 'Two, mayday, and lead you're on fire.' Our call sign is Ram Zero-One. Engine start in 30 minutes. Be locked, loaded, and ready."

✳

On the flight line, the scream of J-79 engines was deafening. Maintenance personnel called it the sound of freedom. Weapons carts loaded with bombs and air-to-air missiles scooted from one protected revetment to the other. Pilots hustled around their jets. The kerosene odor of JP-4 exhaust permeated the air.

Tron and Pepper spoke little as they checked each missile's connections and arming pins. AIM-7 Sparrows hung from the belly and AIM-9 Sidewinders were fitted to pylons under each wing. All were live with blast fragmentation warheads. In a second, they could blast a MiG into confetti. Pepper had never seen a jet loaded live, wall to wall. He had carried only an occasional inert training missile. From his Phantom's belly, in place of the bombs he thought he'd be carrying, hung a 20-mm Vulcan Gatling gun with six rotating barrels. The Vulcan could spew death at 6000 rounds of high-explosive incendiary per minute. The gravity of what he might have to do with this arsenal quelled Pepper's normal banter with his crew chief and weapons troops, who stood by during preflight inspections.

I screw up with this stuff and somebody gets hurt — bad.

Pepper was ready when Raptor checked in on the UHF. They moved out in unison, merging with other fighters on the taxiway. The ramp was busy. Fighters lumbered their way to the arming area with countless red, "Remove before flight" flags fluttering from air-to-air missiles and bombs. Pepper guided his Phantom into a slot next to Raptor's and pressed the top of his rudder pedals to stop the Rhino. Both men held their gloved hands in the air, signaling the arming crew that it was safe to run under the jet to pull all safety pins.

"Tron, I've never seen this much live ordnance in my life. It looks like a Fourth of July parade with all those flags," Pepper said, his fingers thumping an unconscious drumroll on the railing of the open canopy. "You ever flown MiGCAP before?"

"I've flown a couple training missions; nothing for real," Tron remarked. "Man, look at all those pins our crew chief's holding up. I guess we're armed and dangerous now."

Pepper gave the arming crew a double thumbs-up acknowledging that the Phantom was armed. "Wonder what Raptor's doing?"

"Twisting in the seat and rolling his neck around. Maybe he does it to loosen up and get ready."

"I'll try that—"

"Ram Zero-One, Korat Tower, cleared for take-off. Climb runway heading to five-thousand. Contact departure control. Good luck. Godspeed, Ram."

"Ram One." Raptor's terse monotone spoke volumes.

*

At the Laotian border, Ram Flight joined four other fighters already waiting to take on fuel from their KC-135 tanker. The gaggle of tankers and fighters flew in a 30-mile, oval orbit called "Chestnut Track."

"Ram Two, listen up," Raptor called. "There's not much time to talk before we get gas. Air staff at the Pentagon wants Ho Van Chieu before he can rack up another kill. He's already got nine; they don't want him to make the history books as the war's only double ace. Intel says Yellow Star has been boasting he'll finish the 'American War' with at least ten kills. To top it off, he wants to kill us with our own pistol — shoot down an American with an American jet. You understand this mission?"

"Yes, Sir, but can I ask a question?"

"Go, Ram Two."

"Why me on your wing?"

"Nobody else in the squadron has ever gotten a kill shot on me. I just hope it wasn't blind-ass luck."

"No, Sir, I remember exactly how I did it."

"Whoa," Tron chided. "All my frontseater needs is more confidence."

"Pairing experience with inexperience can keep pilots alive," Raptor said, then continued. "Okay, Two, when we leave the tanker I want you in combat spread formation, two- to three-thousand feet out, and line abreast to thirty degrees back. I want you stacked out of my altitude for the best sun angle. When we cross the fence, I want your weapons armed and in tactical formation, six- to nine-thousand feet away, stacked, always stacked. If you're level with me, the MiG will see us both at the same time. Your job is to fly formation and make sure nobody slips a missile up my ass. Got it?"

"Affirmative."

"Remember, Two, it may not be a MiG you're looking for, but an F-5. They're both silver — hard to pick up visually. Figuring range is tough. They're just like these gooks who fly 'em, smaller than we are. That makes 'em look farther away than a Phantom. Under the rules of engagement, you can reach out and touch 'em with a missile if we're cleared to fire, or they're hostile. Today we don't have to wait for them to fire first. Questions?"

"Negative, Sir," Pepper replied.

Tron chimed in on the intercom, "I've never fired live missiles and now we're loaded wall-to-wall?"

"You're also going after the war's leading ace," Pepper said. "Nobody said this shit would be easy."

*

Departing the tanker, Ram headed straight for Saigon, 375 miles southeast with enemy troop concentrations and SAMs scattered along the route.

Nerves on edge, Tron kept running checks on the radar warning receiver (RWR), an instrument that was used to detect enemy radar lock-on. When he pushed "self-test" the system flashed red strobes and rattled like a diamondback, just like it would when enemy radars were locked or launching. The repeated tests were unnerving.

Below, the muddy Mekong River snaked toward the South China Sea. "Okay, Ram, we're crossing the fence, let's green 'em up," Raptor called.

They were now over enemy turf. Pepper flipped the MASTER ARM switch to ARM. The missiles were now poised for combat. Rechecking all armament switches kept Pepper's mind off the fact they were headed directly at the enemy's strongest concentration — Saigon.

More rattlesnakes and red strobes.

"Dammit, Tron! Quit running checks. We're across the fence now!"

"Ah — it's the real deal, Pepper. A fuckin' SAM!"

"Roger!" Pepper shouted. He pushed the nose down, then banked hard left to put the RWR strobe at their two o'clock position to search for the incoming missile. Simultaneously he called to Raptor, "Ram Two's SAM break, takin' it down." Frantically he searched for telltale white missile smoke as his Phantom dived, passing 500 knots. *Should I jettison fuel tanks, get ready to engage the missile?*

"Where is the damn thing?" he shouted.

"I don't see it! Maybe they're dickin' with us."

There was no SAM in sight. Pepper took his hand off the JETTISON switch and pulled the Phantom's nose up to get back in tactical formation.

Raptor called, "They ran the triplets on their radar to make your RWR think they had launched. That's so you'd jettison your tanks and go home."

Tricky little bastards. If I'm lucky, they'll be reading about their "numbah one" ace making a nylon letdown in his parachute today.

The pair of Phantoms continued southeast. Pepper looked below him at a ravaged Vietnam, the lush green focal point of so much world attention. Nearly every crossroads was on fire from ground action. A few miles distant, gray smoke accented hundreds of black, puffy war clouds — triple-A fire at passing aircraft. The lethal war clouds stretched from horizon to horizon as Ram Flight bore in on Saigon.

The war had been going on for so long that fathers and sons had both fought in it. Pepper searched north of the city through a pall of smoke trying to spot Bien Hoa Air Base. He remembered that his father spent a year there fighting the Viet Cong in '68. The base was nearly obscured, but he spotted it through the artillery exchanges between NVA regulars and what remained of South Vietnamese troops. *A lost cause, just like this whole damn war.* All the lives, all the effort to establish and defend the base was wasted. He watched helplessly from 21,000 feet as it became property of Ho Chi Minh's army.

To locate their tanker off the east coast of Vietnam, Ram Flight needed radar advisories and vectors from someone with the big picture. Red Crown Control, the primary radar control for the evacuation, was aboard the USS *Enterprise*, an aircraft carrier off the coast of South Vietnam.

Red Crown controllers monitoring their scopes were overwhelmed by their strenuous task, staring in disbelief at the hundreds of aircraft on their screens. They watched as pilots, all seemingly talking on the frequency at the same time, ditched in the South China Sea, while others ran out of fuel, or simply found nowhere to land.

As Ram Flight headed into this fog of war, they needed fuel for their thirsty Phantoms.

"Red Crown, Ram," Raptor called. "We're a flight of two, with air-to-air missiles, looking for Esso Two-One."

"Ram, roger. Esso is in a north-south track due east of Saigon at angels twenty-five. Vector zero-six-zero degrees for rendezvous. Understand you are loaded air-to-air. We had a probe north of Saigon of two possible hostiles from Cam Ranh about an hour ago. They feinted toward some of our fighters engaged with one of their triple-A sites. The bad guys turned around and went home when we committed two Phantoms."

"Ram, copy, zero-six-zero degrees."

"Ram Two, air refueling pre-contact check," Raptor called to Pepper. "Ensure armament is safe."

"Two," Pepper answered, reaching with his left hand to the weapons section of the instrument panel, and rotating the bullet-shaped MASTER ARM switch down to "safe."

Tron had been quiet in the backseat, absorbing the evacuation action and looking continually behind them for attacking MiGs. "Pre-contact checks are complete, open your refueling receptacle and set your mirrors."

Flying 400 miles across enemy territory meant keeping their speed high and moving the aircraft around more than normal due to ground and air threats. Pepper cycled the fuel switch to check tanks. "Man, where'd the gas go? I guess I've been sightseeing. We're down to eight-thousand pounds. Tron, isn't that our tanker 'bingo' for heading home?"

"Yep. And we'll be down to seven thou by the time we hit the tanker."

"Crap. Raptor should have about the same. That SAM break cost us. How about figuring what we'd need if we get lucky en route and find a tanker as we get back to Thailand."

"We could leave Saigon with about six-thou then, but that's straight line, with no engagements on the way home."

"Okay. Let's press on and bet we either get refueled here, or catch a tanker on the way home. Red Crown might need these missiles. Besides, this is *war*. Gotta push the limits."

Raptor called, "Red Crown, Ram has Esso radar contact on the nose, thirty miles."

"Ram, that's your tanker. Switch to air refueling frequency and contact me when you're complete."

Raptor led the formation in a textbook turning rendezvous with the KC-135. It already had four chicks in tow, fighters waiting their turn to onload JP-4. The boom operator plugged each fighter and filled them. Now it was Ram's turn. Raptor eased into contact position and the boomer seemed to reach out and grab the Phantom's refueling receptacle.

"Ram's contact," Raptor called.

The boomer acknowledged, "Esso contact."

"Boomer, is that Roscoe in your window?" Raptor asked.

"Roger, Sir. Wing commander said he could fly. Last chance and all that."

"Give him a pat from us, will you?" Raptor asked.

"Will do. Ram, I show no-flow on the boom. You're full."

"Ram, disconnect, ready, now," Raptor said, and slid his heavy Phantom up to the wing of the tanker.

Pepper connected with only 7000 pounds of fuel remaining, little more than enough to make it to the next tanker on their way home, if one was there.

Pepper's pulse clicked along at a high rate of fire, but his nerves remained steady. He was stretching his luck. He knew it. He also knew that like combat, air refueling was a game measured in inches. An errant fingertip's worth of pressure and the two aircraft could collide. A glance at the fuel gauge assured him they were taking gas.

Pepper took his eyes off the tanker's director lights indicating he was in optimum refueling position and saw Roscoe looking at him from the boomer's window. Pepper took his left hand momentarily off the throttles and waved. He could see Roscoe peering down at him, panting.

"Boomer, Ram Two," Pepper called. "Would you tell Roscoe that Pepper says hello and that I'll buy him a T-bone tonight?" He could see the boomer move the microphone away from his face and say something to Roscoe. The Lab glanced at the boomer and back to Pepper, then started barking. *Bring us some luck, Roscoe...*

As Pepper's fuel tanks neared full, Esso called, "Ram, Red Crown wants you to contact them immediately. They've got MiG action."

Chapter 13

SPLASH ONE

"So it was that the war in the air began. Men rode upon the whirlwind that night and slew and fell like archangels. The sky rained heroes upon the astonished earth. Surely the last flights of mankind were the best. What was the heavy pounding of your Homeric swordsmen, what was the creaking charge of chariots, besides this swift rush, this crash, this giddy triumph, this headlong sweep to death?"

—H.G. Wells, The World Set Free, *1914*

Refueled, Raptor checked in. "Red Crown, this is Ram Flight with you. Understand you have some work for us?"

"Ram, that's affirmative. How many and how are you loaded?"

"Ram's a flight of two Phantoms, each with four radar missiles, four heat, and 1200 rounds of 20mm. With our fuel, we have approximately 20 minutes of playtime."

"Ram. Roger. We have four unknowns that are airborne Cam Ranh. Refugee aircraft have been heading west to Thailand, but *these* are headed southeast toward you. They're suspected hostiles. They may be trying to attack the tanker you just departed."

"Ram, copy."

"Ram Two, fence check, green 'em up."

"Two."

Pepper flipped on the MASTER ARM again. All missiles indicated armed and ready. "Tron, everything's hot up front. Ready to reach out and touch someone. The sonsabitches are pretty smart. They know if they can take out our tanker, we'll *all* have to turn around and go home. What they don't know is that Roscoe's on that bird and we're the goalie. They ain't gonna get through."

"Yep. That flying fuel pump would make one helluva fireball. Ol' Yellow Star would really like that. It's never been done."

Raptor called, "Ram Two, let's get into tactical spread and eyeballs movin'."

"Ram, Red Crown. Vector northwest. Targets are committed, you are between them and the tanker. We have four unknowns separated in two flights of two."

"Ram, copy."

"Two, stack at least 2000 feet high on my right side."

"Two," Pepper answered, and began to climb. *Unknowns? They could be friendlies. Might be bad guys. Gotta get my act together.*

"Ram, Red Crown, your targets are on your nose, three-zero miles. They appear to be spreading apart to bracket you in the middle."

"Ram One, radar contact, three-three-zero degrees at 28 miles. Red Crown, can you declare them hostile?"

"Red Crown, negative. Still unknowns. Your radar contact is the pair to the west. Look slightly right of them, about three-three-five degrees for the other pair."

Pepper scanned the sky behind Raptor's jet for an attack. "Tron, you have them on our radar yet?"

"Yeah, looks like they're in two groups. We're caught between. Raptor's pointed at the group on the left. They're on our nose, one-five miles."

Pepper glanced at the airspeed indicator. "Raptor's keeping his smash up. We're at the mach just trying to catch him."

"Yep. I'm locked onto the western targets, closure's 1500 knots. They're also doing the mach."

Raptor called, "Red Crown, Ram One is locked to the western targets. Keep us advised on the pair to the east."

"Ram, roger. Command doesn't like them getting that close to the tanker. Esso's in retrograde, trying to escape southeast. Command declares your targets are bandits. They're hostile. Cleared to fire!"

Pepper quickly searched Raptor's six o'clock, high and low. *Holy shit. Bad guys! This ain't no training intercept. Get a missile ready to go. Nobody coming in from our right side. Speed is life. We're mach 1.2 — fast enough.* "Tron, are we locked?" Pepper felt for the Zippo. It was there. *Maybe this is it, Tim.*

"Yep. We're locked to the western pair with Raptor. The other two were off to our right front, about two o'clock."

An AIM-7 radar-guided Sparrow missile dropped from Raptor's Phantom, its rocket motor blasting a trail of bright white smoke. The second followed almost immediately. The missiles accelerated to 2.5 mach above Raptor's launch mach, a closure of 3000 knots per hour (3450 MPH) on their targets.

"Ram's Fox-One," Raptor called. "Fox-One again on targets three-three-zero at 8 miles."

Pepper ached to let his missiles rip, but having never fired one, he hesitated. "Should we fire, Tron?"

"Let's keep 'em and see what happens to Raptor's. We might shoot at the same guy."

"Ram One, Red Crown. The bandits you fired on appear to be turning around, trying to drag you away from the other pair."

Pepper spun his head left, then right, looking for an attack. *I've never seen one of these things launched before, but I know this: those double smoke plumes are going to show every bandit in the area exactly where we are.* "Damn, Raptor's missiles won't catch 'em now, they're going away from us. Where is the other pair? Got 'em on radar, Tron?"

"Negative, we've been locked to the decoy bandits."

Raptor's voice was strained. "Red Crown, Ram. Where are the other bandits?"

"Ram, the second pair is to your right three o'clock, three miles. They're hooking toward you."

Immediately, four helmets swiveled to the right, eyes searching.

They all knew MiG pilots used their radar ground controllers extensively during an intercept. Desperately they searched behind and below each other's Phantoms, then high six o'clock. North Vietnamese ground controllers would watch the American formation closely on radar to determine which aircraft was the wingman. Less experienced wingmen typically flew slightly behind their leaders instead of line abreast. MiGs always attacked them first.

Raptor was first to see him. "Ram Two, break hard right. Bandit your six o'clock high, out of the sun."

It was an automatic. Pepper didn't wait to see his attacker. He slapped the Phantom's wings in a steep right turn and pulled the stick back hard, instantly racking the jet into seven Gs. The wingtips left moisture ribbons and the wings wore fog from the hard turn. *I can't see the sonofabitch yet, but I'm not giving him an easy kill. There he is, up to my right, high five o'clock. What's that thing coming at me?* "Tron, we got a missile tracking at five high. I'm going to try to make it overshoot with more Gs." Pepper turned even harder as the missile stalked deathly close. Both men grunted and flexed under the load, trying to keep enough blood in their heads to see. *Can't black out now!*

The missile couldn't stay with the Phantom. It flashed over Pepper's canopy, close enough to detonate the proximity fuse and explode only feet away. "Damn, Tron. That was *real* close. It's an F-5 with its nose on us!" The detonation shook Pepper; he was frozen in a hard right turn, eyes padlocked to the oncoming threat.

"You better shake his ass, or we're gonna die!"

A break turn a second later and they would have been confetti. *Thanks, Raptor.*

Pepper stifled his sigh of relief as the F-5 pressed the attack. Now inside 1500 feet, its nose glowed orange with 20mm cannon fire. Pepper rolled his jet, but several rounds stitched his left wing. He felt the Phantom shudder, but couldn't tell where bullets had struck. *No damage on the right wing, there're some shredded wing panels on the left. Maybe the foam-filled tanks will seal. Stop the leaks.*

The F-5 rolled to come off Pepper and overshoot to the outside of the turn. Pepper spotted the second F-5 flying 3000 feet behind the leader in a support position.

"Tron, bandit's nose is behind us and his wingman's following. Good. They're off us."

"See'em," Tron replied. "Oh, shit. Not so good. Leader's got a red tail with a star on it."

Pepper slammed his helmet back against the canopy and ejection seat for another look. "Oh, my God. Yellow Star. We just got shot by Yellow Star!"

"Yep. And now I've lost sight of 'em," Tron shouted.

Pepper slapped the wings back hard to the left. *Dammit. I know I'm not supposed to do this, but the sonofabitch is goin' after Raptor.* "Ram One, it's Yellow Star. There's two of 'em. I'm reversing back left."

"Ram Flight, Red Crown. The two bandits that decoyed to the northwest are turning back at you now. They're three-three-zero for ten miles."

Raptor grunted, reflecting the Gs he was pulling. "Ram One copy, we're engaged and anchored with two F-5s. One's Yellow Star."

Pepper saw the two F-5s as he came out of his left turn. *They look like two mockingbirds chasing a hawk. Except these are lethal. I'm afraid to shoot. Yellow Star's too close to Raptor for a missile to tell them apart. All I can do is go for the wingman.* He drew his gunsight to the trailing F-5 and squeezed the trigger. A sickening *thunk*, a white smoke plume told Pepper he'd launched an AIM-7 radar guided missile by mistake.

"Damn, Pepper! We weren't even locked on."

"I know, Tron. Rookie mistake. I still had radar selected from the initial intercept. At least our missile's blind with no lock-on."

"Yeah, well, do some pilot shit up there or Raptor's toast."

Pepper pointed at the trailing F-5 when he fired the Sparrow, and the missile initially flew toward Yellow Star's wingman. The Sparrow appeared to be locked and tracking; the billowing white smoke plume must have intimidated Yellow Star's wingman who rolled his F-5 on its back, and tore into a steep dive. Occupied with chasing Raptor, Yellow Star didn't see his wingman peel off.

Pepper rolled his Phantom over on its back to follow the F-5. The lush green of the rice fields and jungles below was just the background an AIM-9 Sidewinder liked. The heat signature of the bandit's jet stood out like a streetlight on a dark night. Reaching to the lower instrument panel, Pepper's left hand flipped a toggle switch from RADAR to HEAT. While he flew the jet with his right hand, he brought the gunsight to capture the F-5's infrared heat source: its engines.

Tron tried to sound calm, but his voice went up an octave. "Pepper, I'm blind out front. I'm visual on Raptor. He's trying to shake Yellow Star. Hurry."

"The idiot's just diving straight at the ground. There's the growl, nice and loud." Pepper held the sight's inner circle steady. As he centered the fleeing F-5, he squeezed the trigger. A Sidewinder streaked from the left wing pylon and tracked straight at its prey. *Damn! That's a fast missile. It's a big bullet. I better send another one just in case.* He squeezed the trigger again. A Sidewinder launched from the right wing. This time he remembered the radio: "Fox Two!"

"Holy shit, Tron, look at that! He's a fireball."

The first missile flew straight up the exhaust of the F-5's right engine afterburner. The proximity fuse detonated only feet behind, and blast fragmentation from the warhead eviscerated the fleeing jet. The second Sidewinder slammed into the ball of debris, and detonated on a piece of the fuselage. Pepper saw no parachute.

As he passed the fireball, Pepper pulled the Phantom's nose up and victory rolled 360 degrees. He pressed the mike again: "Splash One...F-5."

Raptor called, "Take your time there, Ram Two, I'm just about to be gunned by the North's leading ace — no sweat."

"Ram, Red Crown. Bandits now north of you five miles, inbound."

Raptor's voice strained under the Gs: "Ram...roger...keep advised."

"I just shot down an American jet," Pepper said, mesmerized by the effect of shooting down his first adversary.

"Pepper, come back hard right, Raptor's in trouble. He can't hang on much longer and we got more bandits inbound. He's right four o'clock high across the circle. Let's go!"

"Okay, I've got a visual on him...and the F-5. Sonofabitch, they're close!"

Pepper racked his Phantom hard right and glanced down to check his fuel gauge. He'd been in burner a long time. *Down to 10,000 pounds. We're still okay, but we don't need wing tank drag. We just got rid of a half-ton of missiles. Shed the tanks.* He needed the extra maneuverability. Pepper turned the rotary dial on the weapons panel to tank JETTISON, punched the large red button on the dial to blast them off. He felt the Phantom jolt slightly, telling him the tanks were gone. Pepper rolled out, pointing at the fighters welded in combat, spiraling perilously toward the ground.

"Forget the radar missile, they're too close," Tron said. "You might get a heater, but I bet it's a gunshot if anything. They've got their knives out."

Yellow Star was relentless, although he had to have seen his wingman's fireball, he sensed a kill of another Phantom. The F-5 closed on Raptor for a cannon shot.

"Yep, Yellow Star's up and rolling! That's the damn barrel roll C-tone told us about. Beautiful move. He's right in the saddle for a gunshot on Raptor."

"Ram One, Two's engaged with Yellow Star. Heater in three seconds."

Raptor managed a shaky "roger." His Phantom in heavy buffet, he ratcheted left, then right, ahead of Yellow Star's guns.

The three airplanes spun, one behind the other, ever closer to the ground. They first engaged at 22,000 feet, now they were passing 5000. Pepper saw nothing but jungle and a thrashing F-5 in his windscreen. He steadied his gunsight on the blood-red tail and five-pointed star of the F-5 only 3000 feet in front. Yellow Star. The Sidewinder growl was deafening — *I can't believe this crazy fucking war. American aircraft or no, I'm going to kill your ass...*

Smoke trailed back from the nose of Yellow Star's F-5 as he fired the cannon at Raptor's jinking Phantom. Instantly, Raptor smoked.

Pepper squeezed the trigger and felt the Sidewinder zip from the left wing pylon. Only one heater remained on the right wing station. Either Yellow Star had been watching Pepper's attack or he'd just got lucky. As the Sidewinder streaked toward its prey, Yellow Star racked his F-5 in a sharp right turn. Pepper leaned forward to go from heat to guns. *Damn, I've never seen an airplane turn like that! But he's off the attack and Raptor's still flyin'.* "He made the heater overshoot, Tron. Trying guns." *At best this'll be a high-deflection snapshot. It's a lot smaller than an F-4.*

Shedding the drag from the wing tanks paid off in maneuverability. Pepper could now swing the Phantom's gunsight in front of the F-5 for lead fire. "Tron, keep an eye on Raptor. After guns, we're lookin' for him."

"I've got 'em."

"Ram, this is Red Crown. Those bandits to the north either saw the fireball or got a call. They're headed back toward Cam Ranh."

"Roger...we've got problems," Raptor called. "Stand by...one of 'em's still with us...I've been hit."

Yellow Star slapped the F-5 left, then right, pushed the stick, then pulled it. His jet jinked all over the sky. Pepper knew aiming was futile. *All I can do is let the sight track down toward him, turn my gun on, spray and pray. Trigger's coming down.* Pepper and Tron heard the faint ripping canvas sound as 6000 rounds per minute of high explosive incendiary gushed from their cannon's spinning barrels. Tracers arched in front of the F-5, then drifted down toward the jet. Yellow Star continued his roll to the right as the bullets met him and buzz-sawed through the outboard third of his F-5's left wing. A large piece ripped loose and disappeared close aboard Pepper's canopy. Fuel streamed, turning to fog.

His juices pumping, Pepper banked hard left to separate from Yellow Star's right turn. *Time to find Ram One...* "Where the hell's Raptor?"

Tron jerked his head to the left. "Back at our left eight o'clock. He's headed away from us, trailing smoke."

"Got him. What about Yellow Star?"

"Still heading off to the right, trailing smoke. Maybe it's fuel vapor from the wing you nailed. He's not coming after us."

Pepper called, "Ram One, I have you in sight. Lead, you're on fire...can I come aboard right side?"

"Affirmative. But don't get too close. We may torch. Bad guys are still around. We're headed west now and looking at distance to home plate. It doesn't look good. Both of us are okay...not wounded. Right engine's running real rough. We've got a fire light. We may be turning around to get feet wet over the South China Sea. We may have to punch out. Standby."

"Roger, Sir. We're your right side, 2000 feet, level."

"Ram, Red Crown. You need assistance?"

"Red Crown, affirmative," Raptor answered. "Do you show any threats in our vicinity?"

"Not at this time, Ram One. Looks like three bandits recovering at Cam Ranh."

Raptor continued, "How about our tanker?"

"Ram One, Esso's okay. Retrograde got 'em far enough away from bandits. They're now in orbit 75 miles south of the previous position."

Shit hot! Roscoe's okay...oh, and the tanker too. "Ram One, permission to come aboard and look you over?" Pepper called.

"Two, give me a quick battle damage check and then get back in tactical. We've still got ground threats. MiGs...and F-5s are always a possibility. What's the status on Yellow Star?"

"We got a piece of him. The gun got a good chunk of his left wing. I guess he headed home."

"Good work. I'll confirm a kill on his wingman. Congratulations."

"Thank you. I'm looking at your belly. Lots of oil and hydraulic fluid. Several holes. I'm sliding above you now...you've got big holes topside. I see a small fire on the right engine. Structurally you look okay."

"Okay, Two, I'm shutting down the right engine. Keep an eye on that fire, but move out some in case we blow."

Tron, furiously figuring time, distance, and fuel to Korat told Pepper, "It looks like 350 miles to home plate. Probably two-fifty before we can get a tanker."

Pepper called, "I'm moving away. Fire seems to be out, but you're still trailing some smoke. Tron says it's three-fifty to home plate."

"Ram Two, go to tactical spread. Right engine's shut down; I'm still getting some vibration. Left engine looks okay. Punching out feet wet in the middle of all those refugees off the coast isn't too appealing. Flying three-fifty across bad-guy territory with battle damage isn't good either, but it may be our only choice. There's no place in Vietnam for us to land now."

"Roger."

"Red Crown, Ram. We're heading back to home plate. Tell 'em our situation; we need a tanker en route as soon as possible."

Pepper moved his Phantom out to line abreast formation. He glanced at his fuel gauge: 5000 pounds. With Raptor on one engine they had to fly at 400 knots. It was an hour to Korat, and burning 7000 pounds per hour, they weren't going to make it without a tanker.

Raptor's call confirming Pepper's kill began to weigh as they cruised at 22,000 feet headed northwest. His mind flashed to the missile passing over the canopy. *It was damn close. I felt the concussion when it exploded.* Then he remembered his Sidewinders slamming into the wingman's aircraft. *No chute…That's what they mean by 'only teeth, hair, and eyeballs left.'* A knot like a fist slammed into his stomach. He'd been in a knife fight with North Vietnam's leading ace. *I'm a dead man flyin'.* A wave of nausea rolled up his throat. "Tron, take the jet a minute."

Tron shook the stick. "I've got it."

Pepper thrust his left hand into his G-suit calf pocket to grab the airsick bag. Unhooking his face mask, he flipped it aside. He wretched into the plastic bag until only dry heaves remained. As the jet nipped puffy cumulus, the turbulence reminded him of the Phantom's shudder when Yellow Star's 20mm gun burst ripped its wing. *Just ten feet to the right and it would've been our canopy.* He wiped his face with the thawed towel around his neck. He drank from his water bottle until only ice cubes rattled in the bottom.

He felt for the Zippo. *For you, Tim. That gook sonofabitch was for you.*

The fuel gauge snapped Pepper back to the present: 4000 pounds. Pepper snugged the mask to his face, leaned forward and toggled 100 percent oxygen on the regulator to clear his head. He looked up to see a purple-gray thunderstorm squall line spread in front like the Great Wall of China. The on board radar screen showed several big storm cells. *We need to skirt them. Damn. We don't have the fuel to do it.*

Raptor called, "This isn't looking good, Two. Jet's losing fuel. Are we still smoking?"

"Affirmative, Sir. But it's light, like fuel vapor, not black from something burning."

Raptor called, "Red Crown, we're down to 25-hundred pounds. Weather in front means we have to deviate. We need a tanker — now!"

"Ram, Red Crown. Copy, Sir, we're working on one."

"Good luck finding a tanker," Raptor responded. "By regs, they're not supposed to come from Thailand into Cambodia. It's hostile. Tell 'em we'll be stepping over the side in about 10 minutes and Ram Two in about 15 minutes. Both jets are battle damaged. We're declaring emergency fuel."

"Red Crown, roger."

Pepper feared the worst as they turned right to avoid a towering, anvil-shaped cumulus. At this rate, Raptor would be out of gas before any tanker could join them, if one dared fly into Cambodian airspace. "Tron, could we push 'em?"

"Push who?"

"Ram One. It's been done before. Korea or maybe North Vietnam. Why couldn't they lower their arresting hook? Maybe we could push 'em."

Tron paused. "I'm game, if you are. Maybe it'll liven up this boring day."

"Ram One," Pepper called. "We figure you won't have enough fuel to make it to a tanker. You'll probably flame out before you get gas."

"Tell me something I don't know, Two."

"Well, Sir, how about you lower your hook and we push you since we have more gas? That might keep your motor running until you can onload fuel."

The radio was silent.

Pepper thought out loud, "If they add fuel loss rate to fuel flow on the good engine they'll see they're going to run out before they can get hooked to a tanker. It's either save some gas or punch out over those spooky-lookin' Cambodian jungles down there."

"Roger that," Tron said.

They might be the last prisoners of the Vietnam War...

Raptor called, "Ram Two, a guy named Pardo did that a few years ago over the North. His Phantom took some abuse; so did he. They almost court-martialed him for gambling with lives and equipment. They all four punched out."

"Understand, Sir. We'll take that chance."

"Okay Two, I'll steer us around the buildups. Hook's coming down. Be careful."

"Roger, sliding in below you now." Pepper eased the jet under Raptor's as if preparing for a midair refuel. Much shorter than the KC-135 boom, Raptor's hook angled down beckoning for a push. Pepper knew he'd have to contact it with the sturdy metal band bracing the canopy and windscreen of his F-4. That would allow him to see the hook at all times from a precious few feet away. From Raptor's white underside, Pepper saw oil and hydraulic fluid streaming from several holes. Whether fuel was mixed with it was difficult to tell. He cringed as some of it opaqued his windscreen.

"This is one sick Phantom, Tron. How's this thing even flyin' with so many holes in it?"

"McDonnell-Douglas built a damn good jet."

Pepper felt the airflow off Raptor's wings pushing him away. "Damn, it's turbulent tucked in this close. I bet the Thunderbirds wouldn't even try this."

"Yep, but we're smarter than they are," Tron quipped.

As he eased up under the hook, Pepper thought, *Never seen one this close before. The arresting hook kinda looks like the hoof of a big Budweiser Clydesdale. Okay hook, make love to the canopy bow. Too hard and it's coming through the canopy. Too light and Raptor won't make the tanker. Concentrate. Light touch. Easy.*

Pepper trimmed his Phantom to deal with the unpredictable air currents under Raptor's wounded jet. He gritted his teeth and grimaced as the tailhook brushed the canopy bow to rest on the heavy metal frame.

"Ram One, try pulling your power back now," Pepper called. "I'm shoving you."

"Roger, coming back on the left throttle…it's in idle now."

Whoa, this is like blasting down the road at 80 per, just three feet behind the principal's car. A little turbulence, a ten-degree turn, we're both done. Sure hope Yellow Star and his pals don't show up. We're sitting ducks. One missile, one triple-A round, we're goners.

"Ram One, Red Crown. Emergency tanker's departing Chestnut Track in Thailand. It's headed your way. They say ten minutes. Can you hang on?"

"Affirmative, Red Crown. We don't have much choice. Ram One is down to 1000 pounds of fuel."

Damn. It's hard to hold this jet steady. Must be the vortex off his wings; the hook moves away from the bow. Figure out what's happening. When I'm not pushing him, he slows down. The hook slid aft onto Pepper's canopy. He slowed even more to capture the hook in front again and start nudging. Instead of moving the throttles, he fanned the speed brakes a bit to slow down. *There, ready to rest the hook on the bow. Damn! Too hard. Pepper, you're tearing up the canopy. Move that Phantom easy. Throttle's only an eighth of an inch at a time…*

Raptor called, "Pepper, if you can push us another couple of minutes, I think we can make it."

Tron's tone was incredulous. "Did he just call you *Pepper?*"

"Yeah, I think so," Pepper replied absently. "We just have to do this a couple of more minutes. I hope you're watching our fuel and clearing for threats. I'm padlocked to this hook."

"Raptor must be getting soft in his old age. *Pepper,* jeesh. This push is costing gas. We're down to 1200 pounds."

"Ram, Red Crown. Tanker's on your nose ten miles. They're coming up this frequency for refueling."

"Tron, I can't believe that tanker's entering Cambodia to meet us. I didn't think they could do that."

"Yeah, not supposed to. There'll be plenty of court-martials to go around today."

"Okay, Two," Raptor called. "I'm pushin' the power up on the left engine; we can make it now. Appreciate the push. Tanker's in his turn three miles on our nose. Ops check, Ram One has 500 pounds."

Pepper answered, "Ram Two is 700 pounds."

"Shit, Pepper," Tron said, "if we don't get on the boom soon, we're outta gas."

"In case we don't get hooked up before we're out of gas," Pepper said, looking at the fuel gauge once again, "start storing your stuff back there. Get ready to eject. Put the command selector to AFT INITIATE so you can eject me too in case I'm busy, okay?" *We need fuel. NOW...*

"Roger that," Tron said.

Raptor called, "Esso One-One, this is Ram. Good to see you. We're two Phantoms. Critical fuel on both, single-engine on the lead. I'm cycling both jets for three hundred pounds to keep us running. Can you toboggan? I may not be able to hold refueling position on one engine, and onload gas."

"Esso One-One, copy. Starting toboggan. Cleared to refueling position."

With less than 500 pounds of fuel, he would have to be ready to connect as soon as Raptor took his fuel. Pepper continued to fly off of Raptor's wing instead of easing up to the tanker in the usual observation position.

"Tron, what's *toboggan?*"

"The tanker starts a controlled descent so we can all fly a little faster. That way Raptor will have enough power on one engine. Ain't this fun? Battle damaged, single-engine refueling and out of gas over bad guy country. I don't get paid enough for this."

"Ram One's got 300 offload — disconnect. Ram Two cleared in immediately."

Pepper slid in from the right as Raptor moved out of the way, but stayed close to cycle back in less than a minute. Pepper steadied the Phantom under the refueling boom while changing the aircraft's trim to handle the jet wash and vortices coming off the tanker. Pepper felt the tanker's boom clunk into its receptacle behind the cockpits and confirmed it in his top canopy bow mirror. *Man, that feels good. Now lemme see that fuel gauge climb. There it is. Up to 600 now. We might just make it.* "Ram Two's disconnect," he called.

The Phantoms cycled on and off again, building up their fuel load as the formation headed northwest toward Korat. Once they had 3000 pounds each, they departed the tanker to run for home plate.

Raptor said, "See ya, Esso One-One. We owe you guys. Thanks for your help."

"Anytime. Understand you got the last air-to-air kill in the war."

"Uh, that was Ram Two," Raptor answered. "Hell, I taught him everything he knows."

Chapter 14
MiG Sweep

"Of all my accomplishments I may have achieved during the war, I am proudest of the fact that I never lost a wingman."

—*Colonel Erich "Bubi" Hartmann, German Air Force*
World's Leading Ace, 352 Victories in WWII

When a fighter pilot returns to base from a combat mission, he's drained of feeling. It's from task saturation, sensory overload. He's detached, like he's not flying the jet, just along for the ride. The mind is somewhere else, but the body goes through the motions from endless training. They say God looks after drunks, fools, little boys, and fighter pilots. Sometimes God flies the jet.

When a pilot has killed and survived, he feels more elation for surviving than for the killing. Though the enemy disappears in a detached fireball of fury, it is not without consequences. Killing weighs heavily on the shooter. The holes in his own aircraft remind him how close he was to being a similar explosion four miles high.

*

Pepper taxied his crippled Phantom into its revetment to a throng of maintenance men and women. A few of them pointed to his ripped wing panels. This welcoming committee wouldn't show up unless it was serious. *Are the high rollers gonna nail me for the third jet I've trashed: holes in the wing, mangled canopy?* Next to a fire truck, he saw a base public affairs reporter near Maggot and Paco who stood in the back of the crowd.

The reporter duck-walked forward and snapped a shot of the crew chief hanging the ladder from Pepper's canopy rail. Paco and Maggot slipped through the crowd and peered at the damaged wing.

"Tron, what's that fire truck for? Are we still leaking that much fuel?"

"I don't know."

Pepper guided the jet into the chocks and shut down as the crew chiefs scurried underneath to install safety pins. A chief master sergeant bounded up the ladder clutching cans of red and yellow spray paint and a template cut in the shape of a star.

"Congratulations, Sir! We heard you shot down Yellow Star."

Pepper pulled the helmet off his sweat-drenched head, his hair plastered down in wavy rivulets. He stared at the sergeant through bleary eyes. "Got a piece of him with the gun, but he got a piece of us too. I think we got more of him."

"Sir, we heard on the command net that you got a kill."

Pepper stuffed his helmet, bulging barf bag, and kneeboard into his green helmet bag. "Yeah, we nailed his wingman with a heater." He nodded at the cans. "What's with the paint?"

The chief looked at the can of yellow paint, then tossed it to an airman below. "Okay if we paint a red star on your jet for the MiG? The guys could use a boost."

Pepper pulled off his gloves and stuffed them into the calf pocket of his G-suit. "Well, Chief, it was an F-5, not a MiG…I guess it's commie property now, but we scattered a bazillion pieces of it over South Vietnam." He turned to look out of the windscreen. "Come to think of it, as of today there's no such country. I think the war's going to be over soon. Friggin' lost."

He disconnected his shoulder harness and lap belt. "Hell yeah. Do it."

The sergeant twisted from the top of the ladder, gave a thumbs-up and shouted, "We got us a kill, folks! Paint it on."

A pent-up cheer greeted the chief's words. He turned back to Pepper. "Sir, don't worry about the jet. We've got 'til the next war to fix it."

Pepper handed his helmet bag to the chief and followed him down the ladder. Tron was the last down. The crowd closed in around them to shake hands and offer congratulations. The chief climbed back up the ladder and aligned the star template with the gouged canopy bow. He double-swiped the spray and a blood-red star glistened against brown camouflage. Then he moved the template to the right and used pieces of masking tape to block half the star. An airman tossed him the can of yellow paint and he whisked half a golden yellow star next to the red one.

Pepper stood near the base of the ladder, looking up, his hands resting on his hips.

A voice from the back of the crowd said, "Are we allowed that yellow one, Chief?"

"We're going to leave it on until somebody says we have to take it off," the chief said, still concentrating on removing the template smoothly, careful not to smear the paint. "That sonofabitch bragged about how he was going to shoot down an American with an American jet. You kept him from doing that, and I say the yellow one remains."

"So do I, Chief." The voice from the back was louder now. Every head turned to see whose it was.

Raptor stood at the edge of the group, holding his helmet bag. Tiny stood slightly behind. The crowd parted like the Red Sea for Moses, and a murmur rolled through as people realized it was Raptor walking toward the Phantom.

Pepper set his helmet bag down on the tarmac and stood expressionless, watching Raptor. He should have offered a salute, but he was empty of feeling.

Raptor's flight suit and harness were sweat-soaked dark green, his smooth head glistened from perspiration. A frozen white towel was wrapped around the back of his neck, and tucked into the collar of his flight suit. He stopped directly in front of Pepper and looked up to the top of the ladder. "Chief, that half you just painted nearly cost us two Phantoms. Mine's shot up bad by Yellow Star, but, it's back on the ground — thanks to these guys," he said, breaking into a smile and looking at Pepper and Tron. He extended his arm and firmly shook hands with each of them. "Well done, men," he said.

Relief flooded through Pepper and Tron. They broke into wide grins as a spontaneous cheer erupted.

"Chief, you're only partway done." Raptor looked up once again. "I want you to paint both their names on this jet." He turned on his heel and walked back through the crowd. Tiny stepped forward to shake hands with both fliers.

The crowd grunt-chanted the maintainers' chorus, "Ugh! Ugh! Ugh!" faster and faster.

Pepper and Tron admired the painted addition to their Phantom, while behind them, Paco and Maggot stealthily positioned themselves, dragging a hose from the fire truck.

"Got a kill, huh?" Paco said.

Pepper and Tron turned to see who spoke just as Paco unleashed a torrent of water.

Pepper crossed his arms in front of his face. Too late. Tron spun around backwards and bent over, covering his face with his hands. Paco worked them over, blasting Tron's protruding backside. Cheers and catcalls echoed off the concrete and metal revetment. The reporter snapped away until his camera caught a watery blast.

Pepper leaned against the shower stall with both arms raised. Steaming spray pummeled his head and shoulders. It felt good to be out of his sweat-soaked flying gear, naked, the water washing him clean. He needed solitude and the shower was the only place he could find it.

He was numb from a two-hour session with intelligence debriefers who drew from him every detail of the kill and the engagement with Yellow Star. That wasn't the end of it. An Associated Press reporter was flying up from Bangkok to interview him. Pepper turned the cold water off, turned his back to the showerhead, and let the hot spray sting his back. Colonel Smith, wing director of operations, and the wing commander had him on their calendars for office visits. *Whoopee...* The base photo lab wanted an assortment of poses with his aircraft and the shiny red star. *Shit hot...* To top it off, the Pentagon was playing up the mission to counter all the dismal news about the Saigon evacuation. *Will this ever end?*

Pepper turned to let the water pound the base of his neck. During the engagement, the Gs had been relentless. His neck ached from supporting the helmet at seven times its normal weight. He held his arm out. Broken capillaries from compressed blood speckled it.

The 15-year war left over 58,000 Americans dead and many more wounded. POWs had been tortured and thousands were missing-in-action.

All this hoopla on the day Saigon burns? What's wrong with this? It's total bullshit. Tim's gone. Dad got pounded for a year by VC. Raptor almost got blown away. Does a hero buffoon a Sparrow shot and get his jet stitched? I wasn't even supposed to be on MiGCAP. It was fate I was over Vung Tau when Yellow Star attacked. Weird. I'm almost glad Yellow Star got away. He was a good fighter pilot, flew a helluva jet. Wars need flying legends, even if they are bad guys. I wonder if the pilot I killed had a family?

*

It was dark when Pepper walked the two blocks to the Officers' Club. A monsoon squall had swept through. Puddles were scattered on the path between the hooches and trees dripped. As he neared the club, he smelled the faint stench of wet human fertilizer in the rice paddies outside the base. He heard the rumble of voices and wondered about the mood in the bar.

The noise blasted his ears as Pepper pushed through the worn wooden door to the O-Club bar. The place was packed, standing room only. To the left, two American nurses in starched white uniforms stood at the bar. As usual, a shit-faced fan club of men surrounded them, attentive to their every word. Men in flight suits and casual clothes stood around talking and drinking. A layer of smoke softened the ceiling lights. A Thai house band at the far end of the room mangled renditions of hits from the States. A go-go dancer in pasties and G-string gyrated to the wobbly beat. The lead singer, an Elvis wannabe, replete with sequined jumpsuit, belted out the last stanza of "Brew Suede Sues." His high-pitched, little-boy, oriental voice appealed only to the highly inebriated.

"It's 'Blue Suede Shoes,' you asshole!" Animal shouted from deep in the crowd.

Undaunted, the singer pushed his luck. "What you runderful GIs want hear next?"

"The damn juke box," Maggot yelled.

Three bartenders hustled to keep up with orders from the rabble packed into the bar. One waitress carried a tray loaded with glasses and beer bottles into the crowd. Another stopped to take Pepper's order.

"You want usual? Scotch-nam?"

"No, Li-Li. Tonight I'm going back to Dixieland. Bring me a Jack Daniel's and water."

"Okay, GI. I bring JD-nam."

"Make it a double, Li-Li," Pepper said, pushing through the herd toward Animal.

"Pepper, you be bad tonight?" Li-Li shouted. "You cerebrate? I hear you shot down own plane. That clazy, GI."

"Dammit, is that what they're saying in here? It was American-built, but a bad guy flew it."

"That okay then," she said, turning to the bartender to place orders.

Animal slapped Pepper on the back. "Hey, Pepper. Helluva mission! Nice to see you walk away from one," he said, grinning. "Seriously, congratulations on the kill."

"Thanks, Animal."

The squadron collected at the middle of the bar around Pepper and Animal.

"I won't ask you to go through the whole thing," Animal said, "but how was the F-5 to hassle with, and how good *is* Ho Van Chieu?"

The pilots and wizzos pressed in to hear. Li-Li arched her forearm over Animal's shoulder and handed Pepper his double.

"The Five moves much quicker than the Phantom," he said, stopping to take a long taste of his drink and let his words sink in. "When Yellow Star rolled and turned so quick it watered my eyes. Fives are smaller and much more responsive than we are. Harder to see and harder to hit."

"How good is he?" Paco echoed from behind Pepper.

"Shit, Paco, you're always sneaking up behind me."

"That's what wily fighter pilots do, man. We're all back-shooters."

"He's good," Pepper said. "Real good. C-tone was right. He did one helluva barrel roll behind Raptor." Pepper set his drink on the bar. He used his hands to mimic the two fighters and the barrel-roll attack. "That move put Yellow Star in the saddle for guns. I've never seen anything like it. They were so close I couldn't fire a missile at them. His wingman was close too, in fighting wing position. I had to waste the wingie before I could get to Yellow Star."

"What did his jet look like?" Animal asked. The pilots closed in to hear his response.

"It was a silver F-5, but not flat silver like we're used to seeing. Someone really buffed it. Looked like sterling. After his Sidewinder missed, Van Chieu blew by us to get to Raptor. That's when I saw his red tail and yellow star."

"Were you psyched?" someone asked.

Pepper took another long pull from his drink. The cold, sour mash whiskey had a familiar down-home, delicious bite. "Yeah, a little. That big picture of Chieu on the screen flashed through my mind. I figured we were dead. We managed to duck his first missile, but after that things started happenin' real fast."

A Spectre gunship pilot sidled up to the bar to order ten Singha beers for his table. His pockmarked face looked like someone had put out a fire with an ice pick. He was built like a refrigerator. The nametag on his flight suit read, "Stump." The left sleeve sported the squadron's Ghostrider patch. He turned his head toward the group of Rams and shouted, "Heard you queers shot down one of our F-5s today."

Animal turned to face him. "Oh, Stump. Eat shit and die. We'll take care of you later. When's the last time Spectre shot down anything? We heard you guys just hung out at the Mekong, nice and safe, drinking coffee, boring holes in the sky while 'Automatic George' flew the plane."

Being a good wingman for Animal, Paco slammed his empty glass down, and reached over the bar for a small carton of cream. Filling his glass, he slid it down the bar past Animal. Colliding with Stump's hand, the cream in the glass sloshed over the five-dollar bill he was holding. "Bought you a drink, Stump," Paco said. "Lap it up, Pussy!"

Stump raised his hand and slowly licked cream from his fingers, glaring past Animal at Paco. Exaggerating Paco's southern drawl, he said, "Yum... this tastes just like yo mama's milk, Pay-co."

"You're dead!" Paco lunged from his barstool at Stump, his fists clenched. Maggot grabbed his arms.

Animal leaned back against the bar, eyeing Stump and shaking his head. "Look, we know you trash-haulers have to be breastfed to get your courage up, but it's time you tittie babies got weaned." Pivoting on one elbow, he faced Stump. "Let's see if you can get your courage up without suckin' a titty first.

"Bartender, give us a half dozen eggs out of the fridge there," Animal said. "And two double-shots of Jeremiah Weed."

Hearing the exchange, a larger group pushed in around them. The Thai bartender set a half-carton of brown eggs on the counter. He looked at Animal and Stump. "You throw these, GI?"

"Only if Mr. Stump here blows his grits."

Animal cupped two of the big eggs in his left hand and held a third in his right. He nodded toward the carton on the countertop. "Those three are yours, Stumpy." Their eyes locked, smiles gone. Animal slowly raised the egg in his right hand to his gaping mouth. "No titty this time," he said, never blinking or moving his eyes. He placed the egg on his tongue, his mouth open wide for Stump to see.

Stump stared as Animal's tongue balanced the egg, his eyes held steady as he reached for the carton.

Pepper forgot all about the day's ordeal. "I heard about this, Animal. Shit hot! Eat it, man!"

"Boneless chicken time," Maggot said.

"Eat me, eat me, eat me," the Rams began chanting.

In the middle of Bangkok Elvis's rendition of "Ruv Me Tender," the band quit playing.

Maggot stood up, turned, and faced the chanting mob. When he flashed the engine-cut sign across his throat, the spirits-charged choir fell silent.

Animal's lips slowly closed around the egg like the jaws of a python closing on its prey. The shell crunched. As he chewed, a dribble of yellow oozed from the corner of his mouth. He swallowed the egg in one throat-bulging gulp. He flashed Stump a wide yellow grin, revealing teeth speckled with bits of brown shell. Then he wiped his mouth on his sleeve, downed the second egg, chasing it with the third.

"I hate stinkin' eggs," Stump said, his face chalky as he eased an egg onto his broad, stubby tongue.

One of the Rams started a new chant: "Blow it, blow it. blow it!"

Failing to down the boneless chicken would signal an indelible sign of weakness. Stump cracked the shell with his teeth, forcing himself to chew. He was too slow. Once opened, the mass of shell mixed with a rush of fast-forming saliva. Stump gagged. In seconds the glutinous mixture swelled to twice its size. Just as quickly the crowd backed away. He gagged again, his face turning flush red.

"Uh, oh," Maggot said. "It's pukin'-for-dollars time."

A torrent of egg yolk erupted from Stump's mouth, chased by the partially digested contents of his stomach. The malodorous conglomerate shot six feet.

Maggot applauded. "Chunking at its best," he ruled.

Animal slapped Stump on the back. "Way to go, man! That was a nine-point-five puker."

The Rams resumed chanting: "More eggs! More eggs! More eggs!"

Stump grabbed a napkin from the bar, wiped the drool from his chin, and lurched toward the bathroom.

Animal leaned over to Pepper. "Hang onto your ass and your tits, MiG killer," he said. He stepped on a barstool seat and climbed to the bar. In search of pesky high rankers, he scanned the crowd below. Satisfied there were none, he bent over, grabbed his glass of Weed, and raised it for a toast. "Jeremiah was a railroading man in the eighteen-hundreds." He panned the glass around the bar for all to see. "Like us Rams, he knew the value of hard work, faster horses, younger women, and more money." Shifting his gaze to the Ghostriders he barked, "Jeremiah wants me to say, 'Here's to all you titty-suckin' power-pukers.'"

He drained the glass and belched with masterful resonance. "As far as I'm concerned, if there's a fuckin' MiG pilot flying it, the damn jet's a MiG," he bellowed. Gazing at Pepper, he resumed the soliloquy. "My buddy shot down a MiG pilot today. He happened to be flying an F-5 because the South Vietnamese left the damn thing sitting on the ramp ready to fly. Pepper may have gotten the last air-to-air kill of this goddamn war. He also blasted Yellow Star's ass, then pushed his own leader's Phantom halfway across Cambodia." Animal paused daring anyone to dispute him. All were quiet.

"When *you've* done as much, then you can give Pepper all the shit you like. But right now, pay attention to the only good thing that happened today. We shot down one of the bastards, and we all came back." He glared at the Ghostriders for a long moment, then steadied a big boot on the barstool and bounced to the floor. He spoke so softly only the Rams could hear. "MiG Sweep."

"What's that?" Pepper asked.

"Come on," Animal said, "we'll show ya."

The Rams left the counter 20 strong, and followed Animal toward the double doors. They blocked the only exit from the bar.

Animal leaned over and whispered to Pepper, "We start at this end of the room so nobody can escape."

The Rams lined up along the wall in front of the doorway, with Animal and Pepper in the middle. "Lock arms with your wingman," Animal commanded. Then, loud enough for all in the bar to hear, he said, "Stand by for a fuckin' MiG Sweep!" He looked left and right down the line of locked arms to make sure everyone was ready. Animal commanded, "Rams, MiGs twelve o'clock. Cleared to engage. Clean 'em out!"

Animal plowed forward with Pepper's arm locked on his left and Maggot's on his right. They formed a flying wedge that would trash the room. Tables reeled and overturned, glasses crashed to the floor. People still sitting at their tables tumbled over. Growling like a blitzing linebacker, Animal pressed on: "AAAAAARGH, MiG Sweep, AAAAAARGH!"

On the right flank, a curtain ripped from a window, more tables turned over, beer cans rolled across the floor. A big bowl of popcorn exploded like a Fourth of July bombshell. Spirited cursing rang out in all quadrants. The two American nurses at the bar were swept ahead of the Rams, swearing like longshoremen. One slipped on Stump's upchuck and bailed into the other. Both nurses wallowed in the filthy, wet mess.

Southern gentleman Paco peeled from the wedge to aid a fallen angel of mercy. In her trashed white uniform, she haymakered his jaw. "You assholes belong in a fucking zoo!" she screamed.

American fighting men surged from their tables to join the fray. Some laughed, others cursed. The wisest ducked below the locked arms of the wedge, and shimmied between the Rams for the exit. More curtains ripped from the walls.

A fleeing waitress stumbled, spilling her heavy tray of drinks near the bar. "I no pay for those!" she screamed to the bartender, who shrugged and shielded his face with a pizza pan.

As the stampede bore down, band members unplugged their guitars and scurried off stage, only to be caught against the back wall with others who couldn't escape. One burly Spectre pilot stood stiffly next to his table as if to deny the inevitable in front of the approaching human phalanx. Animal took aim directly at him, and once again sounded the battle cry, "AAAAAARGH, MiG Sweep, AAARGH!" Bunching his enormous shoulders, he pulled Pepper, Maggot, and the rest of the line with him, their arms still locked. Undeterred, the Spectre pilot drew his right fist back and popped Animal's protruding forehead. He had no way of knowing how much Animal enjoyed crushing beer cans against his skull.

The Spectre pilot winced and yelled, "My fuckin' knuckle's broke!" Cradling his right hand with his left, he danced around in a circle until the phalanx swept him and his throbbing hand to the wall with his besieged brethren.

"Take no prisoners!" Animal roared. "No friggin' quarter!"

The Rams bulldozed an assortment of chairs, tables, men, and the two round-eyed nurses to their final destination — the far wall. Most were laughing, and some poured the remnants of their drinks on the heads of the F-4 drivers. The wounded Spectre pilot whined for a flight surgeon to treat his hand. One of the nurses had arrived at Korat just two days earlier. She stared at the ceiling, pie-eyed and shell-shocked, her crisp white uniform only a memory.

Unlocking their arms, the Rams about-faced and surveyed the carnage, patting each other on the backs.

"Now, that's a MiG Sweep!" Animal boomed. Then he grinned. "Anybody have any questions about what the Rams shot down today?"

That drew only muted grumbling. Then someone in the crowd shouted, "Hey, there's Roscoe!"

Second Lieutenant PeeWee stood at attention by the double doors. He wore a baggy borrowed flight suit with captain's bars on the shoulders and "Maggot" stenciled on the nametag. Roscoe sat nobly at his feet, a battle-scarred, WWII leather flying helmet perched on his head. His long, floppy ears dangled through holes in the helmet cut to accommodate them. A dusty pair of goggles nestled above his dark brown eyes, and a silver colonel's eagle gleamed from the helmet's crown like a Christmas tree angel. Roscoe blinked and panted, a study in nonchalance.

PeeWee relaxed from his brace and said loud enough for the rabble to hear, "After the successful combat mission today, the wing commander has promoted Roscoe to colonel."

"Colonelzzz in thuh area," a wobbly Spectre pilot slurred. "Tinchut!" He slow-motioned to a tilting rigidity, leaning ever farther until a bar waitress caught him.

Clearly the MiG Sweep had fulfilled Animal's fondest hopes.

As many began righting tables and chairs, Pepper and Animal sauntered over to Roscoe.

Pepper kneeled to pet the aging yellow Lab, then looked up. "Hi, Pee-Wee," he said.

"Evening, Captain. Roscoe was having a good time until our tanker dived to get away from some MiGs. He got a little anxious, but I calmed him down with that pig's ear you gave me." PeeWee squatted down to pet Roscoe too. "Hey I hear you nailed a bandit."

Pepper shook Roscoe's extended paw. "Yeah, PeeWee, I had to waste one of the bad guys and run off another one."

"He's the closest thing we got to a hero," Animal said. "We did this here MiG Sweep in his honor."

PeeWee looked around the room. "No offense, Sirs, but I've never seen such a mess."

"Oh, it'll get cleaned up," Animal assured. "The worst we've got are some broken glasses and a dirty floor. Nobody but Stump got stomach-pumped or cut up this time. I'll give the club a couple of red notes for the glasses, and the janitor'll mop the floor tonight. They're used to it. The place'll look good as new tomorrow night."

Pepper dropped to one knee and rough-rubbed the dog's back. "Roscoe, you and PeeWee went flyin' today, huh?" The Lab lifted his helmeted head and sniffed. "You remember that T-bone I gave you, Roscoe? Is that why you're sniffing?" Pepper cupped Roscoe's face in his hands and looked into his eyes. "I splashed a bad guy today, pup. Maybe he was the one who got your master many years ago. I'm gonna pretend he was."

Roscoe's arthritic hips trembled and his back legs faltered as he tried to get up. Pepper stood and looped his arms around Roscoe's midsection to help him stand on all fours. Roscoe wagged his tail. "PeeWee, can I take him for a little stroll outside around the club?"

"Sure, Captain," he said, handing Pepper the leash. "It'll do him good. Not much room in that tanker to walk around for eight hours."

"Thanks, PeeWee. I'll bring him back in a few minutes. Come on, Roscoe, what do ya say, let's taxi your jet around the field a few minutes."

Pepper held the door to let the dog limp through; he led him slowly through a breezeway into the balmy night. He let the Lab take the lead to wander wherever he wanted. Roscoe stopped beside a bush at the corner of the club, trying to hike his leg, finally succeeding. They walked a little farther to a treed area with a picnic table. Pepper sat on one of the benches and unstrapped Roscoe's helmet.

"Don't you think you've had this on long enough, my friend?" He ruffled the Lab's ears. "I bet it feels good to get that thing off. You and I had quite a day, didn't we? Your jet was running from the fight and mine was running toward it.

"You know, I've never killed a man. Somebody once said, 'Fighting in the air is not sport. It's scientific murder.' It's weird, pup. Everybody's all fired up about me toasting some guy, and I'm wondering if he had a family. I think about Tim getting killed and my dad being shot at over here. Then I wonder what that pilot felt like for that two or three seconds as his jet came apart around him. I tell myself that's what he gets for being a commie, right? Then I think, hell, he's probably like me, just a wingie doing his job. Probably lost more friends than I have. This stinkin' war killed over a million Vietnamese. He was one of the last ones to die. Maybe *the* last one. Who knows?"

Pepper cupped the Lab's graying muzzle in both hands. A beam shining through the trees from a streetlight illuminated Roscoe's trusting brown eyes. "But it was the bad guy or Raptor, right? That's how I'm thinking from now on. That bastard Yellow Star put his own wingman in my sights. Roscoe...I had no choice."

Pepper said, "Come on, ol' pup." He carried Roscoe's leather helmet in one hand and leash in the other. "We better get you back to PeeWee so he can tuck you in for the night. You've had enough excitement for one day. Thanks for listening."

Ambling back to the club, Roscoe stopped to sniff a bush, then sat and scratched an ear with a stiff hind leg. Pepper let the beloved mascot take his time. He'd heard the stories of how Roscoe had crouched in the back of the commander's jeep during the massive launches of northbound fighters. The dog watched and listened as hundreds of afterburners flared, and bomb-laden jets rumbled down the runway. Roscoe was there when the pilots came back, and when they didn't.

Pepper ruffled Roscoe's head a last time before they passed through the double doors to the bar. "Pup, I bet I'm not the first guy you've heard spill their guts. I bet you could tell some stories."

Pepper handed Roscoe to PeeWee who stood just inside. "He's had quite a day."

"Roger that, Captain, it's sack time now," he said. "I don't know if you've heard, but the wing commander moved Roscoe and me into our own hooch a while back so Roscoe could bed down in air conditioning. He gets his chow in there, and he gets his bath in the communal shower stall."

Pepper grinned. "Hey, he rates it, he's special."

"Yeah, even the hooch maids bathe him. No way in hell would they eat 'Loscoe.' They see how good we treat him. They think he's a god or something."

"You're doing real good with him, PeeWee. The commander thinks so too or he wouldn't bunk you guys together." Pepper patted Roscoe's head. "Let me know if you ever need me to keep him company. Check you later."

Most of the aftermath of the MiG Sweep had been cleaned up. A few people sat at tables while a lone Thai man flipped chairs upside down on tables, and swept the floor. Doctor Lilly, the squadron flight surgeon, waved Pepper over to a stool in the corner where the L-shaped bar counter turned toward the wall.

"Hey, Pepper, congrats on your mission today. I heard you and Raptor did some good work savin' the tanker and shootin' up a couple of their jets."

"Yeah, Doc, just the right place at the right time — and lucky."

"I won't ask you for the whole story, but I'd like to hear about pushing an F-4 like you did Raptor's."

"Well, he was losing gas through the damaged engine. There was no way he was gonna make it across Cambodia, so he dropped his hook. I taxied in and gave him a shove."

"Was it like anything you'd ever done before?"

"Maybe like in college when we used one of our old lunker cars to push-start another one. Someone at the frat house always had a dead battery, and we never had a rope to pull with, so we'd ease up behind and push the other one. The difference today was we were doing four hundred miles per, and were over bad-guy territory. We were lucky; got Raptor to the tanker before he flamed out."

Pepper pulled up a stool and sat down as Doc ordered two beers and then asked, "How in the world did you keep from tearing up your Phantom?"

Pepper took a long pull from his Budweiser. "I did a pretty good job on the windscreen and canopy bow. Raptor's hook carved 'em up enough that maintenance will probably have to replace 'em."

"Well, that's cheaper than buying a new Phantom. How did Raptor handle it?"

"When I suggested a push, he said both of us could get court-martialed for risking two jets. I told him I had to try."

"Your first name's Randy, right?" Doc asked.

"Yeah."

"Raptor had a son who was killed in Vietnam during the Tet Offensive in sixty-eight...his name was Randy. Did you know that?"

"No, I didn't. Maybe that's why the sonofabitch is always on my ass." Pepper stared at Doc, anxious for more. Parts of a puzzle were starting to fit.

"Raptor's kid, Randy, was a Marine fighter pilot flying an A-4 Skyhawk. They were supporting troops on the ground engaged with NVA regulars. He was strafing an enemy position when the gooks surprised everyone and opened up with hidden ZSU-23-4, our favorite goddam four-barrel Phantom shooter. It's probably responsible for more of our guys residing in the Hanoi Hilton than anything else."

"Oh, God. That's a bad-ass gun. Did he get out?"

"No, he was too low when he took the hits. He never ejected. Randy would've been about your age now. Raptor doesn't talk about him much, but he keeps a picture of him in his office. It's the one with them standing in front of Randy's Skyhawk. Raptor said he visited him once on the *Enterprise* when they were in port at Subic, in the Philippines."

"I remember seeing that picture. I didn't study it real hard; I try not to go in there unless I have to, you understand."

"Yeah." Doc shook a half-empty pack of Marlboros and caught one as it slid out. Pepper instinctively reached for his Zippo. The flame was bright enough for Doc to see something engraved on the lighter. Pepper flipped the lid closed to squelch the flame.

"Can I see that?" Doc asked.

"Sure."

Doc paused and sipped his beer, never moving his eyes from the lighter. "Who was Tim? Don't answer that if you don't want to."

"He was my next-door neighbor and best buddy in high school."

Doc flicked his cigarette in an ashtray, looking at the Zippo in his palm. "How'd he buy it?"

Pepper talked to the beer bottle cradled in his hands, peeling the label down with a thumbnail. "He joined the Marines after we graduated. I did college. All he talked about as a senior was getting to the war. He'd been in 'Nam about six months when the NVA got him. They were near the DMZ during Operation Hastings. I heard it was a sniper. He'd just turned nineteen."

Doc shook his head and handed the lighter to Pepper. "July 20, 1966. That was a long time ago, almost nine years."

"Yeah, this war's been too damn long. I've had that lighter ever since. It's my good-luck charm." Pepper slipped the Zippo into his pocket. "It brought my pink ass back alive today."

Doc took another swig, set his beer on the bar, and looked directly at Pepper. "I bet Raptor sees his son in you. You even have the same first name. I didn't connect that until just now. You're both fighter pilots. You're a little bit younger than his son would be. Has he ever called you Randy?"

"No. Just Houston. But during the mission today he did slip and call me Pepper. That was a first."

"You know, the commander picks who flies on his wing. It's not just scheduled that way. He wanted you there today."

"I never thought about it, Doc. Too much goin' on."

"Well, that's the way it works." Doc drained his beer, then took another drag from his cigarette. "There *was* a lot of confusion, but he could have flown with anyone in the squadron. He picked you, and you saved his life. Funny how that worked, huh?"

"You know, Doc, when he was having my ass in his office and harassing me in the air, I never in my wildest dreams thought anything like today could happen."

"Maybe there was a purpose in him sharpening your blade. He knew we were headed for some tough missions with the evacuation coming. He figured you were inexperienced and needed some honing for battle. Maybe that's how you could fly like a wild man and blow that gook out of the sky. Heard you almost got Yellow Star too."

"Yeah, he nearly zapped me with a missile, then stitched my wing. It doesn't get much closer than that."

"Like I said, maybe Raptor toughened you up on purpose. He didn't know you were going to tangle with Yellow Star, but he knew today would push you hard." Doc slid off his barstool and crushed out his cigarette. "Congratulations, Pepper. You did a helluva job. Look, I'm flying in Animal's backseat tomorrow. Make sure that big sumbitch behaves himself for the rest of the night, okay?"

Chapter 15

BONFIRE SAIGON

James Fenton of the Washington Post remained behind after the Saigon evacuation. While he walked through the destroyed and looted American Embassy in Saigon, he cited this poignant inscription by Lawrence of Arabia on one of the walls: "Better let them do it imperfectly than to do it perfectly yourself; for it is their country, their war, and your time is short."

Every combat-ready aircraft and aircrew in Thailand was prepared for take-off at 0500 hours. To support the evacuation, a well-known sequence was established for hundreds of aircraft to get airborne from Thailand. Graham Martin, U.S. ambassador to South Vietnam, was to make the appropriate call to allow the safest possible evacuation of Americans and selected Vietnamese. Having so much invested in Southeast Asia, Martin was reluctant to leave. He delayed the evacuation decision, and by 0600 aircrews and aircraft stood down from launch posture. Most returned to their quarters for much-needed rest. It had been a long week of preparation, MiG Sweeps, and a very long night.

As the aircrews slept, chaos was making Ambassador Martin's decision for him. Wire services at capital cities around the world began to receive reports like this:

APRIL 29, 1975, SAIGON, SOUTH VIETNAM: Ten helicopters, full-burdened with human cargo, ditched into the sea next to the U.S. amphibious command ship *Blue Ridge* because there was no more room on board to land. South Vietnamese pilots crammed their families into military aircraft, flew west and landed them in Cambodia and Thailand. Terrified Vietnamese clung to the landing gear of departing transport aircraft and were crushed as the gear retracted. American newsmen clawed their way atop the U.S. Embassy walls, beating back Vietnamese trying to cling to them. Some people held up their children, begging Americans to take them. The loss of three million Vietnamese and more than 58,000 Americans during the war is culminating this day in chaos of historic magnitude. Some 400 miles away, forces in Thailand have the only U.S. fighter aircraft and AC-130 Spectre gunships left in Southeast Asia. Where are they?

After 15 years of fighting North Vietnamese and Viet Cong, the U.S. was withdrawing its forces. Within two years the North Vietnamese defeated the Republic of Vietnam Forces in the South and were poised today to take the capital as the last spoil of war. Planned as an orderly evacuation of Americans, it would rapidly become a scene of unimaginable chaos once Ambassador Graham Martin finally made a tardy decision to evacuate.

Forces in Thailand, some 400 miles away, had the only U.S. fighter aircraft left in Southeast Asia. They arose in the dead of night, ate a high protein breakfast, and began intelligence and target area briefings shortly after midnight. The target area was Saigon, and the mission never changed. We had been ready for days…Once again we stood down from launch waiting for the ambassador's decision that never came. Most crews headed back to their hooches for some much-needed sleep.

"Where's the damn phone?" Pepper tripped over his boots as he fumbled around the darkened room. "Dammit!" The fog from only two hours sleep left him groggy, like he was in a dream. He finally found it next to the lighted clock. It read 0900.

"Hello."

"Captain Houston, this is Sergeant Johnson at squadron operations. We are under a recall. Draw your weapon and report to the squadron, Sir."

"Okay."

Maybe this was the real thing…

The Rams practiced these recalls many times and had a real one the day before yesterday for the MiGCAP mission. Pepper's mind was numbed due to the alcoholic fog from celebrating the night before in the club. He slowly remembered the evacuation of Saigon was imminent as his body went through the hurried motions of zipping his flight suit and tying combat boots. His mind was on a different track; he wished his head would clear! *Think! Do you have everything? You may not be back in this hooch room for a while.* He jammed a flight cap on his head and checked his watch. It read 0918, the little date window said 30.

April 30, 1975. Pepper's pulse raced as he realized this could be the day the war was finally over. Little did he suspect that just like this screwed-up war, this would be the most screwed-up day of his life. Even though Pepper had survived the MiGCAP with Raptor, he had just enough experience in the Phantom to be dangerous.

First Lieutenant Pete Brown was to be Pepper's backseater, and they were planned to fly a strike mission carrying a full load of 500-pound bombs to use against the North Vietnamese. Signing for the .38 caliber Smith and Wesson at the armory, he wondered if all those plans had changed with another surprise recall.

Steering his bicycle toward squadron operations, Pepper tried to banish the nagging disconnect from his mind. After fifteen years of trying to keep this part of the world free, why were we now preparing to fly air cover as our last remaining Americans fled the former capital?

Intelligence briefings showed the North Vietnamese continued to ring Saigon with more and more surface-to-air missiles, or SAMs, and anti-aircraft artillery, which was called triple-A. Saigon had been transformed into another heavily defended "Hanoi" right before Pepper's eyes. *Had we lost this godforsaken war?* he wondered. *Pepper, you're asking too many questions!*

He then stepped through the doorway of the squadron and once again into pandemonium. The operations desk was surrounded by pilots and navigators copying down changes in missions.

Pepper spotted his backseater, Pete Brown, in G-suit and survival vest, copying data on his line-up card. "Pete, when do we brief?"

"The whole thing's changed," he shot back. "They told us to step to the jets ASAP. Check with the duty officer at the desk to see what's shakin'. We gotta go."

The evacuation decision was supposed to be made during the night so they could be sequenced to get airborne with hundreds of other aircraft in Thailand. However, carefully laid plans went up in smoke as the evacuation decision was delayed too long. Most of the forces stood down from launch status, and now we were scrambling to accomplish the mission anyway.

Mad Dog was on duty. "Houston, glad you're here!" he said. "You are no longer flying strike. You're flying hunter-killer with the Wild Weasels from Okinawa."

"Hunter-killer?" Pepper croaked. "I've been briefing strike for two weeks, and now I'm flying hunter-killer?"

"Here comes your Weasel," Mad Dog said, pointing to Captain Mickey Blane hustling through the area. Blane's call sign was Speedface because of his pointed nose, narrow face, and balding head with hair combed back and flat against his skull. He stood six feet tall, with the thick neck of a wrestler.

The mission involved working with another specialized F-4 called a "Wild Weasel," instrumented to locate signals from enemy radars capable of firing SAMs and triple-A at U.S. aircraft. To be effective, the hunter-killer pair had to work as a team.

Could I make that happen? Quizzing a few Weasel pilots in the Officers' Club about their peculiar mission may just have paid off...

"Let's go, we have to step to our jets. I'll brief you en route to Saigon," Speedface said. Exuding confidence, he quickly finished gathering data they needed for the mission.

On the flight line, pilots hustled around their jets with a sense of urgency bordering on panic. The kerosene smell of JP-4 exhaust hung everywhere and at times made it hard to breathe. Walking toward Pepper's waiting jet, he had to agree that "Rhino" was a good nickname for this beast. With its wingtips bent up, the horizontal tails bent down, and its nose sloped toward the ground, she looked like a rhino ready to charge. It was hung with four mean-looking cluster bomb units (CBUs) that were like trash cans on steroids. Within each CBU were hundreds of small bomblets that would shred or eviscerate anything or anyone in its path.

Pete and Pepper spoke little as they carefully checked each bomb's arming wires and fuses. The gravity of what they might have to do with these cans quelled the normal banter about winning quarters on the bombing range with their scores. These were the real things. Possible scores were only two — life or death.

Aircraft were moving all over the ramp. Fighters lumbered their way to the arming area next to the runway. As with the MiGCAP mission the jets in front of Pepper had countless red, "Remove before flight," flags fluttering from air-to-air missiles and bombs. Stopped now in the arming area, he gazed at Speedface's Phantom in the next slot. *We're next, then these weapons are live!*

Using a call sign of Duster Flight, the two-ship formation joined in the air with KC-135 tankers and took on fuel near the border between Thailand and Laos.

"Departing the tanker, we should be heading southeast for Saigon, 375 miles. There are enemy concentrations scattered along our route," Pete volunteered.

"Roger that," Pepper said, while disconnecting from the refueling boom and sliding over to Speedface's left wing. "'Speed is life,' my crusty old F-4 instructor used to say, and speed will be one of our defenses against SAMs."

The bulky CBUs hanging from the belly of the Phantom made it difficult to keep up with the fast-moving, lightly loaded Weasel. Afterburner would waste precious fuel; Pepper had to cut him off and close during turns.

"Okay, Duster, we're crossing the fence, let's green'em up," Speedface radioed from the lead aircraft.

Duster Flight crossed the placid, slowly meandering Mekong, which meant they were now once again in bad-guy territory. Pepper imagined how much fun it would be to float along with his father and fish those lush green shores. The serenity of the river was a stark contrast to the war raging just miles to the east. Flipping the MASTER ARM switch to ARM made the armament panel "green up" to show his missiles and bombs were poised for combat. Once weapons were armed, special care of what his fingers were doing on the control stick and the throttles became important. One wrong button and either missiles or huge explosives would depart the aircraft. Rechecking all armament switches kept Pepper's mind off the fact that he was headed directly at the enemy's strongest concentration, Saigon. He had read a book called *Into the Mouth of the Cat*, and that is what this felt like. He could see smoke from Saigon on the horizon.

Duster continued southeast and from their altitude of 21,000 feet, Saigon looked like a vast besieged bastion — a giant bonfire...

The fuel gauge shocked Pepper back to reality. "Pete, we need gas!"

"Copy that. Nothing on the radar yet. We're almost to the eastern coast of South Vietnam and there should be a tanker near here."

Pepper rolled the Phantom on its wing for a longer look below. A *bonfire. Saigon's a giant fucking bonfire...*

Duster One tried to contact Red Crown Control on the USS *Enterprise*, a Navy aircraft carrier that was to serve as the radar control. Speedface's voice grew aggravated after three tries with no response. They were rapidly approaching minimum fuel. "Duster Two, if we don't gas up soon, we'll have to fly back across Vietnam and Cambodia without engaging the North Vietnamese," Speedface said over the radio.

Then the radio crackled.

"Duster, this is Red Crown. Your tanker is eighty miles north of your position headed north. Esso Two-One states that he is out of gas and unable to refuel you. There are no additional tankers in the area. What are your intentions?"

So, this must be the fog of war, Pepper thought. It's the confusion that settles on an operation when there are too few resources, like tanker aircraft, and too many people needing them at the same time. *If we don't get gas pretty quick, we are headed for trouble.* It was a long way back across hostile territory and F-4s like to drink gas...oh, do they like to drink gas! Pepper looked back to the west, the way they'd have to go to get home, only to see a line of thunderstorms, between them and the setting sun, blocking their route of flight home.

"Duster Two is pre-strike bingo," Pepper called, advising his fuel was at the point to return to home plate.

Speedface came across the frequency: "Red Crown, Duster. We can't hang around any longer. We're headed back to base and we'll see you next time. Do you have anyone who could use our ordnance on our way back?"

"Yeah, let's get rid of this weight and kill some commies too!" Pepper blurted out loud.

"Red Crown — negative."

Damn! Lugging these CBUs all over Southeast Asia, and we're not going to use them?

Circling off the coast of South Vietnam, Duster rolled out on a northwesterly heading back to Thailand.

"Pete, do you think we should dump these bombs in the South China Sea?" Pepper asked. Pete had been awfully quiet.

"Ah, I think we can keep them a little longer if you want to. They're costing us some gas, but we're not quite to the point where we have to dump them."

"Okay. Maybe we'll get to expend soon."

That was Pepper's first big mistake, courtesy of a severe weather line that crossed the southern part of the country. The squall line of towering cumulus clouds forced them to lower altitudes, which put the flight closer to enemy guns. Reducing the threat, Speedface pushed his throttles forward edging to 500 knots (575 MPH). At this speed, they were turning fuel into noise at a great rate. Jinking the Phantom back and forth to confuse enemy guns used even more gas. Pepper's pulse picked up; the roof of his mouth felt like sandpaper. The situation was getting pretty grim as he reached for the partially frozen water bottle in his right leg pocket.

"I can't get the inertial nav to work and our radios are intermittent!" Pete shouted.

"Okay! Figure out our fuel situation; let's think about options." Pepper wanted to get focused on limping back home with the remaining gas. He unhooked his mask from the right side and took a long pull from the cold water bottle.

"We've got fifteen minutes of fuel left and 25 minutes flying time to base," Pete said after some quick math.

"Okay, we've got to clean off the jet and quit hauling so much iron." Pepper re-hooked his mask and rolled up on one wing and looked down. Heading northwest, the smoke and carnage of Saigon had turned to the lush green, triple canopy jungles of Cambodia.

As a kid, Pepper read nearly every prisoner-of-war book written. Was this the day when he'd find himself falling through the towering trees of the Southeast Asia jungle into the grasp of hostile populace? He stared at the ever decreasing fuel gauge.

Panic started to hot-flush his face. Pepper knew the cockpit temperature had jumped 40 degrees. A bead of sweat rolled into his eye making it hard to see the instruments. Not only was there a bonfire in Saigon, there was a bonfire in his cockpit, too.

"Get a grip!" Pepper said aloud to get focused. His old instructors' words echoed in his ears. *Maintain aircraft control, analyze the situation, take proper action* —

"Duster Lead, Two," Pepper called to Speedface. Lighter and faster, the distance was now opened to two miles; he was walking away.

"Go, Duster Two," Speedface replied.

"Roger. We're emergency fuel and I'm going to jettison ordnance." Pepper looked under his left elbow for the JETTISON switch and rolled over one last time to clear below.

"Nothing but jungle down there," he said aloud, and flipped the JETTISON button to get rid of the four big cans. "What the hell!" Nothing happened! The aircraft should have jumped and felt lighter with all that weight gone.

"Pete, check the circuit breakers back there! Are any popped?" He tried to sound calm.

"What else can go wrong? Now I'm pissed." Adrenaline took over; action kept him occupied. "If we can't get the bombs off this aircraft, we will be on the ground somewhere in hostile Cambodia."

"None are popped," Pete said, his voice as dry as Pepper's.

"Okay. We're going to have to bomb these cans off the jet." Bombing them off wouldn't be as good as a jettison because they would retain the bomb racks. That meant more drag on the aircraft and more fuel consumption than if they were clean. Before that, Pepper had to select whether they would depart *armed* or *safe*. "Armed" meant they would explode when they hit the ground. He hesitated with his hand on the toggle switch. *What's it going to be, Pepper? You have the power of life and death in your hands. Select "armed" and you may get a little payback for all those friends you lost to this stinking war. Not to mention getting stitched by Yellow Star…No one would ever know with all the chaos, and what's more, few people would care. Select "safe," and you do it the way you were trained, to reduce civilian casualties on the ground.* He flipped the switch to ARM. *Why not kill a few commies to even the score?*

Pepper hesitated, his mind flashed to his father's words when he was commissioned a second lieutenant: "As an officer, you'll have to make decisions. Always do the right thing, and you'll never regret it."

Pepper flipped the switch to SAFE. There has to be another day to get even. He hit the "pickle" button four times and felt the aircraft gain altitude as the equivalent weight of a Cadillac left the Phantom. The empty armament panel told him the CBUs were gone. They were now going to use less fuel. Good, there's not much left.

"Duster Lead, Two. I'm cleaned off and need an emergency tanker, now," Pepper called to Speedface, trying to sound *Chuck Yeager* calm.

"Roger that, we're already working on one, Duster Two. We may have a tanker coming down out of Thailand to join us in a few," Mickey replied.

"Duster One, I've got about six minutes of fuel —"

"Copy."

"Pete, can a tanker do that? I thought they weren't supposed to fly into Cambodia."

"They're not supposed to, but it looks like this guy is nuts enough to do it."

"Well, just in case he doesn't get here before we're out of gas, start stowing your stuff back there and let's get ready to eject. Put the command selector to AFT INITIATE so you can eject me also in case I'm busy, okay?"

"Roger that," Pete said.

"I see a red rotating beacon at right two o'clock on the horizon. I'm heading for it. It better be that tanker; we've got one shot to make it," Pepper said, turning the Phantom forty degrees to the right. Dusk had turned to moonless night.

"If that's not our tanker, or if he's headed away from us, we're going to spend tonight in those jungles," Pete said.

"We're not going down there."

"I've got a lock-on to our target and it's headed at us, ten degrees right, twenty-five miles," Pete said.

"Our radio is out. I hope this guy will plug us with no radio. Oh, what the hell, if he doesn't, we'll just pull up alongside and they can watch us eject!" Their radar showed him to be at a range of ten miles from them and closing. "Pete, if this is our tanker, we're in a perfect rendezvous set-up. This may be the first good thing that's happened to us all day!"

"That'd be nice. Our pre-contact checks are complete; just open the receptacle and set your mirrors." His confidence was back at the sight of the tanker — so was Pepper's.

It was now completely dark as Pepper reached down to the right console and lowered the cockpit lighting to reduce glare on the canopy. After opening the refueling receptacle door, he adjusted the three mirrors on the canopy to observe the refueling boom as it made contact behind the cockpit. A feeling of immense relief swept over them when their F-4 slid under the belly of that beautiful KC-135 tanker and they felt the boom nudge the Phantom when it locked onto their receptacle. The thirsty Phantom had very few minutes of fuel left when they plugged. The gas gauge began to increase…

"Pete, we're going to make it."

"Fuck, YES!" he shouted.

That night at the Officers' Club, Pepper's mind drifted to thoughts of home and his folks. They were halfway around the world in Mobile, Alabama. He imagined their day had been typical. They'd probably had breakfast, read the newspaper, cleaned up the house, and gone shopping. Dad, raised on a small farm in North Carolina, usually worked in the yard while Mom cooked.

None of them knew what kind of day this had been in Southeast Asia. That was good because it had been an eerie day. Pepper's second combat mission was apparently closing the door on the war. The onset of problems and the resulting anxiety much different than when he was attacked by Yellow Star. Then, his body and reflexes just reacted and the adrenaline rush left him weak. Today was a slow-motion, near disaster played out four miles high at 500 knots. The worst part was not his problems in the jet, but disaster on the ground — Saigon burning, refugees fleeing every direction except north, chaos in all quadrants.

The squadron was much quieter at dinner that night. They were witness to the end of an era of traumatic conflict for the Vietnamese and American people. Both countries had expended lives and national wealth beyond imagination.

"Here, read this, it'll make you feel better," Animal said, reeking of sarcasm as he handed Pepper an article from the *Stars and Stripes* newspaper. It read:

> April 30, 1975, Saigon. While Americans were evacuated by helicopter from atop the U.S. Embassy earlier today, Vietnamese fled their country in all directions. Almost 150 VNAF aircraft landed in Thailand, most at U Taphao, 350 miles northwest of Saigon where 3911 Vietnamese were sheltered. One single-seat F-5 arrived with three people in the cockpit; a C-47 (civilian version is a DC-3) built to hold 30 people landed and collapsed its landing gear with 100 on board. Another 10,000 refugees were rescued from fishing boats and taken aboard a single ship, the USNS *Greenville Victory*. The USS *Cook* and USS *Tuscaloosa* escorted a flotilla of some 28 Vietnamese Navy ships with nearly 20,000 evacuees to Subic Bay in the Philippines, some 800 miles to the east. Nearly all refugees will end up at U.S. facilities on Guam, and later may enter the U.S. through a refugee camp in Arkansas. The Vietnamese Air Force had grown into the fourth largest in the world with 2276 aircraft. A snapshot of U.S. assets left behind today reveals over $2 billion in serviceable equipment to include:
>
> - 975 aircraft, including 24 C-130 transports, 222 fighter/attack aircraft, and 430 UH-1 helicopters
>
> - Also lost were 550 medium and light tanks, 1330 howitzers, 1.6 million rifles, 15,000 M-60 machine guns, and 48,000 military radios
>
> - 940 ships of various types and sizes
>
> The North Vietnamese communists are now in complete command of this country roughly the size of California.

Staring into his third JD-nam on the rocks, Pepper wondered how he had walked away from this mission today. If it hadn't been for that tanker violating regulations, coming down from Thailand into Cambodia to refuel them, they never would have made it back. He read somewhere that in chaos, heroes are where you find them; some crossed his path today. He owed those guys. He called them the next day and told them.

Big bonfires can burn for days. Saigon might burn in Pepper's mind forever...

Chapter 16

FLIGHT LEAD

UPGRADE

"There is a peculiar gratification on receiving congratulations from one's squadron for a victory in the air. It is worth more to a pilot than the applause of the whole outside world. It means that one has won the confidence of men who share the misgivings, the aspirations, the trials, and the dangers of aeroplane fighting."

—*Captain Edward V. "Eddie" Rickenbacker, USAS*

When a fighter pilot becomes a flight leader, it's not a promotion. He doesn't get paid a dime more for the responsibility. It's a special trust. The chain of command above sees leadership potential in the pilot, but more importantly they see someone to whom others will trust their lives. A bad flight leader can run wingmen into the ground, run them into other aircraft, or run them out of gas. Wingmen must believe in their flight leader enough to fly three feet from his wingtip. They do that at speeds three times those of an Indy race car, through clouds, rain, turbulence, and in the dark of night. That's routine. The flight leader may also have to lead wingmen to war and perhaps death. Leaders are chosen carefully. They are never chosen because of rank, or because it's their turn.

Training requires the new leader to fly with an experienced flight lead on his wing. He will lead air-combat missions, and air-to-ground bombing missions on the practice range. To try the new leader, high-speed, low-level routes and air refueling will be mixed in for realism, resulting in complex missions.

Raptor selects and certifies all new flight leads.

*

After the evacuation, North Vietnamese troops swept through the southern region of the country with ease. The *Stars and Stripes* reported daily that many South Vietnamese were fleeing in boats and on foot. Many stayed behind and were imprisoned in "re-education camps." The paper also ran a piece on Pepper's kill and his engagement with Yellow Star. Even American reporters were intrigued with the North's leading ace flying an American fighter, one painted with a red tail and yellow star. Pepper's shoot-down was the only bright spot in weeks of defeat. They loved it.

Pepper was ready for notoriety to pass. He wanted to do what he liked best — fly Phantoms, especially since Raptor had chosen him for flight lead upgrade training. He had been an instructor in T-38 training aircraft before flying the F-4. Routine things like mission planning and shepherding the flight to and from the working area came easy for him. Owning the only air-to-air kill in the squadron gave him instant credibility.

His final mission for certification as a flight lead was a high-speed, low-level route which would lead to attacking a target on the bombing range. The "alpha" route was the toughest and would require flying 480 knots at tree-top level, skimming jungles and rice paddies for about 150 miles. They would practice flying low to avoid simulated enemy radar, SAMs, and triple-A. Pepper, with Maggot navigating from the backseat, planned the route for 18 minutes, 45 seconds. To certify, they would have to hit their time-on-target (TOT) at the range by plus or minus 30 seconds. Timing could be affected by winds, cloud formations, simulated threats, or getting lost.

The world goes by at eight miles a minute on a low-level route. At 100 feet a pilot can't distinguish terrain features as well as he can when navigating from higher altitudes. Lakes and towns zip by in a blur. He can see only the next mile in front, and must religiously maintain aircraft heading and timing to find turn points. Reaction time is cut to the bone at low altitude. Task saturation for the pilot is a reality.

The primary safety rule is that the wingman never flies lower than his leader. At low altitude, he supports from two- to three-thousand feet away in spread formation.

Pepper's call sign for the low-level mission was "Talon One." Raptor was "Talon Two," Pepper's wingman.

"Okay, Maggot," Pepper said over the Phantom's intercom, "time to get our act together for the low-level."

"Roger, ten miles to the start point," Maggot advised. "It's a dirt crossroads in the middle of some jungle. Our heading should be good right now."

"It's going to be tough to find with these puffy clouds. Maybe it'll be better once we're under them. Time to shake 'n bake," Pepper said as he looked over his right shoulder to check Raptor's position.

"Talon Flight," Pepper called on the radio. "We're descending out of five thousand, going down to the deck for the alpha route. Start point on the nose eight miles. Ops check, go spread formation."

"Push it up to four-eighty while we're descending," Maggot advised. "Our TOT should be good if we hit the start point in exactly one minute."

"Got it. Speed set." Pepper weaved the Phantom back and forth in the descent, dodging clouds to keep his wingman in the clear. The airspeed indicator quickly passed 450 and he eased the throttles forward to hold 480 knots as he leveled the jet above the dark green blur of triple canopy jungle zipping underneath. *An enemy division could be down there and we'd never see 'em.* A quick look over his shoulder confirmed Raptor was in good position, back twenty degrees and stacked slightly high.

"Point's two miles on the nose," Maggot advised. "When you hit it, use sixty degrees of bank, turn left to heading two-nine-two."

Pepper scanned the terrain. "There's a road in front going away — the crossroads are 300 meters off our left wing."

"Talon, abeam start point now. Hack clocks for timing," Pepper called, rolling the jet to a hard left bank.

"Talon Two," Raptor acknowledged, racking his Phantom in an even tighter left turn. As a wingman he had to cut to the inside of the turn to keep up.

"Shit, Maggot! Did you see that bird whip by the canopy?"

"Nearly got us. Looked like a hawk."

"That was a 500-knot bird. Too damn close," Pepper said.

"There's your heading. Check speed. The next turn point is a bridge over the *whoziwhat's* river. I can't pronounce gook names. Should be on the nose, four minutes, eighteen seconds."

"Got it. My clock's hacked. I guess that bird missed Two. He was crossing directly behind us when it blew by." *Perfect. Take Raptor on your flight lead checkride and stuff a friggin' hawk down one of his engines...*

"They're quiet, so I guess it missed 'em," Maggot said. "At this speed, the bird either hits you or it doesn't. Not much you can do either way."

"Okay," Pepper spoke to himself. "Get your cross-check going, juices flowing. Time to bust ass. Radar altimeter reads 100 feet above ground level, airspeed four-eighty, throttles at 90 percent, wing tanks feeding. Damn, this is fun."

Below them an emerald world flowed like a fast running river. Pepper scanned the sky, cotton clouds above beckoned him to come play. *Maybe later. Stay low, below enemy radar...simulated SAM site's near the next turn point.* "I bet we're whipping trees in our wake, knocking monkeys off their limbs. God, what a rush."

"You should have a limestone karst ridgeline angling away from you three miles in front," Maggot said. "The turn point is about four miles on the other side. SAM site's over there too."

"Got it. The ridge is about three hundred feet above us," Pepper said. "Karst, no trees. I'll be rolling across it, Two's in good position." *Gotta time this just right, can't slide up that ridge and balloon over the top. Gotta clear those jagged ones. Time to roll on our back.* Pepper's canopy was only feet from the karst as he pulled the Phantom down to hug the terrain on the other side of the ridge. *Dammit, started that pull-down a little late.*

"We got too high after we missed those rocks, radar altimeter said three hundred feet," Maggot said. "I hope Raptor doesn't call a SAM launch on us."

"I shoulda pulled down sooner, then hugged the terrain down the backside. Gotta do this more than three times in my life — fuck it — no whining, weak dick!"

"We have to get low and stay low. Left turn at the bridge, fifteen seconds, heading will be two-five-zero…ten seconds now. SAM site is just north of it. Jamming pod is on for Fan Song radar."

"Okay, we're back to a hundred feet," Pepper said.

Raptor crackled over the radio, "Talon Two has a missile launch right three o'clock, I'm coming hard right into it."

They wouldn't know which Phantom the missile was tracking. They both had to defend. "Talon One, breaking right." Pepper slammed the throttles to the wall for a full five stages of afterburner. Acceleration and Gs shoved him back, squashing him into his seat. *Grunt! Gotta see. Look out front. Watch out for trees.*

"Raptor's dickin' with us, Maggot. This'll screw up the low-level, and he knows it." *Fly the jet…*

"Chaff, chaff, chaff!" Maggot yelled.

"Roger!" Task-saturated in a hard turn so low to the ground, Pepper struggled to find the CHAFF switch with his left hand. Flipping it dumped a shower of aluminum foil confetti into the air, creating a huge metal target to attract the missile away from their Phantom…*The jamming pod fried their radar. Haul ass.*

"Pod's on, chaff's away," Pepper called, reminding Raptor to do the same.

"Okay, Maggot, we honored the stinkin' missile, let's try to salvage the low-level. I'm coming hard left, we gotta find the course again."

"Good, looks like Two's with us. Try to find the bridge."

"It's left, about two miles. It'll cost too much time to turn and fly over it."

"Yep, parallel our two-five-zero course for now. Maybe we'll see something along the route we recognize. Push it up to five-forty for three minutes. We need to make up some serious time to hit the TOT inside thirty seconds."

Pepper confirmed, "Speed's set, heading's wired. Ten minutes on the route and we've got it knocked. I've never flown this fast, this low. What are we doin', six-hundred miles per?"

"Yep, six twenty-one to be exact."

Pepper laughed. "I love it when you're *exact*. Turns me on." He looked first left, then right, and found Raptor moving back into spread formation off his right wing.

"Ladies and gentlemen, this is your captain speaking," Maggot said. "You may have noticed the ride's a little bumpy. You're probably wearing some coffee about now. I'm afraid it's unavoidable, 'cause you see, at a hundred feet we feel every little heat bump coming off the earth's surface, and at over 600 M-P-H, you are hitting those invisible bumps faster than a forty-four magnum bullet. Sorry we can't slow down and make your ride more enjoyable, but in this business speed is life, and life begins at 600 per."

"You'd make a helluva good captain, Mag. Now, how about being a wizzo?"

"Rogah."

Jungle's a blurred green carpet under the nose. Big rice paddy coming up — it's gone... "I bet those rice farmers just got a thrill. They had their backs turned, never saw us coming."

"Yeah, they love us, right? We're the sound of freedom," Maggot said. "Okay, one minute to turn, watch for a small village with railroad tracks on the north side. There's a pond on the other side of them. It's our point."

"I see smoke off to our left eleven. That may be the town. Yep. What heading do we want over the point?"

"One-nine-eight to the range."

"How's Two look?"

"He's back to our right. Four o'clock. Good position."

Pepper craned his head to the right, but couldn't see Raptor from the front cockpit. He glanced at his instrument panel to check airspeed, then scanned the jungle below and to the left, searching for the turn point. "Okay, there's the tracks. I see a pond out in the open. Turning thirty degrees left, it's on our nose now. How about speed?"

"Over the point, pull it back to four-eighty. We're pretty close on timing. Call crossing the point and I'll check it."

"Three, two, one. Hot damn! We're over the pond, Maggot. Turning hard left to heading." *No power in the turn, let speed decay to four-eighty. Two's crossing inside our turn to our left wing. Good. Check the clock.*

"Bingo! We made up the time. Minus seven little seconds."

"Damn, you're good," Pepper said.

"When you care enough to send the very best — send Maggot!"

"Yeah, you're good, but keep workin', speed's set. Map says we're back on course. Range entry point is about four minutes. Let's get a last timing check in about a minute. We've got to hit that entry point inside thirty seconds or we're fried." He couldn't look at the map any longer, he was too low and too fast. The terrain sloped up in front, but he couldn't see beyond. It could be a drop-off. He turned his left mirror outboard so he could see Raptor in it. "Maggot, I'm betting there's a cliff coming under the nose in a second. I'll be rolling on our back just in case we gotta pull down the backside."

"I remember a drop-off on the route. It goes down about three-hundred feet and flat on the other side."

Like an aerobatic team, Pepper and Raptor simultaneously rolled inverted and started a pull-down before they got to the cliff. Jagged rocks were only feet below their canopies as they zinged over the karst rim. The jungle instantly fell 300 feet, the jets dropped their noses, and up-righted to hug the terrain.

"Talon, ground-launched heater, your right four o'clock," Raptor called.

"Talon One, copy. Breaking right." Pepper slapped the wings into a hard right turn. "Flares, flares, flares!" he called.

"Maggot, I know we're not carrying flares, but I gotta practice finding that damn switch. There it is." *Shit! Almost hit those trees.*

"Pepper, that tree was damn close! We may have clipped it with a wing tank."

"I think we missed it. I hope we did." *At this speed we'd never feel it anyway.*

"Talon One," Raptor called. "Missile overshot, it went for the flares."

"Copy. Coming back hard left to 198 degrees."

"Maggot, our timing just got blown to hell. What speed now?"

"I gotta get an accurate distance and see how much time we have left. Push it up to five-twenty."

"You got it."

Pepper checked his right mirror on the canopy bow and saw Maggot unfold his map, spreading it in front of his face like a newspaper.

"Okay, Pepper, that bend in the river off our right wing says we're nineteen miles from the point. This is important. Check me on it. We got nineteen to go in two minutes, fifteen seconds. At five-twenty ground speed we're doing eight point five miles per minute. We got a headwind component of ten knots. We need five-thirty knots indicated."

"Sounds good," Pepper replied. *I guess. That shit's higher math...*he nudged the twin throttles up a notch. "There's a T-shaped road *intersection* just off the nose to the left. It's on our route, isn't it?"

"Roger that."

"I'm gonna ease over there, then turn back to one-nine-eight," Pepper said, rolling the jet into a shallow turn. "We should be on course, and we're already on speed." *With a little luck we might make our TOT.*

"Pepper, Two's crossing to the right side. We gotta get ready for the pop-up."

Time to arm some bombs. "Talon, fence check," Pepper called. "Green 'em up."

"Two," Raptor acknowledged.

"We should be within radio coverage of the range," Maggot advised.

"Chandy Range Control," Pepper called. "Talon is a flight of two Phantoms, one minute from the entry point and pop maneuver. We've got six bombs each, dropping two at a time."

"Chandy, copy. Cleared in. Cleared tactical pop on the first pass," the range control officer confirmed.

"Okay, Pepper, like I said, we won't be able to see the bomb circle this low, at this entry angle," Maggot said. "We gotta stay low and minimize our exposure to enemy threats. At the entry point it's a five-G pop up to 5000 feet. The target should be off to our left 9 o'clock in the climb if we're at the right place."

"Copy." He took a quick glance down. *Trees still real close. Watch 'em. Looks like we've got the timing made.*

"Ten seconds, Pepper. Entry point is a water tower."

"Got it, it's a little bit right…three, two, one, hack the clock. Low level's done. Starting the pull, taking that elevator ride to the five-hundredth floor."

"Hot damn, I love myself. We're only five seconds late."

"Shit hot! Just don't start making love to yourself." Pepper glanced to his right. "Two's in good position, we gotta find that target in a hurry."

"Passing four-thousand," Maggot said.

Where's the sonofabitch? I don't see it at left nine. "I'm rolling in, we're at five-thousand. You have it?"

"See that building down there?" Maggot asked. "It's the range office and control tower."

"Yep."

"Okay, keep pulling down into it. Now look a half-mile north for the target."

"Got it!"

Pepper pulled the Phantom hard down and pressed the mike button on the right throttle, "Chandy, Talon's in hot with two Phantoms, target in sight."

"Cleared to drop, cleared hot," the RCO advised.

Roll out, put the sight just below the target. Dive angle's thirty-two degrees, a little steep, have to press lower. Speed's four-fifty, power back in the dive. Walk the sight up to that pylon in the middle of the bomb circle.

"Passing thirty-eight hundred, pickle is twenty-three," Maggot said.

"We're steep and fast, I'm gonna press a little below our altitude."

"Twenty-eight hundred…twenty-five…twenty-three…pickle."

"I'm pressin'…there's pickle," Pepper said.

"Pull, pull, pull!" Maggot shouted.

The Phantom bounced and responded quicker, as 1000 pounds of inert concrete training bombs departed.

"Nose above the horizon, jink hard right, then left," Maggot said. "No doubt the gooks would be shooting at us by now."

"Talon Two's in hot," Raptor radioed.

"Two, cleared hot," the RCO called.

"Talon One, your bombs went eighty feet at six o'clock — qualifying."

"Roger," Pepper acknowledged, then shouted over the intercom: "Shit hot! Now if Two can get his in there."

"Don't worry about Raptor. He was dropping bombs before we were born."

"Two, your bombs were a shack," the range officer said.

"Ha! Told you, Pepper. A frappin' bulls-eye."

"Damn, a shack with 500 pounders. Can't be beat."

"You can bet he knows it. It's like holding a royal flush."

"Time for our shack, Maggot."

Pepper keyed the radio: "Talon One's in hot."

"One, cleared hot — hold it! Negative, negative," the RCO shouted. "Talon, hold high and dry. Somebody's on the bomb circle digging bombs."

"Diggin' bombs?"

Maggot understood. "Yeah, sometimes the crazy sumbitches get right out there while we're dropping bombs. They're smart, they know we're dropping training stuff without explosives. One of our little 25-pound training bombs gets them a day's wages from a junk dealer — about a buck and a half. Meantime, we burn fuel and waste a helluva lot more than that."

"Talon, continue to hold high. The Thai commander is driving out to the circle and he's pissed."

"It's an honor thing with them," Maggot said. "The Thai officer thinks this is an affront to his authority. He'll get the digger off the circle, guaranteed."

"Talon, ah…damn! He just shot the digger with his forty-five. Now he's dragging him off the circle."

What the hell? I can't believe there's a guy wasted on the training range! "Well, fuck, Maggot. He could have just left the digger alone. Pretty good chance we'd miss him."

"No way," Maggot said. "Then it would be an international incident. 'American drops bomb on Thai peasant,' the papers would say. Another black eye for Uncle Sam."

"Think the guy's dead?"

"Hell, he was center-punched with a forty-five."

"Holy Christ, he shot him!"

"Don't let it get to you. We better check our gas. We got enough for one more pass?"

"Yeah…and four bombs left. Let's drop all the fuckers and go home."

"Okay, Talon, the range is clear," the RCO called. "There's one mort lying out there somewhere, but you're cleared hot."

"Talon has time for one pass. We'll be expending four bombs."

"Two, do you copy?"

"Roger, copy," Raptor said.

"Talon One's in hot for 45-degree dive-bomb. Last pass." Pepper reached forward to the weapons panel and rotated the bomb select dial to ALL.

"Talon, cleared hot."

"Well, Maggot, if you see a flying body we'll know we got the digger."

"I'll keep my eye out for a flyin' Thai."

"Smart ass. There's four-fifty, throttlin' back."

"Dive angle's forty-three degrees. That's close," Maggot said.

Throttles idle. Sight walking to the target, a little quick, relax the stick, slow the sight down some.

"Passing four-thousand, Pepper. Ready. Ready. Pickle!"

"Two-thousand pounds are away." Pepper pulled the Phantom level to the horizon. Lighter, the jet was more agile, responding well as Pepper jabbed the stick first left, then right, to evade potential gunners on the ground.

"Talon Two's in hot."

"Two, you're cleared hot."

"One, your bombs real short, four-hundred feet at five o'clock," the RCO called.

"Jesus, Maggot, what happened? Those aren't qualifying."

"I don't know, everything looked good from here. Uh, oh…did you reset the sight to forty-five degrees instead of thirty on the first pass?"

"Dammit, no, got distracted by that digger thing."

"Well, that body may have gone flying. Four-hundred feet is damn short."

"Yep."

"Talon Two, your bomb's fifty feet at twelve o'clock, good job," the RCO advised.

"Two."

"Chandy, Talon's departing the range," Pepper called. "See you next time."

"Chandy, roger. Better have maintenance check that sight when you get home."

"Roger." *Thanks, shithead. Raptor's gonna have my ass...*

Chapter 17

DEBRIEFING

...A fighter pilot is a man in love with flying. A fighter pilot sees not a cloud but beauty. Not the ground, but something remote from him, something that he doesn't belong to as long as he is airborne. He's a man who wants to be second-best, to no one.

—Brigadier General Robin Olds, USAF
Korean War Ace, Four Kills in Vietnam

As usual, Raptor wanted the mission debriefing held in his office instead of a briefing room. Pepper and the two backseaters pulled chairs in front of Raptor's desk and sat facing him. Occasionally spinning his chair around to gaze at the flight line, Raptor said nothing as Pepper covered most of the detail.

"Okay, Tiny and Maggot, you're cleared outta here," Raptor barked, interrupting Pepper's debrief of the bombing scores.

"Yes, Sir," they said as they stood and saluted.

"Maggot, I saw that map flying around your cockpit," Raptor said, as he returned the salutes. "Shit-hot on the low-level."

"Thank you, Sir." Maggot executed an about-face and walked through the office doorway with Tiny on his heels.

Raptor rose to look out the window, his hands on his hips. His solid frame was silhouetted by the ambient glow from the window. Sunlight reflected off his shaved scalp as he stood there in silence.

Here it comes. Gonna bust the ride. Keep your mouth shut.

"Sit down, Pepper," Raptor said, still staring out the window. "You know, you can lug bombs for a hundred and fifty miles, roll in and take out your target, but if you lose your wingman while you're doing it, you've blown the mission and your responsibility. You're a worthless fuckin' flight lead. Nobody will fly your wing."

"Yes, Sir."

Raptor turned to glance at the photo of him and his son on the credenza. "If you've got troops in contact with the enemy, that means they're in close combat." He continued his turn and faced Pepper, leaning forward with both hands on his desk to emphasize the point. "When the forward air controller calls for your bombs, rockets, or twenty millimeter, you gotta put 'em precisely on target. Put 'em short, you kill our guys, not theirs." He stood erect and folded his arms across his chest, locking eyes with Pepper. "Those still alive will hate your guts forever. Because you're the leader, where you put them, your wingmen will follow. This ordnance we carry is damn powerful stuff, designed to kill lots of people. A flight puts bombs in short, they kill one helluva lot of friendlies."

"Yes, Sir." *Here it comes.*

Raptor turned and walked to the credenza, never moving his eyes from the photo. "We like to make one pass and haul ass before enemy guns know we're there and open fire." With his voice staccato now like a machine gun, his jaws clenched, and his eyes darting, he battled anger for a moment. "If *your* flight kills *our* troops, that means *less* of us are able to fight. You also didn't inflict any hurt on the enemy. You didn't take them out." Raptor lowered his stare to the desk and glared at Pepper. "Now the gook bastards know you're there, and they'll open up on your wingmen behind you. That means you've gotta make another pass to take 'em out. Get the picture? You missed the target, killed friendlies, and you may lose a wingman or two — all because *your* fuckin' bombs went short."

"Yes, Sir."

"These may be goddam training bombs, but we're training for a reason. We put the ordnance precisely on target, or don't drop. What happened today?"

Pepper swallowed hard and took a deep breath to steel his nerve. "Sir, I allowed myself to be distracted by the digger gettin' blown away. When I changed to the forty-five degree dive bomb pass, I didn't reset the sight. I got the speed and angle right, but the sight was wrong."

"You played football, didn't you, Randy?"

"Yes, Sir."

"Well, this is a game of inches, not yards. Sometimes fractions of inches. The difference between thirty-degree dive-bomb and forty-five is less than an inch on your sight, but as you saw, that's enough to take out friendlies."

"Yes, Sir, it won't happen again."

Raptor came around his desk and sat against the edge. "Let me tell you something: These gooks don't value life like we do. Hell, they think they'll be reincarnated as something better: maybe a water buffalo, a tree, or a friggin' grasshopper. That digger got his shit blown away and you let it rattle you. As a leader, you can't let that happen." He stared at the floor for a moment, then his steel-gray eyes locked on Pepper.

"You know, the French fought the Vietnamese before we did; they had an expression I never forgot: 'Coup d'oi.' In fighter pilot, it means that in battle the leader has to cut through all the crap and focus on the objective, nothing *but* the objective. You gotta be able to do that."

Pepper nodded and leaned forward in his chair, forearms resting on his knees, his fingers laced together. He stared at the floor. Raptor was right. He'd porked those bombs. Had it been a combat situation, he might've taken out friendlies.

Raptor turned to gaze out the window, his back to Pepper. "Are you able to do that?"

"Cut through the distractions and padlock the objective? Yes, Sir, I can do that."

"You're trainable. You guys did well on the low-level," Raptor said, his image reflecting in the glass as he placed his hands on his hips. "You reacted to threats and still made damn good timing at the range. I couldn't've done better."

Pepper listened, fully expecting Raptor to follow up with a tongue lashing, the way his father used to do when he was driving home a lesson in life. *Dammit, Raptor, just lay it on me. I know I screwed the pooch, big time.*

"I've seen your service records. You were the outstanding graduate in your class at Homestead. You should know how to drop bombs." Raptor turned from the window and sat in his chair. "I'm passing you on the flight lead check. But before you take a flight to the range, here's what you're gonna do: drop some more bombs as a wingman. I want a full load of 500-pounders in qualifying criteria. Think you can do that?"

Pepper straightened. "Yes, Sir."

"I want it done ASAP. I'll tell Mad Dog to get you on the schedule. I want you to go to the hooch tonight and think dive-bomb passes. You chair-fly thirty and forty-five degree attacks — the whole damn mission in your mind, over and over, until you fuckin' dream about it. Then go back to the checklist and see if you missed anything."

Raptor picked up his pen and scribbled a signature on the flight lead certification form. "You check and triple check. Leave nothing to chance. There're only two outcomes from what you do with your Phantom. One is life, the other death. Make sure you never lose a wingman, and make damn sure you never kill any of our guys on the ground."

Pepper rose from his chair. "Sir, that won't happen." He took the form from Raptor, stared straight ahead, and held a salute.

Raptor didn't look up, but stared at a pen he was drumming on his desk. "By the way, I was briefed this morning on the accident board findings from your and Jasper's crash. We're off the hook, with them at least," he said, turning the pen end-over-end between his fingers. "They blamed it on materiel failure in the right main gear." He looked up at Pepper holding the salute and staring over his head.

"When you blew the gear down after the hydraulic failure, a valve was supposed to release *all* the uplock pressure. It held just enough to prevent the gear from locking down. No pilot or maintenance error on this one. We got lucky." He returned the salute.

Pepper lowered his arm. He couldn't hold back a grin. "That's the best news I've heard in a long time, Sir."

"As soon as you get qualified on the range, I want you to take a two-day pass. Go to Bangkok, take some R & R and get your mind right. Come back ready to lead missions. Get outta here, Captain."

*

On the range the next day, all of Pepper's bomb scores were qualifying. One pair was even better, his first shack with 500-pounders. During the week he gained experience by leading air-refueling missions and another low-level to the range.

Meanwhile, nearby demons prowled Southeast Asia once again.

***

Chapter 18

BANGKOK

Airplanes are like women — pick what you like and try to get
it away from the guy who has it, then dress it out to the limit of
your wallet and taste.

—Stephen Coonts, The Cannibal Queen

Four months had passed since Pepper first stepped on the tarmac
at Korat. With all the action, it seemed a lifetime ago. Working
continuous six- and seven-day weeks sapped him of the energy
needed to stay sharp. He had to be like the cutting edge of a razor to be
an effective fighter pilot and combat flight leader. He wasn't and Raptor
was right. Pepper needed R & R.

*

Pepper got the two-day pass the day after qualifying on the range. It was
Wednesday morning while the rest of the squadron was flying when
he alone caught the "Klong Shuttle," a C-130 cargo aircraft that made
a daily circuit of the three remaining USAF bases in Thailand. Klong's
final stop was Bangkok. For the 45-minute flight he sat on a bench seat
made of nylon webbing that ran along one side of the aircraft and stared
at the tire of a big John Deere tractor that filled the cargo area.

At the Bangkok airport, Pepper threw his B-4 bag into the backseat of
a bright pink and blue Datsun cab waiting at the head of a long line of
taxis. He had reservations at the Chow Peiea Hotel, a five-story facility
located downtown and leased by the military for R & R.

"How much to Chow Peiea Hotel?" Pepper asked, settling into the backseat.

The driver held up two fingers. "Two hundred baht, GI."

"No can do, Cabby," Pepper held up one finger. "One-hundred baht to Chow Peiea."

"Okay, GI. You cheap."

"Nope. Just no tourist. You good driver, I give you tip."

Weaving through Bangkok's dense, late afternoon traffic, the driver jabbered in Thai while incessantly laying on the horn. A string of faded pastel-colored flowers swung from the rearview mirror. A small bronze Buddha stared at Pepper from the dash, reminding him of his Johnny Walker bender at the Osaka.

Driving on the left side screws me up. I'm looking in the wrong place for traffic…I need to turn that Buddha around to see the wreck that's coming. Maybe what I need is a rub 'n scrub.

"Here hotel," the driver said, stopping the cab at the curb.

Pepper handed the cabby a red note and a twenty for a tip, then leaned forward. "Okay if I rub Buddha's tummy for good luck?" he asked.

"Sure, GI. Good ruck, no charge."

Carrying his bag, Pepper timed his way through a brass and glass revolving door into the spacious hotel lobby. He skirted his way around a bubbling fountain in the middle, noticing the basin was filled with coins. *I bet most of those wishes are to return to the world…*He gazed around the lobby as he walked toward the reception desk. A worker stood on a tall ladder cleaning one of the crystal chandeliers. The rich, deep red and brown tones of teak walls told him he was back in civilization. He set his bag down on the granite-tiled floor and signed for room 302.

Taking the key from the clerk, Pepper heard Tony Bennett crooning, "I Left my Heart in San Francisco" from a jukebox in the lounge on the other side of the lobby. The open double French doors to the bar seduced him. He liked Frisco and Tony's mellow voice. Besides, he was thirsty and wanted a beer.

Pepper walked into the lounge and tossed his bag on a chair as he made his way to the bar. The only patrons were three men sitting at a corner table. A swimming pool adjoined the lounge and Pepper heard a splash and the echoing clatter of a diving board as someone dove in the water. He slid onto a barstool.

"Hello, what'll you have to drink?" the Thai bartender asked in perfect American English.

"Where's your accent?" Pepper asked.

"I get asked that a lot," the Thai said, drying a glass with a bar towel. "Got a physics degree from Southern Cal. My father wanted that. I wanna live in Bangkok. Make more money here working for Uncle Sam than teaching physics. What'll ya have?"

"Gimme a Bud in a bottle if you got it."

"Comin' up," he said, sliding the lid back on a cooler to get the beer. "In for R & R?"

"Yeah. Just in from Korat. Be here for a couple of days." Pepper raised the cold beer and took a long drink.

"The helo pilots in the corner said you guys did good in the Saigon evacuation," the bartender said, wiping the counter.

"It was a lousy end to a lousy war."

"I heard we almost lost a couple of Phantoms fighting American F-5s. We shot them down and almost got Yellow Star. Didn't we?"

"Yeah. I was on that mission. But we only killed one F-5."

"Who got the F-5?"

"I got lucky," Pepper chuckled, and downed another swallow. "Got a two-day pass."

"Got a free beer, too. On the house."

"Thanks! Say, what's your name?"

"Call me Roy. It's really Loi, L-O-I, but GIs think I'm regular Thai and can't say my Rs. They say, 'Oh, Roy.' So that's my name. You?"

"It's Randy. They call me Pepper," he said, turning on his stool, looking around the lounge. "It's kinda quiet around here. What's there to do?"

"Most GIs go to the strip clubs in Pat Pong. They like skinny girls there, except for fighter pilots. I hear they like skinny boys," he said, grinning.

"Like hell!"

"Pat Pong's about fifteen minutes downtown in a cab. Rub 'n scrubs there too."

Pepper saw a woman in fatigues and a tall, lean guy in a flight suit walk in and sit at a table midway between him and the French doors. Cylindrical ceiling lamps subdued the lighting in the lounge, but the woman's burnished red hair gleamed as she passed beneath one.

Pepper thought he recognized her, or was it just wishful thinking? He signaled Roy. "That Bud tasted like another one."

"Comin' up."

"I'm gonna hit the head. I'll be right back. Run me a tab, okay?"

"Sure, GI." Roy popped the cap off another brown bottle and set it on the bar. "Little boy's room is right over there," he said, grinning and pointing beyond the couple.

Pepper stared at the woman in fatigues as he went by. Then standing at the urinal, he tried to place where he'd seen her. *She's pretty. Real pretty. I know I've seen her. Where? That's it. The C-9, the medevac. What's her name? Greer, I think.* Washing his hands, he tried to remember her first name.

Roy was taking the couple's order as Pepper tried to ease by. Stealing another look at her, he stumbled into a pedestal lounge table, knocking it over. An ashtray sailed, hit the floor, and shattered as Pepper tripped and landed in a heap on the floor. At the noise, Roy turned from taking their order and looked down at Pepper. "Sure you fly jets?"

"Yeah, I fly jets."

Pepper saw the woman smiling at him as he scrambled to his feet and dusted himself off. "This is a worn-out line, but don't I know you? Isn't your name Greer?"

She looked down at the nametag on her uniform, then back to Pepper. "It was the last time I checked. Robyn Greer. Did we meet on the Nightingale?" she asked, still smiling.

"I must have forgotten. It was 'classified secret' information at the time."

"Okay, GI." Roy said. "Looks like you're ready for jets again. Want me to bring your beer over with their drinks?"

"Yes, why don't you join us?" Robyn asked.

"Are you sure? I don't want to butt in."

"It's okay," Robyn replied. "This is Steve Miller. He's the pilot on our busted Nightingale."

"I'm Randy Houston," Pepper said, shaking hands as he took a seat.

"Call me Speed. Ran track at the academy."

"I'm Pepper. Makes flowers taste better." He looked at Robyn. "You're busted? What's wrong with the C-9?"

She nodded and Speed answered, "Yeah, starboard engine ate one of its turbine blades and blew a hole in the casing. It's trashed. Another engine's due in from the Philippines tonight."

"Sorry to hear about the motor," Pepper lied, his eyes locked on Robyn. He'd always been a sucker for red hair and blue eyes. He glanced at Speed, then back to Robyn. He hadn't seen a pretty American woman in months. "Did it pop pretty good when it blew?"

Robyn rolled her eyes. "It sounded like a bomb went off."

"Good thing it blew out the side instead of toward the fuselage, or we'd've had parts buzzing by the crew," Speed said.

Roy arrived with a tray of drinks. "Here's your two mai tais and your beer, Pepper."

"Thanks, Roy," Pepper said, reaching for his beer. "Put 'em on my tab."

"Okay."

Pepper leaned back and took a drink from his Bud. He looked at Robyn spinning the paper umbrella that garnished her drink. "How long are you grounded here?" he asked.

Speed rocked forward in his chair and put his elbow on the table. "They say it shouldn't be more than a day or two."

"Hey, that's great!" Pepper smiled and set his beer on the table. "Are you two together?"

Speed grinned and nodded, but Robyn looked at Pepper. "No plans, yet. How long are you here?"

"I've got a two-day pass for R & R."

"Are you by yourself?" Robyn asked.

"Yeah, Raptor said I needed a break since I hadn't been off the base in four months."

"Did you say *Raptor?*" Speed asked.

"Yeah, he's the commander."

"Does he live up to his call sign?" Robyn asked.

"He just barks a lot." Pepper shook his head and took another long pull on his beer. "He's all right. Helluva fighter pilot."

"Glad he's flying fighters. We don't need raptors in medevac," Speed said.

"He's glad not to be in medevac, too, I'm sure," Pepper said.

Robyn sipped her drink holding the frosted glass with both hands. "Didn't I see your picture on the front page of *Stars and Stripes* after the evacuation?"

"Yes, we flew air combat."

"What about the photo?" Speed asked. "You a hero or a goat?"

Asshole...the only shot he's ever fired in anger is a fart in a windstorm. "Call me what you want, Speed," Pepper said, staring at his beer and scraping the label down with his thumb. "But I got the last air-to-air kill of the war."

"Oh, you mean that American F-5?"

Pepper reddened and locked eyes with Speed. "That's the new reality, Captain," he said, icy cold. "Maybe if you were a little closer to the war, you'd know the bad guys own the country, and everything in it — including the South's F-5s."

Robyn stared at Pepper. Her eyes wide. Listening intently.

"I've been close enough to haul off the sick and wounded for the last nine months," Speed countered.

"Well, I'm sure you're good at what you do, but maybe the operative word here is *haul*," Pepper said, draining his now-naked bottle and setting it on the table. "You should try hauling missiles and twenty mike-mike. Mean things. Things that can do some damage and kill people. Then take on North Vietnam's leading ace and have your jet take some hits. Then you can give me all the crap you want."

"Well..." Speed said, taking a drink of his mai tai. The froth left a small white mustache on his upper lip.

Pepper shifted his gaze to Robyn. "Please excuse my mean mouth. I'd rather talk about something else, like where are we going tonight?"

Speed bristled.

Taken by surprise, Robyn replied, "It doesn't matter to me. Where do you want to go?"

"My cabby suggested the Thai Palace downtown for authentic local food."

"That sounds good to me. Speed, don't you want to go with us?" she asked.

Speed slumped in his chair. "Ah, I think I'll stay here in case the maintenance folks have problems with the aircraft. Thanks."

Pepper stood up and looked at Robyn. "I need to clean up. Can we meet in the lobby in a half-hour? Will that give you enough time?"

"That's fine. It'll give me a chance to get into my one and only set of civilian clothes."

∗

Pepper read the *Stars and Stripes* from an overstuffed chair while waiting for Robyn. Since Saigon, there wasn't much of interest to read in the paper, only an occasional piece about boat refugees trying to escape Southern Vietnam. It seemed tragic fallout from the war would never end. Pepper lowered the paper when he glimpsed Robyn walking down the spiral staircase, her hand on the wrought iron handrail, her eyes on his.

Robyn's black slacks and sleeveless white linen blouse went well with her shining still damp red hair. The outfit conformed to her figure much better than fatigues. Her soft cotton blouse curved around her breasts and tucked in tightly at her narrow waist. The slacks fit the flare of her hips perfectly. *God, she's in terrific shape…fresh, clean…still drop-dead gorgeous.*

"Hi," she said, as Pepper rose to his feet and dropped the paper on the arm of his chair. They stood facing each other.

"You look great," Pepper said.

"Thank you. I have to travel really light on these trips. We usually make it back to Clark and don't stay over anywhere. I carry one change of clothes, just in case. It paid off."

"You know what? I'm going to buy you a fine new dress. Let's go to a tailor first thing and let 'em get started on a dress for you. I understand they can make one quick if they know you don't have much time."

"That would be fun," she said, smiling broadly.

Outside, Pepper hailed a cab and held the rear door open for Robyn. A whiff of her perfume quickened his pulse. He rounded the cab and slid into the backseat next to her.

"How much to Thai Palace?" Pepper asked the driver.

He held up two fingers. "Two-hundred baht," he answered.

It's two-hundred to everywhere… "Too much," Pepper said, holding up one finger. "We pay only one-hundred for Thai Palace."

The driver shrugged. "Okay, GI."

Pepper looked at Robyn. "Ripping off tourists is the national pastime. You've gotta set the price before you go anywhere. Pepper pointed to the dash. "Watch, that flag'll stay up, they don't ever use the meter. That's so they can avoid taxes."

"I'm no good at bartering. I'm glad you are."

"The guy I talked to in the lobby said there were tailor shops near the Thai Palace." Pepper looked at his watch. "It's only four o'clock. How about we get a tailor started on your dress before we eat?"

"That'd be great."

"They'll be done, or almost anyway, by the time we get finished with dessert," Pepper said. He hesitated a moment, gazing into her ocean-blue eyes.

"A penny for your thoughts," she said.

"You're beautiful."

"Thank you."

Trance broken, Pepper laid his arm on the seat behind Robyn. "I was thinking how strange it is, us riding in this cab together. Only a few weeks ago I had a hard time getting you to tell me your first name. Remember?"

"Yeah. I figured you were just another horny fighter jock hitting on a round-eye."

He grinned, surprised by her candor. "What's wrong with that? It's normal ops."

She chuckled. "It's like the same song playing all the time. After a while you get tired of the tune."

Through the window, Pepper saw a market area with dried meats hanging, tropical fruits in storefronts, and brightly colored oriental goods for sale. In an open quadrangle two women in ornate dresses, with six-inch fingernails were dancing to singsong Thai music. "Look, Robyn. Those must be the Thai dancers I've heard about."

Robyn turned to see. "Oh, aren't they pretty? I saw pictures of them in my hotel room. They're so graceful."

The cab driver continued down the street and stopped in front of a restaurant with two big golden columns supporting an inverted arc. The arc's tips curved up like a pagoda temple.

"This Thai Palace, GI," the cabby said.

"Thanks!" Pepper handed him a red note and a 20-baht tip. Grinning at the tip, the cabby hustled out and opened Robyn's door. Pepper stepped around the back of the car and reached for Robyn's hand. "Cabby, do you know a good tailor around here?"

He pointed across the street and down a few shops. "You go Hong Kong tailor. They number one, GI." Pepper could see mannequins in the window, some with unfinished suits and dresses on them.

"Okay. Let's go to Hong Kong," he told Robyn.

"Always wanted to go," she said, smiling.

They entered the store to find the right wall stacked to the ceiling with bolts of cloth. They were every color imaginable.

"Sawadii," the traditional Thai greeting came from a small man sliding off a stool behind a wide wooden countertop. There was a bolt of shiny white cloth spread across the counter. He laid a large pair of scissors down next to an adding machine and walked around to meet them.

"Sawadii," Pepper answered, holding the palms of his hands together at his chest and bowing slightly.

"You no tourist," he said, bowing in like fashion. "My name is Billy, real name too hard for Amelicans."

"My name is Pepper. Real name too hard for Thais," he said, grinning. "And this is Robyn."

"Nice to meet you, Lobyn," he said, bowing again. "What I do for you?"

"We need a nice dress, in a very short time," Pepper said, scanning the wall of colors. "Can you make one in a couple of hours?"

"Oh, sure. No ploblem."

"What kind of fabrics do you have?" Robyn asked.

"All silk. Only have Thai silk here."

"You mean all this is silk?" Robyn asked, gazing about the store.

"Yes, Lobyn," he said, panning his arm all around. "Everything silk." He turned and walked behind the counter, rummaging underneath for something. "I find," he said as he pushed aside the white cloth and placed a thick catalog on the table. "Lobyn, you look in Sears Catarog for dress. I go find you pletty silk." Billy hesitated for a moment studying her features. "You have pletty eyes, I use them," he said, turning toward the wall and lifting a ladder.

Robyn looked at the front of the catalog and first opened it to the tool section, then found the dresses. "I haven't seen a Sears Catalog since I left the States," she said, excited. "I'm in Bangkok, looking at the current spring catalog. Unbelievable. I'll finally get to see what they're wearing."

Pepper slumped into an easy chair by the store window. He watched Robyn at the counter as she leafed through the catalog. *Trained killer one day, getting a dress made the next. Better watch it. You're falling…*

"A lot of these are nice, but they wouldn't look good in silk," she said.

"Look in back, Missy," Billy said, climbing up the ladder with his eye on a bolt near the top. "See dressy ones."

Robyn turned to the end of the section. "Oh."

"You find, Missy?" he said, pulling a bolt of blue silk out of the bin, and starting down the ladder.

"These are real nice. You can't make one of these in a couple of hours, can you?" she asked.

"Sure, Lobyn," he said, walking toward her and cradling the bolt in his arms. "You come back two hours. I do final fit for you."

"Oh, that's a pretty color," she said.

"This cock pea brue."

"What?" Pepper asked, getting up from his chair and walking toward them.

"Best coror for you. Cock pea brue."

Robyn grinned at Pepper, shook her head and shrugged. "It's a pretty color. I like it."

"Billy-san," Pepper said, reaching for the bolt, "do you mean peacock blue?"

"Yes. That what I say."

Pepper looked at Robyn, they broke into laughter.

"Yes, Billy," Robyn said, covering her mouth with her hand, fighting laughter. "It's a beautiful color. Can you make this one?" she asked, pointing at a knee-length cocktail dress.

"Yes, can do easy."

"Do you like it, Pepper?" she asked, holding up the catalog.

"That'd be real pretty, Robyn. Let's get it made."

"I've always wanted a silk dress."

"I take measurements now." Billy took the yellow tape from around his neck and pointed toward the three-section, full-length mirrors in the corner. As he and Robyn walked toward it, Pepper returned to his chair and settled in again. He listened intently for the measurements, then frowned. *Damn!* They made no sense in centimeters.

*

"This is elegant," Robin said as the two walked up to the hostess holding menus, arms crossed and bowing from the waist.

Black lacquer tables inlaid with mother of pearl, stood beneath paper light globes in the middle of the room. Booths, with hanging ivory beads, bordered the room. Ornate gold and brass framed temple rubbings of Thai dancers hung from the walls. A spicy scent of smoldering incense drifted from a small Buddhist shrine in the corner of the room. It was early. Only two couples were dining.

The hostess held the beads back so Robyn could slide into a secluded booth. Pepper ducked under and sat across from her.

"Dlinks?" the hostess asked, handing them menus.

"Another mai tai, Robyn?" Pepper asked.

"Yes."

"A scotch-nam, ah, scotch and water, please," Pepper said.

"Speaking a little local?" Robyn asked as the hostess turned to leave.

"Yeah, I guess it's kinda hard to shift gears from Korat to Bangkok," he said, fumbling with the menu, looking into her eyes. For the first time they had no distractions, only each other. *Why was he nervous?*

"What's it like there?" she asked.

"Pretty much all we do is work and fly," he said, shifting his gaze to see if the drinks were coming. "But, Saturday nights and Sunday the place turns into a zoo. Everyone blowing off steam. It sorta reminds me of my college frat house — wild and crazy."

"Sounds like fighter pilot heaven," she said, smiling.

"I guess so. There's a war on. People act different."

"I don't know what any of this food is," she said, looking at her menu. "Do you?"

"How about I order?"

"Please."

A waitress in a pale green kimono brought their drinks. Holding the tray, she bowed. "Sawadii," she said, and placed the drinks in front of them, then stood by silently, waiting to take their order.

Pepper pointed to the menu. "We'd like the Thai combination, please. This one with Cow Pot, Thai fried rice with water chestnuts."

"Velly good choice," she said. "It come with green tea, anything else to dlink?"

"A small bottle of saké, please."

"Chi, cup (yes, Sir)," she said, bowing again and turning to leave.

"I'm freezing," Robyn said, rubbing her arms. "Are you cold?"

"There are so few places that are air conditioned here, when you get to a place that has it, you feel like you're at the North Pole," Pepper said, looking up. "And those ceiling fans make it feel a little cooler too."

"Maybe that warm saké will break the chill."

"It'll warm you up." Pepper looked at the table and noticed their fingers were only inches apart on the table.

"What are we eating?"

"I ordered a noodle dish with all kinds of things mixed in." He glanced at their hands again. *Should I?* "You don't want to ask too many questions about what's in it. Guaranteed it'll be spicy with some garlic. All Thai food has garlic, I'm afraid." *What are you scared of MiG killer? Do it.*

"We'll smell really good, huh?"

"We'll get some mints. It won't bother me, if it doesn't bother you." Pepper slid his hand under hers and lifted it. "That's a nice ring," he said.

"Thank you."

Cradled in his hand, her fingers were shapely, supple, and soft. "Is that a garnet?" he asked, feigning great interest in a rectangular, blood-red stone in a rich gold setting.

"Yes, it's my birthstone. January. We had a stopover here a while back and the taxi driver took us to Johnny's Gems."

Pepper gazed at her, still holding her hand. "Did the cabby want two-hundred baht?"

"Yes!" she laughed. "We didn't know. Thought it was normal."

Pepper looked down at her ring again. He took a chance and lightly stroked the back of her hand with his thumb. "It's very pretty," he said, easing their hands down to rest on the table. Touching her made him hunger for more. As she leaned forward and sipped her frothy white drink with a straw, Robyn left her hand in his.

"Dang cabbies. It's always two fingers," he said, then chuckled, relieved she didn't reject his touch.

"Your hand is so warm. It feels good," she said, wrapping her other hand around his.

Pepper reddened. "Thanks. So does yours." He wrapped her hands in his own. Amazed, Pepper told her, "You just say things."

"It's what I feel," she said, stirring her drink with the straw.

Pepper looked over the top of his glass as he took a drink. "So, you'll tell me just as easy when you don't like something?"

"Yes. What I really like is that dress we're getting." Her eyes widened with an expectant look. "If I'm still here tomorrow night, can we go somewhere so I can wear it?"

"Sure. I can wear a new white leisure suit and a fancy shirt I had made in Korat," he said, smiling.

"Great. Hope my plane stays busted."

"If an engine's coming from the Philippines, it'll be a miracle if they get it changed in one day," he said, continuing to stroke her fingers.

Robyn took a sip of her mai tai. "Am I inviting you on a date?"

"It's okay. I accept." Nervousness faded. He was suddenly at ease, comfortable.

"Can I come around there by you?" she said, sliding out of the booth, but still holding onto his hand. "Your 98-point-six might warm me up."

"Sure," Pepper said, holding her hand, not wanting to let go.

"There," she said slipping into the booth next to him.

*

Later, in the hotel lounge, Pepper and Robyn took a secluded table near the dance floor and ordered drinks from a waitress. The band belonging to the empty instruments on the platform played only on the weekends. So this night's music came from the juke box on the opposite side of the dance floor.

At the Thai Palace, Pepper enjoyed Robyn's perfume and was intoxicated by her childlike openness. He had put his arm around her to offer warmth; she snuggled in close and rested her hand on his leg. He longed for more.

"Would you like to dance?" Pepper asked, reaching for her hand.

"Yes," she said, entwining her fingers in his as they walked. Only one other couple shared the hardwood dance floor as the mellow sounds of "Moon River" began to play.

Pepper was surprised how easily he and Robyn fit together; she molded in closer than he expected and eventually laid her head on his shoulder. Her hair smelled like fresh-cut lilacs and was soft against his cheek. She let go of his hand and softly wrapped her arm around his back. They swayed, in a comfortable embrace, slow and rhythmic, the dance step forgotten.

"Are you unwinding?" she asked, turning her head, searching for him. Her eyes were deep blue and captivating in the subdued lights. Her firm body pressed close. His left hand rested in the curve of her lower back. *I want her.* The thought crept up on him and wouldn't leave his head. For the first time in a long time he was getting hard and couldn't control it.

"Yeah," he said. "I haven't been thinking about Raptor or the war."

"Good." She tightened her embrace, ever so slightly. "Do you think it's over?"

"Probably," he answered, pulling her closer. "But, there's still a lot of stuff going on in this part of the world."

"Do you think you'll see any more combat?" Her voice was low as she put her head to his chest.

Under the soft illumination of a ceiling light, they continued to sway even though the music had finished. "Could happen, I guess." He unintentionally pulled away ever so slightly. Like waking from a wonderful dream, his mind fought to not return to combat mode. He wanted to stay right here, right now with this beautiful woman, but he had to answer her. "Intel says the Vietnamese may soon be making a push into Cambodia. They call it 'the domino effect.' If that's true, the gooks are right next-door."

She turned and looked up at him, apprehensive of the unknown. "You mean they will send you to battle again?"

"It's possible," he said, holding onto her arms. Alone on the dance floor now, they stopped swaying. "That's what I do. Fly fighters."

"I know," she said, putting her head back on his chest.

"Such a nice night. I hate the thought of spending the rest of it alone."

Robyn stopped and gazed into Pepper's eyes. "You don't have to."

Robyn left her purse on a chair at the vanity. She walked past the canopied bed, with deeply carved oriental figures embedded in tall, black wooden posts. An oscillating fan blew long white ribbons hanging from each post. She opened French doors and stepped out on a small balcony ringed in wrought iron. In the dark street the noises weren't as loud as before.

Pepper eased up behind her, sliding his arms around her waist and they stood gazing out into the night and the street below. The heat enveloped them like a steam bath. There was a salty-sweet smell of vegetables in soy sauce cooking somewhere.

"The city doesn't look so mysterious from up here. Just lights," she said.

"They all look alike at night. Especially from the air."

"I had a good time," she said.

"Me too."

Robyn turned in his arms and put her hand on the back of his neck, pulling his face down closer to hers. Her lips were warm and soft as they parted ever so slightly. Pepper's pulse rushed. She was delicious. He eased from the kiss and gently touched the outline of her lips with his tongue. "I want you," he said, and swept her into his arms. He kissed her harder this time, then slowly moved to her cheek and kissed it, lightly as a feather blowing across her face. He nudged her auburn hair back from her ear and breathed into it. Pepper melted as he felt her delicate, warm hand on the back of his neck. "I need you," he whispered, then laid her gently on the bed.

She rolled on top of Pepper and pinned his arms against the bed. "I need you, too," she whispered and she kissed him, her tongue probing. Releasing one of his arms she began to unbutton his shirt. Pepper's hand went to her breast as they kissed like starving people devouring a feast. The two rolled back and forth on the bed, shedding clothes until there was only white-hot skin touching white-hot skin.

Robyn cupped Pepper's head in her hands and brought his lips down to hers. Then she moaned as he slipped into her.

Pepper stood on the balcony in a white terrycloth hotel bathrobe, his hands buried in the pockets. He stared across the bustling, early morning Bangkok streets. Below him, merchants were busy opening their shops, pedestrians darted to and fro through the traffic, horns mixed with bicycle bells, and the air had a faint, unmistakable smell of diesel fumes.

"You look like you're in another galaxy." Robyn stepped onto the balcony with a cup of coffee in each hand.

Pepper turned, his face blank, preoccupied with the impending storm in neighboring Cambodia and Vietnam. He tried to tune into what she said. "Ah, room service must have arrived."

She smiled and nodded. "There's some great fruit and breads. The best is this coffee." She handed him a cup. Her smile broadened. "I cheated. I already took a sip."

"Thanks. I need it to get my jets started this morning," he said, squinting from the steam, relishing the first taste.

"Okay, which galaxy?" she asked.

"I was just remembering last night," he lied, looking out on the city and taking another sip.

"What about it?"

"I loved making love to you," he answered, turning to gaze at her. He knew it was hard to commit to anybody in a combat environment and wondered if he would ever see her again — would she want to see him again? "You were wonderful," he said, trying to get back on track.

"You were too, both times," she said, with an impish grin. Slowly her smile faded. "What's on your mind? You look like you're a thousand miles away. Any regrets?"

"I have to be honest with you. I actually was thinking about something else."

"Okay, spill your guts, or draw iron," she said, making a play gun out of her hand and pointing it at his face.

"Let's sit down," he said, looking at a plastic chair for her and pulling one up beside her. Pepper leaned forward, resting his elbows on his knees and staring at the cup cradled in both hands. "I really did enjoy last night. I've never felt this strongly for anyone. It's special. I know that. I was thinking about all the talk on base that the war's over. That we'll be pulling out before long."

"Then why the long face? Isn't that good? You can go back to the world."

"Yeah, that part is." Pepper took a sip, hesitating.

"I'm curious, why did you have that cigarette lighter on the nightstand? I haven't seen you smoke anything."

Pepper pulled the Zippo out and handed it to her. Robyn rolled it over in her hand and read the inscription.

"Is that what you were thinking about? Who was Tim?"

Pepper sat back in his chair and looked at Robyn. "We were best buds in high school. He was a Marine. Killed in Vietnam."

"Didn't it say 1966? That's a long time ago."

"Yeah. I've been trying to get to the stinkin' war ever since then. Now it's over, before I can pay a debt."

"You shot down an enemy pilot, didn't you?"

"It's not what I planned to do all these years. I wanted to put some hurt on the North Vietnamese Army so I could go back to Tim and tell him I made it over here too. Paid 'em back."

"It must have really affected you. It's ten years later and you're still thinking about it."

"Yeah, it's still with me."

"You did what you came to do. Let it go," she said, bending down for a small bird feather on the concrete floor. "Open your hand," she said. She placed the feather on his palm. "You have to pretend this feather is all the bad emotions you feel about losing your friend. Wrap them all up in that feather, then hold it over the railing and blow it into the air."

Pepper stood, looking at the feather in his hand, the light breeze moving it back and forth.

"Now, let it go," she said.

He stepped to the edge of the balcony, stared at it for a few moments and blew the feather into the air. It floated on the gentle currents across the rooftops.

Robyn waited until the feather was out of view and stepped to the railing. She put her arm around his back. "Is it gone? Did you let it go?" she asked.

"I tried. I think there's too much here to let it go that easy." Pepper put his arms around her shoulders and pulled her close. He leaned down and gently kissed her. "I felt a calmness there for a minute."

"That's your mind wanting to let go, but then your heart won't let you," she said, putting her head on his chest. Their arms circled each other, a silent embrace said all that was needed.

*

A fighter pilot has many facets, like a diamond in the rough. They're uncut angles that beg for tempering, cutting, slicing to make them shine. The right woman can do that without tampering with the inner core that is common to all fighter pilots — passion. Fighter pilots love flying and their machines; they also love their women like no one else on the earth loves another. To them passion is passion, whether it be an aircraft, or a beautiful woman. They mirror each other and are special.

His aircraft and his lover both have a great shape, nice curves, a softness in their exterior, and a rigidness inside. That's what Pepper saw in Robyn — something special.

＊

The rickshaw driver leaned back, his leathery, gnarled hands pulling on the crossbar. Using his weight as a brake, he stopped the buggy in front of Hong Kong Tailors. Pepper thanked him in Thai as he paid. The old driver bowed repeatedly and jabbered in Thai when Pepper handed him a tip.

"That was a lot of fun," Robyn said, as they walked toward the shop. "Sure beats a cab. Gives you a chance to look around."

"Yeah, and enjoy the smells," he said, holding the door open for her.

Robyn stepped into the shop and saw Billy hurrying toward them, smiling. "Sawadii, Billy," she said, clasping her hands in front and bowing.

"Sawadii. I see pletty girl now Thai," he smiled, and returned her bow.

Looking at Pepper he said, "I see you get reisure suit made at Kolat. Nice job," he said, holding the white jacket open to inspect the seams. "You no wear sissy shirt. That good. Some tourists have pink flowers on shirt. Not good for man."

"You don't have to worry about him wearing pink, Billy," Robyn said smiling. "Fighter pilots don't do that sort of thing."

Pepper laughed. "Too much like pink-o commie for me."

"Is my dress finished?" Robyn asked.

"Have all finish," he said, pointing to a door in the corner of the room. "It in dlessing loom, waiting for you."

Pepper let out an exaggerated sigh of relief. "Thank God, she's been bugging me all day about it."

"Stay there. I'll be right back," Robyn said, disappearing through the dressing room door. I can't wait to try it on."

She can't wait to put it on. I can't wait to get it off her...

In a few minutes, Robyn stepped from the dressing room and stopped in front of Pepper, beaming. "I love it," she said, looking down and smoothing it in front.

"God, you're beautiful. The color really brings out your blue eyes."

Robyn looked up with a broad smile. "Thank you."

Pepper held both arms out to the side, ran his eyes up and down her figure, devouring her.

"Look nice pletty girl," Billy said, easing around Robyn and inspecting the fit.

Pepper took Robyn's hand and spun her slowly around as if they were dancing, admiring how the dress gathered at her slim waist, then flowed over the curve of her hips. "It's a keeper," he said.

Robyn draped her arms around his neck. "Thank you for the dress. You're a keeper too," she whispered as she kissed him.

Billy clapped. "Glad you rike keeper," he said, giggling.

Pepper and Robyn sat in the orchid-adorned gondola as if glued together, his arm around her shoulders while they enjoyed a river tour. The gondolier was silent as he poled them past lights hanging from sampans and fishing boats. The night was balmy with thunderstorms rumbling in the distance every now and then. Although darkness covered the city, the sun had not yet set at 40,000 feet. Snow-white tops of towering cumulus stood like brilliant icebergs in contrast to the blackness below. Some boat people were cooking in woks on small hibachi grills. Wonderful aromas of frying vegetables, garlic, and exotic spices rode the gentle breeze. Singsong oriental music drifted from a sampan's radio as they eased past.

"This is beautiful," Robyn sighed, leaning her head back on Pepper's arm.

"This has been the best twenty-four hours of my life," Pepper said.

"Does it have to end? It's been the best time of my life too."

"My pass is up tomorrow; I'll have to leave on the Klong shuttle at oh-eight hundred," he said.

"I know. The Nightingale is supposed to be ready tomorrow too."

The gondola sliced quietly through the river; the only sound now was the bow wave as it lapped against the wooden hull. "I want to tell you something," Pepper said, turning to face her.

Robyn's eyes met his.

Pepper blushed, suddenly nervous, but alive like he'd never been before. "I've…I've fallen hopelessly in love with you. There, I've said it."

Robyn hesitated an eternity. Her eyes darted back and forth searching his. She took his face in her hands and gently kissed his cheeks and forehead.

"I was hoping you felt that way, too," she said.

She slowly kissed her way to his lips. "I love you, too," she whispered.

Robyn's warm, inviting kiss locked his pulse in five stages of afterburner. He felt like he was falling with no parachute.

Her auburn hair brushed his face, the light fragrance of Chanel consumed him. *She's the one…*

Chapter 19

PAY BACK

"He put on righteousness as a breastplate, and a helmet of salvation upon his head; he put on garments of vengeance for clothing, and wrapped himself in fury as a mantle. According to their deeds so will he repay, wrath to his adversaries, requital to his enemies..."

Isaiah 59:17-18

O nly two weeks had passed since the fall of Saigon; the enemy wanted still more American blood. At 2:20 p.m. on May 23, 1975, off the coasts of Cambodia and Vietnam, a Khmer Rouge communist gunboat circled the SS *Mayaguez*, a U.S.-flagged container ship belonging to Sea Land Corporation. For the Khmer Rouge, the U.S. was weak from the loss of the Vietnam War and the debacle of Saigon. When one of the gunboat's machine gunners triggered rounds across the *Mayaguez*'s bow, he sparked a firestorm that would never be forgotten. While the Khmer Rouge hijacked the ship, they forgot their own adage: "One should not wake a sleeping tiger." The next four days would define U.S. stature in Southeast Asia for decades.

At a small, remote base like Korat, news and rumors of the *Mayaguez* hijacking traveled at lightning speed. At the squadron dinner table that evening, talk focused on one subject: the taking of an American ship in the Gulf of Thailand, 300 miles to the south. With the exception of the afterglow from Pepper's kill, morale was in the toilet. The news left the flight crews frustrated and bitter. Were they headed for another defeat in Southeast Asia? Would this be like the captive *Pueblo* in North Korea, whose crew was incarcerated and tortured for months? That image both energized them and made them mad as hell.

"Pass the goddam salt," Animal barked at no one in particular. Paco shoved the salt and pepper shakers down the table. Animal used them to create a black and white coat over his meatloaf. "If I ever get back to the U.S. of fuckin'-A, I will never eat meatloaf again. I know this ain't beef. It's water buffalo, monkey meat, or dog. Hell, you never know in this godforsaken place. Hey, is Roscoe still around? Hope his hind leg ain't in here."

"Hey, Animal, don't let your MEAT…LOAF!" someone shouted from the end of the table.

"Cute, real cute," Animal replied, cramming a large piece into his mouth. "The first time I heard that one I wet my diaper." He kept talking, cheeks bulging. "As bad as this dog-loaf is, I bet the crew off that American ship would like some right now. Hope they send us down there to kick some ass."

Pepper grabbed the salt shaker. "Is the crew off the ship?"

"Yeah. When I left the squadron, an intel puke told me the gooks forced them to drive the ship to some island. They took the Americans off the boat there."

Animal caught a waitress's arm as she passed by. "Hey, Lieia, bring me a JD and Coke, will you? And lots of pepper, please. My friend here wants to eat some more carnations." Grinning mischievously, he scooted a flower arrangement toward Pepper.

"I'm full, Animal," Pepper said. "No room for flowers tonight. I heard a couple of our F-111s diverted from a training mission to find the ship. They watched it anchor off some island named Koh Tang in the middle of nowhere."

"Well, that'll be a helluva lot of fun," Animal said. "What possible good could F-4s do to get the crew back from some jungle-choked sand pile?" He crammed another chunk of meatloaf in his mouth. He chased that with a scoop of reconstituted mashed potatoes that looked like wet concrete. "Go down there and make a lot of noise," he mumbled. "Shake the place up with 2000-pounders? I think we should go bomb the gooks' presidential palace until they give the crew back. That'd be more effective than killing a bunch of monkeys on some friggin' island. What'd you call it? Crap Tongue?"

"*Koh Tang*," Pepper said.

"Sounds like that powdered orange juice I drank as a kid. Tang," Animal said.

As Lieia set his drink on the table in front of him, Animal twisted around in his chair and opened his mouth wide to display an amalgam of meatloaf and mashed potatoes.

"You ugly Amelican, Animal," she said.

"But I ruv you, Rieia. Marry me, I take you to States, buy you Cadirack car."

"You clazy-man. I not melly you. I melly him," she said, winking at Pepper.

"Aw, Rieia, Pepper have girlfriend everywhere: in States, in Air Force, downtown. I no have plitty girlfriend like you. Melly me, I make you satisfied woman."

"Peppah — not *you*. You clazy as hell. Pay for dlink. I vely busy. You get ship back tomollow?"

"How did you know about that?" Animal asked, sipping his drink. "Never mind. You ladies know everything before we do. You spy, Lieia?"

"What spy?"

"Give her a break, Animal," Pepper said.

"Lieia, I not save ship," Animal said. "Pepper save tomorrow. He my *he-ro*. How many men on the ship, Lieia?"

"I think thirty-nine."

Animal rolled his eyes. "Damn, we haven't even been briefed and she already knows how many were in the crew.

"Okay, Lieia, this is a test. What's the name of the ship?"

"Name *My Guess*, but no militaly ship. Civilian. Khmea Louge have."

"How you know so much, Lieia? Who the hell is Khmer Rouge?"

"On Thai ladio tonight. Khmea Louge vely bad communist. They mean, kill many people. Like chop heads off."

"Okay. More test. How do we get the crew and ship back?"

"Go to Gulf of Thairand in Phantom. Kill many Khmea Louge, they give ship back."

"Then you melly me?" Animal's face flushed from the Jack Daniel's.

"Ugh," she grunted, taking his money for the drink. "You clazy-man."

"Okay, I get ship back, you make love to Animal?"

"No way!" she snapped, then smiled. "I make ruv Pepper."

"You're a slam-dunk, Animal!" Maggot chipped in.

"Two points, Lieia," someone said from the far end of the table.

Pepper blushed.

Animal shook his head, then leaned forward and tried with no success to stir his hardened mashed potatoes.

Sirens sounded a base-wide recall for a mass briefing the next morning. Everyone was seated in the base theater by 0500 hours.

"Ladies and gentlemen, the wing commander!" a lieutenant shouted from the back of the theater. Boots slapped the floor in unison as the crowd stood at rigid attention.

"Take your seats," the colonel said from halfway down the aisle. Near the podium he turned to face his people, the big American flag covering the wall behind him. He scanned the room. A mixture of flight suits, fatigues, and faces spread before him. Pepper sat beside Animal in an aisle seat about six rows back. The rest of the 34th Rams filled the next two rows.

The colonel, dressed in a crisp, dark green flight suit and gleaming jungle boots, folded his arms in front, turned to his right and walked slowly across the stage. "Ladies and gentlemen, commanders aren't supposed to say this, so give me some leeway." Silence. He stopped to face the audience again. "I'm really pissed..." His voice rose. "I'm so damn mad I could spit nails. I asked you to evacuate Saigon and we thought it was the end of the Vietnam War. I asked you to do it regardless of your feelings about losing friends over here. You did it and you did a damn fine job. I thank you for pulling together and doing it right. You made me proud to be in this Air Force."

He paced across the stage and stopped under the bright ceiling light. "We worked hard and did our duty well — while the whole world watched us lose a long war," he continued. "I know morale has dipped in the two weeks since Saigon. Some of you may see this as the lowest point in your career."

He turned to his left, glanced at the flag and walked back toward center stage, arms still folded. "I can't blame you for feeling that way. Hell, sometimes I feel it too. But this has been my experience: when good people hit bottom, given a reason they bounce back on top real quick. We've been given that reason.

"Yesterday afternoon in the Gulf of Thailand, Khmer Rouge naval forces fired upon, then hijacked the SS *Mayaguez*, an American-flagged container ship. They forced it to anchor off an atoll called Koh Tang." His icy-cold stare swept the room. He jabbed his right index finger, poking it into the audience's chest. "I'm here to tell those Khmer Rouge — you don't screw with America and you don't take innocent Americans. Not now, not ever!"

Grins spread across faces in the audience. The colonel turned to his left, hands on his hips, and took a few steps without saying a word. Three hundred pairs of eyes watched his every move.

Pepper sat transfixed. He'd never heard a wing commander talk this way.

Our lives are in his hands. Raptor said, where the leader's bombs go, so do the wingman's. If the old man's pissed, everyone's pissed.

The colonel turned again to face them. "As of 2400 last night, President Ford has given us clear rules of engagement: No Khmer Rouge goes to, or leaves the island. As I speak, AC-130 gunships from Korat are over Koh Tang. They're searching for the crew with low-light TV and infrared sensors. Just before coming here this morning, I was briefed that Spectre destroyed a Cambodian gunboat. Ladies and gentlemen, once again we're in a shooting war. We'll save our ship and its crew. It won't be easy, but we're the only ones who stand a chance to rescue them." He seemed to make eye contact with every person in the room as he hesitated. "Now…you're the best trained, and you've got the most recent combat experience in the entire Air Force. We'll perform this mission with absolute precision."

He glanced stage left. "Captain Bonham, you may start the intelligence briefing now."

As the flag retracted, C-tone stepped from behind the curtains to the podium. Her fatigues were starched, nearly cracking when she walked. Her honey-blonde hair was pulled tightly back in a twist. Simultaneously, the theater lights went dark, leaving her illuminated by a single ceiling beam. She pressed the control button on the podium, filling the screen with an out-of-focus, black and white photo of a Y-shaped island.

"This is Koh Tang," she said. "Tang means island in Cambodian, that's why you won't see the word *island* after it. I apologize for the poor quality. This is the only photograph we have, taken late yesterday by an F-111 wizzo with his hand-held personal camera. Note that the island is generally shaped like a slingshot, its forks extending north."

C-tone left the podium and strolled into the beam of the picture, appearing ghostly in the mottled light. She pointed a pencil-beam flashlight at the screen. "You can see the SS *Mayaguez* anchored close on Koh Tang's eastern side." She circled the area in the crotch of the slingshot's forks. "Spectre's infrared shows a collection of human images in this general area of hooches and grass shacks. We think this is where the crew is being held, though we can't count them individually. Our infrared can't distinguish Khmer Rouge from Americans."

She pointed offshore to the bay formed by the forks. "These four objects are Cambodian gunboats based at the island. From what the wing commander just said, only three remain. The threat of gunboats is real. There are more available on the Cambodian mainland, only thirty-five miles away. The larger vessel here is suspected to be a Thai fishing boat. They may have hijacked it for the food on board." She turned and walked back to the podium.

"Gentlemen, the distance is such that you'll have to refuel over the Gulf of Thailand before entering the target area. Tankers will be on station, but there is no radar control to assist your rendezvous. Our aircraft carrier, the *Enterprise*, just arrived in the Philippines from the Saigon evacuation. It's still at least three days away.

"You should also know that an HH-53 with nearly two dozen security policemen on board crashed last night in eastern Thailand. They were responding to the hijacking. No one survived.

"This morning, more than two-hundred U.S. Marines are being airlifted to U-tapao in southern Thailand. Air Force CH-53 and HH-53 helos from all over Thailand are assembling there as well."

She eyed the wing commander in his front-row seat. "Sir, that's all we have at this time. Are there any questions?"

The colonel rose and strode to the stage as lights came to full bright. "Thank you, Captain."

He turned to face the audience once again. "Ladies and gentlemen, we are at a defining moment for United States presence in Southeast Asia. Vietnam has fallen and bad guys in this part of the world made the mistake of thinking us weak. Khmer Rouge have killed a helluva lot of their own people. Given the chance, they won't hesitate to kill Americans. You and I are the business-end of the sword in this part of the world. We save the crew, or they don't get saved."

The colonel strolled across the stage and nodded to C-tone. She hit a button that brought a detailed flight schedule to the screen. He continued, "In two hours, A-7D Sandys will launch, followed by Phantoms, then Spectre. We will be flying to the Koh Tang area all day in case we are needed. 'Cricket' will be over the island in a C-130, providing battlefield command and control. Even though President Ford has given us carte blanche — use care. We don't want any more Americans killed in this part of the world. Unless you are receiving fire, or see someone else in imminent danger, get clearance to expend your weapons. Remember, you are professionals. Do it right. Carry on."

Everyone snapped to attention. The only sound was the creak of theater seats rocking back and forth.

*

With a call sign of "Killer," Mad Dog, the operations officer, chose Pepper and Maggot to fly his number four Phantom, tail-end Charley. Their flight would be the third group of Phantoms to launch for Koh Tang. Preflight briefing done, the eight crewmembers suited up in life support. It was quieter than usual. The warriors weren't tight or loose, just serious.

Pepper stood in a section of lockers isolated from the rest. He pulled all Velcro patches off, "sanitizing" his flight suit in case he was shot down or captured. He stowed all unnecessary items in the locker. He removed his Alabama class ring and placed it on the top shelf. He then propped his wallet open to the picture of Robyn, his favorite, a close-up in her Air Force nurse's uniform. Her seductive smile always swept him away for a moment. Pepper tore small strips of electrical tape to cover the shiny plastic captains bars stitched on the shoulders of his flight suit. He placed his military ID card and a few dollars into a zippered plastic pouch to keep them waterproof.

Donning his survival vest, he walked to the bright red gun-clearing barrel. With the word "WARNING" stenciled on it, the sand inside would stop an ill-fired bullet. Drawing the .38 Smith & Wesson hanging under his left arm, he pointed the pistol into the barrel and released the cylinder. He pulled five rounds from the vest and slid them one at a time into holes in the cylinder. He left one hole without a cartridge so the pistol's hammer would rest on an empty chamber. He pulled open the right breast Velcro pocket to check the blood chit. A white silk handkerchief with an American flag printed at the top, bore an inscription in several Asian languages stating that the bearer would be paid handsomely for the safe return of the American. He felt for the Zippo in the chest pocket of his flight suit and zipped the survival vest. Stopping by the fridge, he stuffed two frozen water bottles in each leg pocket of his G-suit. He was ready.

PeeWee stood curbside; Roscoe lay beside him, head resting on his paws. As the fliers trailed out the life support door to catch the crew van, each flight member patted the Lab for good luck, and stepped into the van.

Last in line, Pepper knelt and set his helmet bag down. As Pepper ruffled the old dog's ears, the Lab raised his head. He didn't lick Pepper's hands this time. "Roscoe, buddy. Do some of your magic to help us get that crew back."

As if on command, Roscoe barked three times at a flight of A-7s thundering overhead.

"That's it, PeeWee," Pepper shouted above the jet noise. "Just the sign we needed!"

"Must be, Sir," PeeWee replied, hands cupping his ears. "It's good to see him show some spirit. He hasn't eaten in a couple of days. And I've never heard him bark at jets before."

Pepper climbed aboard the waiting van, turned and stuck his head out the door. "You come by the table tonight, Roscoe. Bring PeeWee. I'll buy both of you a steak. See ya. Gotta go to war." He winked at Roscoe and his control officer, and grabbed the overhead handrail.

As the van lurched ahead, Pepper shuffled to the only vacant seat, next to the cooler of frozen towels. At 0800, the day was fast warming; an early morning thunderstorm had turned the air into a stifling, muggy steam bath. Pepper, used to the fertilizer smell, noted that it seemed particularly strong today. He cracked open a frozen towel and draped it around his neck. He wrapped a second one in a plastic barf bag and shoved it into his G-suit leg pocket.

As Killer Four, Pepper, and Maggot were last to be dropped off at their Phantom. The familiar love-hate feeling swept over Pepper when he saw his jet. Adrenaline mainlined his veins as the steady rumble of launching fighters blasted the flight line and weapons trucks hustled around the ramp. The prospect of action excited him, but seeing his aircraft loaded to the max served as a sober reminder that an enemy waited to be engaged.

"You just became a flight lead and you're already back to flying number four," Maggot chided, glancing at Pepper and shaking his head while they walked toward their Phantom.

"Screw you. I'm lucky to be on this mission. Look at the brass out here. It's serious when everyone but us is a major or light colonel."

Pepper set down his helmet bag, exchanged salutes with the crew chief, and took the aircraft forms from his hand. "Hi, Chief. How's the jet?"

"She's code one, Sir. Ready to kick some tail."

Maggot fished his checklist out of his helmet bag and started inspecting the four LAU-3 rocket pods hanging under the F-4's wings. He crouched to inspect the larger pod holding the multi-barreled Vulcan Gatling gun bristling from its belly.

Pepper glanced at his preflight checklist periodically as he made the walk-around inspection. As the pilot, it was his responsibility to check overall condition, looking for leaks or loose panels.

"Maggot, those rocket pods look like trash cans on steroids," he said as he inspected the afterburner exhausts. "I fired one rocket in training. Somehow its fins were bent. Damn thing went haywire and killed a cow grazing a thousand feet at twelve o'clock from the target. Unlucky cow, unlucky me — no more rockets. Now we're carrying seventy-two of 'em." *The gun's awesome. We could thump commies pretty good with this load — if I can put it where it's needed...*

Maggot slid under one pod to check the next one. He screamed over the nearby engine noise. "You fire them pretty much like twenty mike-mike, but it helps to be bunting. You know, pushing forward a tad on the stick until you're a little light in your seat. When the rockets blast out of the tubes, the fins don't get bent leaving the launcher under Gs."

"Thanks for the tip. I knew I brought you along for some reason."

*

The heavily armed Phantoms found their tankers over the Gulf of Thailand and topped off with fuel before pointing toward Koh Tang.

Southeast bound at 21,000 feet, Mad Dog checked in with the command and control aircraft. "Cricket, Killer, flight of four fox-fours departing the refueling track. We're en route to the island, about fifteen minutes out."

"Cricket, copy. Go ahead with your line-up."

"Roger. All aircraft have twenty mike-mike and LAU-3 rockets, all white-phosphorous. We have about thirty minutes playtime in the target area."

"Cricket, copy...we need you ASAP. We want you to look at a boat headed to the mainland, about ten miles north of Koh Tang."

"Roger. Pushin' it up."

"Shit-hot, Maggot!" Pepper hollered. "No hangin' around pickin' our noses today!"

"Sounds like action to me."

From continually looking toward number three and flying the wing position, Pepper's head was welded left. His neck was getting sore. "I got used to looking around as a leader. Can't now."

"That's okay. You fly good position, I'll look around."

"Thanks, asshole. At times like this, it doesn't pay to be the nose gunner," Pepper said.

"Killer Flight," Mad Dog called. "Fence check, green 'em up. Remember, guns are hot."

"Don't you love it when Mad Dog mothers us?" said Maggot.

"Hi-viz mission, I guess." *Finger's pointing straight out, nowhere close to the trigger. MASTER ARM on. Rockets selected. We're hot.*

"All my checks are done back here. Fuel looks good, tanks feeding."

"Cricket, Killer's five minutes out," Mad Dog said. "What's the situation?"

"Killer One, two Khmer gunboats have been sunk by previous flights. A Thai fishing boat left the island and is underway toward mainland Cambodia. We're working with the command center to get clearance for you to attack the boat with rockets. We'll let you know ASAP. Continue east on present heading for now."

"Shit-hot!" Maggot howled. "White phosphorous gonna make you burn, baby burn."

"Hell, I've never shot at a boat before. Do I ever get to do the same thing twice in this business?"

"Piece of cake," Maggot said. "Think of it like a truck going down a road, only slower. Or, it's like Joe Willie Namath throwing a pass. Lead it just a little, then *rock and fire*. This may be the first time we've done this, but it sure beats stackin' widgets in some factory in West *Vagina*."

"Hey, you can't say that word in the cockpit, you lecher. Too much of a distraction. Time to be *exact* again. Let's plan thirty-degree rockets first. What's the setting?"

"My captain, you need exactly thirty-seven mils."

"I love it when you're *exact*." Pepper cranked the sight down and adjusted the illumination.

"I know; turns you on."

"Ladies and gentlemen, this is your captain. Hang onto your asses and tits, and whatever else you've got. And remember: Nothin' could be finah than to be in West Vagina in the mornin'!" Pepper sang.

"Cricket, Killer One: I've got the boat in sight, it's about twelve northeast of the island. It's white with the wheelhouse in the stern. About seventy-five feet long."

"Killer, roger, that's the one. Your flight's cleared to expend rockets in front of the boat. We need to turn it back to the island if we can. If it won't turn, we'll have to take it out in accordance with the rules of engagement."

"Killer, copy. One's in for a full pod of Willy Petes about fifty meters in front of the boat."

"Hell, Maggot. We're really going to do this!"

"Remember, it only takes one 'Aw, shit' to wipe out all your attaboys."

"Yep."

"Killer One's off the boat. Dry. No rockets."

"What the hell?" Pepper said. "Somethin' wrong with his jet?"

"Could be a lot of things. It ain't Mad Dog. He's on his third combat tour like Raptor."

"Killer Two's off. No rockets."

"Killer Three's off. No rockets."

"Jesus, Maggot. What's going on here? It's our turn. What if we're the only ones in this whole flight to get rockets off?"

Pepper rolled the Phantom into a steep left turn and pulled the nose down toward the boat. "Killer Four's in hot for rockets."

Triple-check. Armed. Sight's thirty-seven mils. Boat's moving left to right. Sight's just below it and to the right — perfect. Speed four-fifty. Dive angle twenty-nine degrees.

"Okay, Pepper, lay some hate on 'em. Thousand feet to go…five hundred. Ready, ready, pickle."

Okay, 'precisely' fifty meters in front. Pickle. "It looked good, Maggot," he said, pulling the Phantom's nose to the horizon to stop the dive. "But nothing happened."

"Shit! We're just like the rest. What gives?"

"Don't know. I show we're armed. Check the circuit breakers back there."

"They're all in."

"This is Killer One. Something real queer's going on with these rockets. We're gonna try one more time, then jettison them."

All four aircraft again tried their rockets. Not a single one fired. The small boat continued motoring toward the mainland, undeterred in the face of the American bluff.

"Okay, Killer Flight," Mad Dog barked, "jettison all rockets. They ain't workin', folks."

"What the hell?" Pepper groaned. "Not a single rocket off the entire four-ship?"

"There's only one way that could happen," Maggot said. "The weapons crew at the runway didn't arm them. There's a wafer switch on the back of each pod that has to be rotated to ARM before take-off."

"Damn…you're right."

"Cricket, Killer won't be expending any rockets today. We're dumping them in the Gulf. Request clearance to strafe in front of the boat."

"Killer, you're cleared for strafe."

"One's in with the gun."

Pepper reached forward to the weapons panel and flipped the toggle switch to GUN. He confirmed a tenth time that the MASTER ARM was on, and changed the sight to 30 mils for strafe. He selected WING STATIONS on the JETTISON switch and blew the pods off their pylons.

"Pepper, confirm sight at thirty," said Maggot.

"Set."

They watched as the three Phantoms in front of them ripped strings of 20mm rounds in front of the boat. It never slowed or turned.

"Stubborn sombitch. Boat's not going back," Maggot said.

"The captain must have a hot date on the mainland tonight. It's our turn."

Pepper then keyed the mike: "Killer Four's in for strafe."

Of all air-to-ground attacks, strafing was his favorite. He was top gun of his training class. He was a deer hunter and firing the Gatling was similar to triggering a high-powered rifle. The Phantom's sight had to be held steady like the crosshairs of a scope and the trigger squeezed smoothly.

Pepper set the speed and dive angle. He then walked the sight to a spot 50 yards in front of the Thai fishing boat. *Steady, steady. There's 2000-foot range. Trigger's comin' down. Nada, nothing, zip, zero.* "What the fuck?"

"I hate it when pilots say that!" Maggot said. "What happened?"

"The damn gun didn't fire!"

"Oh, good. I thought it was something serious."

"It *is* something serious, you little shit. No rockets off this jet, and now no fuckin' bullets either. What we got here is a weak dick Phantom."

"I'll check the circuit breakers." Maggot looked down at the consoles on his left and right. "There's three of 'em popped. Centerline armament circuit breakers. That's the gun. Turn off the MASTER ARM and I'll reset 'em."

"It's off."

"Okay, they're reset. You can turn the MASTER ARM back on. Shit! They popped again. One more time...there they go again."

"Godamnit! It's our turn to strafe. All we can do is drop down and take a good look. Hell, we can't shoot a thing at 'em."

"Yeah we can. I'll shoot the mothers a finger as we go by."

Pepper rolled the Phantom on its back and pulled the nose down. In a few seconds they were skimming the waves and pointed directly in front of the boat. Just before they got to the bow, he rolled the jet on its left wing and pushed his right leg forward on the rudder pedal in cross-control. It kept the nose from falling with the left wing down, allowing a longer look as they passed overhead.

Maggot held both hands to the top of the canopy in one-fingered salutes to the Khmers below.

"Killer, Cricket. If it doesn't appear to be turning, you are cleared to strafe the vessel itself. You can eliminate it on your next pass."

"Killer One, copy."

"Maggot, did you see all those guys crouched along the edges of the bow?"

"Yep. I also saw those gooks in the back firing automatic weapons at us."

"The people along the bow didn't have black pajamas like gooks. They wore all kinds of clothes and colors. They were bigger, too."

"Killer One, this is Four."

"Go."

"Sir, our gun keeps popping circuit breakers when we arm. Couldn't shoot anything so we dropped down and took a good look at the boat. There're people lined up all along the bow. They're in the fetal position. Hands behind their heads."

"Copy. Anything else, Four?"

Pepper kept his Phantom in a loose left turn as he climbed. He saw the three other jets ahead in a box pattern. Killer One rolled in.

"Sir, those people are bigger than Orientals and have multi-colored clothing. I think they might be friendlies. Maybe the *Mayaguez* crew."

"Okay. One's dropping down to take a look. The rest of the flight hold high and dry."

They continued flying their box pattern with the boat at one corner of the box. Mad Dog made a pass directly over the boat at about 300 feet. "Cricket, there's a lot of people on the boat. Are you sure you want us to waste it?"

"Killer One, we're checking, Standby...how many souls on the boat?"

"I'd estimate about forty. Like Four said, they're outlining the bow rail with their hands over their heads, air-raid position. Some of them looked up as we went by. They were Caucasians."

"Killer, this is Cricket. Command says you are *not* cleared to expend. I say again, you are not cleared to expend on the boat. Copy?"

"Killer, copy. Will comply."

"Pepper, looks like we stopped the whole show," Maggot said.

"Maybe we did. Hell, we can't fire anything anyway. Let's try those circuit breakers one more time. MASTER ARM is off."

"Okay, but there's something wrong electrically, that's why it pops those breakers. We could get us a fire."

"Killer, Cricket. You're cleared for strafe in front of the boat. We need to turn it back to the island, particularly if the crew is aboard. You are *not* cleared to expend on the boat."

"Roger, Killer One's in for strafe."

"Okay, Maggot. MASTER ARM is back on. Tell me the breakers are not popped."

"They stayed in. Wait! They popped again. *Shit!*"

"We gotta get some twenty millimeter across that boat. I want you to hold in those circuit breakers when I get ready to fire the gun."

"Can't do it, Pepper. We'll start a fire."

Pepper pounded his fist on the fiberglass glare shield above the instrument panel. A broken piece flew to the floor. "Goddamit, Maggot! Hold in the fuckin' breakers. Those are Americans! I know that's the *Mayaguez* crew…we're next."

"Four's in for strafe," he called.

"I pushed 'em, Pepper. They wouldn't stay. I hold 'em in, we get a fire. I know it just like you know the crew's down there."

"Fuck me."

"A few more rounds of twenty millimeter won't make 'em turn if they haven't already," Maggot said.

"Maybe so. You know what? I don't care if this piece of shit Phantom burns like a fireball."

"Me either, but I'd like for it to carry my pink ass home. Besides, I can't swim."

Pepper chuckled. "I can't either. We're just not gettin' anything off it today." He pushed the jet's nose toward the dark blue ocean below. "We gotta do something. Might as well give the *Mayaguez* crew a morale booster—the sound of freedom, two J-79s in afterburner." He skimmed the wave tops at 500 knots, the Phantom aimed straight at the fishing boat.

Movement in the mirrors caught Maggot's eye. He twisted in the seat to look behind at a saltwater rooster tail from the jet's engines. "Shit, we're low."

"The gooks on this boat won't forget today," Pepper said. "They'll think this Rhino is gonna ram 'em." *I wanna be rolling thunder, fifty feet away.*

A quarter mile from the Thai fishing boat, Pepper shoved the twin throttles outboard, then jammed them to the wall. All five stages of afterburners lit at once. At such a low altitude and high speed, acceleration kicked them in the back like a size-12 combat boot in the ass.

"Whoowee, Pepper, that gook just went swimming," Maggot shouted as a black-clad figure threw his AK-47 over the side and followed it in.

Pepper pulled the big jet's nose up at the last possible second. Thirty thousand pounds of pissed-off Rhino streaked across the open bow, mere feet above the deck. The over-pressure under the Phantom's wings rocked the boat side to side.

Eat shit and die, scumbags…

Several *Mayaguez* crew members uncovered their heads as the ear-shattering noise passed. They looked up and saw Pepper's jet blast skyward, orange-hot afterburner cans spouting twin blow torches. He slapped the Phantom's stick full right for continuous victory rolls.

Americans lining the bow no longer cowered. Together they stood, waving their arms, others turned and shook fists at the wheelhouse. A tattooed young mate held both hands high, thrusting one-fingered salutes at his captors.

While Killer Flight joined on a northwest heading to Korat, the Thai fishing boat plowed a frothy white wake in the deep blue sea as it headed toward the mainland.

The world watched…

Chapter 20

Roscoe

"A dog is something special to a fighting man. A dog's eyes look into a man's soul for corners where softness remains."

—Anonymous

Pepper looked left and right, checking each wingtip for clearance from high metal walls as he guided his Phantom into the revetment. The crew chief crossed his arms in front of his face to signal a stop as the nose wheel rolled precisely onto the parking mark. He gave the cut across the throat sign, then Pepper raised both throttle levers and slid them full aft, shutting down the engines. As the whine of big J-79s wound down he began unstrapping from the impotent Rhino.

"Maggot, I bet heads are gonna roll over these rockets."

"Yep," Maggot said, unstrapping his kneeboard and sliding it into the pocket of his helmet bag. "We didn't do anything wrong. Hell, it's way above our pay grade anyway. Let the big brass duke this one out."

The crew chief hung the ladder from the cockpit railing and climbed to the top rung to help carry flight equipment. "How'd it go, Sir?"

"Not good, Chief," Pepper said, as he leaned forward to unhook the ejection straps on his calves. "Jet's code three — busted. This jet's grounded." Pepper unhooked his shoulder harness and threw the straps back against the ejection seat. He jerked the lap belt loose, then crammed his kneeboard and gloves into his helmet bag. "I still can't fuckin' believe what happened. None of us got any rockets off, and we couldn't fire the goddam gun."

"Sorry to hear that, Sir," the crew chief said, taking Pepper's helmet bag from him.

"Me, too. We blew it. Nobody could fire any rockets and this piece of shit couldn't fire the gun either. The *Mayaguez* crew was on a boat that we couldn't turn back to the island. They're on the mainland now. Captives."

"Damn."

"The rockets may have failed because they weren't armed at the runway. Somebody screwed up," Maggot said, as he handed the chief his helmet bag. "The gun is a different story. It's got an electrical problem. Keeps popping the breakers back here."

"Chief, I want you to get the weapons troops on it ASAP," Pepper said, climbing out of the cockpit. "We need this jet yesterday."

The crew chief shook his head. "Damn," he repeated. He took Pepper's helmet bag and gear in one hand, and held onto the ladder with the other. As he started down he said, "Yes, Sir, we'll get 'er fixed ASAP."

Pepper climbed out of his cockpit and stepped to the ladder. He paused to look at Maggot sitting in the rear cockpit, his hair sweat-matted, eyes glazed. "You look like shit."

Maggot snapped out of his trance, leaned forward and stuffed his flight gloves in his G-suit pocket. "This blows. I never felt so absolutely fuckin' worthless in my whole life."

"Everybody was counting on us to get that crew back," Pepper said, starting down the ladder. "Hell, we were fifty feet from them. We saw their faces and couldn't do a damn thing."

"Do you think it's over?"

"Maybe."

*

Killer Flight gathered in a briefing room to go over the mission. Mad Dog, as lead, stood at the head of the table, while the others sat around it. He leaned on the lectern, his face blank. The chalkboard behind him had three large letters: "A-F-U," scrawled across it. Reticent flight members took seats around the table.

"Gentlemen, some days you just hope a mission ends before another disaster happens. This is one of those days." Mad Dog backed away from the lectern and turned to face the board, then pointed. "Anybody know what that stands for?"

"All fucked up," Maggot droned.

"That's affirmative, Four. And it was worse than we thought. The two four-ships of Phantoms in front of us couldn't get rockets off either. That's twelve Phantoms. Every jet the thirty-fourth flew this morning. Not one of 'em got a damn rocket off." He erased the letters and wrote "864" in their place. "Gents, I did the math. That's over eight hundred white-phosphorous rockets that didn't fire.

"Pepper, have you ever seen a Willy Pete hit the ground?"

"I've only fired one, Sir. It had bent fins and went crazy."

"Anybody else fired any?" Mad Dog asked, looking around the briefing table. No one answered.

"Well, let me tell ya, if you were on the ground, or in this case, on the water, you'd be amazed. First of all, when they leave the pod, all nineteen of 'em accelerate through the speed of sound, making a loud crack when they break the barrier." He leaned forward with his forearms on the lectern. "That alone is unnerving as hell on the ground, not to mention a boat. That's followed by instant impact and explosion of all of 'em at once. The last thing in the detonation sequence is acrid, billowing, white phosphorous smoke that mushrooms like a small A-bomb." Mad Dog's face reddened as he fought to control anger. "If that occurs fifty feet in front of you — you either stop, or you fuckin' turn back. Even an idiot would have to figure the next bunch was going to blow his shit away."

Pepper leaned forward to make a note on his mission lineup card: Learn more about 2.75- inch rockets. He took a long sip from his cold, sweating bottle of Coke.

"Let this be a lesson," Mad Dog said. He turned to the board and added the bold letters, TRAIN/FIGHT, and underlined them. He turned back and tapped his stick of chalk on the lectern with each word: "You-must-train-like-you-fight. I didn't like this ordnance configuration. We haven't used LAU-3s since the U.S. signed the peace accords with the North Vietnamese in Paris nearly three years ago. No one on this base has ever handled them. Hell, we've turned over personnel two or three times since they were last used. The gouge is this: we have no close air-support ordnance left in Southeast Asia — except rockets. When we have to get close to people, it's rockets and twenty millimeter. That's it."

"Sir, what do you think happened with the rockets?" Pepper asked.

"We know what happened. Our people didn't arm them. It's in the checklist, but in our hurry to get jets loaded and airborne, we missed it. That's what happens when you don't use the damn things. It's too late to practice with them when you're in the middle of a fight."

"Are we gonna get another chance?" one of the wizzos asked.

"Who knows? With the crew on the mainland, it's going to be tough. They can hide them anywhere. We have to get smart. Be prepared in case there's another chance."

Mad Dog looked at each of the seven around the table. "Like the boss said, this is a defining moment, and it's not over 'til it's over. You need to know everything there is to know about delivering rockets, including the equipment. Next time we'll make sure the weapons troops know how to arm the pods. They'll also plug in their headsets so you can verbally confirm the jet is armed prior to take-off.

"Did anyone get any photos of the crew? Cricket's concerned there are still some Americans on the island."

Shit. I had a Nikon in the map case. Never crossed my mind to use it. We could have counted faces, known if they were all off the island.

"Any questions?" Mad Dog asked.

Steam-room moisture hung heavy in the night air as Pepper made his way to the party hooch in the middle of the compound. He stepped through the beads hanging full length in the doorway, edged his way through the crowd of Phantom drivers to the bar. He ordered a double scotch-nam. "Anybody seen Roscoe?" he asked the Thai bartender.

The Thai avoided Pepper's eyes. He scooped ice into a glass and poured a hefty slug of Johnny Walker Black. "No see Loscoe," he said, still looking down.

Jumpin' Jack Flasch was bent over the pool table in the middle of the room. He slid a cue stick back and forth, drawing a bead on the cue ball. "Roscoe died today, Pepper."

Pepper went cold. "What? Are you serious?"

Jumpin' sidestruck and miscued the cue ball. It shot the length of the table, skirting the wedge of racked balls. "Damn!" he said, walking down the table to retrieve the ball. "PeeWee said Roscoe was lying down in the back of the commander's jeep while they were next to the runway watching us launch," Jumpin' said, striking the cue ball hard for the break. "After we rolled as the last four-ship, Raptor leaned back to pet him and he just wasn't breathing any more. He called the command post and they put the word out on the crash net like a major accident. Shit deal. Helluva dog."

"It's true," Paco chimed in from across the table. "It *would* happen today. We probably need ol' Roscoe around now more than any day I've seen. This place is on its ass."

"Well, goddammit," Pepper muttered, then turned his back, leaned on the bar, and drained his Johnny Walker in three gulps. He signaled to the bartender. "Give me another one. Make it a double and forget the fuckin' water."

Pepper grabbed the rope hanging from the ship's bell over the bar and banged the clapper back and forth. "I'm buyin' a round for Roscoe. Belly up. Let's get shit-faced."

He downed his second drink faster than the first. "Hey, bartender, another one, just like that one," he said, slapping the glass on the bar. *Fuckin' Roscoe! Just like goddamn Vietnam — lose your best, then lose the war.*

Carrying his drink, Pepper walked over to the juke box and dropped in a nickel. He punched "R" then "10," having no idea what song would play, his eyes were too blurred to read the selection. "R" was for Roscoe, "10" for how old the yellow Lab was thought to be. A mechanical arm placed the 45 RPM record on the turntable and Otis Redding sang, "Let Me Come On Home." His soulful voice, deep and gravelly, belted Georgia blues from the ten Sony speakers in the room: "Honey, I'm gonna come home to you…Baby, you're one-thousand miles away…"

The dozen or so in the room drifted to the bar and ordered their free drinks. Pepper leaned both hands against the pulsating juke box, staring down as if searching for another song. Something wet rolled down his face and splattered on the glass.

Damn humidity…

Pepper didn't know how he got in the stinking pit. It didn't matter. It was dim, and he couldn't see a way out. Dozens of snakes slithered and hissed all around him. A huge king cobra raised its head six feet, a third of its 18-foot body. Eyes probing his, the cobra flared its hood and flicked its forked tongue. Pepper shifted his eyes, searching for a way out of the pit. He would have to make a stand. Here. Now. Not daring to move, he coaxed his pistol from its holster. He raised it and aimed at the cobra's head. He pulled the trigger flinching as the hammer fell. *Misfire! Dammit!* He dropped the .38 and felt for the handle of his survival knife. He found the sheath, but there was no knife. He gulped, fighting panic.

What was that noise? Thunder? His head throbbed. Had someone hit him with a baseball bat or squeezed him with giant vise grips? Pain shot to the base of his skull when he moved. His mouth felt like he'd downed a glass of sand. So dry. Nothing left to swallow. *Use this big stick. I can beat the cobra away. What's that noise? They're closing in on me…*

The window rattled in Pepper's hooch room. He turned his head and a low moan escaped. He squinted through gritty eyes. A sliver of light between the curtains oriented him and he realized it was jet noise that shook the window. Temples throbbing, he rolled over to check the room. No one there. The big Seiko on Pepper's left wrist told him it was 0800.

Gotta drink something. Need Alka-Seltzer. What the hell happened last night?

Pepper slid his aviator sunglasses on and flung the door open to face bright sunshine. Clutching two packets of Alka-Seltzer and a glass, he steadied himself against the doorframe with one hand. This would hurt like hell, but he had to do it. He crept down the sidewalk to the communal bathroom. Rubber thongs flopped on his feet; a towel was slung over his shoulder. Seeing him, two Thai maids saw him and jabbered something to each other, giggled, and hustled out of the bathroom as he shuffled and groped his way to the sink. He splashed water into a glass, plopped in four tablets and watched them fizz. *Get 'em down, maybe I won't barf. Fuckin' snakes. Hate 'em. I'll never drink again.*

As the tablets dissolved, he let a shower steam and tried to recall what happened the night before. He remembered being at the party hooch and tossing down a drink or three after hearing about Roscoe. After Animal joined him he'd had a few more drinks to be sociable. It seemed like everyone who walked into the hooch had a favorite Roscoe story.

Fizz popped from the glass as he held it up to make sure there weren't any milky white chunks left at the bottom. He downed the bubbling elixir in three gulps. Then he reached down with both thumbs to hook his boxer shorts and step out of them. His thumbs found nothing to hook. *What the hell? I slept naked? Haven't done that since Osaka. Maids got a charge, I guess. Hey, how you boys doin' down there? Still with me?* He stepped into the hot shower. He remembered three slugs of Jeremiah Weed after Animal shook the dice and challenged everyone to play Twenty-One Aces for drinks. He lost count after that.

He let the hot water beat on his head and prayed for the Alka-Seltzer to kick in. A monstrous belch boiled up from his stomach and echoed off the walls. The stuff was starting to work.

"Pepper, that you in there?" Tron called, turning on the water in the adjoining stall.

"Yeah, but please hold it down."

"HA! HOW'S THIS? IS THIS TOO FRIGGIN' LOUD?"

"Man, give me a break. I'm dyin' here."

"Yeah, I bet you are. The squadron was in rare form last night. There hasn't been a night of walling around here in a long time."

"Walling?" Pepper turned to let the steaming water beat on the base of his neck.

"Yeah, don't you remember? Animal and you guys walled Maggot pretty good — the best I've seen in the ten months I've been here. Damn, I just realized, I'm getting short, less than sixty days to the world. Hallelujah, Lord. Amen!"

"Tron, there's a law against you being so happy while this ax is stuck in my forehead."

"Take some Alka-Seltzer."

"I did. I'm code three, busted. What's wallin'?"

"You don't remember? You, Animal, and a bunch of us found out Maggot was balling a Thai chick in his hooch. Stupid shit made the mistake of telling us he's engaged to a round-eye nurse in Okinawa. Anyway, his roommate let us in their room and someone had a Polaroid. We caught 'em butt naked, asleep on top of the sheets, wrapped around each other like snakes."

"Man, don't say snakes."

"You don't remember what we did?"

"Nope, not a thing after the third dice game. Did I get stupid? Need to apologize to anybody?" Pepper stepped from his shower stall and reached for his towel.

"Naw. It was just a standard whiskey front blowin' through. We better see if Maggot's still alive, though. About ten of us had our hands on the bedframe. After the Polaroid flash, we picked one side of the bed up and slammed it against the wall, while both humpers were still asleep. Animal snapped an *after* picture, then we stampeded outta there."

"Pictures turn out?"

"Yeah, they're great. Animal's gonna blackmail Maggot's ass to do anything we want. If he doesn't, we're gonna send the evidence to Okinawa."

"Shit hot!" *Thank God the stuff's workin' on my head.* Pepper leaned down to the sink for a long drink of tepid water.

"Since you don't remember any of that, you probably don't remember that A and B flights got tapped for the first launch this morning. We in C and D have an oh-nine-hundred intel briefing."

"Oh, shit. I forgot. Thanks."

"You're welcome, and by the way, you look like hell. Man, you'd need two heads to be any uglier."

"Eat shit and die, Tron."

*

The squadron briefing room was less formal than the base theater. It held 50 seats. With two flights of Phantom drivers it was only half full. Pepper sat three rows back on the aisle, nursing his second Coke, thankful for the miracle of carbonation. Between swallows he munched on a Baby Ruth. Maggot stepped over him to roll into the next seat.

"Hey, Pepper. Thanks for the wall-job last night, you prick. Really appreciate it."

Pepper downed the last of his Coke. "I don't remember a thing. I am innocent, lily-white, virgin clean."

"Who's got the pictures?"

"Pictures?"

"Yeah. I remember at least one flash before the bed hit the wall. I figure it's the ol' blackmail next. You got 'em?"

"Don't know what you're talkin' about. Maybe you should ask Animal."

"Oh, shit. Not Animal! I'm a dead man."

"You do what he says, he might show mercy."

The room fell quiet as Mad Dog walked to the front of the stage. The blue uniform cap sticking out of the leg pocket of his flight suit bore the silver leaf of lieutenant colonel, second in command of the Rams. He turned to face the crowd, arms folded across his chest. "Gentlemen, we have the LAU-3 arming problem fixed, but today we've got a whole different situation at Koh Tang. I've asked C-tone to give us an update and then I'll tell you what the flying schedule looks like.

"Dana, you have the floor."

"Thank you, Sir," she said, bouncing up the single step to the small stage. "Gentlemen, a major battle erupted this morning. Just after dawn, eleven

CH-53s — call sign Knife — and HH-53s — call sign Jolly — carrying two hundred Marines approached Koh Tang from the northwest. Three of the helos separated from the rest and unloaded a reinforced Marine platoon onto the USS *Harold E. Holt*, a Navy destroyer escort nearby. Their mission was to board and secure the *Mayaguez*." C-tone paused to check her notes. "The other eight helicopters, with 170 Marines aboard, continued in pairs to Koh Tang."

The willowy blonde placed a slide on the overhead projector and switched on the machine. "Koh Tang's this slingshot-shaped island. The helos split up in a two-pronged assault as they approached the island's northern end. One prong came around the left arm of the slingshot to LZ two, or landing zone two. The other prong went directly into the crotch area at the base of the slingshot's forks. That was to be LZ one."

Maggot leaned toward Pepper. "I love it when she talks about crotches."

Pepper smiled and swallowed the last bite of his Baby Ruth breakfast, never shifting his gaze from the photo.

"At LZ one, the helos made it in without resistance, but ran into a trap. As the first two hovered to offload Marines, they were caught in a hellish crossfire. Those flying behind the leaders watched as Knife 23 took punishing hits to its rotor system. To his left, Knife 31 took a pounding, burst into flames and crashed on the beach. The pilots of Knife 23 wrestled their wounded helo to the beach just as the tail section tore off. The twenty Marines on board fought their way to the tree line."

Maggot leaned toward Pepper again, and said, "Holy shit! This is gettin' serious. Are you sure Animal's got the pictures?"

Pepper leaned over and whispered, "I'm gonna find 'em and send 'em straight to your honey if you don't shut up."

"Okay, okay," Maggot said, slumping in his seat.

C-tone put a second slide on the overhead. "Gentlemen, this photo was taken from an RF-4 this morning right after the shoot-downs. You can see Knife 23 on the beach pretty much intact except for the tail rotor section." She walked to the screen and used a pointer to encircle a pile of green and black debris, part of it in the surf. "This is what remains of Knife 31. A survivor said they took hit after hit from automatic weapons and rocket-propelled grenades. He saw the copilot fire an M-16 out his window until he was killed by an RPG. There were numerous casualties in Knife 31. Somehow thirteen of our guys escaped. They swam away in a hail of bullets and were picked up at sea."

C-tone turned from the screen and faced the audience. "A survivor from a third helo said they had a lot of holes and an engine shot out. They skipped along the wave tops on one engine. They took on water each time and finally ditched a mile west of the island. One crewmember was killed. A fourth helo made it to the mainland before being forced down. Two more were heavily damaged and can't be used again.

"Gentlemen, over half of the available helos in this part of the world were lost in the initial assault. That's the bad news. Here's the worst: there are only fifty-four Americans now on Koh Tang, in two groups. They're facing approximately two hundred well-armed and fanatical Khmer Rouge — on their home turf. The only way for more Marines to get on the island is by helo. Questions?"

Paco raised his hand. "Why didn't we know the gooks were there?"

"There are no intelligence sources on the island and there wasn't enough time for overhead reconnaissance. We loaded the only available resources, helos, to the max with Marines and hoped for the best. Command couldn't be sure all of the *Mayaguez* crew had been taken to the mainland. Some might have been left on Koh Tang."

Pepper flinched. *Damn, camera was in the map case. I could have gotten a photo...*

"Do we know any more about the *Mayaguez* crew?" Animal asked.

C-tone looked at Mad Dog in his front row seat. "Sir, do you want me to elaborate?"

Mad Dog rose and stepped to the stage. "No, Dana, I'll take it. Thank you for your briefing. You're welcome to stay."

"Thank you, Sir, but I'm due at the command center to update Colonel Offal and the other squadron commanders." C-tone packed her slide case and hustled through a nearby door.

Mad Dog faced the group, hands on his hips, face somber. "While our helos and Marines were getting carved up by the Khmer, a Thai fishing boat approached the USS *Henry B. Wilson* under a white flag. They returned the entire crew of the *Mayaguez*. The crew was subsequently transferred to our ship and it's about to get underway. That's the good news.

"But gents, the situation on Koh Tang has gone to hell in a handbasket. Now, we'll have to get more Marines on the island to help extract the ones who're there. Our forces are scattered in the jungle in close combat. That means our jets can't do much to help, but A-7 Sandys from Korat did some heroic work against pockets of Khmer they spotted, which was tough. Remember, these guys run around in black pajamas, in a jungle they know real well. Anyway, we took out a couple of their gunboats trying to make it to Koh Tang, but the rest of our flights brought their ordnance home."

With the room shrouded in silence, Mad Dog folded his arms and walked slowly across the platform. "I'd like to give you guys a flying schedule you could plan on, but the situation is too fluid, and communication from Koh Tang is hard to come by," he said and turned to face them. "What I want you to do is this: pilots will be paired with their backseaters, so get your crew briefings out of the way. Then I want all of you to hang close in case you're needed on short notice. No errands, no leaving the squadron unless I approve. We'll have your meals brought over from the chow hall. Questions?"

There were none.

Mad Dog started to leave, then hesitated. "Oh, yeah, I nearly forgot. There'll be a memorial ceremony for Roscoe day after tomorrow, *depending* on how the operation goes. It'll be in front of the O'Club at noon. We're going to do an F-4 flyby with a missing-man formation. We'll be dedicating a statue to the best damn dog in Asia."

Not long after the intel briefing the squadron public address speakers paged Pepper to operations. His head had ceased throbbing. His eyes were clear.

Mad Dog sat at the ops counter. "Pepper, Raptor wants you to meet him in the command post right away."

"Yes, Sir. Should my wizzo go too?"

"Yeah, it wouldn't hurt. I'll sign you and Maggot out. Hustle it up."

Minutes later Pepper and Maggot jogged across the compound to the command post and after being cleared, were allowed in through the coded electric door. It was dark except for the large Plexiglas flight-following board covering the left wall. The board was illuminated and had multi-colored flights and times written in grease pencil. About midway across the room, a bank of telephones faced the board. Raptor sat, talking on one of the dozen telephones. Labeled "Cricket," his was the only red handset. Pepper and Maggot stood quietly, waiting for Raptor to finish his conversation.

"Okay, understand you need my best four-ship loaded for close air support. When? ASAP? You got it." Raptor paused, listening.

"Understand. Yes, Sir, we'll do our best. We can have them there in two hours." Raptor hung the receiver on the console.

Pepper stepped forward. "Sir, we were told you wanted us right away."

"Yep," he nodded. "You and Maggot pull up a couple chairs."

They each rolled a chair over and sat facing Raptor.

"Guys, it's getting ugly. We try to insert more Marines by helo, but they keep getting their shit blown away. Of the initial eleven helos, eight are done for. Our maintenance guys are doing their best to get a couple more put together and flyable. Anyway, our only close-air support ordnance is rockets and twenty mike-mike. Pepper, you got Top Gun for strafe in training."

"Yes, Sir."

"You probably have the most recent experience and they're going to need some good shooters." The gray metal chair squeaked as Raptor leaned forward to place emphasis. "Here's what I want you to do. Give me a lineup of the guys you want in your four-ship and the ordnance configuration you want. I don't need the crews right now, but I do need the configuration so maintenance can be loading the aircraft. Gentlemen, you have thirty minutes to brief and be at your aircraft."

Pepper gazed at the flight-following board for a moment, absorbing the information. "Sir, I think all our jets have the gun loaded on the centerline. I'd like to keep the gun on all and have number one and three loaded with LAU-3, Willy Petes; two and four loaded with Mark-82, 500-pound bombs, in case we need to bust something up."

"Okay. We already have two jets loaded with rockets and gun. We'll load the other two with six Mark-82s each."

"Sir, those are Marines we're supporting, right?"

"Affirmative, Pepper, about two-fifty."

"I know it's not the usual squadron call sign, but do you think we could use *Firehammer* for this mission?"

Raptor looked away at the flight-following board and hesitated. "Yeah, go ahead, use it. Do some good work down there. Meanwhile, don't let the doorknob hit you in the ass on the way out. Your thirty minutes are now twenty-five."

*

Pepper chose Animal as his deputy flight lead in the number three Phantom. The 10-minute briefing covered only essential items, but Pepper made a point to discuss the ordnance they'd carry. The rockets would be crucial if they found Marines in close combat on Koh Tang.

Pulling their four Phantoms into the arming area before take-off, the pilots felt a sense of urgency they hadn't seen the day before. There were "zebra-striped" super-sergeants everywhere. A lieutenant colonel confirmed that this time all pods were armed.

Firehammer was airborne in record time, only 45 minutes after Pepper got the tasking from Raptor. With no radar control for vectoring, they had difficulty finding their tankers over the Gulf of Thailand, but hook-ups were routine. Soon, they were full of JP-4 and approaching the target area.

"Hot damn, Maggot!" Pepper said. "We're on the pointy-end of the sword now."

"Yep. The cavalry to the rescue, boys. The Four Horsemen of the Apocalypse are ridin' hellbent for leather...and justice is comin' with them."

"Did you feel a whole different attitude from everybody? I mean the guys in the flight are serious as hell, like they're leaning forward in the saddle," Pepper said, looking left and right to check the positions of his three wingmen. "And the maintainers busted their tails getting these jets ready so fast." *Gotta get pumped. I'm leading four Phantoms into battle with the best guys in the squadron. Ass kickin' ordnance, too. Firehammer. Shit hot!*

Pepper keyed the mike button on the right throttle: "Cricket, Firehammer, flight of four fox-fours with you, sixty-eight miles northwest of Koh Tang."

"Firehammer, proceed inbound pronto, we've got work for you with Nail 47 and 68, forward air controllers overhead the island presently."

"Roger. Pushin' it up."

Pepper alerted the flight. "Firehammer, fence check. Green 'em up. Go to spread formation. Stand by to check guns on my call."

Test firing the Gatling guns was not usually done, but with the weapons problems the day before, Pepper wanted to know the guns would fire before committing them for close support of Marines. He reached down and moved the weapons select from HEAT to GUNS, then flipped the MASTER ARM toggle to ARM. The jet was hot.

Okay, everybody's spread out. Should be ready. "Firehammer, guns, guns, guns."

Pepper squeezed the trigger on the control stick and watched tracers arc in front. He quickly looked left and right to see tracers from the other three. "Shit hot. All guns are workin'."

"Firehammer, Cricket, need for you to enter overhead the island at five thousand feet. We've got Klong 960, flight of four C-130s above us. They're packin' BLU-82B on board, fifteen-thousand pounders to blow LZs in the jungle if we need 'em."

"Firehammer, copy. We're out of twenty thousand for five."

As the island came into view, Pepper developed a mental picture of the airpower stacked overhead to make extraction of the Marines possible. He needed a playbook to keep the players straight.

Going vertical from the island, there should be two Nail FACs, one low, one high in OV-10 Broncos. We should be next in the stack, followed by Cricket as command and control. Klong will be above them. All these aircraft, and we're the only shooters...

"Firehammer, this is Nail 47. High FAC. Go ahead with your lineup."

"All four Phantoms have twenty mike-mike. Numbers one and three have LAU-3 rockets. Numbers two and four have Mark-82s."

"Nail 47, copy."

Pepper brought the flight over the south end of the island and began a sweeping left-hand turn around the atoll. For the first time he was able to get a good look. The "slingshot" pointed north, just as C-tone had said. White sand beaches bordered the island's lush green jungle. Emerald green shallows deepened to dark blue. Two CH-53 carcasses lay on the beach, in stark contrast to all the natural beauty. To the north end of the island a gray OV-10 Bronco circled. Gone from its anchorage east of Koh Tang, the SS *Mayaguez* steamed northwest.

There goes the ship. What the hell are we fightin' for now? A couple of grenades just flashed. Mortar rounds cookin' off. Tracers back and forth. Looks like a cauldron of pain down there.

"Firehammer, this is Nail 68. I'll take over now. Do you see me over the north end of the island?"

"Roger."

"I want your rockets and mike-mike first; then we'll see if we can use the Mark-82s."

"Firehammer, copy.

"Three, join my right wing. We're going down to work with Nail. Two and Four hold high."

"Okay. FACs into mark," Nail 68 called. "Your target will be where my rocket goes."

Pepper watched the Bronco roll sharply on its back, then upright. A single Willy Pete streaked toward the edge of a clearing near the "crotch." A thin column of bright white smoke billowed among the jungle growth and coconut palms near the water.

"Firehammer's 'tally ho.' Looks like the hooches are the target."

"Affirmative. Hit my mark with your rockets, Firehammer. You're restricted to a run-in heading to the southeast only. Pilots off one of the helos, and some Marines are just to the northwest — close. Can you put your rockets where I just put mine?"

"Firehammer, affirmative. How many do you want?"

"Let's try two pods on the first pass. Knife Two-Three from one of the downed helos is close to the target with a radio. Knife, keep your heads down."

"Roger. Bring it on."

"Firehammer, you're cleared hot."

Maggot coached Pepper: "Thirty-seven mils on the sight, twenty degree dive, four-fifty knots, twenty-five hundred feet slant range. Remember, light in the seat when you pickle."

"Sight set. We're armed. Rockets are hot. Outboard pods selected on both wings. Time to rain death and destruction. The Prince of Peace is in, to the southeast."

Now, smartass, put this stuff where it needs to go, give 'em some peace.

"Firehammer's in hot," Pepper called, a hint of anger in his voice. He rolled the Phantom in a hard left, descending turn, then slapped the wings back right to level. The sight was now below the drifting smoke. He pushed the throttles forward to grab 450 knots as soon as possible.

Maggot started the altitude cadence: "Thirty-five hundred...three thousand...twenty-five hundred, check slant range. Pickle anytime."

Sight's just below the smoke. Need more nose down trim, get light in the seat. Four-sixty, power back. Dive angle good. Sight's on the smoke. Let 'em rip. With his right thumb, Pepper smashed the red button on the control stick. "Pickle!"

Thirty-eight rockets screamed from the jet, turning the air brown with exhaust, their heat waves obscuring the target. If he watched them hit, Pepper knew his Phantom would hit right behind them. Pulling hard on the stick to lift the big jet's nose above the horizon, he jinked the Phantom right, then hard left to evade ground fire. From the jungle a Khmer rocket arced toward Pepper's Phantom. *Not even close, asshole...*

"Felt good. How'd it look?" Maggot asked.

"Awesome! Those *Petes* are faster than the speed of heat. Better than Sidewinders. Last I saw they were headed to the smoke."

"Perfect. William Peter's gonna burn your house down, Khmer queers."

"This is Knife Two-Three. Those were real close!"

"Firehammer Lead, those were fifty feet short," Nail called. "You hit the smoke, but it's drifting. You gotta hit the target — the hooches."

"Firehammer One, roger," Pepper sounded calm, but his heart rate shot off the charts. The heat of self-doubt flushed his face; sweat rolled into one eye. He continued the climbing left-hand turn to enter a box pattern around the island.

"Firehammer Three, you got the hooches? Can you put your rockets right on 'em?" Nail asked.

"Three, affirmative," Animal replied.

"Firehammer Three, cleared hot. Restricted heading."

"Three's in hot. Hooches in sight. FAC in sight."

Put it on 'em, Animal! Smoke 'em.

Chatter between the cockpits stopped. Pepper fingered the Zippo in his chest pocket and fished it out. Glancing at the inscription, he rubbed his gloved right thumb — his pickle finger — across it for luck. Slipping the lighter back into his pocket, he looked down and left to see Animal's rockets explode in a mushroom cloud inside the enemy's compound.

"That's it, my friends, that's it!" Nail shouted. "Firehammer One, you're cleared hot."

"One, copy. Target's in sight. FAC's in sight. I'd like to expend twenty mike-mike *and* rockets on this pass."

"Firehammer, cleared rockets and mike-mike," Nail confirmed.

"Guns and rockets are selected, Maggot. If it looks good, I'll fire 'em both."

"Roger. Lay some severe hate on'em."

Pepper continued in the box pattern until he was ready. He rolled the Phantom into a hard left turn and began sliding down the 20-degree slope toward the target. *Nothing much to shoot at...*It was like drawing aim on a white-tailed buck when all he could see was its shoulder outlined in the brush. The cross hairs had to be dead steady or there would be a miss, or worse.

Friendlies are close, real close.

"Maggot, call the pickle, but I'm gonna press closer than last time. Call my pull point too."

"Roger. Just don't watch the rockets hit."

Dive's wired, speed's set. Sight's just below where the hooches should be. Jet's trimmed. Light in the seat. Perfect. Precise.

The billowing plume from Animal's rockets drifted slowly toward the bay, away from the target. As the target cleared, Pepper flew straight as an acrobat sliding down a wire. As he closed, he spotted burning hooches. Soldiers in black pajamas scurried out of them and dodged into the jungle. One Khmer's clothes were afire as he ran, then tumbled into a ditch. Another stopped, shouldered his AK-47 and began firing at Pepper head on.

"Thirty-five hundred...three thousand...twenty-five hundred...there's slant range. Pickle!" Maggot yelled.

"Pressing."

"Two thousand feet — you better FIRE!"

Pepper pressed the pickle button with his right thumb and squeezed the trigger with his finger. A second cluster of 38 rockets screamed from his wings. Again the air turned hot and brown in front of him. The faint sound of ripping canvas as the Gatling gun's six barrels spun to 6000 rounds per minute signaled blazing death.

"Thousand feet. Pull — Pull — PULL!" Maggot shouted.

Pepper had already started the stick aft at six and a half Gs in less than two seconds. Moisture ribbons trailed his wingtips; the Phantom's wings fogged. Both men neared blackout and grunted loudly to keep some vision.

Here come the trees, we're gonna be damn close.

As he got nearer, the rush came faster. Pepper fought the stick to get the jet's vector above the tree line before it was too late.

Peering out the sides of the canopy, Maggot saw green whipping by under the wings. "Did we clip 'em?"

Pepper racked the jet erratically, right, left, right, pulled the nose up, then slapped a hard left turn to avoid ground fire. "Nope," he said.

Firehammer One's red fireball tracers arced across an emerald carpet of tropical treetops. They flew toward the Khmer Rouge with hundreds of invisible high-explosive incendiary rounds. A few hundred feet farther, all rounds merged with 2.75-inch rockets to cut trees in half and rip through hooches and grass shacks. Burning white phosphorus splattered in all directions.

The 20mm was dense and furious. At close range, it gutted everything and everybody inside an area the size of two tennis courts. Three more structures burst into flames; several black-clad bodies burst apart, arms and legs flying through the acrid, smoke-filled air. At this patch of jungle in Southeast Asia, Armageddon had arrived.

Years of repressed anger bubbled to the surface. Pepper wanted the target annihilated. He rolled his jet left in a climbing turn for another look. White smoke mushroomed from the heart of the compound. Secondary explosions cooked off from stored ammunition. Tracers arced in all directions like star bursts on the Fourth of July. His ordnance spent, Pepper slammed the throttles into burner and victory-rolled the jet over and over.

That's for our buds that didn't make it, you bastards...

"That's it, Firehammer!" Nail shouted. "No need to hit that one again. What's still standin' is burnin'."

Pepper leveled his Phantom and looked over his left shoulder at Koh Tang. He transferred the control stick to his left hand, and brought his right one to his helmet visor to salute.

...Semper fi, Tim.

Nail called, "Firehammer Three, we're gonna move your rockets fifty meters northwest. There's a machine-gun and mortar emplacement there. We gotta take it out. FAC's in to mark."

"Firehammer Three, copy."

Nail 68 circled left to set up for his rocket pass. Close to the action, he could spot movement, but he made an easy target just 1,000 feet above the fray in his slow-moving Bronco.

"Firehammer, stand by," Nail said. "Taking ground fire near the western LZ. Gotta defend."

The last part of his transmission was strained, almost drowned by a background of revving twin turboprops. Pepper looked down to his left. Nail had stopped his arcing circle, rolling the Bronco on its back, jerking the nose toward the ground. Smoke trailed the aircraft from the 7.62 minigun, a miniature Gatling. Its barrels swirled, spitting tracers and high-explosive lead down the throats of Khmer gunners.

"Okay, Firehammers, they're quiet. I'm visual. Cleared hot, Three."

"Three's in hot with Willy and mike-mike. FAC's in sight."

Pepper leveled his Phantom at 5000 feet. From the left side of his canopy, he had a good view of Animal's attack, and he could see the Nail's gray Bronco circling south of the smoke plume created by his attack. Animal's jet flew straight and smooth as a launched arrow.

"This is like one kid watching another zinging down a slide on the playground," Maggot said. "Hope he puts some precise hurt on 'em."

Rockets streaked ahead and 20mm cannon smoke streamed behind Animal's jet as it tore into the Khmer gun emplacement. Sand, dust, and hundreds of sparkles erupted in the small clearing as Willy Petes turned the air white hot.

"Looks like hell on earth down there!" Maggot said.

"Shit-fuckin'-hot, Animal!" Pepper shouted.

"Their officers' club will be closed tonight!" Maggot was ecstatic. "Turn out the lights, the party's over," he sang.

"I think we created a new attack with this twenty millimeter and Mr. William Peter," Pepper said. "Let's call it 'Shake 'n Bake.'"

"Perfect."

Pulling up from the attack, Animal jinked his Phantom left, then right, and called, "Firehammer Three's off, Winchester." He was out of bullets and rockets.

The flight was low on fuel, particularly Firehammer One and Three. Two and Four had time to make one pass each. Nail wanted to keep their 500-pounders clear of the Marines, so they rippled all six into the jungle beyond their position. The bone-jarring noise dwarfed Khmer mortar explosions. Their intended effect would be psychological: Khmer would wonder what devastation will rain on them next; Marines on the isolated atoll would know that America's airpower was alive and well.

"Nail, this is Knife. I don't have much battery life left in this survival radio. Before I lose comm, those last two passes hurt 'em bad. We might be able to get out of here before long if we have any helos left."

"Knife, this is Nail. Copy all. We have two choppers standing by and another one on the way."

"Good. We need 'em…"

✳✳✳

Chapter 21

THE CRUCIBLE OF

VIETNAM

...Sunward I've climbed, and joined the tumbling mirth
Of sun-split clouds and done a hundred things
You have not dreamed of—
wheeled and soared and swung...

—John Gillespie Magee, "High Flight"

A fighter pilot often flies great distances to targets he's never seen. He drops into battle for a few minutes and does his best to kill the enemy or destroy their fortifications. They call it close-air support, or CAS, because friendlies are very close to enemy forces. Infantry units think of CAS as "airborne artillery." When employed properly, it reduces the combat pressure on them.

Koh Tang was such a place and one of the roughest CAS missions a fighter pilot could imagine. On a small, distant island, opposing forces locked at each other's throats. Marines had no place to maneuver to take advantage of airpower's full arsenal. With their backs to the sea, they were surrounded by a well-trained and numerically superior force. No trucks waited to take the Marines to safety; no landing craft stood ready to storm the beach. Extraction could be done only by helo and only three of eleven choppers remained. They were battle-damaged as well.

The *Mayaguez* crew was returned. A long, arduous war in Southeast Asia was nearly over. There was no reason to stay engaged in combat on Koh Tang, but downed Air Force crewmen and stranded Marines remained to be extracted. The ground commander decided to leave the island and not remain engaged with the illusive enemy throughout the night.

It was late afternoon when Firehammer Flight departed Koh Tang. Their attack had killed a third of the Khmer Rouge force and set the compound ablaze. As darkness fell, the fire became a beacon in the ink-black expanse, serving as a navigation fix for the helos and Marines as they fought their way off the island.

Enemy resistance remained fanatical. The remaining helos worked to save over 200 Marines as darkness descended. At one point a Khmer Rouge platoon — seeing the Marines escaping — stormed the helicopter and reached hand-grenade range. Just as a Khmer started to hurl a grenade, he and his entire group were cut down by the only functional minigun left on the chopper. After that burst, the minigun jammed and Marines aboard fired their M-16s as they lifted off. The few helos remaining made repeated trips into this vortex of hell to extract all Marines. "Take 'em all," one HH-53 pilot shouted as they took off with 54 Marines — twice the maximum allowable load.

As the last helo lifted off from Koh Tang, the men aboard saw only the eerie wink of an abandoned strobe light on the beach. All that had been the crucible of the Vietnam War was over.

Because the war-weary, battle-damaged Phantoms had been shot through and patched so many times, they no longer enjoyed the luxury of a routine flight. Weird things continually happened and Firehammer's flight from Koh Tang was no exception. Pepper departed the target area with adequate fuel on the gauge, but while he checked the jet's individual tanks on climb out, he noticed that his internal wing fuel was trapped. It would not be usable. As in the Saigon mission, he headed once more to an emergency tanker.

"Maggot, the internal wings aren't gonna feed."

"Maybe we took a hit from the gooks."

"Yeah, maybe. The other tanks are feeding, but there's not much left in 'em."

"Not good."

"I'm gonna tell Animal. Firehammer Three, we've got trapped fuel in the wings. How about lookin' us over and see if we took any hits."

"Roger."

Animal moved behind and below Pepper's left wing. He slid under Pepper's Phantom searching for telltale signs of external damage or leakage. Sliding up to Pepper's right wing he called, "You're clean, Pepper. I've had fuel trapped like that. Blowin' the empty tanks off changed the internal wing pressurization. That made 'em start feeding."

"Okay Two, move out to spread and I'll blow 'em."

Pepper looked down to the left console to find the red WING STATION JETTISON switch. He checked that Animal was a safe distance away. Numbers Two and Four flew beyond him to the right. He raised the covered switch and flipped the toggle. He heard a muffled "thump" as two empty 370-gallon tanks peeled away and fell toward the Gulf of Thailand.

"Whoa," Pepper said, looking at the fuel gauge. "Look at those tanks feed now."

"Yee haw, that did it," Maggot said. "We ain't taken a swim today. We're headed to the party hooch tonight!"

Pepper dipped his wing to the left, signaling Animal to cross under and resume his position as they returned to Korat. Pepper called Cricket and checked out of the battle area.

After hours of being cinched tight, the outline of Pepper's oxygen mask was etched on his face. That outline always marked who'd been flying and for how long.

Lieutenant Colonel Stump Collins was the first person Pepper saw as he entered the squadron.

"Raptor wants a debrief of the mission ASAP," he said. "He's in his office."

"Yes, Sir. I'm headed there now."

Pepper still found the commander's office intimidating. Raptor had the power to give and the power to take away.

The admin sergeant ushered him in immediately. Pepper stopped in front of the commander's desk and held a salute. "Captain Houston reporting, Sir."

"Have a seat, Pepper," Raptor said, returning the salute. "How'd it go?"

"Maintenance did a terrific job giving us jets on time and our ordnance worked," he said, taking a chair.

"How did the tanker guys do on the rendezvous?"

"Fine, Sir. We had trouble finding them visually, but finally got all four hook-ups, and topped off before heading to Koh Tang. My radar was weak, but Three finally got a contact and called the tanker's turn." Pepper leaned back in the chair and crossed his legs.

"How'd it look when you got to the island? Reports from there have been scarce."

"Well, Sir, you were right. Things had gone to hell. It was tight in a small area." Pepper intertwined the fingers of both hands and held them up. "The friendlies and gooks were all mixed up together. It was tough to figure out where our guys were. We had two Nail FACs overhead who did a super job. I just trusted them to put us on the target and they did. That's the first time I'd ever worked with a FAC."

"First time, huh? I guess they don't let us train with them anymore."

"He was close to the action and marked the target. I hit his smoke with the first set of rockets, but the smoke had drifted. They were about fifty feet short."

"Hell, I think a qualifying rocket is inside seventy feet," Raptor said.

"Yes, Sir. I guess so. I've never qualified in rockets."

"No shit?"

"I fired one in training and it went berserk. Anyway, it was familiarization only. I didn't have to qualify. They said we'd probably never shoot rockets for real with all the high-tech ordnance in the inventory."

"Did your flight hit any friendlies?"

"I don't think so. I know my rockets got pretty close because one of the guys on the ground said so. I think it was Knife Two-Three."

"That was probably a pilot from one of the CH-53s that were shot down."

"Could've been. Animal adjusted from my rockets and put his right on 'em." Antsy, Pepper uncrossed his legs and put both feet on the floor.

"You guys should have had two pods left. Did the FAC use 'em?"

"Yes, Sir, and the twenty millimeter. My instructor told me once that the gun and rockets have the same trajectory. He said it was possible to fire them at the same time. Since we were short on gas, I decided to try both if the pass looked good."

"Yeah, you can, but you better have a lot of experience." Raptor gazed steadily at Pepper as he leaned back in his chair and crossed his arms. "Most pilots get channelized doing both, and point their jet at the ground too long." His eyes narrowed. "Did you?"

"Sorta. We, ah, got a little closer than I would've liked."

"Clip any trees?"

"No, Sir. No branches stuck in the belly on post flight."

"Good. I'd hate to fire your ass for trashing *another* Phantom after all of this."

Is the ol' man grinning? "Not necessary, Sir. We done good — I think. Nail said there wasn't anything to shoot at after my second pass. Lots of secondary explosions and stuff. He moved Animal's rockets to a gun pit and hammered 'em real good."

"What about the Mark-82s?"

"Two and Four made one pass and pretty much dumped them well beyond the —"

There was a knock on the door, then the wing commander strode into the office. Raptor and Pepper shot to their feet.

"Take your seats, gents," the colonel said, grabbing the chair next to Pepper.

Pepper's brow broke into a sweat; his leg began to jiggle. Nerves. He had never been face to face with a light colonel and a full bird. They didn't ask him to leave, so he sat quietly.

"Just got an intel report from Cricket, Bill," the colonel said. "The Nail FAC says it was very *close* close-air support, down there. Did our boys put some rockets on 'em late this afternoon?"

"Yes, Sir. That was Captain Houston's flight. He was just briefing me on the mission."

The colonel shifted his eyes from Raptor, stared at Pepper and hesitated.

Here it comes. Too close, we got some friendlies. They stared at each other, the colonel's face expressionless. Pepper's right hand went to the left chest pocket of his flight suit and he felt the outline of the lighter. His mouth dry, he couldn't swallow.

No! Damn it! Tell me we didn't kill any Marines. Tell me that, Colonel!

"The report said hooches and the entire compound area are still burning from the white phosphorous. After dark, it was the only thing the helos and Marines could use for a reference. There were no navigation aids, no way to locate people except for taking bearings off the fire."

The colonel stood and walked to the big window, holding the ever-present FM command radio in his left hand. He placed his right hand on his hip gazing at the ramp and blue taxiway lights. Raptor's chair squeaked as he rotated to face him.

"Got any Wild Turkey?" the colonel asked.

"Yes, Sir." Raptor leaned forward and opened the bottom left drawer of his desk. He placed three shot glasses on the desk and filled them. Raptor handed one glass to the colonel and one to Pepper.

"Two pieces of news," the colonel said, touching his glass to Raptor's, then holding it toward Pepper, who walked around the desk to clink his glass with the colonel's. "The first is…the Vietnam War is finally over. This was the last battle."

The three pilots held their glasses high, then downed them in the traditional gulp. The colonel grinned and said, "How about one more, Raptor?"

"Yes, Sir.

"Pepper?"

"Yes, Sir. Thank you." *The prisoner's last wish before he's executed.*

"Another bit of news came from Nail," the colonel said, setting his radio and hat on Raptor's desk. "He reports that our Firehammer Flight did some good work. They set the place on fire, and using his words, 'kicked some serious ass.' He counted thirty-nine KIAs in the compound area alone.

"Best news of all, the Marines are off the island and scattered to three ships." The colonel reached for his glass and held it up to toast. "Raptor, you and your squadron did a helluva job on a tough mission today. Thanks...and congratulations."

"Thank you, Colonel, but Houston and his flight did the work and with very little preparation." Raptor drained his glass and set it down. "I'd like to put 'em in for Distinguished Flying Crosses."

"Do it. They deserve 'em," he said, smiling at Pepper.

"Sir," Pepper hesitated, but stared at the colonel, "if I could make a request...I'd like to trade the DFC."

"For what, Captain?"

"To fly the number three position tomorrow in Roscoe's flyby."

A slow grin spread across the colonel's face. "You want to do the pull and be the missing man, huh?"

"Yes, Sir, I do."

"What if I told you that I picked A-7s to do the flyby?"

"Sir, I'd say that's okay, let 'em do the flyby — right in front of the F-4s. We should be last and do the pull."

"Why?"

"Because Roscoe was a Ram dog, Sir. He flew here from Taiwan in a 34th pilot's lap. He rode to the runway in the Ram commander's jeep for every launch and recovery during the war. He was always there. Roscoe was a Ram, Sir. He won't get a DFC, but he should get Phantoms."

The colonel looked at Raptor, then back at Pepper. "You drive a hard bargain, Houston. You're right, Roscoe was a Ram." The colonel set his shot glass down on Raptor's desk and thought for a few seconds, then said, "Okay, here's what we do. I can only approve one flyby. It'll be F-4s. Raptor, you lead. Houston, you fly number three. Be on timing for the pull." The colonel turned his back to them and again looked out the window.

"Pepper, just before you pull up, have the throttles outboard. Then go to burner just as you start the pull. I want lots of noise."

"Raptor, after he pulls, you three close your formation and light your burners too. I need for this thing to be a morale booster. Make it look good. Make it sound good."

"Yes, Sir," Raptor acknowledged.

"Sirs, one more request?"

"Damn, you're full of 'em, aren't you, Pepper?" the colonel said, turning from the window.

"Can Lieutenant Penix fly in my backseat?"

"PeeWee? Good idea. Do it." The colonel grabbed his hat and radio from Raptor's desk. "Gotta go. Good job. Do another good one tomorrow," he said, then paused as he turned for the door.

"Who's with you in the picture there with the Skyhawk, Bill? Did you have an exchange tour with the Navy?"

"No, Sir. I didn't fly off a carrier, but my son, Randy, did. He was an A-4 pilot off the *Kennedy*, Gulf of Tonkin."

"Hey, super! What's he doing now?"

"He was killed in a close-air mission with Marines. A ZSU got him."

"Damn, Bill. Sorry. This war got to all of us in one way or the other," he said, bending to take a closer look at the picture. "Not much longer.

We're going home soon. What's that on the canopy, in quotes under his name?"

"It's *Zippo*, Sir. That was his call sign. Anybody needed a light, he always had his Zippo."

That's why Raptor hesitated when I asked for the "Zippo" call sign.

Pepper stood quietly as two battle-scarred, weary warriors faced each other. Sheer guts and dedication had carried them through three combat tours. Their losses weighed on them. Finally, it was over.

"Sorry about your son," the colonel said, extending his hand once again. "Do you want to use 'Zippo' for your call sign tomorrow?"

Raptor shook hands and thought for a moment, glanced at Pepper then back to the colonel. "Thank you, Sir, but tomorrow's Roscoe's day. How about we use Roscoe Zero-One?"

"Sounds good. Later, gentlemen." He keyed the radio as he walked out through the office door: "Command Post, Korat One is mobile."

Raptor and Pepper heard, "Command Post, roger, Sir," as he walked down the dimly lit hall.

There would be a base-wide, one-hour stand-down for Roscoe's memorial service. The dedication flyby was planned for 1100 hours, just as the service ended.

A local Thai woodcarver performed a miracle. In two days he produced a life-sized sculpture of Roscoe sitting upright, mouth open and panting in what looked like a smile. The light-colored teak was unvarnished and placed atop a special brick platform in front of the officers' club entrance where gardeners created a small quadrangle under the flagpole. An engraved brass plaque was to be dedicated and hung at the service. Hundreds would attend.

Before the mission was briefed, Pepper took PeeWee to life support where he was fitted with G-suit, parachute harness, and helmet. They also trained him in the Phantom's ejection system.

At the squadron, Raptor called for the flyby briefing to be held in a regular briefing room instead of his office. Out of character, he covered all the routine items himself, then elaborated on the missing-man portion. "Okay, Three, as we approach the flagpole I'll give you two *ready* calls. At five seconds to TOT, the first *ready* means to ease your jet slightly high in the formation. They won't be able to see it from the ground and it'll put you above our wing vortices when you pull. You won't bobble the formation that way."

Pepper nodded.

"The second *ready* means to get the throttles outboard and stand by to go to burner. The last call I'll make is *pull.* I want a sharp five-Gs and afterburners cookin'. Once you're vertical, you can do aileron rolls until PeeWee pukes."

Raptor chuckled as PeeWee's face turned pale.

Raptor looked at Paco and continued, "Four, once Three has pulled, I want you to close the formation and get ready to go into afterburner. The Wing King wants us to look good and sound good. Let's do it."

"What's jingling in your flight suit?" Pepper asked PeeWee as they walked to life support.

"That's Roscoe's collar and dog tags. I figured we ought to have him along."

"Good idea. It's nice to know with all this crap going on, that we can do something for Roscoe." Pepper glanced at PeeWee as they walked. "I'm glad we're flying the Three position."

"Roger."

At 1055 hours plus 20 seconds, Roscoe Flight of four Phantoms departed its holding point at 360 knots. Timing would place the aircraft over the officers' club flagpole precisely at 1100, while the flag was lowered to half-staff.

Raptor keyed his mike: "Korat Tower, Roscoe Flight is departing the holding fix. Be over the flag in four plus forty seconds."

"Roscoe Zero-One, roger. You own the airdrome, Sirs. Weather clear except for one small cloud overhead. Winds light and variable, altimeter two, niner-niner, two."

Raptor rolled out on the heading that would take them to the flag, then eased the flight down to 1000 feet altitude. They were in classic "fingertip formation," close and lined up like the fingers of a person's right hand. Raptor flew middle finger in the lead position. Pepper flew as Three, the ring finger. Animal and Paco were the pilots in numbers Two and Four. When Pepper pulled to vertical, the ring finger would be gone, leaving a space in the formation, signifying a missing man. Today it was Roscoe.

The four held "Thunderbird" tight formation, wingtips overlapping and in perfect alignment as Raptor powered up for 360 knots. As he called "Roscoe — Ready," Pepper eased his Phantom three feet higher than the rest. He could see Raptor's jet below. At the second "Ready," Pepper moved both throttles outboard, working hard to maintain precise alignment. He didn't dare move his eyes from Raptor's jet to see the flagpole.

"Pull!"

Pepper buried the control stick in his lap and shoved the throttles to the wall. "Hang on, PeeWee," he grunted. "This'll be over soon."

"It's…okay," PeeWee said, straining to get the words out as his oxygen mask sagged on his lips. "We're Roscoe, goin' to Heaven."

Raptor called, "Roscoe Zero-One, flight of three, burners now!"

Pepper's Phantom arced to pure vertical. Sunward he climbed, afterburners shooting fire, trailing hundred-foot blow torches.

"PeeWee, am I seeing things?" Pepper said. "That cloud ahead looks like a dog's head, an ear, a muzzle."

"Yeah, I see it."

Pepper moved the stick full to the right and the Phantom corkscrewed in roll, after roll, after roll. They burst through the cloud on their way to 10,000 feet. The Phantom climbed like it was shot out of a cannon. In a few seconds, and nearly out of sight from those below, Pepper rolled the Phantom on its back as it ran out of airspeed. Their timing was perfect. The jet was spent.

"Ol' Roscoe would've barked at that," PeeWee said weakly.

Inverted with the world upside down, Pepper looked down at the cloud. "Yeah. So long, buddy."

Raptor called, "Roscoe Three — Pepper, you're cleared to join my right wing for landing."

*

As Pepper and PeeWee walked down the sidewalk from life support to the squadron, PeeWee stopped for a moment and reached for the leg pocket of his flight suit. A dog tag and vaccination tag jingled on Roscoe's collar as he pulled it out. "Captain, I think you should have this," he said.

Pepper stood holding the thick, brown leather collar. He turned it over and watched the tags swing. Roscoe's name was engraved on the back of a tag shaped like a Ram squadron patch. Only two weeks ago, Pepper had looked up from refueling under the tanker. Roscoe's face, with his tongue hanging lazily out of his mouth, had stared at him through the boom operator's window, PeeWee by his side.

I fought for my life against Yellow Star that day. Seems so long ago...

"Thanks, PeeWee. I know how special this is to you," he said, setting down his flight bag. "How about you keep the collar and I take the tags? That way we both have something of Roscoe's."

"Okay, good idea. Maybe that's why you're a captain and I'm still a second lieutenant, huh?" he said, smiling.

"You'll be wearing those bars before you know it," Pepper said, twisting the S-shaped hook to remove the tags. He handed PeeWee the collar and removed the dog tag chain from his own neck. He took it off and threaded Roscoe's tags on with his, bent the hook back and shook the chain. "Sounds better," he said, retrieving his flight bag and walking toward the squadron.

"War's over, PeeWee. Let's go home."

***

Epilogue

THE WALL

This is earth again, the earth where I've lived and now will live once more...I've been to eternity and back. I know how the dead would feel to live again.

—Charles Lindbergh
On sighting Ireland after his first solo Atlantic crossing, 1927

As if gathering for a mass military formation, they came from all directions to be there at the appointed time. Along nearly every street in Washington D.C., men wore whatever still remained of their uniforms as they made their way on foot, on crutches, or in wheelchairs. Proud, their heads up, they were silent. Thousands were drawn to the Vietnam Veteran's Memorial on the day of its dedication: November 13, 1982.

Robyn, an Air Force nurse, and Pepper, the commander of an F-15 Eagle squadron at Langley AFB in Virginia, arrived early with their two children. Now a lieutenant colonel, small crow's feet radiated from the corners of Pepper's eyes and a touch of gray frosted his temples. All things considered, the post-war years had been kind to him. Pepper wore civilian clothing except for his father's old and faded brown leather flight jacket from World War Two. The jacket honored the year his father had served in Vietnam.

Pepper and Robyn stood at a distance on a low, tree-covered hill, watching as the muted crowd gathered in the grassy bowl between them and the memorial. From his perch, Pepper marveled at the elegant simplicity of the long, black wall, a magnet drawing together a throng of warriors.

The wall formed a large, horizontal "V" as it angled downward into the ground. Its shiny granite panels bore the names of more than 58,000 young men and women who died in America's longest war. Bedecked in red, white, and blue bunting and American flags, the speaker's stand stood above and behind the wall.

Pepper remained on the rise away from the crowd. As a pilot he had flown over the carnage and fought in the last battle of the war, but unlike most of these men, he hadn't been in the trenches for months on end. Although, it was time for those who had served in Vietnam to honor dead friends and comrades. It wasn't yet time for him to go forward. Hanging back, lost in his thoughts, he heard the speakers' voices, but not their words.

He leaned and whispered to Robyn, "Tim was funny. Siphoning gas out of my folks' car. He gagged and coughed; we figured we'd get caught. We got lucky." Pepper hesitated, fighting back the lump building in his throat. "We didn't have any money and had to replace some of the gas we used joy-riding all night in his parents' new Plymouth."

She gazed up at him. "Did he have a girlfriend?" she whispered.

"Yeah. Dory. She was Tim's first and last love; neither one of 'em ever wanted anybody else," he said…his mind drifting. He remembered Tim wearing his Marine dress blues to church the day before leaving for Vietnam. Always muscular from lifting weights, he looked especially hard and lean after boot camp at Parris Island.

Older than the rest of us…

They flinched as the first of three volleys from seven rifles echoed across the long reflecting pool between the Lincoln and Washington memorials.

"Daddy, why did they shoot those guns?" four-year-old Janice asked, her red hair in pigtails, her bright blue eyes searching for an answer.

"That's the way they remember people who can't be here," he answered, kissing her cheek, and putting his arm on Scotty's shoulder. The rounds faded to the mournful refrain of a lone trumpeter playing "Taps."

Pepper recalled the time he heard those sounds, on a hot August day in 1966 when they buried Tim at a beautiful cemetery in the country near Mobile.

Tillman's Corner, Alabama. A lifetime ago.

As the trumpeter finished, the crowd dwindled.

"Are you coming to the wall with me?" he asked Robyn.

She hesitated and squeezed his hand. "You go. Tim was your friend. Take your time. We'll wait here."

He gazed directly into her eyes for confirmation. "Okay," he said, squeezing and releasing her hand. He squatted and hugged both children.

"I'm going down there to tell an old friend good-bye. I'll be back in just a few minutes." Both children nodded.

Pepper made his way to the panels for 1966. Scattered along the length of the wall, people stood, their eyes teary, staring at beloved names. As he drew closer he saw a veteran in jungle boots and fatigue pants, probably from Vietnam days. His threadbare field jacket bore the Big Red One of the First Infantry Division on its shoulder. Pony-tailed and bearded, he leaned against the wall with one arm, his other hand covering his eyes as he wept.

Pepper stopped in front of panel 9E, searching with longing and dread. His eyes finally found what he was looking for: "Timothy Scott." For long moments his fingers traced Tim's name.

Buddy, you're in the company of heroes...just like you.

Pepper reached into his pants pocket and withdrew Tim's Zippo. He held it in the palm of his right hand, rubbing the inscription with his thumb, just as he had done seven years before over Koh Tang. He read the words he'd etched on Tim's lighter: "Tim Scott Died 7-20-66 Vietnam." Leaning over, he placed it at the foot of the panel, took a step back and snapped a salute. Staring at Tim's name, he inched the salute down to his side.

"There's your Firehammer, old friend, good-bye," he whispered. "Semper Fidelis."

He turned in the November chill and walked briskly down the path toward the Washington Memorial. Robyn joined him from the hill with the children in tow, her arm wrapped around his waist as he rested his on her shoulders.

They never looked back.

The End

ERSON

RNARD A GREEN · TURN

N A ZUKOV · JAMES F A

E · TIMOTHY S DAVIES

PENTER · BRENT I GRIO

BILLY D NELSON · DC

HELL · RONALD J KINK

DAVID S PETERS

ACKNOWLEDGEMENTS

I discovered that writing and publishing this book was a labor of love. It spanned many years and nobody does it alone — neither did I. FIREHAMMER started as an effort to see if I could go the distance and complete a book-length piece of work during the time I participated in a critique group in Panama City, Florida. I credit this august group of writers, novelists, and editors with molding and shaping this English language challenged fighter pilot. Some folks came and went from the group but the most productive deserve my heartfelt thanks. Norris McDowell, Mike and Karen Helms, and Nadine Collins were there every time we met and provided priceless guidance and editing for both magazine features and this book.

A story like this would never have been told without the courage, dedication, and total professionalism of the brother fighter pilots and weapon systems officers I was honored to serve with for twenty-seven years. I particularly want to thank the men and women, both past and present, of the 34th Tactical Fighter Squadron, as it was called in 1975, who formed the basis of the characters in FIREHAMMER. Ours is a rare breed and given the chance, I would go back and do it with you all over again.

A gathering of young fighter pilots once asked me to talk about what I, as a former F-15 C Eagle squadron commander, would change if I could do it again. My answer was that given another chance, I would thank my family a lot more for their sacrifices and courage in following me around the world and moving every two or three years. I told them that I would also show much more gratitude to my aircraft maintainers. They spent untold hours in the cold, heat, rain, ice, and snow to give me a quality machine to fly. All my landings equaled my take-offs. I never had to eject during 4000 hours of high-performance jet time.

My wife, Jan, never lost faith in this book getting published. She is to credit for making the dominoes fall resulting in publication. Her discussion with author Janie DeVos led to Pat Avery and Joyce Faulkner of

Red Engine Press reading the manuscript and deciding to publish. Joyce Gilmour's editing and gentle nudging were priceless in the production of FIREHAMMER. Hugh Smith's work on the cover was simply masterful. My heartfelt appreciation and admiration goes to all of you. Kill MiGs!

Notes

HISTORICAL NOTES

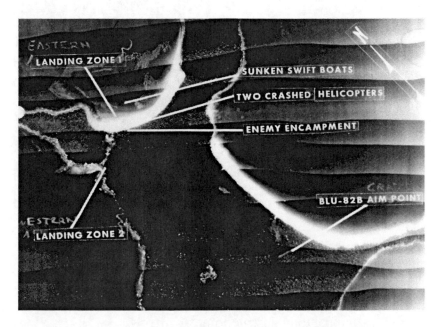

Photo of mosaic of the northern part of Koh Tang shows the area where the most action occurred. An analyst has penciled a change to the names of the landing zones. The distance between the eastern and western LZs across the island neck is only 400 yards and Khmer gunners had clear fields of fire at both areas.

At the eastern landing zone, Khmer gunners held their fire to the last minute when they unleashed a fierce cross fire of automatic weapons and rocket propelled grenades that brought down Knife 23 and Knife 31. This photos shows the severed tail section of Knife 23 and the total destruction of Knife 31.

Stats

From The Wall

www.TheWall-USA.com

Interesting Veterans Statistics off the Vietnam Memorial Wall

There are 58,272 names now listed on that polished black wall, including those added in 2011.

The names are arranged in the order in which they were taken from us by date and within each date the names are alphabetized. It is hard to believe it is 38 years (as of 2013) since the last casualties.

The first known casualty was Richard B. Fitzgibbon, of North Weymouth, Mass. Listed by the U.S. Department of Defense as having been killed on June 8, 1956. His name is listed on the Wall with that of his son, Marine Corps Lance Cpl. Richard B. Fitzgibbon III, who was killed on Sept. 7, 1965.

There are three sets of fathers and sons on the Wall.

At least 25,000 were 20 years old or younger.

12 soldiers on the Wall were 17 years old.

5 soldiers on the Wall were 16 years old.

One soldier, PFC Dan Bullock was 15 years old.

997 soldiers were killed on their first day in Vietnam.

1,448 soldiers were killed on their last day in Vietnam.

40 sets of brothers are on the Wall.

Thirty one sets of parents lost two of their sons.

54 soldiers attended Thomas Edison High School in Philadelphia.

8 Women are on the Wall. Nursing the wounded.

244 soldiers were awarded the Medal of Honor during the Vietnam War; 153 of them are on the Wall.

Beallsville, Ohio with a population of 475 lost 6 of her sons.

West Virginia had the highest casualty rate per capita in the nation. There are 711 West Virginians on the Wall.

The Marines of Morenci — They led some of the scrappiest high school football and basketball teams that the little Arizona copper town of Morenci (pop. 5,058) had ever known and cheered. They enjoyed roaring beer busts. In quieter moments, they rode horses along the Coronado Trail, stalked deer in the Apache National Forest. And in the patriotic camaraderie typical of Morenci's mining families, the nine graduates of Morenci High enlisted as a group in the Marine Corps. Their service began on Independence Day, 1966. Only 3 returned home.

The Buddies of Midvale - LeRoy Tafoya, Jimmy Martinez, Tom Gonzales were all boyhood friends and lived on three consecutive streets in Midvale, Utah on Fifth, Sixth and Seventh avenues. They lived only a few yards apart. They played ball at the adjacent sandlot ball field. And they all went to Vietnam. In a span of 16 dark days in late 1967, all three would be killed.

LeRoy was killed on Wednesday, Nov. 22, the fourth anniversary of John F. Kennedy's assassination. Jimmy died less than 24 hours later on Thanksgiving Day. Tom was shot dead assaulting the enemy on Dec. 7, Pearl Harbor Remembrance Day.

The most casualty deaths for a single day was on January 31, 1968 — 245 deaths.

The most casualty deaths for a single month was May 1968 - 2,415 casualties were incurred.

For most Americans who read this they will only see the numbers that the Vietnam War created. To those of us who survived the war, and to the families of those who did not, we see the faces, we feel the pain that these numbers created. We are, until we too pass away, haunted with these numbers, because they were our friends, fathers, husbands, wives, sons and daughters. There are no noble wars, just noble warriors.

"The wars are long, the peace is frail, the madmen come again. . . ."
Diogenes

GLOSSARY

BINGO: A predetermined amount of fuel that, when reached, requires termination of the mission and return to base for landing. The flight leader can adjust this fuel based on factors like weather, threat, distance to base, etc.

BURNER: Short for the afterburner section of the engine.

CALL SIGN: A name and number that a flight of aircraft uses for their mission. It can also be a nickname for a person in the business of flying fighter aircraft.

CBU: Cluster Bomb Unit, a collection of smaller bomblets contained inside a larger bomb. More info: http://www.fas.org/man/dod-101/sys/dumb/cluster.htm

http://www.youtube.com/watch?v=cKeabA0BvgE

CHAFF: A radar countermeasure in which aircraft or other targets spread a cloud of small, thin pieces of aluminum which appears as a cluster of secondary targets on radar screens. Chaff can be used to distract radar-guided missiles from their targets.

ELEPHANT GRASS: Elephant grass is a tall grass that grows in dense clumps of up to 10 feet tall. It grows along lake beds and rivers where the soil is rich. The edges of the leaves are razor-sharp which make stands of elephant grass nearly impenetrable.

EWO: Electronic Warfare Officer is not a pilot. Analyzes signals and uses countermeasures to defeat them. More info: http://en.wikipedia.org/wiki/Electronic_Warfare_Officer

F-4 Background

F-4 site: http://www.fighter-planes.com/info/f4.htm

F-4D model specific: http://www.globalsecurity.org/military/systems/aircraft/f-4d.htm

F-4 Photos: http://www.globalsecurity.org/military/systems/aircraft/f-4-pics.htm

F-5A/E Freedom Fighter: http://www.fighter-planes.com/info/f5.htm

Video — Marine F-4s in close air support of ground Marines using a FAC. Shows Da Nang:

http://www.youtube.com/watch?v=aCzio8WpkCs

Video — USAF F-4s firing cannon, Thunderbirds in the Phantom, good music, A/B take off,Eglin finflash Phantoms in cammo, landing with drag chute: http://www.youtube.com/watch?v=VIyzK6x8lNA

Repeated low passes by Phantoms, shows landing hook down, breaking the sound barrier (fog), AB glow at dusk, Navy and AF F-4s:"The Best of F-4 Phantom." http://www.youtube.com/watch?v=ixd1wvOq234

* = should see, some of the best

*"Cockpit Audio of SAM Shootdown of F-4." Good photos and videos with a chilling audio recording of Dodge 2 being shotdown by an SA-2. Only one guy got out, the backseater, pilot didn't make it. http://www.youtube.com/watch?v=G0kAJunnnGQ

*Season II of :Dogfights," has an awesome video animation and personal interviews with F-4 vs MiG dogfights in Vietnam. Starts with A-1 Skyraider first MiG kill of the war, then at about 14 minutes it focuses on the Vulcan Gatling Gun kills of Air Force F-4s. Great depictions!

http://www.youtube.com/watch?v=qn5YtuYkTow

*F-5 video simulation of F-5 Freedom Fighter with lots of statistics and Beatle music in the background. Shows F-5s in Aggressor cammo with red stars on the tail to look like MiGs!

http://www.youtube.com/watch?v=DnAemMfTOjA

FIGHTING WING: A fluid, mostly offensive formation that allows the wingman to maneuver as necessary behind his leader. Like a kite maneuvering on a string.

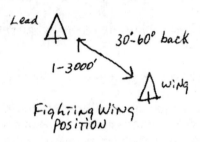

FINGERTIP: Close formation about three feet apart. Used to penetrate weather or at night where seeing each other would be difficult. Also used with several aircraft in the formation so they are not strung far apart.

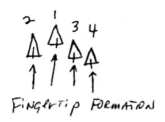

FINGERTIP FORMATION

*

FOX ONE/TWO/GUNS: Actual air-to-air or simulated missile shots. Fox One is a longer range radar guided AIM-7 "Sparrow" missile. Fox Two is a heat/infrared seeking closer range missile. See missile photo below. The F-4 could carry four of each type. "Guns" is used when employing the six-barreled Gatling gun at up to 6000 rounds per minute. More info: http://www.youtube.com/watch?v=zQvObtxH2EY

*

GUNS DEFENSE MANEUVER: When defensive, it is a maneuver used to defeat an attacker's gun shot. Can involve nearly forcing the aircraft out of control.

*

KLONG GRASS: Also commonly spelled Khlong; is the general name for a canal in the central plain of Thailand sometimes used for sewage. Grass growing in these canals are long, tough reeds.

*

MiG: Mikoyan-and-Gurevich Design Bureau of the USSR that developed fighter aircraft, thus the MiG abbreviation. Sometimes used as a term for any enemy aircraft. More info: http://acecombat.wikia.com/wiki/Mikoyan-Gurevich

This USAF Aggressor F-5 painted to look like a MiG, would have looked very much like Yellow Star's F-5 with a red vertical tail and yellow star.

MiGCAP: Abbreviation for MiG Combat Air Patrol missions whose objective is to engage and destroy enemy aircraft. More info: http://en.wikipedia.org/wiki/Combat_air_patrol

http://search.aol.com/aol/image?q=MiGCAP&v_t=wscreen50-bb

MiG SWEEP: An alternative slang term for MiGCAP mission above. The term can also be used to describe a group of people locking arms and "sweeping" a bar of tables, glasses and people to one end.

MIKE: Can be used as an abbreviation for minutes, microphone or millimeters, like in "twenty mike-mike" for the 20 millimeter cannon.

MILITARY POWER: Sometimes abbreviated MIL, and refers to 100% power setting not including the afterburner.

NOSE GUNNER: Slang term for the front seat pilot position.

PADLOCKED: Brevity code for unable to move your eyes off a target or threat because you will lose sight.

PITCH-BACK MANEUVER: Turning while climbing maneuver to change direction 180 degrees while climbing to a higher altitude. A slice-back is the opposite, losing altitude while changing direction 180 degrees.

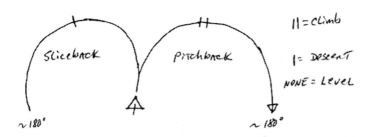

PIPPER: The predicted impact point (PIP) is the location that a ballistic projectile (e.g. bomb, missile, bullet) is expected to strike if fired. The PIP is almost always actively determined by a targeting computer, which then projects a PIP marker (a "pipper") onto a combining glass (see glass at eye level where pipper is displayed) in front of the pilot in the F-4 aircraft. Also called a gun sight. Photo taken from actual F-4D flight manual.

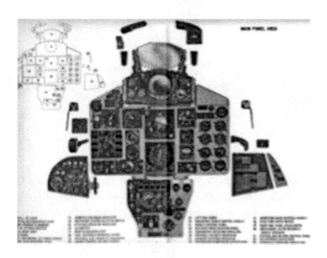

PRC-25 RADIO/PRICK: The major field radio of the Vietnam War. It was referred to as a "Prick Twenty-Five" by GIs, or "Prick" for short, and was about the size and weight of a case of soda. More info and below image from: www.tourofdutyinfo.com/ToDAdvisorwebpages/fieldradio2.html

PRC-25 Backpack Radio used in the Vietnam War. (Photo from http://olive-drab.com/od_electronics_anprc25.php)

RADOME: A radome (the word is a contraction of radar and dome) is a structural, weatherproof enclosure that protects a microwave (e.g. radar) antenna.

More info at: http://en.wikipedia.org/wiki/Radome

RIG: Part of the "Rig/Stab Aug" check where the pilot checks the alignment (or rigging) of the aircraft flight controls prior to maneuvering.

SIDEWINDERS/AIM-9 J/P: Very fast, short-range, heat/infrared seeking missiles that guided to the threat aircraft exhaust. The F-4 could carry four Sidewinders.

More info: http://www.fas.org/man/dod-101/sys/missile/aim-9.htm

Armorers work on AIM-9 Sidewinders to be loaded on the F-4D behind them. Missile in foreground is AIM-7 Sparrow. (Photo from site above)

SMASH: Brevity code for airspeed. More info: http://www.ausairpower. net/TE-Sidewinder-94.html

SPARROWS/AIM-7E-2: Radar-guided medium range air-to-air missile with high-explosive warhead. The F-4 could carry four AIM-7 Sparrow missiles. See photo above.

More info: http://www.fas.org/man/dod-101/sys/missile/aim-7.htm

STAB-AUG: Short for stability-augmentation. The F-4 had three stab-aug switches for pitch, roll and yaw. They assisted the pilot when making inputs to the flight controls.

ROE: Rules of engagement. Higher headquarters determined ROE for missions based on the situation. An example of ROE was when the pilot must visually identify a threat aircraft before employing weapons.

RWR: Radar Warning Receiver. An instrument that tells the pilot/WSO that a threat radar has locked-on to them.

TALLY HO: Brevity code for visual sighting of an enemy aircraft. Sometimes used for sighting any aircraft or object on the ground.

TARGET FIXATION: Occurs when the pilot is concentrating so hard on the target or aircraft he is attacking that he loses situation awareness of how close he is getting or how fast he is overtaking. More info: http://en.wikipedia.org/wiki/Target_fixation

Also: http://www.youtube.com/watch?v=lbKLB7xNWhs

TOT: Time Over Target.

WING TRIM: The pilot has the ability to "trim" pressures from his control stick by using a 4-way button. Wing trim means pressures reduced to the ailerons/spoilers to reduce roll tendencies. The same can be applied to the pitch and yaw axis.

WSO: Weapon Systems Officer. Flies in the rear cockpit of the F-4 and manages several systems for navigation, radios, radar and weapons. Usually pronounced "wizzo." More info: http://en.wikipedia.org/wiki/Weapon_Systems_Officer

YAW: An axis of the aircraft where the nose can be moved back and forth by fish-tailing the aircraft with the rudder pedals.

YAW AUG: An augmentation system that assists the pilot in controlling the rudder during turns. Usually turned off in the F-4 when heavy maneuvering was expected.

CPSIA information can be obtained at www.ICGtesting.com
Printed in the USA
LVOW10s0419210714

395198LV00008B/13/P